USS Hamilton
Miasma Burn

Mark Wayne McGinnis

Other Books By MWM

Scrapyard Ship Series

Scrapyard Ship (Book 1)

HAB 12 (Book 2)

Space Vengeance (Book 3)

Realms of Time (Book 4)

Craing Dominion (Book 5)

The Great Space (Book 6)

Call To Battle (Book 7)

Tapped In Series

Mad Powers (Book 1)

Deadly Powers (Book 2)

Lone Star Renegades Series

Lone Star Renegades (also called 'Jacked') (Book 1)

Star Watch Series

Star Watch (Book 1)

Ricket (Book 2)

Boomer (Book 3)

Glory for Space Sea and Space (Book 4)

Space Chase (Book 5)

Scrapyard LEGACY (Book 6)

The Simpleton Series

The Simpleton (Book 1)

The Simpleton Quest (Book 2)

Galaxy Man Series

Galaxy Man (Book 1)

Ship Wrecked Series

Ship Wrecked (Book 1)

Ship Wrecked 2 (Book 2)

Ship Wrecked 3 (Book 3)

Boy Gone Series

Boy Gone (Book 1)

Cloudwalkers Series

Cloudwalkers (Book 1)

The Hidden Ship

The Hidden Ship

Guardian Ship

Guardian Ship

Gun Ship

Gun Ship

Copyright

To join Mark's mailing list, jump to:
http://eepurl.com/bs7M9r

Visit Mark Wayne McGinnis at:
http://www.markwaynemcginnis.com

Prologue

Somewhere within the Andromeda Galaxy ...

Grish Junior Officer, Sub-Capitaine Porskel, led his small procession, himself and two deck-sergeants, across the desolate, rocky landscape. Scattered bones of indeterminate species, some smallish in size and others quite large, littered the terrain out to as far as the eye could see. Obviously, feeding frenzies were a common occurrence around here, Porskel thought.

The three Grish crewmen wore heavily insulated environment suits to compensate for the planet's double-digit sub-zero degree temperatures. There was no sunlight here. No warmth. Everything had a purple-bluish hue to it – the ground, the distant rocky ridgeline, even the sky above them.

Porskel jumped back as a small, rodent-sized, creature with

three heads scurried across their path. Clearly, different forms of life *did* manage to survive in this place, Porskel thought.

"So fucking cold here, I swear I can no longer feel my snout," Deck Sergeant Langar said to no one in particular. He blew a steamy snot blast onto the inside of his faceplate.

Sub-Capitaine Porskel shot him a disapproving glance. "Don't start with that complaining shit, Sergeant Langar . . . hold your tongue."

The other Deck Sergeant, Screal, huffing and puffing and languishing several strides behind them, said, "I think there's something wrong with my oxygenator unit."

Langar chuckled, "That, or maybe it's those constant late-night visits to the feeding trough, eh?"

Eventually, they reached a vertical wall – a dead end. Sub-Capitaine Porskel stood craning his neck to look upward, "Solid rock . . . must be a thousand feet tall."

"Now what? I think we missed a turn back there," Langar said, glancing back the way they'd come.

"Uh-huh, yeah, maybe we should just head back," Screal said, agreeing with Langar and looking nervous.

"Quiet! Both of you. We're to wait here until we're contacted," Porskel ordered.

And so, they waited. Certainly, this was not a place one would visit without an invitation.

Looking about the barren expanse with trepidation, Porskel suspected that the three might have been chosen for this mission because they somewhat *expendable*. Porskel glanced up toward the sky where Fleet Commander Prog Hongly, onboard *The Hortnick*, currently sat in high orbit.

"Look!" Langar said, pointing to a lone dark figure ahead. He'd somehow emerged from a shadowed cleft there within the cliffside.

The three stared nervously as the ominous-looking figure approached – one who appeared to be floating more than walking. Robed and hooded in black, his shadowed face seemed mostly featureless, except for an exposed, skeletal-like jawline. The bright white of his jawbone and teeth contrasted with his otherwise stark black appearance.

"He's going to kill us and eat our flesh . . . that's what they do here, you know. They're ravenous fuckers . . . always hungry."

"Shut up, Screal," Sub-Capitaine Porskel spat in a hushed voice. "I don't think the Varapin even eat meat. Their physiology isn't like ours . . . or like anyone's."

Sub-Capitaine Porskel, along with his two bumbling sergeants, were here on Devastin as little more than emissaries. Their Grish ship had traveled two long months to reach this god-forsaken planet. Their presence here, at this specific time, had been worked out well in advance.

The figure's hands and feet were exposed, protruding from his robe. Steam rose into the atmosphere like a kind of wafting perspiration, exuding from his crinkled, obsidian-black flesh. Porskel couldn't see the alien's eyes, squinting through the haze; he saw only two, tiny, pinpoint reflections of light.

"I can smell your stink even through your environment suits," came the Varapin's menacing, high-pitched voice.

Langar and Screal, making dull-witted expressions, glanced at each other. Sub-Capitaine Porskel said, "To whom am I addressing, please."

"You can call me Tome."

Porskel said, "My name is – "

"Your names are of no importance to me," the Varapin said.

"I see. Um . . . so, your Council of Nine . . . have they made their determination?"

Silent, and with a predatory leer, the dark figure began to hover around them. "Will the Varapin come to the aid of the Grish? Have they signed the Alliance? The contract?"

Tome made a *hissing* sound. "The Council members are listening as we speak . . . yet no decision has been made."

Capitaine Porskel had pretty much relayed everything he'd been told to say. Improvising was not his strong suit.

Tome said, "We do not trust the Grish . . . such an unpleasant breed you are. Hmm, perhaps it would be best if we simply sent several Ravage-Class Landers to *your* home world, instead. Mass harvest the life forces of your pathetic populous there . . . and be done with this bothersome business."

Porskel knew better. This offering – an agreement for the Grish to quadruple production of life-energy containment cisterns for the Varapin – could not have come at a more opportunistic time for these aliens. Not with their ever-expanding predominance within their galaxy. No, as unpleasant as the Varapin might find the Grish, Porskel knew his people were phenomenal manufacturers. And only a select few could supply their ghoulish need for cisterns.

Porskel waited as the looming Varapin came closer to him. Suddenly, Commander Prog Hongly was yelling in his ear; he only now remembered the fleet commander had been eavesdropping from the *Hortnic*. *"Make the deal! Do not jeopardize the deal, you imbecile!"*

Porskel said, "Excuse me . . . Tome . . . the Humans, along with those disgusting worms, um . . . the Thine, they are becoming a dominant presence within their small corner of space. And with the powerful Pleidian Weonan now joining forces with them, there may be no stopping that Alliance." He eyed the hovering figure. "Who knows . . . even this area of space could someday come under their scrutiny." Porskel tried to ignore the verbal berating now coming from Commander Hongly. Evidently, making threats to the Varapin was a very bad idea. But surely, nothing he could say would be any news to this Tome character, of the Council of Nine.

Sub-Capitaine Porskel continued, reciting his well-practiced instructions. "To reiterate . . . the Grish will indeed quadruple cistern production. We will do so quickly and ensure timely delivery. In turn, the Varapin Empire will come to the aid of the Grish, honoring our new unilateral and equitable war-pact, one that commits to the destruction of the Alliance forces. All we ask is that Earth and another nearby planet . . . one of little importance, Juno 5, remain as Grish territory and off-limits to the Varapin or anyone else. Is this acceptable?"

The menacing figure seemed to contemplate the proposal.

The silence did little to calm Porskel's nerves. "Certainly, with your superior technology, your vast fleets, your countless warships – "

"Do not patronize me, Grish piglet!"

"Of course, yes, yes. . . the Sub-Capitaine apologizes," Deck Sergeant Screal interjected, bowing his head in an exaggerated display of submission.

Sub-Capitaine Porskel suspected that the Varapin Council of Nine had already agreed to the contract and the war pact... and that this was all some kind of dramatic posturing.

After a long minute, Tome said, "Fine. You can convey to your superiors that the terms are agreeable. A fleet of our most powerful warships will embark within three-star cycles. All Human, Thine, and Pleidian Weonan warships will soon come face to face with the Varapin Empire's might. As specified, Earth and the Humans – as well as Juno 5 – are to be left to the Grish. Thine and Pleidian Weonan will be offered up as givers of life to our greater cause. As our fleet departure and subsequent invasions are imminent, the confidentiality of our intentions must remain secret. Deviate from this agreement at your own peril, snouted creature. I assure you, the Grish would not want to face the wrath of the Varapin. Do we have an understanding?"

Porskel, again hearing his superior's thundering voice in his ear, said, "Yes. You can count on us, Tome. You and the Counsel of Nine can trust the Grish."

The hooded figure raised his head. "Fine. The signed

agreement has already been sent to your technologically obsolete battle cruiser." The Varapin gestured upward to the sky.

Sub-Capitaine Porskel was flabbergasted at how well things were progressing. *I might survive this day, after all.* He felt today would certainly affect the trajectory of his long-stalled military career. He turned to his deck sergeants, Langar and Screal. Both looked relieved and more than ready to head back to their shuttlecraft.

But Tome had yet to leave. In fact, his hovering form had drifted closer to them. *Sudden movement.* Porskel glanced to his right, over to Screal, where he'd caught a blur of motion. Tome, having moved with incredible speed, had now wrapped himself around the upper torso of the deck sergeant, like some kind of parasitic cloak. Paralyzed with fear, Sub-Capitaine Porskel stared in horror. Tome's black, claw-like fingers now ripped and shredded at Screal's faceplate. The sound of terrified squeals filled Porskel's helmet – the sergeant's desperate pleas being broadcasted into the open comms channel.

With fear restricting his throat – even his breathing – Porskel raised a feeble, restraining, hand, "Please stop, Tome . . . please stop hurting him . . ."

But Tome was already using his far superior strength to force Screal's head backward – as far back as it would go – so Screal was now looking straight up into the Varapin's deathly face. Ice crystals had already begun to form on Screal's exposed chubby cheeks, his bulging eyes glazing over.

Porskel then watched as an electrified stream of blue energy coursed forth from Screal's gaping mouth up into Tome's equally open jaw.

Perhaps what was even more frightening to Sub-Capitaine Porskel at that moment, was the knowledge that he, too, might very well fall victim to Tome's wrath. It made sense. This had always been a part of it... a prearranged sacrifice to seal the deal.

Chapter 1

Walter Reed National Military Medical Center, Bethesda, Maryland

Captain Galvin Quintos

I was waiting for the nurse to come back for me. Dressed smartly in my Captain's US Space-Navy uniform, fingers tapping on my hover-chair's armrest, I was eager to get going – get out of here. I'd been a patient at the Walter Reed Military Medical Center, recovering for the better part of three-and-a-half months. I wiggled the toes on my left foot. It still felt strange – like I possessed someone else's body parts. Two toenails hadn't grown back in yet, but I'd been assured that, in time, they'd show up, just like my other toenails had. *Suppose I should be grateful, only three toenails missing, after losing my left hip, along with my left leg and foot.*

Only recently had my memories returned. Doctors informed me that this was normal; I had experienced a form of retrograde amnesia – common, after enduring catastrophic incidents such as the one I'd been through. The horrific course of those past events was all too present now, playing repeatedly in my head. Truth was that a part of me wished I'd never regained those recollections. But, as it turned out, retrograde amnesia would not be my only emerging mental concern. In this year of 2171, the US Space-Navy had measurably improved the diagnoses of mental issues. Apparently, after several in-depth hypnosis sessions, I was diagnosed with something called Delayed Onset Post Traumatic Stress Disorder, or DOPTSD. Oddly, it had not stemmed from any of the recent cataclysmic events onboard the *USS Hamilton*, although that had been what is commonly called a *trigger*. In fact, I'd undoubtedly had DOPTSD for a good portion of my life – since childhood. Before my leg surgery, Dr. Lopez, (a friendly, perhaps overly-empathetic psychologist), told me that my particular type of DOPTSD most certainly would have affected my life since childhood. Well, he wasn't telling me anything I didn't already know. *I needed to get back to work.*

"Captain Quintos, Delayed Onset PTSD impacts different people, well, *differently*. Tell me, do any of these symptoms sound – or feel – familiar to you? Depression?"

I inwardly said, *Check.*

"Mood swings?"

Check.

"The inability to make deep and long-lasting relationships?" *Check.*

"Are you experiencing, of late, a racing heartbeat?"

That and the onset of debilitating anxiety . . . check!" Yep, all of those.

I shook my head, "Nope. I feel fine. But as you said, Doctor . . . um, what did you call it, Late Onset PTSD? It impacts different people, differently, right? I guess I was just one of the lucky ones."

By his disappointed expression, I could tell he wasn't buying what I was selling. Hell, I'd already been diagnosed by modern science. We both knew I had *issues*. Unfortunately, I was more aware of them now since they'd been triggered. But it wasn't anything I couldn't deal with. I wasn't thrilled that my service file would now mention all this. There again, there was nothing I could do about it. And whatever DOPTSD bullshit Dr. Lopez wanted me to deal with . . . it would have to wait.

The concerned looking doctor leaned forward and placed a hand on my shoulder, "I'm going to approve your return to active duty, Captain, but I'll be keeping an eye on your mental state. At some point, you'll need to deal with this. There are therapies that work; exposure therapy comes to mind. This helps patients face and control their fears. It gradually exposes them to the trauma they experienced earlier, as a child . . . in a safe way. The therapist uses various tools to help patients with DOPTSD cope with their feelings. Captain . . . Galvin, deal with this soon, I fear your ability to lead, to captain effectively, may be impacted . . . perhaps at the most inopportune, time."

* * *

A few of us were lined up, side-by-side, hovering in the hospital's corridor like Arrow fighters within a flight bay, awaiting permission to launch out into space. Next to me, sitting within his own hover-chair, was an elderly man. Stooped and round-shouldered, wisps of white hair tried to lie flat upon his pink scalp. Age spots covered most of his forehead. From what I'd overheard him say in a casual conversation with another patient, he was Admiral Glen Howard, Retired. Recuperating from kidney surgery, he too was now waiting to be discharged.

A phlegmy cough erupted from his throat as he pointed a crooked finger in my direction. "I know who you are . . . hell, everyone around here knows who you are. You're that famous Quintos fella . . . Uh, Galvin Quintos."

The admiral hadn't spoken my name like it was a good thing.

"That's *Captain* Quintos," I said.

He snickered then continued, "You're the one who got us pulled into this damn war with the Grish."

Normally, I would be content with allowing the old coot to think what he wanted to think; no skin off my nose. But as I sat there, steadily tapping my fingers, I became more and more irritated. And I could see him glaring back at me in my peripheral vision. *Fucking old barnacle.* Much of the official record of the events that transpired those months earlier had been sealed. The public had just a barebones accounting of the actual facts, facts that didn't fully explain how many thousands had died under my watch.

"So, you want to know what happened . . . what really

happened, Admiral? Or are you content to spew out the same ignorant disinformation as everyone else?"

The old man's face reddened. "You pissant. . . how 'bout you show me the proper respect – "

Ignoring his feigned indignity, I waved his comment away as if it was a pesky fly.

He said, "Fine. You tell me, Quintos. Go ahead and tell me your side of things. Let me be the judge."

I studied the old man, the smirk on his wet lips taunting me to go on.

"It all started three-and-a-half months ago . . . prior to Earth being drawn into its first intergalactic war."

The admiral rolled his eyes.

I continued, "It was supposed to be a simple diplomatic mission into the Auriga Star System. Fleet Command had deployed the 3rd Fleet – eight once-powerful, but older, in need of maintenance, U.S. Space-Navy *EUNF* warships."

"Christ! I'm an admiral! Don't you think I know what the damn 3rd Fleet was, boy?!"

"Anyway, the entire fleet was dispatched. Little more than window dressing, an inflated show of force, whereas in reality, only the barest minimal crews were actually deployed for what was sure to be a cake-run of a mission."

I now had the old man's full attention.

"When we arrived at the Auriga Star System, the Grish were already there, waiting for us. Cloaked, they were invisible to our less than optimal sensor arrays. At the time, I was the XO of the *USS Hamilton,* once the pride of the U.S. Space-Navy."

The admiral's brows shot up. "A fine old dreadnought . . . . immense proportions. She was one of three huge ships ya know. All built just like her . . . some sixty-years-ago."

I nodded. "Soon were decimated by these alien forces. Our Bridge was nearly destroyed. Our skipper at the time, Captain Eli Tannock, was nearly killed – struck in the head by a falling girder. So... being the ship's XO, I was elevated up in rank to become the new acting Captain. It wasn't long before the Grish destroyed all but three of our warships. And that's when I remembered *Hamilton's* Broadsides . . ."

"Decommissioned . . . Nah, those big cannons didn't work anymore," the admiral interjected.

"Well, we got them working. Found the old munitions and unleashed them on the Grish . . . destroyed a number of their warships . . . drove them out of the Auriga Star System."

The admiral smiled. "Never heard that part... would have liked to have seen that. Broadsides, huh?"

I nodded back. "Our last three remaining ships were pretty torn up. Loss of life within the decimated fleet was close to ten thousand. We needed to get out of that System fast. We'd been played! Didn't know who we could trust, and we were also low on fuel."

The old admiral looked thoughtful. "Outside of Auriga Star System you're not going to find a nearby fuel depot."

"We determined where we could find fuel... off limits; it was within Pleidian Weonan territory. The fuel depot was located within a space station called Ironhold, occupied by Pylor pirates. We stormed the station; externally, with Arrow fighters – and internally, with several small Marine units. In the end, we took over the station and got our fuel. We also rescued a number of Pleidian Weonan hostages, one of whom was Empress Shawlee Tee."

The older man said, "So, that was you . . . I'd heard bits and pieces about that rescue. And the reason why Earth's now allied with the Pleidian Weonans."

"Anyway, the *Hamilton* was finished – so battle-damaged she couldn't move another inch. Extensive deck breaches, her drives were shot to shit. We abandoned the ship, transferred across to the *Union*, which as. at that time, the last remaining vessel of the 3rd Fleet."

"That's quite a story, young man. You obviously made it back to Earth . . ."

"Yes. It took some time. The *Union* wasn't in great condition either, but her propulsion system was capable of FTL . . . we arrived back here during the Grish's prolonged bombardment of Earth. Within minutes, we were taking fire from multiple Grish warships . . . The *Union's* shields were weak, incapable of defending her already battered hull. I don't remember the exact moment that Grish smart missile struck the bow of the *Union* . . . the final blow, one that decommissioned her . . . also took off my left leg. I woke up in here."

"But that wasn't the end of the battle, was it?" the admiral asked. "You brought with you a fleet of Pleidian Weonan warships . . . warships far more advanced than anything the Grish had to offer. Earth was saved from certain annihilation."

I shrugged. "You already knew all that, didn't you, Admiral? You just wanted to hear the story from my own lips."

"Guilty as charged . . . yes, guilty as charged, Captain. Thank you for giving an old man your time. Now tell me, before you are the next to be pushed out of here," he placed a hand on my knee, "Some word of your crew . . . and where are you off to next?"

"I honestly don't know for sure, sir. From what I've been told, my crewmembers were each given a pick of new ship assignments. So, I imagine they've all dispersed; the lot of them could be halfway around the galaxy by now. I've had very few visitors since awakening from my two-month sleep stasis . . . while my left leg and foot grew back." I didn't share with the admiral that I was surprised (also a little hurt) that nary a one of my fellow crewmembers – some of whom I thought were close friends – had come to visit me: Not Lieutenant Wallace Ryder, nor Chief Craig Porter, nor other Bridge crewmen. Neither had Doc Viv. Sure, I'd been in stasis for much of the time, but I'd been wide awake for these past three weeks while undergoing physical therapy.

The admiral made a *pfft* noise. "You mean, other than Admiral Cyprian Block! EUNF U.S. Space-Navy's new Executive Five-star Fleet Admiral."

That was true. Admiral Cyprian Block, a friend and long-time mentor, took a chance and promoted me to captain when we were on the *Hamilton* months earlier. Then, he had been promoted, as well. One week ago, he'd visited me here – bringing with him a contingent of other high-ranking Naval officers.

Block, himself, pinned the Space-Navy Cross onto the front of my hospital gown, promising a more formal ceremony would be held in the future when the war with the Grish had settled down. Block had also informed me that my next post was nearly ready. "Prepare for deployment within one- or two-days' time." Now, here I sat, waiting to be released from Walter Reed, ready to be told what my next command would be. I didn't really care which ship I'd be assigned to, as long as the deployment was soon. I had a bone to pick with the Grish – they'd stolen a sizable percentage of my anatomy. Yeah, a reckoning was coming.

As it turned out, it wasn't a nurse who arrived to push my hover-chair out of the hospital corridor into the mid-Spring morning air.

The old admiral and I watched as a waifish, attractive, junior officer stepped through the double-glass doors. Seeing me, she smiled.

"Lieutenant Pristy," I said, somewhat dumbfounded. Gail Pristy had proven herself to be an amazing Bridge officer, probably more valued than any I'd ever served with. She was smart, remained cool under pressure, and was devoutly loyal. Onboard the *Hamilton*, it was brought to my attention that she might have had a small crush on me. I never pursued that. If anything, she was more like a little sister. And right now, I couldn't be happier to see anyone.

Looking equally glad to see me, she made a beeline for my hover-chair. "Captain, so good to see you . . . you look fit as a fiddle!"

"Thank you, Lieutenant. I'm surprised and happy to see you, too." I introduced her to Admiral Howard – now sitting far more erect in his chair and looking far less elderly than just moments before.

"So nice to meet you, Admiral," she said. "You commanded the 8th Fleet, back in forty-nine. Am I right, sir?"

The admiral beamed. Since this was 2171, the admiral was on active duty some twenty-two years prior. How Pristy knew about Admiral Howard, I'd need to discover some other time.

"That is correct, Lieutenant . . . back when you were still a small child."

Lieutenant Pristy refocused her attention back to me. "We have a lot scheduled on our agenda today, sir. Are you up for it?"

"A lot to do? Agenda? So, then, you're not just here to say hello?"

"No, Captain . . . I've already been here to visit you multiple times before. Of course, you were in stasis during those times."

I stood up. "Let's get out of here."

"Supposed to wait for the nurse," the admiral admonished, looking a bit vexed.

"If you know anything about me, sir, you'd know I tend to break the rules sometimes."

Leaving the admiral after a firm handshake, Lieutenant Pristy and I headed for the exit. She gazed up at me, "Not even a limp . . . well done, Captain."

After three weeks of painful physical therapy, I was close to one hundred percent back. But if Pristy asked me to take a jog around the block with her, she'd see I wasn't totally there yet.

I said, "So, new uniform . . . I like it. Is it specific to your new post?"

Dark gray in color, it had crimson piping, running down the sleeves, lapels, and the front of the shortened jacket. Her uniform slacks, maintaining the same overall gray coloring, also bore crimson detailing. A crisp white dress shirt and tie completed the ensemble. "Can you tell me about your ship . . . have you been deployed yet?"

We emerged outside into a beautiful, breezy morning. A long time had passed since I'd last felt the sun's warmth on my face. Birds chirped away in a nearby tree. I stopped and glanced up and noticed several hovercrafts cruising past overhead.

"This way, sir," Lieutenant Pristy said. "To answer your question . . . yes, I can tell you about my new post. I'm very excited about it. And I have my orders . . . I embark tomorrow."

She must have spotted the disappointment on my face. She said, "I know we don't have much time to catch up before it's back to military business as usual." She glanced at my chest. "Where's your new medal? I wanted to see it . . . never actually seen a Space-Navy Cross before."

"Admiral Block let me wear it for about five minutes. He then put it back in its box and left with it."

"Hold on . . . where are we going? Why are you *really* here, Lieutenant?"

"I'm delivering you to Halibart Shipyards. Admiral Block

thought you'd like to see a friendly face, so he signed off on a short leave for me so that I could accompany you there."

Halibart Shipyards was the U.S. Navy's primary space warship manufacturing hub, situated in high orbit around the Moon.

"Thought that was destroyed during the Grish attack on Earth? Actually . . . I'm pretty sure I saw it explode."

"It's all new . . . and we had some help getting it operational again. Actual shipbuilding already commenced; it's open for business, sir."

As we turned the corner along one side of the hospital – and just about to ask her why we'd be going to Halibart Shipyards if no ships had been completely built there yet – what I saw up ahead made me stop in my tracks.

Six people stood on the sidewalk, clustered together in a small group, a welcome wagon of greeters. On seeing us, they all waved. I stopped, uncomprehending, albeit happy to see each of them – Lieutenant Wallace Rider, Science Officer Stefan Derrota, Chief of Security Alistair Mattis, Chief of Engineering Craig Porter, SWM Crewman Lasalle, and a seven-foot-tall ChronoBot named Hardy. Fellow officers and crew from the *Hamilton,* they were – more importantly – my closest friends.

As we approached the group, I told Lieutenant Pristy, "They all have the same fancy new uniform as the one you're wearing. Something tells me that you've all been posted to the same warship."

She gave me a sideways glance, "You really don't know, Captain?"

I shook my head.

"When we were given the option to choose our next post, our next space vessel, almost all of us chose to stay with our Captain . . . with you. That made things difficult. We've been on temporary assignments, awaiting the build-out of our new ship . . ."

Only half-listening to her now, the one person missing from the group ahead was Doctor Vivian Leigh – *Doc Viv* – a beautiful, highly intelligent surgeon, who probably wasn't as interested in me as I was in her. *Why would she be here?* Her unique skill-level would hold her in high-demand within the fleet.

Now approaching them, Hardy seemed to be the most excited to see me.

Lieutenant Pristy said, "He's been here the entire time, Captain. They wouldn't let him back inside the hospital . . . his constant vigil – the pacing and his thousand-pound girth destroyed the floor coverings."

"He was here?"

She gave me an exasperated look. "He was ordered to stay away by Admiral Block, but Hardy ignored him. Said all Space-Navy demands ranked second behind his internal LuMan directives."

Only a select number of these seven-foot-tall, highly advanced ChronoBot killing machines were left in the known universe. What made them different from other kinds of robots was their incredible intellectual capacities, partly due to a living, organic AI brain component. Originally, this bot was characterless – robotic – and went by the name LuMan. Then, through a kind of bazaar mishap onboard the *Hamilton*, the memories of a decades-long dead crewmember, John Hardy, infiltrated the ChronoBot's psyche. Thus, Hardy was reborn, although LuMan was also still there too – typically satisfied to remain in the background.

I braced for what was coming next. Hardy strode forward, his mechanical arms extended outward. Next, lifted in the air, I was enfolded into him. "Easy, Hardy . . . you're crushing me!"

Hardy set me back down. In his Boston-accented voice, he said, "Sorry, Cap . . . ah, it's just so damn good having you back with us again!"

Stefan Derrota said, "Captain, we need to board our transport now . . . and you'll need to change clothes. I'm sorry to break up this happy reunion so quickly, but we have a tight schedule to keep."

I smiled upon seeing the friendly-mannered, Mumbai, India-born, science officer again. His tie looked slightly askew, and his shirt was not as crisp or wrinkle-free as the others'. The man always appeared somewhat disheveled. I nodded, "It's good to see you, too, Stefan. Let's go. I want to get far away from this hospital as quickly as possible."

Chapter 2

We made our way over to an adjacent parking lot where a small transport ship awaited us. Its aft drive unit idling, twirling trails of steam rose into the air from several lift thrusters beneath its two stubby wings. We all clambered up a ramp and through a side hatchway that closed behind us.

Immediately, the craft ascended as its lift thrusters became fully active. Being jostled about, I fell into a seat and strapped myself in. To my left sat Chief of Security Alistair Mattis, and to my right, Ship-Wide Maintenance Crewman Lasalle. Originally from Louisiana, the muscular, somewhat imposing, albeit soft-spoken Black man was an unequaled expert when it came to knowing everything Hamilton, included both the spacecraft, the *USS Hamilton*, and America's 18th Century Founding Father, Alexander Hamilton.

Mattis swiped strands of thinning dark hair back into place atop his head. Typically, dour, he attempted a smile. "Welcome back, Captain. It's awfully good to see you again."

I knew this greeting from Mattis, who had a glass-half-empty kind of personality, was as warm a sentiment as I would get. Yet, easily forgiven, considering he'd recently lost his daughter, Gunny Zan Mattis, one of several crewmember victims murdered during my brief stint as Captain on the *Hamilton*.

I returned his smile. "Okay, Alistair . . . where the hell are we going? Enough with the mystery."

Mattis laughed, bringing his hand up to cover his mouth. Before he could answer, Lieutenant Pristy, somewhat off-balance, was standing in front of me.

"I've been instructed to tell you to get properly attired, sir," she said, lifting a garment bag.

"This is getting tiresome, Lieutenant . . . I get it, all the matching uniforms, since yeah, we're all being deployed to the same ship. It's far too early for the *Hamilton* to be fully repaired . . . if that's even possible, after the beating she took. So, what kind of ship is it to be? Maybe a battlecruiser . . . destroyer, frigate? Or maybe a carrier of some kind?"

Bemused, Lieutenant Pristy lifted her brows and thrust the garment bag into my chest, "Just get changed, sir . . . we're already running late for a meeting with the Brass. Once we arrive at Halibart, we'll need to move fast." She noticed my reaction to that. "No time like the present to get that new leg of yours moving."

I stood clutching the garment bag. "You know, you've gotten a lot cheekier since I last saw you, Lieutenant."

She shrugged, "The head's back that-a-way . . . all the way aft."

We arrived at Halibart Shipyards while I was still in the

head pulling on my boots. Jostled about, I felt restraining clamps engage and heard the transport ship's drive begin to wind down. I stood up and looked at myself in the mirror. The dark gray dress uniform, with its updated styling and cut, was a bit different than I was used to but I liked it. As I placed my officer's cap atop my head, a thunderous knock banged on the door. When I opened it, Hardy said, "Time to go, Princess. You look fine."

* * *

Lieutenant Pristy hadn't exaggerated. After disembarking from the transport vessel, we were indeed running. The rebuilt Halibart Shipyards was clearly larger, more massive, and modernized than I remembered. Large diamond-shaped glass windows flanked both sides of the corridor that we were now sprinting down. Planet Earth lay off to our left, the far larger-looking moon to our right. So far, my leg was holding up okay – sure, it hurt like a son of a bitch, but at least it hadn't given out on me yet. I spotted no less than a dozen US Space-Navy warships situated on fabrication platforms, at various construction stages. There was a battlecruiser, three destroyers, four smaller and more nimble-looking corvettes, and even a large spacecraft carrier in the distance – a fine-looking vessel – perhaps that would be our new posting.

"This way, Captain!" Pristy said, making an abrupt left turn at an intersecting juncture. I was tiring, but Hardy's heavily clomping footfalls – mere feet behind me – kept me from slowing down.

I recognized Derrota's accented voice without glancing his way. "Do you need to stop . . . take a breather, Captain?"

"No, I'm fine. Let's pick up the pace . . . I can do this all day," I said, attempting to hide the fact I was dying inside. And that's when I spotted her. The sun was illuminating her form – golden rays spotlighting the ship's majestic design. I stopped running, my chest heaving, and moved closer to the window. Yes, it was the *USS Hamilton*, but not the same ship I'd captained some three-and-a-half months earlier. She'd been revamped; *hell*, rebuilt from the ground up, and what a transformation this was. At just over three miles in length, her hull now literally glimmered with a high-polished sheen. And all the usual messy extraneous implements – cable conduits, junction boxes, antenna clusters, exhaust vents, weaponry stations – all were now gone. Triangular, with multiple propulsion exhausts at her stern, this breathtaking vessel, this colossal-size dreadnought, was even more beautiful than the first time I'd seen her.

I felt a heavy hand on my shoulder. Hardy said, "What do you think, Cap . . . those Pleidian's do us right?"

The last time I'd seen the *USS Hamilton,* she'd been on her last legs – first, having been savagely battle-damaged by the Grish after entering the Auriga Star System and, just days later, finished off by Pylor pirates within Pleidian territory at Ironhold Station.

"We need to go, Captain . . . Admiral Block just messaged

me again," Lieutenant Pristy said, gesturing to her latest-generation TAC-Band on her wrist. "And yes, we need to get you outfitted with one of these newer bands too . . ."

We jogged a bit, then walked the rest of the way. When I caught up to SWM Crewmember Lasalle, I asked him, "How much of this reconstruction were you privy to?"

"Pretty much all of it, sir . . . I stayed with her during the entire reconstruction."

"So, you went to the Pleidian's shipyards? Near Weonan?"

"Correct. I stayed on board the ship throughout. It was quite something. I can't say I understand the technical aspects, all the upgrades, and modifications, but I'm well-versed on the mechanical . . . the functional changes that took place."

"Good to know."

"Captain . . . you should know, *Hamilton* now utilizes a substantial amount of advanced Pleidian technology. Pretty much everything that had comprised her insides. . . well, most of that has been shit-canned. She now has a new FTL propulsion system and a separate jump drive component. Its weaponry and shields are new, too." Lasalle didn't seem thrilled with the present situation.

I said, "Sounds like I have a lot to learn about. Look, change can be hard. I know you had a strong connection to the ship the way she was before, but she was an old rattletrap. You knew that better than anyone. Let's try to embrace these new modifications. I'll be counting on you to assist me in getting reacquainted with this new, improved, *USS Hamilton*."

"There's another individual who may be better suited at doing that, sir," Lasalle said.

We arrived at the mid-ship portside entrance gangway, where the group had held up for us. "After you, Captain," Lieutenant Pristy said. "Welcome home, sir."

I hurried up the ramp and stepped onto the deck of the *USS Hamilton*. I'd probably entered through this same hatchway a hundred times before, stood on this same spot too many times to count. But what I saw now was all new – the passageway's former tarnished metal bulkheads and grimy deck plates were gone. Everything was now a glistening bright white. The old overhead lights and other fixtures were all gone. I reached out and touched a nearby bulkhead, subtly-illuminated from within. It was soft to the touch – coated with a familiar substance, a substance we'd found back within Ironhold Station. I knew you could fire a Shredder pistol point-blank at this stuff from firsthand experience, and it wouldn't so much as leave a mark. Orange block lettering high on an adjacent bulkhead indicated we were on Deck 14 – Zone D. I proceeded further into the vast ship, immediately almost getting lost, attempting to find the once familiar bank of elevator lifts.

Lasalle, hurrying to catch up to me, said, "GravLifts are right up ahead. Over there, sir."

"GravLifts?"

"Yup. Pleidians ripped out the old elevator systems. Said they were too slow . . . also dangerous. These new lifts utilize push-pull antigravity technology. Have to admit, it's a lot nicer ride than those old buckets of bolts we used to travel around in."

The group converged into some kind of circular vestibule, which wasn't there three-and- a-half-months earlier. I pursed my lips and waited, still nobody volunteered anything. "Okay . . . I give up. Where's the damn elevator doors . . . uh, I mean the GravLift doors?"

Derrota, looking pleased with himself, reached out and placed his palm onto the bulkhead; a glowing, blue ship's legend appeared. He tapped at Deck 10, Zone D, Captain's Conference Room. Nearby, the blank, solid wall magically spread open. Again, I remembered seeing this same type of technology on Ironhold Station.

We all rushed into the car. I leaned over toward Lassalle and said, "Your first task . . . I want all these hidden doorways, or hatchways, outlined with a border."

"Um, sir . . . regular paint won't stick to this SmartCoat . . . that's what everyone calls this stuff. But I'll talk to my Pleidian counterpart. Add it to my list of things that need changing."

I probably would have missed the subtle motion of the lift car if I hadn't been paying attention. Within seconds, we were already slowing down. Coming to a gentle stop, the wall before us once more spread open into a doorway – we'd arrived.

Lieutenant Pristy's, as well as all the other TAC-Bands, were now vibrating. "Admiral's getting impatient," she said, stepping out into the ship's largest main passageway – commonly called Whale's Alley. I was pleasantly surprised to see it looked even more like the inside cavity of a giant whale. The massive, curved overhead beams were now coated in that same glistening, white SmartCoat as everything else.

First to reach the Captain's Conference Room, Lieutenant Pristy made a swiping motion with one hand, causing the door to slide open. *Good, at least some of the original ship technology hadn't been scrapped.* We all filed in behind her. About one-quarter of the seats, positioned around the translucent Jinhong crystal table, were filled. I nodded, seeing Bay Chief Frank Mintz and Chaplain Thomas Trent – one person I was less than thrilled to see. I had hoped he would have retired by now. There were several other new faces I didn't recognize.

We took our seats and focused our attention on the front of the compartment where Admiral Cyprian Block was standing and not looking particularly pleased. Directly to his right stood a young male Pleidian Weonan. Dressed in a new, smart, *USS Hamilton's* junior officer's uniform, his rank designation was *Ensign.* My eyes moved upward to his face – a face characteristic of all Pleidians. Basically, their heads were oblong, with an open void within the skull's middle section – an opening that one could see through – somewhat like the head of a tennis racket (although this open area wasn't nearly as large as that.) He had two widely-spaced eyes on each side of his head, and a mouth running along its bottom contours. There wasn't a real nose, per se, but several small nasal cavities were set below each eye. Pleidian flesh glowed blue, giving them a kind of ethereal affectation. It had something to do with their cellular physiology . . . light-emitting molecules called *lumivale*, similar to luciferin, found on Earth in such organisms as jellyfish and fireflies.

The admiral glanced around the room, his eyes hesitating momentarily on Hardy. Block's brows knitted together, the ChronoBot still being an anomaly to high command. A mechanical being, the bot was not considered an actual member of the crew. But since the advanced robot maintained the memories and personality of one John Hardy, a long-departed *Hamilton* crewmember who'd lived five decades earlier, he was far more than just a robot. He had proven to be a pivotal aspect of our combat success on Ironhold Station. Hardy's loyalty to me was unwavering – his inner LuMan counterpart had been programmed to protect me at all costs – even above and beyond ship and crew.

Admiral Block said, "Captain Quintos, welcome aboard the *USS Hamilton* . . . currently the most advanced warship within the sector; hell, maybe the entire galaxy." Block glanced at the ensign. "According to Fleet Commander Twinwon, Pleidian master shipbuilders included every technological advancement they possessed, into this warship's renovations. She's powerful, fast, and intelligent. Although I have been briefed on such items, I'll leave it to your new ensign here, Lorric Plorinne, to provide the details – all the technical specs you'll undoubtedly want to know about."

Ensign Plorinne shifted his weight from foot to foot, looking uncomfortable with having so many eyes focused upon him at one time. He raised a hand, "Hello . . . I am Ensign

Lorric Plorinne. I am proud to serve with you onboard this great starship."

Hardy yelled out, "Welcome, Lorric! So, who do you really answer to? The *EUNF* US Space-Navy, or is it Pleidian Weonan's Fleet Commander Twinwon?"

Admiral Block looked annoyed at hearing the question, but surprisingly, not annoyed enough to say anything. He glanced toward the ensign, waiting for his to answer.

"I have taken an oath of service to your *EUNF* US Space-Navy . . ." Lorric looked directly at me, "My loyalties are to the *USS Hamilton* and her skipper . . . Captain Galvin Quintos."

I nodded and looked around the table. Reflected on my officer's faces was mostly skepticism. Curiously, it was the same expression Admiral Block currently shared. No, this Pleidian Weonan junior officer was most likely little more than a Pleidian mole, sent here to keep tabs on two essential things: their massive financial investment, and us humans, their new military ally.

Chapter 3

Admiral Block glanced toward the entrance as if expecting someone else to arrive. "I suppose I should just get started. Let me begin by saying, what I'm about to tell you is classified. No one beyond these walls is privy to this information." He turned his gaze to each of us. "As the war with the Grish continues, there is a new player in the mix. Our intel informs us the Grish have recently signed a war pact with the Varapin."

Murmurs broke out all around the table. There were few people alive today who hadn't heard of this ghoulish-looking, downright evil, alien race. For half a century, stories of their misdeeds had been the fodder of childhood nightmares – a modern-day boogie man incarnate.

"Quiet! the admiral barked. "I have a lot to go over with you and not much time to do it in. Needless to say, the Varapin are a highly advanced – not to mention *ruthless* – adversary. A bit of history about these vile creatures. Mostly verified through third-party alien accounts, some say that a Varapin's blood is composed, primarily, of ethylene glycol, an organic compound that doesn't easily freeze or crystalize. That, and that the Varapin species has evolved over millions of years, thriving within their home's dark and frigid environment. A subatomic spacial anomaly transformed their nearby blue hypergiant star into something completely different –a rare neutron star – a radiant blue pulsating sphere that emanates cryogenic methane hydrate. Whereas most organic life spread across the universe requires the consumption of caloric compound nutrients, there, on the Varapin home planet of Devastin, the Varapin, along with other species, do not. Their unique physiology requires just one thing – the inhalation of another's life-force energy. To survive, they literally need to rob, to *steal*, the life essence from another being."

The Admiral let that sink in. No one spoke, so he continued. "We're thinking that their deal with the Grish would have undoubtedly involved some sort of negotiated trade. A tit-for-tat aspect. The Grish could offer Earth up with its nine billion inhabitants . . . that's an enticing incentive. Hell, the day may soon arrive when their Ravage-Class Landers are descending from the skies above Earth. And remember this . . . the Varapin do not take prisoners, they take one's life force . . . their very soul."

"Surely, with the aid of the Thine and the Pleidians, we're still capable of defeating these ghouls, no?" Ryder said. "Look how we've been kicking the Grish's ass for several months now."

Block said, "Please, keep your comments and opinions to yourself, Lieutenant, until I'm finished. But to address your statement, you couldn't be more wrong. The way things are looking, we'll probably be outnumbered and outgunned when it comes to warships and firepower."

I said, "Even with the new and improved technology of this dreadnought, sir? From what I've heard —"

Cutting me off, Block shot me an annoyed look. "Didn't you hear what I just said to Lieutenant Ryder about interruptions? Anyway, that leads to a recent, important discovery." The admiral gestured to the Ensign with the jutting of his chin.

A projected 3D video feed suddenly filled the space between the Admiral and Ensign and the rest of us sitting at the table. "This impressive-looking vessel is the Varapin Empire's *Sintchu*. Four miles long and a third of that wide. And like the revamped *USS Hamilton*, she is a dreadnought of unfathomable technology and power. Make no mistake about it; the *Sintchu* is the Varapin's direct counterpart to the US Space-Navy's *Hamilton*."

"Like two gods at war," Lieutenant Pristy said under her breath — barely loud enough for anyone else to hear.

"Not a bad analogy," Admiral Block said. "Undoubtedly, the time is soon coming when these two behemoths will come up against each other. Yet, I must admit . . . as of right now, I have my doubts the *Hamilton* would survive a direct confrontation." The admiral noticed late arrivals were standing at the entrance. "Come in . . . the perfect segue to what I'm about to discuss."

My breath caught in my chest at seeing Major Vivian Leigh striding into the conference room — her long, blonde, wavy hair cascading down to the center of her back. She looked confident, aloof, and just as beautiful as I remembered her. *Interesting* – she was wearing the *Hamilton's* same new gray officer's attire. Two others entered behind her. I recognized the well-tanned middle-aged man with long silver hair, dressed in an impeccably-tailored business suit. He strode into the room with an air of confidence that comes from being a trillionaire – having substantial business and real estate holdings on Earth and numerous other worlds within the sector. Investor Talco Wentworth, 48, and the brother of the recently deceased Milo Wentworth – who had been murdered on this very ship less than four months earlier. The third one to enter the conference room, much shorter than Doc Viv and Wentworth, was wearing an elaborate-looking tan-colored environment suit. The three situated themselves on the opposite side of the table from me, but my full attention was on the shortest of the newcomers, who's helmet's faceplate was darkened. The individual tilted his head to one side and then waived at me. Hesitantly, I waived back.

"It is me, Captain Quintos . . . you would remember me as Coogong Lohp . . . although I now go by Coogong Sohp." His faceplate suddenly transitioned from opaque to transparent. After a moment, an alien's worm-like face pressed closer to the faceplate, becoming more apparent. His voice, more accurately, a synthesized voice, was being transmitted, *somehow*, via helmet speakers. Large expressive eyes could be seen through the murk of the surrounding Ambiogell – a dark mud-like substance surrounding the Thine, just as oxygen would be for a human. I took in the familiar broad smile. Coogong Lohp, like Milo Wentworth, had been another murder victim here on the *Hamilton* – his segmented worm body chopped up in his quarters and left for dead. What the murderer, young Ensign Hughes, hadn't realized at the time, was that the Thine weren't so easily killed. In fact, all that Hughes had accomplished was an expedited Thine reproduction cycle. I flashed back to seeing several small segmented baby worms within the ship's HealthBay; evidently, Coogong Sohp had been one of them, and now, already grown to full size with Coogong Lohp's memories still intact.

"It's good to see you, Coogong," I said.

The admiral cleared his throat, "If I may continue . . . I do have other time considerations today."

"Sorry, Admiral, please go on," I said.

Doc Viv was now fiddling with her TAC-Band – she had yet to acknowledge me. *Whatever.*

The admiral said, "Welcome, Mr. Wentworth, Major Leigh, Coogong Sohp . . . I was just about to speak about this vessel's inadequacies the rest of our new Space-Navy assets."

"Not even out of the spaceport, and this newly updated ship is already inadequate?" I said.

"May I, Admiral?" Wentworth said in a condescending tone.

I already didn't like this man, and I didn't even know him yet.

"I am here to continue the good work of my late brother, Milo . . ."

"Just a whole lot of trouble, if you ask me." Chief Craig Porter interjected.

Wentworth shot Porter an annoyed look. "He and others were directly involved with negotiating with the Junops for mineral rights on their home world. But, of course, the Grish had disrupted those negotiations when they attacked the 3rd Fleet at the Auriga Star System . . . where thousands of our good men and women were killed."

"I understand your continued investment interests, but what does this have to do with those military inadequacies that the admiral refers to?" I asked.

Admiral Block said, "Captain, Juno 5 is our closest intelligent-life neighbor within the galaxy. And it's a world rich with several unique minerals . . . certain minerals not found anywhere else in the universe, at least to my knowledge."

For the first time, Doc Viv spoke up, "Goriom, Zathium, and Pilorium . . . to name a few." She still hadn't looked up from whatever she was doing with her TAC-Band.

Wentworth continued, "Exactly. They're actually more than simple minerals; they're exotic quantum particle elements and will soon be added to the Periodic Table of Elements."

"Okay . . . and how does all this affect the fleet's . . . *Hamilton's,* battle readiness, again?" I asked.

Wentworth smiled, "What if I told you there was a means to enhance the *Hamilton's* shields . . . provide ten times the protection against any of our enemy's energy weapons, rail munitions – or even smart missiles? And that the output of your new Pleidian FTL HyperDrives could be tripled, if not quadrupled. And, that newly installed jump drive components could double your manufactured wormhole distances?"

I shrugged, "I'd say you're probably exaggerating. . . maybe making shit up?"

"That's uncalled for, Captain," Admiral Block said.

"It's fine, Admiral," Wentworth said with a wave of his hand. "The captain has every right to be skeptical of these outlandish claims. I probably would be, too."

Wentworth placed a hand atop Doc Viv's shoulder, "We've just spent a fascinating three weeks together on Juno 5." Wentworth looked at the doctor with an appreciative, bemused smile, as if he was privy to something more intimate between the two. *I really don't like this guy.*

"I was there, too," Coogong Sohp added good-naturedly, "with my team of scientists, and I can substantiate Mr. Wentworth's claims."

"And what? These minerals . . . elements, they need to be mined? Like from the ground on Juno 5?" I asked.

"Yes, from many miles beneath the world's rocky crust. An elaborate and expensive proposition," Wentworth said.

"So, this is all just academic at this point. Excavation hasn't really even started."

"On the contrary, mining has already begun. Within the next thirty days, I expect Earth's Space-Navy assets can begin circulating through the renovation process. Here at Halibart Yards, as well as other shipbuilding ports."

"I still don't like the idea that my HyperDrives are to be experimented with," Chief Porter said, clearly not pleased.

"Hell, it's taken me the better part of a month to understand the new Pleidian technology as it is!"

The Admiral said, "We're all going to have to make certain adjustments here. What you don't know is that minimum quantities of stabilized Zathium have already been acquired from the Junops. The *Hamilton* will be the first vessel to have the enhancement upgrade for multiple ship-wide systems. With the assistance of Thine scientists already onboard, the retrofitting will commence immediately – today, if possible."

"So . . . we're to just wait here at Halibart while these upgrades are installed?" I asked.

Admiral Block looked at his TAC-Band. "On the contrary, Captain Quintos. *Hamilton* will be leaving port today, along with the 2nd fleet . . . due here within the hour."

Coogong Sohp said, "The upgrade modifications will need to be made en route. It should not be a problem."

"Wait . . . En route to where?" I asked.

Doc Viv glanced my way and snickered. Christ, she was almost as annoying as Wentworth.

The Admiral said, "En route to the Varapin Empire's most prized and powerful fleet, called the *Rage of the Gonjun Ract* . . . a fleet centered around the *Sintchu* dreadnought. And a fleet that absolutely must be halted before reaching this sector."

"And where is this Rage of the Gonjun Ract, now?"

"Soon to be leaving neighboring Andromeda Galaxy."

As the meeting broke up, I watched as Doc Viv was the first to hurry from the conference room with Wentworth close on her heels.

Chapter 4

Admiral Block signaled me over. "Captain, I apologize for the expedited timeframe here. There's much we still need to discuss, but that can happen over encrypted micro-wormhole laser-link." He gestured to the young Pleidian Ensign awkwardly standing alone nearby. "I'd like you and Ensign Plorinne to get better acquainted. Nobody on board the *Hamilton* will be more familiar with these new Pleidian Weonan modifications."

Ensign Lorric Plorinne joined our conversation, "I would be honored to provide you a tour, sir."

Now looking at the young alien with his strange apertured head, I spotted Hardy in the distance – through the open void – looking at me. He had configured his myriad of facial sensor lights into a spinning pinwheel design. Annoyed, I turned back to the admiral. "You don't think we're rushing things a little . . . deploying before all the kinks have been worked out, not just for one ship's upgrade, but also two?"

Ensign Plorinne said, "From what I understand, the stabilized Zathium modifications are not so much hardware alterations but core hyperpower mods stored within the ship's reactor modules . . . a kind of subatomic conditioning . . . whereby the Pleidian Weonan modifications are more structural and mechanical."

"I haven't even assessed the crew yet, sir, other than those who were in this room; I don't know who's on board. Normally, as you well know, I would have been a part of that decision-making."

The admiral's face grew stern. "Damn it, Galvin! We don't have time. We don't have an extra fucking minute to waste here. The Varapin are coming for us . . . coming for Earth AS WE SPEAK! If the 2nd Fleet can't detour them, it's "game over" for humanity. Our Thine and Pleidian Weonan allies won't be able to save us!"

I let that sink in. "You're putting a lot of eggs in one basket, sir. The 2nd fleet being the one and only safeguard to saving mankind?"

The admiral looked to the others, now standing around us. "I didn't want to say this out loud, and I'm sorry to have to put this so bluntly, Galvin . . . but the 2nd fleet isn't the only safeguard to save humanity. It is simply a means to give us *more time*. Time for our mining operations on Juno 5 to catch up, time to get our other Space-Navy assets battle-ready for when the Varapin's *do* arrive here in this sector."

"The sacrificial lamb."

"Perhaps, but you've beaten the odds before, Galvin." He

shrugged. "War is a bitch. Get to know your new ship. Get to know your new crew. And as soon as the 2nd fleet arrives here, make haste toward Andromeda."

Admiral Block left the conference room looking as if the weight of the world was upon his shoulders – *perhaps it was.*

The others now approached, those same crewmembers that I'd arrived here with. I said, "You heard?"

Lieutenant Pristy said, "How could we not . . . the admiral wasn't exactly discreet. He looked scared, Captain."

"I got the feeling he didn't really expect us to survive . . . and that's why he was angry," Derrota said.

"Then we have to make sure that we *do* survive," Lieutenant Ryder said. The Arrow fighter pilot looked over to Coogong Sohp, who was getting up from his seat at the table, just now, with difficulty.

I hurried over to him, giving him a hand. Considering the Thine people had little more than useless nubs for legs and arms, I wondered what kind of robotics beneath his environ suit enabled him to be even this mobile. I said, "Coogong . . . can I ask you a question?"

"Of course, Captain."

"This here is Captain Wallace Ryder. He's in charge of our fleet of Arrow fighters."

Ryder shot me a surprised look, having gone from the rank of Lieutenant to Captain in the blink of an eye. It had been long overdue, and I had a feeling that Ryder would earn every bit of this promotion within days to come. I had put the paperwork through to the Brass close to four months earlier, even before the Grish attack within the Auriga Star System. The sign-off came while I was agonizing through physical therapy.

"Talk to me about these Zathium modifications – the kind of subatomic conditioning your scientists are doing. Specifically, can these alterations be made to our individual Arrow fighters, as well?"

Coogong pondered the idea. "I believe your Arrows utilize single HyperDrive components capable of FTL . . . no?"

Ryder said, "Yeah, FTL is possible with an Arrow Class Space Fighter. . . but not recommended."

"I will take a look. There are minimum quantities of Zathium to consider."

"Can you get more? Like within the next few hours?"

"Perhaps. I must go . . . talk to my people." Coogong Sohp's faceplate went opaque as he headed out of the conference room.

"Perhaps now is an appropriate time to tour the new and improved *USS Hamilton*, sir?" Ensign Plorinne said enthusiastically.

"First, I want to see what the hell you've changed on my bridge."

It was not the same bridge I remembered. Sure, the basic layout was similar, with the adjoining Combat Information Center (CIC) off to the left, and there was roughly the same number of console stations here – but everything was new and different. At the forward section of the large compartment was a 3D Halo Display of incredible clarity and resolution.

Currently being displayed was the *USS Hamilton* itself, slowly rotating around on its center axis. In the middle of the bridge was the raised "Captain's Mount," an ascribed historical reference back to a period when officers were on horseback, usually atop a hill or ridgeline, observing an ensuing battle below. Sure, they'd changed out the actual seat for something new with more complicated controls on the armrests, but it looked comfortable enough.

Lieutenant Pristy moved past me to her Tactical Station console.

"You know how to use that new-fangled interface control board, Lieutenant?"

"I do . . . we all have been well trained, Captain," she said, gesturing to the others now taking their seats. Crewmember Don Chin was seated at the Weapons Console, while Crewmember Grimes took up the Comms Station's controls. Chief of Security Alistair Mattis and Science Officer Stefan Derrota both stood nearby appraising the compartment. Typically, Derrota would occupy the CIC next door. Now that he had an actual security department to manage again, Mattis would do double-duty here on the bridge, or within his own rebuilt department up on some other deck. I had a lot of catching up to do. Hardy had taken a position at the rear corner of the bridge. He looked to be in a sort of recharge or stasis mode.

A melodic, almost musical, series of sounds emanated down from above. A woman's voice was being broadcast, "High-priority incoming hail from the *USS Capitol* . . . Fleet Commander Roger Brice."

I looked to Lieutenant Pristy, who smiled back at me.

It was the Main Artificial THought Resource – commonly called *MATHR* – the *Hamilton's* central AI system, located physically within her own nook over in the CIC compartment. Her voice was new now, younger, far more pleasant.

"Open the channel, MATHR," I said, taking my seat at the Captain's Mount.

The Halo Display came alive with a replacement feed of the Fleet Commander.

The man was completely bald on top, which was strange in and of itself since male-pattern baldness had been cured over seventy-five years prior. Apparently, this look was by choice. His beak-like nose was long, and his artic-cold blue eyes were small. The man could not have looked any more like a bird than if he'd grown feathers and flapping wings. His uniform was pristine white with teal piping details. Now, it seemed that each US Space-Navy warship's attire was different for each vessel – making its own kind of fashion statement. Or maybe, it was more like sport's teams' uniforms. I noticed the Fleet Commander's lapels had the unmistakable twin Sun Bursts. This man had the newly created officer military rank of *Elitetan*.

"Captain Quintos, you look well-rested. I assume you are prepared to break port?"

I didn't like his tone or inference that I was just standing around like someone schmoozing at a cocktail party. "Thank you, Elitetan Brice –"

"You can address me as Fleet Commander, Captain."

"Yes, sir. There are a few last-minute technical issues that still need addressing."

Brice was already shaking his head. "No, no, no . . . I have been forewarned about you, Captain Quintos, how you like to play by your own set of rules and how you have no problem bending or breaking those same rules in the process. You will ready your ship for immediate departure." Brice looked at his TAC-Band. "I'm feeling especially gracious today. You have one hour, and not a minute longer. Brice out." The feed disappeared, quickly replaced with the slowly-rotating *USS Hamilton.*

Chapter 5

Sitting within the mostly unchanged confines of the Captain's Ready Room, I was reviewing the technical specs for *Hamilton's* new Pleidian modifications. In addition to basic structural repairs – those required from the battle damage the ship had endured – there were countless other additions and improvements made that could take me weeks to review in detail.

Lieutenant Pristy stuck her head in the entranceway, "Captain . . . Elitetan Brice has disseminated the fleet's mission parameters."

I waved her in. "Come on in and take a seat."

Doing as asked, she scrolled through the data and information on her tablet. "You want the good news – or the bad – first?"

"Always start with the bad news first."

"Well, I spoke to my counterpart, onboard the *Capitol,* Lieutenant Tammy Rye. She says working under Elitetan Brice is more than challenging. Both ambitious and competitive, he's a petty and insecure officer. Admiral Block's selection of you to captain *Hamilton* practically gave him a stroke. Felt the Fleet Commander should be skippering the fleet's primary asset . . . this dreadnought."

"Kind of does make more sense," I said.

"Yeah, well, that wasn't part of the deal with the Pleidian Weonan," Pristy said, chewing on the inside of her lip and looking a little cagey.

"What? What do you know that you *aren't* telling me?" I asked, checking my new TAC-Band. I'd received several messages from Wallace Ryder and one from Chief Porter.

She pursed her lips, looking as if she may have said more than she should have. "I can't keep this a secret any longer, even though the admiral made me promise to. Said it would compromise the mission. Captain, I've known about this for weeks."

"Uh-huh," I said, tapping a response to Ryder.

She said, "Word has it that *Hamilton's* USA ownership was actually forfeited over to the Pleidians as part of our war pact deal."

"Okay . . . well, the ship was pretty much worthless at that point, right? And the US Space-Navy probably would have scrapped her for raw materials anyway."

Pristy added, "Yeah, but when she was returned here, all bright and shiny . . . ownership of this amazing vessel that we are now occupying was not deeded back to the US Space-Navy."

"So, she's what . . . on loan to us by the Pleidian Weonan?

That makes sense to me. Hell, the ship was rebuilt at their expense."

"No. You're way off base, Captain. You were supposed to be told about this. Was part of the Pleidian conditions."

"I was in stasis. Again, to me, it's all understandable."

"Captain, there was supposed to be a celebration, a special kind of christening extravaganza. Empress Shawlee Tee wanted to perform the symbolic handing over of ship keys, herself."

Only half-listening to her as I now continued to peruse the ship's new tech specs on my desk halo-display, she suddenly had my full attention. I looked at her. "Wait. What is it you're going out of the way not to tell me fully?"

"Okay. Well, here's the good news aspect. This ship . . . it's all yours, Captain." Wide-eyed, she covered her mouth with both hands and squealed. "The *USS Hamilton* was a gift from Empress Shawlee Tee to you . . . personally! I guess you not only saved her life, which was a bigger-than-big event, of course, but you also helped bring her world out of a prolonged despondency. You are a true hero among the Pleidian Weonan people."

"Wait . . . go back just a little, before that whole hero-to-the-Pleidians thing . . ."

She said, "This ship, you *own* it."

"No! No way. This ship must be worth billions and billions of dollars."

"Uh, try more like trillions and trillions of dollars," she rebuked.

"Who else knows about this?"

"Of course, Admiral Block does. All the brass. Also, Fleet Commander Elitetan Roger Brice surely knows too. Also, my friend, Lieutenant Tammy Rye, and of course Derrota, he knows —"

"So pretty much everyone in the world but me?"

"Pretty much."

I sat back in my chair and thought about the new implications. Musing out loud, I said, "Fuel is going to be expensive. Upkeep and maintenance, oh God . . . and port fees. Fuck, no! I can't afford to own a dreadnought."

"I just told you that you own the most advanced, amazing, starship in this entire part of the galaxy, and all you're worried about is port fees?"

"I didn't ask to be given ownership of this ship! It's going to cause problems, conflicts. It already has."

"I thought you'd be happy. Thrilled, even."

"Look, I don't even own a HoverCar back on Earth. Never owned a home, and I leased an apartment. I don't *own* things, Gail . . . owning things scares me."

"Then, I imagine you are outright petrified right now," she said, not looking sympathetic to my situation. I thought back, recalling how Doc Viv acted in the meeting. She'd looked pissed off – annoyed at something – wouldn't even look at me. *Hmm.* Due to the fact, maybe, she'd been ordered to serve on my personally-owned starship. I almost laughed out loud at how ludicrous this all was.

Lieutenant Pristy said, "There's more."

I raised my brows.

"All those things you mentioned . . . maintenance expenses, and such, are covered by the Pleidians in perpetuity. Not only for you, but for your heirs, as well."

"I don't have any heirs."

"I'm available," she said, giggling. "Sorry, bad joke."

I let out a breath. "Can we talk now about the real reason you came in here? The fleet's mission parameters?" I checked the time on my TAC-Band. "We're already ten minutes late leaving port."

The lieutenant stood and stared down at me. "Are you going to keep her?"

"No, of course not. I'll donate the ship to the US Space-Navy . . . should look good on my next Officer's Peer Review."

"Don't think you can do that, Captain . . . be a slap in the face of our most powerful ally."

"Close the door on the way out."

"What do I tell Elitetan Brice when he calls in again?"

"Tell him I fell down an elevator shaft . . . or maybe say I got sucked out an airlock; that one always works well."

She rolled her eyes at me, then left me to ponder my odd predicament.

I spent the next half-hour reviewing the upcoming mission parameters. I learned the 2nd Fleet had grown substantially – a Battle Group that maintained eleven powerful warship assets: foremost, the *USS Hamilton,* a dreadnought. Also, the *USS Capitol*, a Heavy Battleship – the second most powerful vessel within the fleet. There also were four Jericho-Class Destroyers: the *USS Billings, USS Kennedy,* the *USS Gallaher,* and the

USS Starlight, as well as two big Spacecraft Carriers, the *USS Enterprise* and the *USS Louisiana*. Finally listed were three fast and nimble Corvettes: the *USS Gun*, the *USS Brave*, and the *USS Mighty*.

I looked closely at the proposed flight directives. The distance between Earth and the edge of the Andromeda Galaxy was about two-and-a-half-million light-years. That vast expanse was well beyond anything an Earth Battle Group Fleet had traversed before. It required four refueling stops, but since there were no fueling depots along the way, the two Spacecraft Carriers had been specifically configured, adding massive holding tanks. *Huh . . . so we'd be carrying the required amounts of fuel needed with us.* Preliminary calculations showed us making nine manufactured wormhole jumps. Hey, even moving multiples of FTL speeds, it would be painfully slow, considering the prospect of traveling so many millions of light-years.

I noticed that the nine jumps were not in a straight line toward our objective: a convergence point with the enemy, that Varapin fleet. The directive looked to be well- calculated – dropping the 2nd Fleet into outer boundaries, or even into open *frontier* space. Some territories were known to be open shipping lanes that were more or less friendly, while other drop locations were unfriendly, about as hostile as we could find ourselves in. For subsequent jumps, those between wait times, the transitioning times would need to be expedited. Unfortunately, there was no getting around the *JDTR* – Jump Down-Time Requisite – a calculation of progressive light-year distances – along with the size and power diversity of the manufactured wormholes.

Add to that a whole slew of other metrics I've long forgotten, and you arrive at the JDTR. The wormholes we would be manufacturing to accommodate the entire fleet, would be massive. So, I suspected that our subsequent JDTR timeframes would require no less than six to seven hours of wait time, twiddling our thumbs. That's an *eternity* when showing up uninvited within unfriendly space.

I noticed the slightest rippling effect upon the liquid in my coffee cup. I closed my eyes and listened but heard nothing. Checking the ship's status on my desk's Halo-Display, I saw – sure enough – that *Hamilton's* new HyperDrives were cycling up. I shook my head, recalling how obtrusively noisy *Hamilton's* old drives were, causing the deck plates to jump and vibrate.

My TAC-Band was vibrating again, but none other than Fleet Commander *Elitetan* Roger Brice was calling this time.

I accepted the call. "Yes, Elitetan Brice."

"Please . . . that's Fleet Commander Brice. What is the damn delay? Eleven US Space-Navy warships and twenty-three-thousand personnel are waiting. Am I going to have a problem with you, Captain?"

"Sir . . . for all intents and purpose, this is a brand-new warship. Added onto that, this crew is unfamiliar with much of the new technology . . ."

"Enough! I want that dreadnought out of port, joining formation, within ten minutes. Have I made myself clear?"

"Crystal . . . copy that, sir." I closed the channel.

Melodic tones cascaded down from above. MATHR's voice

filled the space around me, "Captain Quintos . . . Chief Craig Porter requests your presence in Engineering and Propulsion."

"Tell him I'm on my way."

Emerging from the Captain's Ready Room into the Bridge, I found Hardy and the young Pleidian Ensign Plorinne waiting for me. I was fairly used to Hardy shadowing my movements, but Ensign Plorinne – not so much.

"Captain . . . would this be a good time for me to start escorting you around? A quick tour."

I quickened my pace. "Have a lot on my plate, right now . . . walk with me, Ensign."

Lieutenant Pristy yelled across, "Captain, you still haven't met your new XO."

"When I get back."

"And *Elitetan* Brice? He's hailing the Bridge again!"

"Tell him we're having a problem getting our portside restraining clamps to release. But that we're working on it."

"You want me to lie to our new Fleet Commander?"

Already well into Whale's Alley by then, I didn't think an answer was warranted.

"Come on, Ensign Plorinne . . . try to keep up."

"Yes, sir. You and the robot have long strides," he responded breathily.

"Don't call me *the robot*," Hardy said.

"Sorry . . . I meant no disrespect."

"Yeah, well, I'm just *Hardy*."

We arrived at the location where the banks of new GravLifts were situated. I knew this because I saw Crewman Lasalle and a maintenance worker, already hard at work, painting a new orange border around where the hidden doors were located.

"I see you found the right kind of paint," I said.

"Yes, sir . . . Ensign Plorinne here actually steered me to the right storage compartment. But it's not paint, just another color of this same SmartCoat stuff."

"Got it."

Reaching over, Ensign Plorinne placed a palm onto the bulkhead. The same blue, glowing ship legend appeared just like before. "Where are we going, sir?"

"Zone G, Engineering and Propulsion."

The ensign tapped in the destination, and an opening expanded outward, becoming an entrance door. As we strode inside the car, I said, "Ensign, this routine seems overly cumbersome, having to place a hand on the bulkhead first. I liked it better when I could just wave at it, like I do at the other hatchway doors within this ship."

The ensign quickly went to work, tapping away at the set-up-level menu display. "Okay, sir . . . I'm reconfiguring all the ship's GravLift passageway doors to be triggered by a wave-of-hand motion. Also, MATHR will ask the lift's occupant where it is he or she wants to go. Does that work for you, sir?"

"Yes. Thank you."

The lift gently came to a stop. The door opened, revealing Chief Craig Porter waiting there for us. He didn't look happy.

"What's up, Craig? What's all the hubbub about?"

"We have a problem . . . a big problem."

Chapter 6

Varapin Empire Warship, Sintchu – Exiting M31 (Andromeda) Galaxy

Conductor Sprin-Rop Kyber

Conductor Kyber, Sr. Varapin officer of *Rage of the Gonjun Ract Fleet*, glided soundlessly through one empty passageway after another – the fabric of his long black robe fluttering mere inches above the deck. The hour was late, and all but a few of his loyal crew had long since adjourned into their respective, coffin-sized, Ebom-Pods. The next wormhole leap was imminent, and he needed to get back to the *Sintchu's* bridge.

He'd spent the last two hours within the detention center. More answers were required. The foul, repugnant Grish officer had proven to be weak – had moaned and whined even before any real torture had begun. Technically, the Varapin and the Grish had just entered a war pact, but Kyber trusted no foreigner, no alien, at face value. Just one more reason the Varapin were still the dominant force within their own galaxy – and soon, another. If Sub-Capitaine Porskel was an example of all Grish officers, they would prove to be poor allies. He'd put up little resistance, and mere minutes into the questioning, the fearful, odoriferous Grish officer had shit himself. More information would be needed from Sub-Capitaine Porskel – but that would have to wait until later. Conductor Kyber had wanted to indulge his voracious appetite, to force the Captain's head back and inhale the fleshy being's life force energy. This act would have, undoubtedly, left a nasty taste in his mouth. These Grish were disgusting. But alas, he had restrained himself. What he had learned thus far had given him pause. The Human, Thine, Pleidian Weonan alliance was clearly a force to be reckoned with – adversaries not to be underestimated. And this refurbished dreadnought he learned of, this *USS Hamilton* – if the Grish Sub-Capitaine's intel was correct, was a vessel of formidable prowess. Not in the same league as the *Sintchu*, but a concern just the same.

Entering the *Sintchu's* bridge, his second-in-command, Regent Malimand, relinquished the command post. Bowing his hooded head, he gestured to the forward display, "We have entered uncharted territory, here, within this desolate void between galaxies. While preparing for our next leap, sir, a large fleet . . . seventeen Tafmolly warships in all, have decloaked and gone to battle stations. They have weapons locked onto all of our ships . . . evidently, prepared to fire. The fleet's commanding officer is demanding our immediate surrender."

Considering the situation, Conductor Kyber extended his

skeletal jawline, whereby a thin tongue, black and forked at its tip, curled upward to moisten the Conductor's thin upper lip.

Regent Malimand said, "What are your wishes, sir? Shall I awaken several teams . . . dispatch our Ravage-Class landers, perhaps? There is ample availability within our cistern tanks. There again, these are small creatures with insignificant life forces, perhaps closer in size to small rodents."

Kyber shook his head, "Let our crew rest. Destroy the rodents, we have a schedule to keep. That, and my Ebom-Pod calls to me." He offered his second-in-command a skeletal, toothy grin.

"As you wish, Conductor." Regent Malimand immediately barked off a series of high-pitched commands to the sparse bridge crew, which, in turn, was communicated to the bridge crews of each warship within the fleet. "Shields up! Fire at will!"

In a brilliant show of Varapin force, powerful Dual Vortex Laser Beam weapons, *DVLB's*, came alive. These particular death beams, when fired, overlapped and combined in a cork-screw effect. Damage propagated by the DVLB weapons were always catastrophic – quickly overloading an enemy's energy shields. At that point, exposed ship hulls were super-heated to 30,000,000 degrees Fahrenheit –melting within a nanosecond. All life within: incinerated. To date, the Varapin had yet to lose a space battle of any real consequence – and Conductor Sprin-Rop Kyber was confident that on this day, victory would soon be his.

Even before Conductor Kyber had moved toward the

Bridge's exit, he witnessed the last of the Tafmolly fleet being annihilated. *What a pathetic, insignificant, species . . .*

Chapter 7

Halibart Station, USS Hamilton, Engineering and Propulsion

Captain Galvin Quintos

We followed Chief Porter aft, deep into the bowels of Propulsion and Engineering. My head swiveled back and forth, taking in all the changes having been made here. Everything seemed to be new, including four large clear-walled reactor domes, and several new HyperDrive units that, at eighteen feet tall, were actually smaller than the previous ones, but looked far more impressive and modern-looking.

We came to a stop in front of two large glass spirals that stood about my six-foot height. Both were filled with some sort of sparkling, energized green liquid. I'd never seen anything like them before.

"Captain . . . these are our new state-of-the-art Pleidian Weonan Jump Springs," Chief Porter said.

"Huh, they look like springs," Hardy said.

"They're not actual springs in that sense," the chief said. "Between the two of them, that one there being the primary, the other, the backup, they're now responsible for the manufacturing of *Hamilton's* . . . hell, *the fleet's* jump wormholes. MATHR is no longer involved with making any of the jump calculations. All AI functions, calculations and such, are self-contained within these Spring units."

"Okay . . . that's super interesting, Craig," I said. "So, you brought me down here just to tell me all this?"

"No. I brought you down here to show you *that*." The chief pointed to an area on the deck, glistening with something wet and green. I leaned over to get a better look.

"Best you keep your distance, Captain. Stuff is probably unstable," the chief said, looking irritated.

Hardy moved closer and knelt down. He reached a mechanical hand out while extending a long chopstick-like probe. "It's a sub-atomic soup mix of variant quantum particles called HydraQuant . . . that, and something else. Hmm."

Then, I noticed the group of five, short, environment-suit-wearing beings all huddled together, not ten feet away from us. The Thine scientists. They all had their faceplates in opaque mode. One of the little aliens stepped forward, his faceplate going from black to transparent. "Captain Quintos . . . I can explain."

"Is that you, Coogong Sohp?"

"Yes, sir, it is I."

"Did you have something to do with this . . . this leakage here?"

"Yes. Well, maybe."

"Does this have something to do with those elements, um, Goriom, Zathium, and Pilorium you were speaking of earlier? How you were going to supercharge the ship's various power sources?"

"It seems the Zathium, which is provided in a gaseous state, does not react well with the rubber-like sealing gaskets used by the Pleidians."

"So, you've already started your upgrades?"

"Uh, well, yes, we thought we'd get an early start on things."

"And how many of the ship systems have you messed with so far?"

The five scientists looked to one another and quietly conversed. Coogong said, "All of them. All ship systems that utilize HydraQuant, as well as ADAP."

I knew ADAP was the ship's primary fuel – an Exotic-Derivative Antimatter Proton mix. I looked over to Chief Porter, questioningly.

He said, "Shit . . . ADAP's used for all the basic propulsion system components, the HyperDrives . . . add to that, the ship's shields are discretely powered by ADAP."

"But we have added very minimum quantities of Zathium to the ships ADAP reservoirs," Coogong said, looking encouraged.

"So, only this Jump spring's system has that more concentrated mixture? Is that what you're saying?" I asked.

"Yes, Captain . . . but we had no idea this –"

I cut him off. "What can you do to fix the problem? We're now well over an hour late jumping out of the system."

The Thine alien stared at the two Jump spring units. "I'm sorry, but those two devices should be replaced. Be scrapped."

"Do we even have replacements for these onboard?" I asked.

Ensign Plorinne nodded, "Most definitely! These things blow out all the time, supposedly."

"That's at least something. So, how long?" I asked.

"They're pretty much plug-and-play . . . an hour, maybe two," Chief Porter said.

"And the other systems you introduced Zathium in to . . . the ADAP reservoirs?"

Once again, the Thine conversed between themselves. "I believe the quantities are low enough that no adverse reactions will take place. At least not for the short-term," Coogong said. "We'll have to keep an eye on the reactors . . ."

Now the question was, do I convey this shit storm of information to Elitetan Roger Brice? My initial thoughts were yes, of course, I should. The blame rested squarely on high command and Wentworth's shoulder for introducing this experimental mixture before it was thoroughly tested. Maybe this stuff worked well enough on traditional US ship mechanics, but clearly not on Pleidian Weonan ship mechanics. No, I'd be more than happy to pass the proverbial buck here, placing the blame on Wentworth and his cronies. Then I thought of Doc Viv. She seemed to have had some kind of involvement with this project. *Maybe that's what she'd been assigned to for the last few months while I was recovering.*

"What do you want to do, Cap?" Chief Porter asked, still looking disgusted at the two Jump springs.

"Swap them out ASAP. And don't speak of any of this to anyone yet." I looked to the Ensign and Hardy, and then to the five scientists. "This stays between us until I say otherwise, am I clear?"

Everyone nodded, looking unsure that it was the best course of action.

"Copy that," Hardy and Porter said.

Chief Porter said, "These are heavy MF-ers . . . we could use Hardy's help swapping them out."

"Stay here, Hardy. Do what you can to help. After that, use that high AI intellect of yours to better assess the other ADAP systems. I need to know just how fucked we really are here."

I arrived in HealthBay eight minutes later, having ignored no less than six TAC-Band and four MATHR hails – all requesting me to contact Fleet Commander Roger Brice. He'd waited this long – he could wait a tad longer.

I found Doc Viv within the laboratory adjacent to the Surgery Center. She was wearing a white lab coat and had her hair tied back into a tight ponytail. Leaning over, she had one eye pressed into the eyepiece of a microscope. She looked up, sensing my approach. She didn't look happy to see me. "I'm very busy, Galvin –"

"Knock it off, Vivian . . . you're going to tell me what the hell is going on."

"Don't call me that. And nothing's going on."

"Okay, so, I can contact Elitetan Roger Brice, tell him *Hamilton's* jump springs are toast because of that Zathium shit? That the whole mission may need to be scrubbed because someone didn't do their homework?"

She glared at me but said nothing.

"What's your involvement with Zathium . . . and with Wentworth?"

"That's none of your business."

I've never hit a woman. Never ever wanted to, but this was about as close as I'd ever come. "Look, I'm the captain of this ship. This mission just may decide the fate of fucking humanity, and you have the audacity to say that this is none of my business?

Her face flush, and she looked away.

"I've just returned from Engineering and Propulsion. That Zathium crap the Thine scientists are injecting into our power systems is breaking down –"

"Yeah, yeah, the sealing gaskets. I already know all that. What do you think I'm doing here? There's a problem with the molecular binding elements. It can be fixed."

"Again, what is your part in all this?"

She crossed her arms over her chest. She looked as if she was considering telling me. What I didn't expect was her eyes filling with moisture and a lone tear now making its way down her left cheek. She swallowed hard. "I'm sorry, Galvin." She shook her head, "But it's partially your fault."

"Mine?"

"Yes! Yours!"

Chapter 8

Major Vivian "Viv" Leigh – Ship's Primary Physician

She stared back at Galvin, her expression giving nothing away.

"Why is this *my* fault?" Quintos asked. "Up until a few weeks ago, I was lying in stasis growing back my new leg. In other words, totally oblivious to the world around me."

She turned her attention back to her work – her microscope.

Galvin continued, "Come on, what's your involvement with Wentworth? What's that all about? You certainly weren't a fan of his brother when he was alive."

She said, "It's your fault because they were coming after you, hell-bent on taking everything from you, including your freedom." Viv reached over and tapped at a nearby console. The object she'd been observing through her microscope's lenses was now being displayed in all its 3D glory via a hovering

Halo-Display. She watched Galvin as he took in the energized, colorful subatomic nexus.

"It's beautiful, but what am I looking at?" he asked.

"I'll give you one guess," she replied.

"Zathium."

"Yup, Zathium. That and HydraQuant . . . right out of that busted jump spring unit."

"I'm glad it's being looked at, but why is *Hamilton's* primary physician looking –"

"Galvin, I'm a highly-educated scientist. And for your sake, you should be glad that I am."

He shut his eyes, clearly frustrated. "What is going on, Viv?"

She said, "Talco Wentworth, the man you saw me with this morning, did not take the death, the murder, of his brother well. In fact, he has sworn his considerable financial means to make those at fault pay; and pay dearly."

"Good! Between the Grish and Ensign Hughes, he should have no shortage of people to direct his anger at."

Viv was already shaking her head. "That's not how people like Wentworth and his army of lawyers think. The Grish are, well, the Grish, and not anyone he can easily sue. And the murderous Ensign Hughes is dead . . . again, not someone Talco can go after."

Galvin shrugged. "Oh, well."

"No. Not, *oh, well.* The way Talco Wentworth and his legal team see things, the US Space-Navy and *Hamilton's* skipper were to blame for allowing that to even happen." She held up her forefinger, "First, the *Hamilton*, being in her decrepit state, should never have been allowed out of space-dock. What Wentworth is referring to as a 'rickety death trap with a compromised AI.' An AI that provided almost zero security."

"Okay, I can almost see his point on that one," Galvin said.

"Second," Viv said holding up two fingers, "Following the Grish battle and Captain Tannock's grave injuries, one Commander Galvin Quintos, a very young XO with multiple disciplinary infractions, should never have been put in command . . . especially not given the responsibility of such a large warship."

"Wait . . . Milo Wentworth was already dead before that Grish attack. Prior to my taking command."

Viv shook her head. "There is no unmistakable evidence to prove that. And let me tell you, I've spent the better part of three weeks trying to do so."

Galvin's expression softened some, "Really . . . you did that for me?" He offered her a crooked grin.

"Shut up. This is far more serious than you realize. You were in big trouble and, most likely, upon waking up from your prolonged nap, headed to the brig for years."

She hesitated before going on. *Talking about making a deal with the devil – what will he think of me after this?*

"Go on."

"During those three weeks of trying to find a way to clear you – and the US Space-Navy – I spent a good portion of my time looking into the Wentworth's. Galvin, there are few people I've come across in life who are slimier, more abhorrent, than that family. They take self-preservation and greed to a level unheard of for a hundred-and-fifty years." For the first time, she almost smiled. "Then, it hit me. I wasn't going to help you by playing defense. I'd have to appeal to his core, narcissistic primal urges."

Galvin looked at her with a raised brow.

"No, not sex . . . although he's certainly tried to get me into his cabin several times over the last few weeks. People like him want two things even more than sex; that's power and money."

"And you figured out how to get one of two of those for him?"

"My research on the two brothers led me to what Milo Wentworth was doing onboard when *Hamilton* was attacked in the first place, near Bon-Corfue, within the approaching Auriga Star System. It was all about the Wentworth's gaining mineral rights on Juno 5, a mere two light-years from Earth."

"I think most of us knew at least that much," Galvin said.

She nodded, "Well, after the Grish attack, and Earth formally declaring war on the Grish, Wentworth's high hopes of capitalizing on that backward world's amazing mineral and exotic element deposits fell apart. Earth resources all went toward the war effort. There wasn't a mining ship to be found that would risk traversing open space while the Grish were attacking more and more regularly."

"So, what did you do, Viv? Why am I not sitting in a brig somewhere wondering what's for dinner tonight . . . rice gruel, flour gruel, or maybe millet gruel?"

"What the hell is millet?"

"I'm not sure. Go on."

This time, she did smile. "I simply asked Talco to meet me for drinks one night. Told him I had a proposition for him. One that would make him the wealthiest man on Earth."

"Wow, you don't mess around. And I take it he agreed to meet with you?"

"Sure did."

"Don't keep me guessing, what was this earth-shattering brainstorm you presented to him?"

"That if he could see fit to drop his legal suits against both you and the US Space-Navy, I promised to help him reestablish his mining ventures on Juno 5. And that I could almost guarantee sales contracts far beyond anything he and his brother had dreamed of prior."

Galvin, looking thoughtful, rubbed the stubble on his chin. "It was your idea to use the three Juno 5 elements – Goriom, Zathium, and Pilorium – to boost warship power outputs."

"Uh-huh, mostly Zathium. I'd gotten hold of several tiny samples earlier. Samples that practically cost me my life savings, by the way."

"I'll pay you back."

"Oh, sure you will . . . with what? Your goofy looks?"

"You don't know?" he asked.

"Know what?"

"Um . . . never mind, I'll tell you later. So, Talco obviously went for the deal."

"Oh yeah, he jumped on it. Within a few days, he'd drawn up papers for me to sign. A new LLC was formed with me as a minor contributing partner. I was to continue my research on how, mostly using Zathium, I could enhance US Space-Navy propulsion systems. Even the early test results were mind-blowing, Galvin. Zathium and ADAP seemed to be a match made in heaven. And since most spacefaring vessels use ADAP as their fuel source, the prospects were enormous. Talco and I gave a real-life demonstration using an old beat-to-shit thirty-year-old corvette gunship on its last legs. We showed before and after comparison results. The Zathium gaseous additive so improved performance, the military brass couldn't get a contract signed fast enough. Wentworth's mining operations were back in business and with the protection of the 8th fleet. There would be just one possible roadblock."

"What's that?"

"A real, actually-new warship test was required. Something far bigger than an old corvette."

"Tell me it's not the *Hamilton*."

Viv's temper flared. "Why not? I knew that the ship still, for the most part, utilized that same fucking fuel she always had . . . ADAP. I'd tested Zathium every which way but Sunday on ADAP. And I'd specifically asked that Coogong Sohp and his Thine scientists be on board to assist me. There was no reason to think things wouldn't be anything but successful! How was I to know Pleidian Weonan shipbuilders use a kind of rubber-like gaskets that turn to paste when mixed with Zathium?"

Galvin let out a long breath and shook his head. "What a clusterfuck."

"You're telling me? If US Command finds out about this, they may cancel the contract with Wentworth. And he'll . . ."

"Come on, what can he do? Fuck him!" Galvin said.

"I don't think you know the length men like him go to get even. I told you, I researched him and his family. He'll come after me. More likely, pay a professional to do it. I have zero doubt about that."

"So, you're saying we have to keep this a secret."

"Just until I can figure out how to neutralize the destructive effects of the Zathium."

"Viv, we're minutes away from jumping out of system. We're going into battle, and that Zathium shit is already coursing through this ship's veins, causing who knows how much damage."

"I just need a little more time. I think I'm close."

Galvin didn't look convinced. Viv heard his TAC-Band vibrating and saw he was being hailed. Ignoring it, Galvin said, "You need to guarantee that you and those Thine scientists can fix all the ADAP issues. It's not like we'll have replacement parts for reactors and drives, light-years from here."

She said, "The jump springs cannot be repaired, as you know, but I'm confident the fuel system, with its much-diluted amounts of Zathium, *can* be repaired."

Galvin continued to look at her as he raised his TAC-Band, which was vibrating again. "Talk to me, Craig."

"We got the two new jump springs installed. Ran a quick diagnostic on the system. Should be good to go for manufacturing wormholes."

"Why is it you sound less than confident, then?"

"It's fine . . . I say we give it a go."

Galvin said nothing for several beats.

"Galvin?" said the Chief of Engineering.

"Fine . . . keep me and Doc Viv up to date on any other issues."

"And the little scientists running around here?"

"Give them anything they need."

"Copy that, Cap. Chief out."

Another hail announcement was coming from MATHR.

"Captain Quintos, your presence is required on the Bridge. Captain Quintos, your presence –"

"I'm on my way," he said. He gave Viv one last look, "Keep me apprised, Doc." Galvin turned to leave.

She wanted to tell him she was sorry again. That it hadn't been her intention to make things worse instead of better. She got herself situated behind her microscope and continue her work.

Chapter 9

Captain Galvin Quintos

Entering the bridge, I saw the face of Fleet Commander Elitetan Roger Brice dominating the forward Halo-Display. Still birdlike, his beady eyes locking onto mine in the same second I saw him. Lieutenant Pristy was standing at her station, making excuses for my absence.

"Captain Quintos!"

"Yes, Elitetan Brice, how can I help you?"

The Fleet Commander's nostrils flared. Although I could not see all of the man via the feed, I was certain his hands were balled into white-knuckled fists.

"We are three hours late . . ." he looked at his TAC-Band. "Make that three-and-a-half hours late, leaving this system. I warned you, Captain, I would not idly stand by while you disrupt this mission. It is too important . . . far bigger than your disruptive antics."

Then, I saw the two large MPs making their way toward

me. I glanced over to Chief of Security, Alistair Mattis, who the MP's technically reported to. Looking sheepish, he mouthed the words, *I'm sorry . . . had no choice . . .*

I smiled and winked before turning back to the Halo-Display. "Oh, by the way, Fleet Commander . . . Admiral Block wishes you a safe and successful mission."

Elitetan Brice held up a hand, gesturing for the MP's to hold up. "You spoke to Admiral Block?"

"Yes, just now over secure laser-link comms," This was actually a stone-faced lie. No conversation had taken place between the admiral and me. "I felt there were issues I needed to make him aware of – the same mission-critical issues you hadn't been interested in hearing about earlier."

"You're treading on thin ice, Captain. I assure you, you don't want me as an enemy." Brice hesitated, perhaps choosing his next words carefully. He attempted a smile, which didn't really work. "So . . . can I take it the *USS Hamilton's* technical issues have now been resolved?"

I gave a half shrug. "Sir, this is, for all intents and purpose, a new ship. Rebuilt from stem to stern. There are going to be issues. The crew is tirelessly working out the various kinks as we speak. But I am encouraged to say, *Hamilton* is now ready to take her place within the 2nd Fleet."

"Good, good, glad to hear it. Our first wormhole drop location will be near the spiral nebula Sh 2-289. The location should provide little danger of hostilities or attack."

I held my tongue. That far out, there would be no way of knowing if we were dropping into a dangerous sector of space until we actually got there. He was making assumptions that could easily come back and bite him, all of us, in the ass.

The Fleet Commander attempted another smile, "And I have good news for you, as well, Captain. I'd like to introduce you to your new Executive Officer. I believe you two are already acquainted?"

As if on cue, two individuals entered at the back of the bridge simultaneously. The one on the left I knew and disliked immensely, Chaplain Thomas Trent. Striding next to him was none other than Captain Eli Tannock. The same Captain Tannock who had skippered the *Hamilton* before me – having been near fatally injured during the Grish battle at Auriga Star System. He looked healthy enough now. A barrel-chested man with a salt and pepper close-cropped buzz cut, he raised his chin, as if in defiance of the scrutinizing eyes upon him at that moment.

I looked back to Fleet Commander Brice and saw the satisfaction in his eyes. He said, "I'm sure you are aware, Captain Quintos, it is not unheard of for a ship's Captain to, um, fill in as XO, when circumstances call for it. And as you so alluded to yourself, the *Hamilton* is an immense responsibility. Having Captain, XO, Tannock's many fine years of service behind him, well . . . it will only improve our odds of success."

Had it been possible to pull that virtual image of Fleet Commander Brice out through the Halo-Display and show him my true level of appreciation, I may have done just that. The pompous shit didn't realize this was a huge mistake, not only affecting me and my ability to command, but the crew, as well. This was guaranteed to cause split loyalties – contention and strife. I watched as the two close friends approached. Just as the Fleet Commander's eyes showed satisfaction at my displeasure, Chaplain Thomas Trent did not try to hide his utter jubilance. *Fucker.*

"I'll let you get reacquainted. Please, have your helmsman bring *Hamilton* into formation, Captain Quintos. Signal the fleet when you have established a jump wormhole out to our first designated spacial coordinates. Fleet Commander Brice out."

"This is a blessed day," the chaplain said, all smiles. "To see this good man back on his bridge and in such fine form . . . well, it almost brings an old cleric like me to tears."

Tannock said, "Thank you, Thomas. As always, your friendship and support, has made all the difference. But please, go now, and let us all get back to work."

The two shook hands. The chaplain offered me a slight bow of his head and rueful smile, then turned to leave.

I glanced about the bridge. What I saw was disturbing and precisely what I'd feared: a bridge crew who were doing their best to look pleased. But their forced, pasted-on smiles didn't fool me.

"Captain Quintos, would it be possible for me to address the bridge?"

I hesitated a moment before answering. "Of course, XO."

"Thank you, sir," Tannock said, then looked from one crewmember to the next. "Many of you know me and have served with me in the past. I hope some of you would consider me a friend, or, at the very least, respect the relationship we held. I want to thank you for your service. Going forward, this ship has but one Captain, and that is Captain Galvin Quintos. He, alone, skippers this fine vessel. He has proven to be a resourceful leader, one that I, too, will be proud to serve under. Understand, I am not here to cause problems, to cause any kind of allegiance issues. That would be counterproductive. I will be loyal to this captain as you must be, as well. The truth of the matter is, I simply was not ready to retire. Felt I still had, *have*, more to give the US Space-Navy. Doing so as your XO will be both my pleasure and my honor."

His words were spoken sincerely, and I could tell that the bridge crew accepted them without hesitation. When Tannock turned away from them to face me, his face was like a block of stone – impossible to read. So, I would reserve judgment for now and just keep an eye on the situation.

I said, "Helm . . . report."

Crewman Don Chen said, "All port restraining clamps have disengaged, sir. Propulsion Systems operating normally without issues. Request permission to join the fleet, sir."

"Permission granted, Helmsman. Proceed into designated formation placement."

I signaled Lieutenant Pristy with a nod of my head. I had prearranged with her what she was to do next. She changed the Halo-Display feed to that of Earth – the blue world with its surrounding cotton-like wisps of white clouds seemed more beautiful than ever. "Look alive, everyone. Our actions over the next few weeks just might determine the longevity of our home-world. We fail, Earth's population will face a terrible, unthinkable fate at the hands of a powerful alien race . . . the Varapin."

The feed changed, this time showing a three-dimensional view of space – the Milky Way Galaxy and part of the distant Andromeda Galaxy, next door. I said, "The craggy green line indicates the fleet's course out to the very edge of the Milky Way. The nine red dots along the line represent our proposed manufactured jump points. Those four red dots circled in blue are designated refueling stops where the fleet's two spacecraft carriers, the *USS Enterprise* and the *USS Louisiana,* will get to work replenishing depleted fleet asset fuel levels."

I said, "Science Officer Derrota, do you have anything to add concerning the first jump location?"

"Stop off one will be on the outskirts of a planetary system centered around the blue B-type star, LSS 86, located near the spiral nebula Sh 2-289, which is at the far edge of the Cygnus – or Outer Arm of the Milky Way. Note that this is right on the rim of the galaxy. The star is an extremely bright blue B-type, a young main-sequence star with a mass sixteen times that of the Sun."

XO Tannock stepped forward, "And there will be sufficient reserves to take the fleet all the way there, as well as back home again?"

I said, "It will be close, XO. We have a mere twenty-percent over-allowance."

I inwardly smiled knowing something Tannock, apparently, did not. That with the Zathium additive, as caustic as it was to the propulsion system's inner workings, it purportedly added an additional twenty-five percent to the *Hamilton's* FTL fuel mileage. But we'd just have to see if that was true or not.

A new and unpleasant tone emanated down from above. I anticipated hearing MATHR's voice, but it was that of Fleet Commander Brice. His face had replaced the view of space and our prescribed mission course.

"Good morning, and congratulations to all crewmembers of the 2nd Fleet. Soon we will embark on a journey out to the farthest reaches of the Galaxy. We will come face-to-face with an enemy like none other . . ."

Only half-listening to Fleet Commander Brice prattle on, I saw that Ensign Plorinne and Hardy were at the back of the bridge, both trying to look overly-casual at getting my attention. I nodded back at them, letting them know I'd join them in a minute. But first, I moved over to the Helm Station and watched, on Chen's console Halo-Display, the disposition of *Hamilton*, now carefully making its way between several of the fleet's massive battlecruisers. As Brice's voice droned on, I leaned down and said, "Have you received the exact final first leg jump coordinates near LSS 86?"

"Yes, sir. Came over from the *USS Capitol* a while ago."

The Capitol was the fleet's command ship, a Heavy Battleship. "And *Hamilton* is still designated to manufacture the jump wormhole?" I said, just loud enough for Chen to hear.

He nodded. "The Chief assures me the new jump springs

are operating normally . . . no issues reported." Chen looked at me with alarm. "Should another vessel within the fleet be –"

"No. It's fine. Continue on, Chen," I said, stepping away from the Helm Station and heading for the back of the bridge. I could almost feel Commander Brice's eyes boring into my back. I'm sure he was less than pleased with my lack of attention to what I was sure was supposed to be a motivating speech. I reached Hardy and the Ensign, "What is it?"

Ensign Plorinne spoke first, "We may have a problem, sir."

Chapter 10

"Stowaway?" I repeated.

Hardy said, "Wentworth was supposed to have left the ship along with all other nonmilitary or nonessential personnel back at Halibart Shipyards." The ChronoBot glanced up – his face display, comprised of numerous rearranging sensor lights, now took on a thoughtful faux expression.

"And you know he's still on board the ship?" I asked.

Alistair Mattis stepped into the conversation. "I'd previously configured MATHR to give me a heads-up for just such circumstances. There were just too many non-crewmembers of late for me to personally keep track of. Granted, several individuals have, indeed, submitted the necessary request forms to stay onboard . . . like our Thine scientists. But Talco Wentworth, no, he wasn't cleared for this mission."

"Just have MATHR track his TAC-Band," I said.

"Gee, thank you, Galvin. I wish I'd thought of that," the Chief of Security said, heavy with sarcasm. "He's a tech wizard.

He'd have no problem deactivating the tracking component on his Band. And before you ask, yes, I'm sure sensors or ship-wide video surveillance will eventually locate him —"

"My sensors are more accurate than those onboard *Hamilton*," Hardy chimed in. "Wentworth is indeed on board this ship . . . he's on the move, mid-ship, upper-level decks."

Mattis said, "I'll send a security team to find him."

I remembered Doc Viv's warnings about Wentworth and his capacity for revenge. I wasn't sure what harm the egocentric investor could still do to Viv or even the mission. "Tell your team to keep things, friendly . . . no need to make this overly combative."

"Fine," Mattis said. "But we can't have the guy wandering around the US Space-Navy's principle warship, unattended. He'll need to stay in his quarters for the duration."

I nodded, "Agreed."

My new XO was making his way toward us. To my knowledge, he was still unaware of the issues with Zathium and the propulsion system. For now, I would keep it that way.

"XO . . ." I said.

"Captain. We're in position within the fleet. Elitetan Brice has given us the go-ahead to manufacture the wormhole."

"Brice gets pissy when you call him that . . . he likes being called *Fleet Commander*," Hardy said.

XO Tannock eyed the robot. "Good to know. And what rank are you, um, Hardy?"

"No rank . . . I guess I'm rankless." The robot looked over to me. "You know, I would like a proper rank. One that is commensurate with my outstanding contributions aboard this ship."

"See what you've started, XO? Hardy, why don't you find something to do. We have a jump to make."

I made my way back to the Captain's Mount and took a seat. Lieutenant Pristy had the mission course logistics back on the Halo-Display. She said, "Orders, sir?"

"Helm, initiate wormhole manufacture. Comms, keep the command ship apprised of our actions. Lieutenant, let's go to battle stations."

I felt everyone's eyes on me. Brice had explicitly said that our first drop location would land us into non-hostile territory.

A new feed appeared on the display. The formation of a manufactured wormhole never ceased to amaze me. It was both beautiful and awe-inspiring. I watched as the confluence of brightly colored prismatic spacial distortions formed into a yawning wormhole mouth, a slightly narrower throat beyond taking shape beyond. Although it wasn't visible, I knew another mouth was forming at the opposite end. As the fully-formed jump wormhole took shape, and without a reference to compare it to within the vastness of open space, it was hard to tell just how big the thing was. Considering the comparative size and mass of the entire 2nd fleet, I knew it had to be colossal. It took immense amounts of energy to form this wormhole and maintain it open.

Still looking at her board of indicators, Lieutenant Pristy said, "I'm getting a tactical inquiry. Looks like Brice wants to know why we're showing battle-ready conditions, Captain."

Ignoring her, I said, "Helm? What order does the Fleet Commander have the *Hamilton* entering that wormhole?"

Crewmember Chen said, "Um . . . it looks like eighth, sir, right behind the *USS Louisiana.*"

"Can you move us up in line?"

"How far up in line?"

"Like, first?"

Chen stifled a laugh, "Sir, but we're not supposed to –" He cut himself off.

XO Tannock said, "You have your orders, Helm."

I exchanged a quick look with the typically always-by-the-book Tannock. He gave me a bemused nod.

Crewman Chen said, "Moving us to the front of the line now, sir."

I felt, more than heard, *Hamilton's* powerful new drives come alive, as subtle vibrations coursed up through the deck plates.

Lieutenant Pristy turned in her seat and looked at me with a scowl. "You know that you're not making any friends, Captain. My tactical board is already lighting up with complaints."

"We're at the front of the pack, sir," Chen said.

"Excellent. MATHR, hail Chief Porter."

A moment later, the Engineering and Propulsion Chief's voice filled the bridge. He said, "Go for Chief."

"Tell me one more time those two new jump springs are fully operational . . . and ready for business."

"I'm a little busy here, Cap. But yes, as you said . . . the two jump springs are fully operational and ready for business . . . Chief out."

I saw a displeased-looking Fleet Commander Brice appear on the Halo-Display. Before he could say a word, I said, "Helm, jump the fleet."

It's never a pleasant feeling, transitioning in through a manufactured wormhole's yawning mouth, only to be spat out the other end. It's as if one's very molecular structure has been compressed and compacted; one's mind goes fuzzy, as if the whole ordeal goes far beyond what can be mentally comprehended. And then come the feelings of vertigo and nausea. You don't so much get used to it; you just learn to tolerate the experience.

I expected to see something nearly identical to what we'd left behind: inky black space with millions of glimmering indistinguishable stars.

Lieutenant Pristy was the first to say something – actually, not say – but yell something. "Incoming! Two smart missiles. Both are establishing a lock on us!"

What I was looking at was an in-process space battle of epic proportions. Blue and red energy-weapon fire crisscrossed between no less than two dozen warships. A series of bright yellow explosions peppered the hull of a hulking, odd-shaped, vessel off our portside. Another warship, perhaps some kind of battlecruiser, was firing rail munitions at another vessel, causing chunks of hull-plating to break free like giant flakes of dried paint.

Pristy said, "Impact in three, two, one!"

The ship shook as both smart missiles buffeted *Hamilton's* shields – one right after the other.

Mattis and Tannock took hold of the Captain's Mount. I caught sight of Derrota coming out of the CIC. He missed his footing and ended up on his rear-end.

That's when it happened. Wide-eyed, like a dear caught in the headlights, I froze. My heart rate was skyrocketing, and I couldn't move my arms, my legs – anything! I tried to catch my breath. I tried to at least look normal, to look like I wasn't losing control. *"Galvin, deal with this soon, I fear your ability to lead, to captain effectively, may be impacted . . . perhaps at the most inopportune time."*

"Damage report!" I yelled, snapping out of it – sounding far more in control than I felt.

"Negligible . . . shields holding at 99 percent," Pristy said. "Crap! But both the *Billings* and the *Kennedy* took serious hits before going to battle stations and raising shields."

Hardy was now standing on my left. "Any ideas? Who are they? What have we dropped into the midst of?" I asked.

"I've made quasi-positive ship identifications. If I was to guess, we have the Ramdei on one side and the Clouse Veng on the other. At present, Earth - nor our allies – have any kind of trade agreement, treaty, or war pact with either. Seems we simply stumbled into a skirmish. The two alien species have been at war for close to a hundred years."

"How much of a threat are we dealing with here?"

Technology-wise, they are not as capable as that of the US Space-Navy. Add the technological prowess brought to

Hamilton by the Pleidian Weonan, even having twice as many combined Ramdei and Clouse Veng warships, they would be no match for the 2nd fleet. One more thing, neither culture has progressed to the point to have any kind of interstellar jump capability."

Fleet Commander Brice appeared on the Halo-Display. "Apparently, we have emerged from our wormhole into a battle situation."

"No shit," Hardy said under his breath.

Brice said, "We will defend our ranks. Those vessels fired upon; you will return fire. Prepare to go FTL . . . make haste out of this system . . . all fleet helmsman, you will prepare . . ."

I interrupted the Fleet Commander, moving up to Lieutenant Pristy's tactical station to get a better look at the fleet conditions. "Sir, there's no way the *Billings* still has FTL capability. And it looks like her shields are failing. May I make a suggestion?" He and I both knew he had made a grave tactical error by not following our lead, going to battle stations before jumping. It was customary practice to, at a minimum, raise ship's shields prior to jumping into suspect territory.

After a flicker of irritation, Brice said, "Go on, Captain. Make it quick."

"We still have several hours before our jump spring system has sufficient recharge levels. And no other vessel can jump all of us at once. I suggest the *Hamilton* stay behind with the *Billings* and bring her in close. We can do a shield-wrap around her hull, and together we'll get ourselves clear of this mess via standard FTL propulsion. Catch up to the fleet several light-years on. We don't have a dog in this fight. I recommend not, I repeat, not, returning fire. We certainly don't need another intergalactic enemy right now."

Chapter 11

I heard Tannock let out a heavy breath, and I turned in time to catch the wary glance he'd shot me. Reconsidering my overt gumption, yeah, perhaps I'd pushed things a tad too far. But, hell, if left to his own instincts, Fleet Commander Brice was sure to further jeopardize more lives, not to mention this mission.

Brice pursed his lips but had yet to commit either way.

Lieutenant Pristy said, "The *Brave's* shields are down to ten percent. Her propulsion system going borderline."

"Fine . . . take good care of the *Billings*. We lose that asset, and there will be hell to pay, Captain." His feed went black.

I said, "Helm, move us in close to the *Billings*."

We watched as the US Space-Navy's 2nd Fleet, including the damaged *Kennedy* and *Brave*, quickly move off. The Ramdei and the Clouse Veng continued their battle, but seemingly, they were now content to let our warships pass unaccosted.

"Captain, we're being hailed," Crewman Grimes said.

"By?"

He gestured toward the Halo-Display. "Uh, Prime Centurion Goben of the Clouse Veng Empire."

I looked to Hardy, "Who's currently winning that battle?"

"I'd say the Clouse Veng . . . but it's close."

"Put him through, Crewman Grimes."

The feed came alive; it took me a moment to understand what I was looking at. The many deviations of alien forms never cease to amaze me, and what I was looking at now was no exception. Prime Centurion Goben was a big ball of matted brown fur with skinny tree-branch-like protruding arms, both with a knotted clump that worked as a three-fingered hand. There was a kind of face amidst all that hair – two eyes, a nose, and a large mouth. What I didn't see was any kind of legs or feet. I briefly wondered if the Clouse Veng species simply rolled around from one place to another when mobile.

I said, "Prime Centurion Goben . . ."

"Captain Quintos, welcome to our small corner of space."

"Thank you. Sorry for the intrusion . . . our intent was to pass through here unnoticed."

It looked as if he'd momentarily lowered his head or face, like a bow – but it was hard to tell. He continued, "And my apologies for any damage incurred by ours, or our enemy's, warships. It appears we both were under the impression you were hostiles that had come to assist the other. I would like to thank you for your restraint . . . your advanced technological prowess has not gone unnoticed."

"There's been no loss of life. We'll make repairs and be out of your . . ." I was about to say *out of your hair,* but said, "way," instead.

Lieutenant Pristy said, "Ramdei warships are skedaddling out of the system, Captain."

"Congratulations on your apparent victory, Prime Centurion Goben," I said.

He used one of his tree branches in a casual wave-off gesture. "They'll be back. They always come back. This narrow corridor of space has been hotly contested for as long as our two cultures have had spaceflight capabilities."

Another ball of fur entered the feed and handed Goben what looked like a tablet. After glancing at it, he said, "Captain Quintos, it has come to my attention that all of your vessels have interstellar jump capability, and the ability to manufacture wormholes at will."

I said nothing.

He said, "Please, let me be blunt here. We have a great interest in acquiring such technology and will pay handsomely for it. The advantages of such capabilities would – "

Smiling, I interjected, "Prime Centurion Goben, I'm sure your people have similar directives . . . that that kind of *interference* with foreign cultures would not be permitted. But what I can do is get the ball rolling for our two civilizations to begin a conversation. Perhaps, in time – "

It was his turn to cut me off. "Captain Quintos, I am sorry."

"Sorry?"

"There is no way I can allow your vessels to leave here. As advanced as your warships seem to be, I seriously doubt your dreadnought and failing corvette can match the might of twenty-eight capable warships."

Lieutenant Pristy said, "Oh my, the Ramdei are back . . . and they've fallen into formation with the Clouse Veng ships."

Having had a few minutes to observe the big furball, I was better able to see the alien's mostly-hidden face; right now, I could tell he was smiling. It was strangely contagious, and I smiled back. I let out a breath and shook my head.

"Prime Centurion Goben, I like you. I appreciate your crassness . . . your gumption. So, when I tell you that you're making a grave mistake here, it's coming from one simple ship commander to another. You don't want to go down this path with me."

"And I like you as well, Captain Quintos, but my allegiance is to my Emperor, so the offer still stands. Why not simply sell us the jump technology and be on your way, while you can? Leave behind the vessel you call the *Brave*. That will suffice. You have ten of your chronological time minutes to decide." The feed went dark.

Rumpled-looking Science Officer Derrota, coming out of the CIC, was hurrying over toward me. In his Mumbai-accented voice, he said, "Captain, hold on, I may have a non-combative solution." Out of breath, he reached the Captain's Mount.

"What do you have, Stephan? We don't have a hell of a lot of time to be chatting."

"MATHR . . . as you know, she's been significantly enhanced by the Pleidians."

I had heard that, and she certainly had a more pleasant voice, but I hadn't actually witnessed any discernable difference with her capabilities.

XO Tannock said, "Captain, I suggest we make several strategic hits upon the enemy. Perhaps take out two or three enemy warships. Let them know, decisively, what they are dealing with."

That wasn't all that far off from my own considerations.

Derrota was shaking his head, "No, no, this will be far better, Galvin. A good test of our new and improved cyber capabilities."

"I'm not following. Make it quick, Stephan."

"MATHR is an AI now capable of much more, including breaching of the Clouse Veng's – as well as the Ramdei's – secure ship-wide networks."

"That's more than I can do," Hardy said, making a surprised faux expression.

"What, specifically, did you have in mind?"

Derrota said, "We have direct access to virtually all of their on-board systems. Environmental, comms, navigation, shields, weapons . . . even their ship AI's will come under our direction."

Lieutenant Pristy said, "Closing in on eight minutes now, Captain."

XO Tannock ran a hand over his buzz-cut. "I don't like it. It's a nonconventional and unproven plan. In my many years of experience as Captain of this ship, it was always our ability to strike fast and strike hard that saved the day. Not any kind of new-fangled, untested concept."

I was wondering how long it would take for Tannock to say something like this. His resistance to new ideas didn't bode well. I said to the Science Officer, "How long would it take to set things up . . . to breach their —"

Derrota shook his head, "No, it's already in place. MATHR has infiltrated their networks. Give the command, Galvin, whatever it is you want to do . . . and it's done."

I thought about that, feeling XO Tannock's eyes boring into me. "Okay . . . on my command, I want each of those alien warship's shields to drop. After that, have them lock onto and fire upon the propulsion systems of each another. Preferably non-lethal strikes. And I want it all to happen simultaneously. Can MATHR do that? If not, we stay with more conventional tactics."

Derrota glanced up, "MATHR, do you have enough information to proceed with these orders?"

"Affirmative, Science Officer Derrota. Regulations require such a command come directly from a senior-level officer, such as Captain Quintos or XO Tannock."

Tannock still didn't look pleased with any of this. Lieutenant Pristy gestured to her TAC-Band, "Time's up, sir."

I said, "Go ahead, MATHR. Implement the cyber-attack."

All eyes went to the Halo-Display and the two alien

warship fleets. Nothing was happening. I heard Tannock cluck his tongue, reasonably sure he was looking more than a little pleased with himself.

Goben was back on the display. "Captain Quintos, have you made your decision?"

"Indeed, I have." I hesitated long enough to shoot Derrota an annoyed look. So much for his brainstorm of an idea. About to give the order for Lieutenant Pristy to bring *Hamilton's* powerful weapons to bear, I saw there was a sudden commotion on board the Prime Centurion's now shaking, turbulent bridge. The big ball of fur was abruptly rolling around to his left, and then, right. The Halo-Display showed a split-screen view of the two alien fleets now firing their energy weapons at one another. The mélange of crisscrossing multi-colored plasma bolts was breathtaking and strangely beautiful. Then, a single warship's aft area explosion seemed to ignite all the rest of the vessels to follow suit and explode. Soon, the crippled ships of both alien fleets were drifting out of formation – some were careening into other ships, other's hulls fractured and broke apart.

Prime Centurion Goben had apparently regained his footing long enough to stand upright. It was apparent his bridge was in turmoil. Loud voices, not accurately translated by MATHR, were coming across as extended barks and yipping sounds. Goben turned to the camera and spoke, "I will not forget this, Captain Quintos . . . this day, you have made an enemy of both the Clouse Veng and the Ramdei."

"I warned you, Prime Centurion, you were way out of your

league. Be thankful you avoided a far worse response from the US Space-Navy."

My eyes were drawn to another split screen; at first glance, it looked as if a cluster of tumbleweeds had been blown out into space from a fissure on one of the alien ships. Realization struck – they were Clouse Veng crewmembers.

Goben said, "Leave this sector of space, Captain, and never return." The feed went black.

Lieutenant Pristy said, "Sir, shall we assist with . . . helping them?"

XO Tannock said, "I think we've done enough damage here. Don't you, Captain?"

I wanted to lash back at the older officer. Remind him he had preferred to destroy several alien vessels – an action that would have caused far more loss of life. But I held my tongue.

Crewman Grimes said, "Sir, Captain Styles from the *USS Brave* is reporting minimal repair success to his HyperDrive. He believes FTL propulsion will be possible within the hour."

Chapter 12

We had several hours before we'd catch up to the 2nd Fleet, and *Hamilton's* Jump springs were still recharging for the mission's next leg. I seemed to have a bit of extra time, and my new Ensign was champing at the bit to show me something. I extricated myself from the Captain's Mount and stood. "XO, you have the bridge."

"The Bridge is mine, Captain," XO Tannock said, taking my place upon the raised chair. I sent Lieutenant Pristy a sideways glance, which I knew she'd understand: *Keep an eye on our XO and let me know if I need to get back here.*

Both Ensign Plorinne and Hardy were waiting for me at the back of the Bridge.

"We can go? I can show you now, sir?" the young, overly-exuberant Pleidian Weonan asked.

"Yes, Ensign, I have a little time. But let's not make this an all-day event. I do have a ship to captain."

"Yes, sir . . . it's just that, well, this is kind of a surprise. It's special."

As we walked, I looked up to Hardy and saw that the spinning pinwheel was back, dominating his virtual face display.

"Sir . . . I hope you don't mind, but several others have requested to be present," Ensign Plorinne added.

Annoyed, I stopped within the expansive and busy Whale's Alley. "Ensign, are you going to tell me what this is all about? Sure, I understand you want to take me on some kind of tour, but now you're inviting spectators, too?"

We'd approached the bank of GravLifts. A small crowd had assembled there, and instead of looking at the lift doors, they were all watching the three of us as we neared. From behind, I heard running footsteps. I looked back to see Stephan Derrota, looking out of breath, hurrying to catch up to us. "I'm coming too!"

Only now did I realize the cluster of people at the GravLifts were those crewmembers I was closest too. My friends, and mostly the same ones who'd been waiting for me outside the hospital. Newly promoted Captain Wallace Ryder, SWM Crewmember Lasalle, Security Chief Matti (who I thought was still on the Bridge, but evidently not), and one more person – who had not been among those who had met me at the hospital – Major Vivian Leigh.

I said, "What the hell is going on here? Just so you all know, my birthday isn't for another four months."

The lift doors expanded open, and we all stepped inside. Ensign Plorinne tapped in our destination.

"We're all just excited to see it," Lasalle said. "It's the only part of the ship I wasn't privy to see during reconstruction."

Standing directly behind Doc Viv, I saw that she was tapping away on her TAC-Band. *Probably messaging one of her people in HealthBay.* She looked tan, and her hair looked even more golden than I'd remembered.

Tap, she continued. It was then that I noticed the ring on the fourth finger of her left hand. And not just any ring; the finger clearly sported a large diamond. It was an engagement ring; my heart skipped a beat. Although the pretty, brilliant doctor and I had never dated, I'd thought there was a connection. At the very least, the possibility of one. Perhaps that had been more in my head than hers, I supposed. Still, things between Viv and whoever her mystery man was must have moved lightning-fast while I was recuperating over the last few months.

She glanced up over her shoulder and caught me looking at her hand. Immediately she lowered it, looking self-conscious. "I'm having to postpone a surgery. Just working out a time to reschedule things," she said.

"Didn't have to do that on my account . . . it's just a silly tour."

"Uh-huh . . . you just keep believing that, Galvin," she said with a smirk.

"What do you know about this?"

She made a zippering-of-her-smiling-lips gesture and turned away. She reached a hand back, grabbing her hair tight in her fist and lifting her locks to expose her long neck. "Getting hot in here," she said.

Some men are all about a woman's legs or breasts, but for

me – it's the back of a woman's neck. Like catnip to a tomcat. I looked away and tried to concentrate on something else.

Ensign Plorinne tapped on the GravLift's glowing legend, and I felt the car slow and then ease to a stop. "Okay . . . we're almost there."

I rolled my eyes, "And where is that?" I asked.

"Decks that had previously been seventy-two and seventy-three . . . which have now been combined."

"I wasn't sure what those decks previously were used for. Then, suddenly worried, I said, "No . . . not Cherry Park!"

Cherry Park had taken up much of the ship's top decks. It was a one-hundred-meter-wide by two-hundred-meter-long cherry tree-lined promenade amidst rolling grasslands. A meandering stream ran down its center. Overhead, a projected azure sky and heat-emitting yellow sun slowly trekked across the sky each day, from east to west. Setting late every afternoon, the sun descended beneath a distant horizon into brilliant hues of crimsons, blended with oranges and purples. You would typically find off-duty crewmembers lounging here on any given day or night – often couples lying on blankets, and nearby, open coolers stocked with cocktail beverages. And for the ship's senior officers above the rank of lieutenant, such as Department Chiefs, the XO, and the Captain, there was the Sanctuary – two full acres of solitude. Within the Sanctuary, there were five rustic log cabins, situated within dense, wooded patches. My mind flashed back to Cherry Park one specific night, to the softly illuminated Japanese tōrō lanterns and the path that eventually led to an intimate garden area called a

Korakuen. There, a hot springs pond billowed with steam. And it was there, in the near pitch-darkness, that I'd had an encounter with a still unknown woman. She'd made love to me, while never speaking a word, and never making herself known to me afterward. I had speculated it could have been Doc Viv, perhaps I even hoped it was her, but tossed the idea away as being far too unlikely.

"No, Captain," the Ensign said. "Cherry Park and the connected Officer's Sanctuary areas are still intact – I believe the crew would have mutinied at losing such a valued recreation area to escape to when off-duty."

"Okay . . . so these decks, seventy-two and seventy-three . . . they've been repurposed? Can I ask under whose authority?"

Instead of answering, Ensign Plorinne tapped on the legend, and the lift continued on again. Less than a minute later, MATHR announced that we had arrived. I noticed above the ships glowing legend the words:

RESTRICTED AREA – NO UNAUTHORIZED ENTRY PERMITTED

. . .which repeatedly blinked on and off.

I said, "Seriously? This is some sort of top-secret section of the ship?"

The others in the car were blank-,faced; apparently they

didn't know the answer, either. They wanted to know, probably more than I did, what secrets this section of the *Hamilton* held.

The GravLift doors opened. Standing in front of us was none other than Empress Shawlee Tee, herself, of the Pleidian Weonan Empire.

Like Ensign Plorinne and all Pleidians, there was an oval, see-through, void in the middle of her head. The alien anatomical differences to that of humans were far less startling to me now. And I knew the Empress was considered beautiful among her people – besides her being revered and loved. I had saved her life. Aided by a small band of Marines, we had ended her captivity onboard Ironhold Station, a station occupied by abusive Pylor pirates. Freeing her and her compatriots had earned me much fanfare and personal gratification, like the ownership of this very vessel having been signed over to me. So, why was this immensely important Pleidian Empress standing here in front of me?

She smiled with delight at seeing me and then acknowledged the others with a slight lowering of her head. Perhaps what was most odd was her manner of dress. If I wasn't mistaken, she was wearing blue jean overalls over a red flannel work shirt. She also wore heavily scuffed work boots. She brought her hands together in a steepled praying gesture and bowed. "Welcome Captain Quintos . . . welcome to all of you."

I said, "Empress . . . I'm bowled over, seeing you here. Astonished, really. What, um . . ."

She raised her palms, "Please, let me explain. I have so much to tell you. First, Captain, I am not Empress Shawlee

Tee . . . not exactly. I am her representative. One of only fifty ultra-advanced Symbio-Poths in existence. I assure you, a more advanced, self-aware machine would be hard to find within our galaxy, and perhaps, the Universe."

Intuitively, I knew her words would strike a chord with Hardy, standing somewhere behind me. Because Hardy was a one-of-a-kind ChronoBot, a robot designed and built mostly for battle, his biological AI and human memories made him an enigma. But was he the most technically-advanced robot around? Probably not.

"At this moment, Shawlee is seeing you, experiencing this moment from afar. She would not, I believe the Earth expression is, have *missed this for the world*."

Science Officer Derrota said, "Fascinating."

Doc Viv leaned forward and narrowed her eyes, "No way she isn't real."

The Shawlee Symbio-Poth laughed, clearly taking the comment as a compliment. "I assure you; I am a *manufactured* being . . . but much care has gone into my *presentation*, if you will. What you must know, from the start, is that all Symbio-Poths are based on real people, alive or deceased. There are no Symbio-Poths in existence that are unique to themselves . . . an important distinction, and one we Pleidians take very seriously. In time, I'd be happy to explain this further, but for now . . . it is time for the tour to begin."

Chapter 13

Until now, I had paid little attention to where we were
standing. And as if on cue, a medley of loud and oddly
familiar noises came alive around us. One unmistakable sound
was the repetitive whine of an impact wrench. Now, like the
opening scene of a professional stage performance, dimmed
lights around us began to brighten. We were standing within
the confines of a garage – a garage where old-fashioned automobiles were being repaired. No less than three men wearing
grease-stained overalls were hard at work; one man stood
beneath a raised car, peering up at engine area's bottom. Another
was half-buried under the hood of what I recognized to be a
classic T-Bird. The third man was making all the noise, finishing tightening the nuts on a wheel with his impact wrench – a
wheel that sported a brand new white-wall tire.

Over and over, the same question swirled in my mind, *why
is this here . . . why is this here on my ship?*

Still gleeful, the Shawlee Symbio-Poth leaned in closer. "I know you have a few questions. Come . . . so much to see." With Ensign Plorinne at her side, they led the way out of one of the roll-up garage doors and out into the daylight. *Daylight?* As realistic as the faux sky within Cherry Park, here was a robin's-egg blue sky with a bright yellow sun beating down on us.

Like nervous tourists in a strange country, we moved as a group, not wanting to stray too far from one another. Shawlee, seeing my expression, was laughing now. She took my arm in hers. I felt the warmth of her body pressing in close. *How could she not be real?*

"Galvin . . . take a look around. Really look . . . look and remember."

I turned to my left and then to my right. We were standing smack-dab in the middle of small-town USA. A town that did seem *strangely* familiar. Directly across the street, which I remembered as Prairie Oysters Street, was an old-fashioned barbershop with its slow-turning helix sign of blue, red, and white stripes. Next door to that was 'Jerrys Pawn,' and next to that was 'Meats,' which I supposed was a butcher shop. To my left, and on this side of the street, was the 'Rocket Diner,' all clad in reflective, shiny metal. A black automobile, dark smoke emanating from its tailpipe, cruised by in front of us. The man behind the wheel, wearing a suit and tie, waved a friendly hand in our direction. At the back of the vehicle, I saw the license plate had been issued from the state of Indiana. Then I knew exactly where I was and why I had an eerie feeling of Déjà vu.

The Shawlee Symbio-Poth had her arm around my waist and turned to face me. "So, you know where you are?"

I tried to match her enthusiasm with a broad smile of my own. "Yes . . . uh-huh, for sure, I do. This is Clairmont! Where I grew up . . . until I was –"

"Eleven!" she said.

I said, "Back in the year 2150 . . . um, but this looks to be maybe like the 1950s . . . maybe two-hundred years earlier than that," doing my best to keep smiling. In 2150, there were very few automobiles left, and those were more like hobbyists' novelties. HoverCars dominated even the smallest, rural towns by then – even in Clairmont.

A man wearing an apron came out of 'Meats' across the street, wiping his hands on a blood-stained hand towel. Seeing us, he raised his head, "That you Galvin? Say hi to your Pa for me when you get home!"

I waved to the man, "Sure thing, Mr. Springer."

The butcher disappeared back into his shop while the others nearby stared at me, slack-jawed.

Doc Viv said, "You know him, Mr. Springer?"

I continued to stare at the closed butcher shop door across Prairie Oysters Street. "I do. I did." My smile was gone now. "Shawlee . . . who else is here from my childhood? And how much of my hometown did you replicate?" Without thinking, I gazed back down the street toward the South, a mile or so in that direction where I knew a small dilapidated four-acre farm would have been.

"Anyone you knew . . . is here. As to your second question,

yes, that quaint little farm is indeed right down this road. And before you ask, yes, that farmhouse is occupied. You can go and visit your Ma and Pa at any time you wish."

I felt sick, fighting back the urge to throw up on the curb.

"Let me get this straight," my close friend, Wallace Ryder, said. The one person here who knew the most about my less-than-rosy childhood. Having graduated from Space-Navy's Flight Training together, we'd been inseparable – I knew his sorted past, and he knew mine. He said, "And you know all the historical details . . . the complexity of the relationships?"

Ensign Plorinne said, "May I address this one, Empress?" looking to the Shawlee Symbio-Poth.

"Of course."

"When recreating this town, this place of wonderful child-hood memories, no stone went unturned, as you humans say. We compiled every known video clip in existence for the time period you were here, every personal diary entry, every year-book message, every newspaper obituary, and that's nothing compared to the one-on-one interviews of those still alive. You'd be surprised at just how much humans like to talk about one another."

"I believe that's called gossip," Doc Viv interjected.

"Go on," Ryder said.

Ensign Plorinne pointed down the street to a distant marquee. "Every detail is perfect. Like the movie playing at that theater at the time . . . *Twelve Angry Men*."

Doc Viv was already shaking her head. "I know my movies. Directed by Sidney Lumet and starring Henry Fonda and Lee

J. Cobb. That's a black-and-white 2D movie from the late nineteen fifties. Maybe 1957. Not 2150, when Galvin would have been alive around here."

Ensign Plorinne glanced over to Shawlee. He said, "It was a decision we went back and forth on for quite some time. We had the most historical visual information for the period of the 1950s when this town had been at its . . . well, let's just say *its peak at that time.* So, yes, the actual era – or time period – represented here was indeed 1957. But all the town's inhabitants, the people young Galvin would have known and grown up with, are from his era in the 2150s."

"But that's a two-hundred-year time difference. Sure, I understand taking some creative license, but that's no small deviance of reality," Ryder said.

I saw Shawlee's shoulders sag, her eyes now brimming with tears.

I said, "I love it! It's ingenious! The best of two worlds . . . the people I knew as a child, and the town itself when it was most alive and, frankly, fun! Great job . . . I can't even imagine the time and expense poured into this . . . this . . ." *What was this?*

"Gift!" Doc Viv declared. "A wonderful gift."

I took both of the Shawlee Symbio-Poth's hands in mine and looked at her. "You have already done so much for me. This ship . . . I was just recently made aware that you put the ownership into my name. That, alone, is beyond conceivable to me. It's a gracious, but underserved gesture. And now this? Why, Shawlee . . . why so much?"

"Back up . . . you own this ship?" Doc Viv said, looking baffled.

Ignoring the doctor, I felt the Symbio-Poths fingers tighten around my own. She was now close enough that I could smell the sweet breath she'd finally let out. "It's simple, really. I love you, Galvin. As much as I would love my own brother – or even my parents. I was destined to live out my life on that horrid station, to endure a lifetime of pain and humiliation. And there's something I'm sure you are unaware of . . . something I'm still not comfortable speaking of. Those things, all the rapes . . . the indecencies that that Pylor pirate, Cardinal Thunderballs and his ilk transgressed upon me personally, as well as to the other young female hostages; we had also been filmed." She hesitated and closed her eyes. "Every few days, the pirates would transmit the horrific video-feeds over to the Pleidian Weonan Fleet of ships nearby, so my people could suffer along with me, with us. For close to two years, my home's Pleidian society spiraled deeper and deeper into despair -a world on the brink of collapse. You, my dear friend, changed all that. So please, do not talk of undeserved gestures . . . I am nowhere near done showing you my, *our*, full gratitude. Galvin, I know about you, your past. And I've read your recent medical file."

Oh, for shit's sake, is nothing private anymore? I felt my heart rate elevate – my breathing start to restrict. It passed as fast as it started, though. I nodded and finally 'got' where she was coming from.

"Well, thank you again, Shawlee. I look forward to spending a lot of time here. Getting to know these people again." *Not.*

"And your parents . . . they are here for you, too."

My stomach twisted and knotted all over again. "Wow! That too."

"I hope you will share this place with your crew. Let them come here and interact with the Symbio-Poths. There are close to fifty of us here."

"Sure . . . in time, I can see the crew coming here and enjoying this place. For now, perhaps it will be just those here." I glanced at the others around me.

Derrota said, "I imagine there some kind of out-of-the-way maintenance areas . . . for the Symbio-Poths and such? Even the most advanced robots require a little upkeep, no?"

Hardy chimed in, "Not ChronoBots."

Ensign Plorinne said, "You are correct, Science Officer Derrota. Behind King Pins bowling alley. It's an off-limits area we'd prefer your crewmembers not visit. Best to keep the secrets of the magic . . . magic."

"And you have personnel there?" I asked.

"Yes, Captain. We have four of our brightest and most accomplished Pleidian Engineers, and four technicians staffed here. They have been instructed to stay out of sight during normal Clairmont visiting hours. During the hours between 2:00 am and 5:00 am, they move about the town and surrounding areas at will, doing repairs and making adjustments to things." Ensign Plorinne gestured to an old Ford pickup truck parked across the street. "Those are actual Earth automobiles, Captain . . . poorly designed, I'm sorry to say, and requiring much attention."

I noticed pedestrians were now more prevalent, strolling along the sidewalks. Several cars passed by us on the street. The level of reality here was breathtaking.

"I must leave you now, Galvin," the Shawlee Symbio-Poth said. "If you need anything, please ask any one of the townsfolk . . . they'll know how to reach me." She gave me a hug and kissed my cheek. "That was from me, Shawlee, not the Symbio-Poth in front of you." She smiled at the others, then looked back to me. "Enjoy your gift, Galvin." She moved off down the sidewalk and soon was gone from sight.

My TAC-Band began to vibrate, as did most of those around me who wore the bands. "Looks like we've caught up with the fleet. Time to get back to reality, everyone," I said. They looked like wistful children at an amusement park, being told their favorite ride had been closed for repairs. "How about we come back tomorrow?" I said.

Chapter 14

As I entered the Bridge, I saw that the entire 2nd Fleet was depicted on the Halo-Display, and XO Tannock was speaking with Fleet Command Brice. Approaching the Captain's Mount, I heard Tannock say, "Yes, sir, I will ensure that happens." The XO stood and said, "The Bridge is yours, Captain."

"Thank you, XO . . . The Bridge is mine." I sat and acknowledged a smaller feed with the fleet commander's unpleasant face staring back at me. "Elitetan Brice."

I knew he wanted to correct me – order me to stop calling him *Elitetan* – but he let it go.

Brice said, "If I had guessed the Ramdei or the Clouse Veng warships would be turning their attention to the *Hamilton* and the *Brave*, I assure you . . . I would not have ordered the 2nd fleet to proceed."

Was that an apology? I'd almost lost count of the Fleet Commander's errors in judgment, and it was only day one of the mission. "The situation was handled, sir. The *Brave* is nearly back to being fully operational. No lives were lost."

"Excellent. And *Hamilton's* jump springs, fully charged I take it?"

I glanced over to Crewman Don Chen sitting at the Helm Station.

He nodded. "Yes, sir. Charged and ready."

Lieutenant Pristy said, "Captain, the next jump coordinates have been loaded."

Thanks to Pristy, now projecting up from my armrest, another far smaller 3D Halo Display provided a brief synopsis of our next jump location. I'd previously reviewed the information, but the refresher was welcome. Scanning the information, we'd be dropping into the 11-billion-year-old Pisces II Dwarf spheroidal satellite galaxy of the Milky Way. Pisces II was one of the smallest and faintest satellites of the Milky Way – the stellar population of Pisces II consisted mainly of moderately old stars formed 10–12 billion years ago. Distance from our own solar system was 0.6 million light-years.

"Is there a problem, Captain?" The Fleet Commander asked, his tone somewhat accusatory.

"No, sir. Just making the best guess as to if we'll be dropping into contentious territory again."

His eyes narrowed. "If you had been here a few minutes earlier – and not taking a leisurely tour of your own ship – you may have heard my fleet-wide orders. For this next jump, we have already gone to battle stations. As of this moment, your vessel is the only one not complying."

Glancing back at me, Lieutenant Pristy said, "Going to battle stations . . . sorry, sir."

MATHR announced;

"Battle stations…Battle stations . . ."

I simply smiled back at the Lieutenant. Turning to Chen, I said, "Helm, initiate wormhole manufacture."

Five minutes later, all eleven 2nd Fleet Warships emerged into the Pisces II Dwarf spheroidal satellite galaxy.

Nearby was a planetary system devoid of color. Situated around a dim red dwarf star were nineteen small, mostly rocky-terrain, exoplanets.

Chief of Security Mattis was at my side with his tablet. He said, "I don't think I've ever observed a less interesting, more lifeless, planetary system. Little more than a cluster of rocks circling a dying star. There's no danger here that MATHR can detect. He looked up and around, finding Hardy at the back of the Bridge.

Hardy shook his head, "As far as my sensors tell me, we are completely and utterly alone here."

I noticed the Fleet Commander's feed was still active. He moved into view. "Captain, a word, please. Best that we speak in private."

I ignored the speculative glances from my Bridge crew as I headed into the Captain's Ready Room. Upon entering the compartment, I discovered it was already occupied. Chaplain

Thomas Trent was seated in one of the armchairs – his Bible open to an indeterminate passage on his lap. "Ah, Captain." He closed the Bible and stood. "I know you are a busy man; this will only take a moment."

I looked over toward my desk. "And the Fleet Commander?"

"He is leaving this . . . um, delicate discussion in my hands."

"Really?" I said. "I didn't know the two of you were in such close communication."

The chaplain sat, placing a palm on his Bible. With his head slightly tilted to one side, and his expression grave, he said, "Captain, it has come to my attention that another House of God, a *chapel,* in this case, has recently opened its doors to the crew."

I stared back at him. "I have no idea what you are talking about. And yes, I am a busy man."

"I believe a new house of worship is indeed somewhere up there on the combined decks of seventy-two and seventy-three."

Shit. Clairmont. "No. That's not a real town. Nothing is real there."

"Are the doors of the small chapel there not open to the crew? Are there not pews inside, and is there not a lectern for one to lead a congregation?"

"I have no idea. And I'm not one hundred percent sure there's even a chapel there," I lied. I knew perfectly well there was a small church on Clairmont's outskirts; growing up, I'd spent many fidgety Sunday mornings attending services there.

"Well, per my contract with US Space-Navy, I am to have

unilateral administration rights over all onboard sanctuaries. It is in my contract."

"Look, Chaplain, I don't believe any crewmembers will be attending services – "

"As I said, my contract is quite definitive."

"Even if the congregation is a bunch of robots? I'm sorry, Symbio-Poths?"

"The Lord works in mysterious ways. He does not discriminate as to who or what shall be his faithful flock."

"You're kidding me, right?"

"Do I look like I'm kidding you, Captain?"

My molars were on the verge of biting through my tongue. "Fine. As of right now, though, the town is not open for business. Other than for a few select inspectors, the general crew is still not permitted in Clairmont . . . or its chapel. As soon as that changes, I assure you, you will be the first to know."

The Chaplain stood. "That is all I ask. Thank you, Galvin."

I watched him leave and, only then, went behind my desk and sat down. *Why do I care if the old coot gives a sermon to a bunch of bored robots?* I chuckled to myself. Perhaps I was getting fatigued; it had been a long and stressful day. A few hours of sleep was what I needed. I checked the time; it was 10:30 pm. I eyed the nearby leather couch – it was calling to me.

I awoke, feeling my TAC-Band coming alive. I checked the incoming message.

Capt. Ryder: There's a cheeseburger, fries, and a vanilla shake waiting for you. Clairmont's Rocket Diner. Hurry up!"

Passing through the Bridge on the way out, I saw that the third duty shift was present. The Halo-Display showed the fleet's relatively slow FTL progression toward our next jump location. Everything was quiet.

"Where to, boss?"

I spun around to see Hardy standing at his usual back-of-the-bridge station.

"Heading up to grab a bite to eat." I knew full well it would be impossible to dissuade the ChronoBot from escorting me, so I didn't try.

We walked in silence. I liked moving about the ship when it was quiet like this. It was the only time I felt I could really listen to her. Every warship had its own internal noises – its own personality. And now that the *Hamilton* had been recon-stituted with a new propulsion system, it sounded different. It would take me a while to get to know her again.

We reached Deck 72/73 and entered through the same entrance as we had earlier. The garage was quiet now; the mechanics were gone, and their tools were all put away. The T-Bird was still there, with its old flat tire needing replacement. There were only so many props available for this shop, and I guessed that 1950-era tires were just a few. The large garage door remained rolled up, and Hardy and I strode out into the night. The moonless sky above was filled with stars – the

Milky Way was as bright a swath of murky light as I'd ever seen. Looking about the town, all the little shops were lit from inside – some still had people milling about within.

I said, "This way, Hardy. Diner's just a couple of blocks this way."

A minute later, reaching the 1950s era eatery, I said, "You coming in?"

"Nah . . . think I'll do some nosing around out here. Although, the thought of eating an actual *real* cheeseburger is almost enough to make me cry." Fake tears streamed down the robot's animated face display.

I made a sympathetic expression and pushed through the front door.

Immediately several of my senses jumped into overdrive. Foremost, I was hit with so many wonderful smells. Wherever the kitchen was, ground beef, onions, and mushrooms were simmering on a hot grill. A fresh lemon meringue pie was being displayed in all its glory on the nearest countertop. As for sounds, Elvis was crooning out *Don't Be Cruel* on the jukebox, and a Hamilton Beach was churning milk and ice-cream back in the kitchen.

"Over here, Galvin!" Wallace Ryder said, waving a hand from a booth along the front windows. I passed by a *Leave-it-to-Beaver* family of four, the youngest in the midst of telling a schoolyard story. They looked up, and I smiled, "Evening, folks."

Ryder was not alone in his booth. Doc Viv was seated across from him – a plate of French fries in front of her. It wasn't a hard decision choosing where to sit. I slid in next to Viv, "Hey, Doc."

"Hey, Galvin."

A burger in hand, Ryder used his other hand to pluck a menu from behind the condiments caddy, offering it to me.

"No need, you've already brainwashed me."

A middle-aged waitress dropped off several Cokes at the other table before heading over to take my order. *Dorthey* was inscribed on her brass nameplate. To my surprise, she said, "Hi, Hon. Aren't you out late for a weeknight? Your parents know where you're at, Galvin?"

"Uh, yeah, I think it's fine."

"All righty, what can I get you tonight?"

"Cheeseburger, fries, and a vanilla shake."

Dorthey scribbled the order onto her notepad. I noticed she'd rushed the application of her lipstick and that she wore a floral-smelling perfume that transported me back to another time.

Doc Viv was sitting with her legs crossed, one leg keeping beat to *Fever*, a steamy number by Little Willie John that was easily two-hundred years old. I was surprised to see she was wearing a sleeveless white blouse tucked into jeans and hand-painted cowboy boots. Her long hair was tied back into a high ponytail. Her hips were swaying just enough to conjure illicit thoughts of what she would look like, *not* wearing anything at all.

Ryder said, "Don't be mad, man, but I've shared a bit of your, um . . . past history here in Clairmont."

Chapter 15

Viv placed a hand on my arm. "I'm sorry, Galvin. I didn't know. How terrible it must have been for you. How old were you - if you don't mind me asking?"

"When it happened?" I said, feeling my heart rate jump into overdrive. Suddenly I felt clammy, as a chill came over me. She nodded.

I realized she probably would have already read my most recent medical file and was aware of the late-onset PTSD diagnosis. *Shit!* "I guess I was around eleven."

"What happened? Ryder didn't know the specifics."

"The specifics of how my father became a murderer?"

"Hey, if you don't want to talk about it . . ." Ryder said with a mouthful of cheeseburger.

Of course, I didn't want to talk about it, having spent nearly twenty years not dealing with it. *Why am I dealing with this DOPTSD bullshit?*

"It must have changed everything for you . . . growing up here, in this perfect little town," Viv said.

I let out a breath. "I guess I was about eleven. It was late . . . my family was driving home from the 4th of July festival here. Each year a rinky-dink fair would come to town, you know, with all the scary rides and game booths."

"With your mom and dad?"

"And my older brother, Eric."

"Go on," she said.

"Anyway, as I said, it was late. We were all crammed into my dad's hover-truck, an old Ford HO-250 pickup." I smiled, remembering that night and how we were all singing along to a song on the radio. My dad had won me a stuffed bear at the squirt-gun shooting gallery – or maybe it was a dragon. I knew I was too old for it, but I loved it anyway. "Leaving town, going south toward home, we came up fast on another car. An automobile, not a hover-car."

"Like the ones here in town?" Ryder asked.

"Stop interrupting, Wallace!" Viv said.

"It's okay. Yeah, like these – but more modern."

Dorthey was back with my order. She positioned the plate and shake in front of me. Before bustling off, she tussled my hair. "Enjoy, sweetie."

I lifted the top bun of my cheeseburger and poured on a heaping mound of ketchup. Then, I did the same for my fries. I shoved several of the way-too-hot fries into my mouth and reached for my shake.

Viv rolled her eyes. "Go on, what happened next?"

"As I said, we came up to another vehicle. It was dark. That patch of road didn't have streetlights or anything. The car, a Volvo, was going slow. Real slow. And it was weaving back and forth over the yellow lines. My dad wanted to pass and cursed. Even hover-cars were required to stay on the road . . . basically, the same rules applied to hover-cars as the wheeled cars. Twice, he tried to pass the weaving car, and twice, we'd almost been clipped. I remember Mom telling my dad to calm down, that we'd be home soon; we lived just down the street. But dad had become unhinged. When the Volvo swerved to the right again, my dad punched it, trying to maneuver around the right side. But the Volvo swerved right back again."

I stopped to take a sip from my milkshake. I closed my eyes, not wanting to see their faces.

"What happened?" Viv said.

"We were even with them, Dad's pickup and the old Volvo. I could see into the backseat. A boy, a year or so younger than me."

"'That's Scotty Miller,' I said to my Mom, recognizing the kid from school. He was wearing an Indianapolis Coyotes baseball cap. Damnit; I can still see it all so clearly. The Volvo jerked to the right and clipped our truck. Tore off the driver's side mirror. My dad went from angry to furious. Instead of slowing, letting the car have the road, he swerved left."

"The Volvo got knocked off the road?" Ryder said.

I nodded. "It practically went airborne. One moment it was there, right next to us, the next it was shooting off at an angle out into a field. I saw it dip – like it had rocketed into a ditch or something. The car exploded. Yellow light filled the truck's cab. I saw my mother's face at that moment, the shock and terror on her face. She screamed for my father to stop, to turn around. My brother and I began to cry, and Mom beat my father's arm and shoulder, but he kept driving. His only words were, 'No one could have lived through that. I'm sorry, it's too late.'" My heart was racing, and I was struggling to breathe. Thankfully, Viv and Ryder didn't mention it.

"I'm so sorry, Galvin," Viv said. "That's awful. What happened next?"

"We got home that night and packed up everything that would fit into the bed of the truck and a flatbed hover-trailer. My father strapped everything down. Back in the house, he shut off the water, the gas to the furnace, and boarded up the windows. Even before the sun was up, we were gone from Clairmont, never to return."

"What happened to you? Where'd you go?"

"Few different towns. Dad tried to find work. Two years later, he was killed in a bar fight. A year after that, my mother killed herself. That was the end of Lori and Carl Quintos." I let my own words sink in. It had been a long time since I'd let myself think about such things. I said, "Eric and I became the ward of the state of Colorado. Miraculously, I did pretty well in school."

Ryder said, "A few years later, Galvin and I met at Annapolis. Two screwed up kids changing the course of our screwed-up lives . . . for the better." He held out a fist.

I bumped his knuckles. "The Space-Navy has been my real

home for quite some time. I thought I'd left my past in the rearview mirror. I guess not."

Doc Viv, her brow furrowed, said, "Why, for God's sakes, did the Pleidians, the Empress, build this fucking place?"

Her words took me by surprise, and I laughed out loud. It was funny, in a sick and twisted kind of way.

"There would have been no way for Empress Shawlee Tee to know what had happened. No way for anyone to know. It's not her fault. She's under the impression it will be, um, therapeutic for me."

"So, what are you going to do?" She said, gesturing to the fabricated world around us.

"I'm going to go with it. Actually, I have a lot of great memories of Clairmont. Growing up here. Much of my life was storybook perfect . . . and I'll concentrate on those."

"Good for you, Galvin," She said.

A deep rumbling emanated from outside. The three of us looked out the window as an 18-wheel tractor-trailer passed, heading down Prairie Oysters Street. I heard the little boy yell from another booth in the diner, "Look Ma . . . that's the Mega-drop Tower! I recognize it from last year."

"I think you're right, by golly . . . sure looks like it," his mother said.

No one at our table spoke. The uncomfortable silence was interrupted by Dorthey's return with the check. "It's on the house, Galvin . . . say hi to your Ma for me." Again, came the hair-tussle.

I said, "Thanks. Um, Dorthey?"

"Uh-huh?"
"What day is it?"
"It's Wednesday, of course."
"I mean the day of the month . . . the number date."
"It's the first. First of July."

Chapter 16

Varapin Empire Warship, Sintchu

Conductor Sprin-Rop Kyber

Early, the *Sintchu's* bridge was quiet, as the Varapin *Rage of the Gonjun Ract* Fleet entered into deep and desolate space – a space, an expanse, really – that spanned millions of lightyears between two massive galaxies.

Conductor Spin-Rop Kyber was impatient to make the next jump, to bring this campaign to fruition. But he would need to reign in his hunger for battle and conquest for a little while longer. Not two hours earlier, had his second-in-command, Regent Malimand, conveyed the latest orders coming in from Imperial Command: Maintain current course and speed. No more jumps. Two additional fleets, *Wrath of Power* along with *Revenge of the Heart*, will be joining with *Rage of the Gonjun Ract,* forging the most daunting, powerful, space-fleet armada in Varapin history. Some sixty mighty warships in all – soon, all to be under his direct command.

The *Sintchu's* commander studied the star charts and their predetermined interstellar course toward Earth. Three combined magnificent fleets would require more sustenance for such a long journey. Depleting their life-energy containment cisterns so early into their mission would be irresponsible. No . . . they would be making other strategic stops along the way. Soon, unsuspecting alien societies would be coming into contact with the Varapin – with the expanded *Rage of the Gonjun Ract* Fleet. And they would have the great honor of offering up their life-energies to the most exalted cause within the Universe – to the most deserving and venerated of all beings.

Kyber took his leave from the bridge, leaving Regent Malimand on watch. Now, gliding along a muted, dim-lit, passageway, he felt he should be more jubilant – even ecstatic – at his future prospects. But this was not the time to revel. Not yet. First, he must vanquish this alliance uprising before it gained any more strength. Fortunately, recent intel confirmed Earth's 2nd Fleet had already suffered minor losses. Kyber had watched the events, a mere skirmish, taking place in real-time as they unfolded. One of the smaller warships, perhaps a gunship or a corvette, had nearly been destroyed by a less-advanced alien fleet, or maybe two fleets – the details were still somewhat unclear. Even so, the humans were already proving to be a less-than-competent opponent. Still, Kyber would continue to stay several steps ahead. He inwardly smiled – the primitive humans had no idea they were being watched (actually, *shadowed*), at this very moment. How clever he had been to forward-deploy that lone Cyclone Death Fighter, with his most prized warrior pilot, Haite-Caheil, at the controls. The near-constant stream of intel had been most enlightening.

Kyber's thoughts turned to his other source of inside information. They had no clue they had a traitor amongst them. He was right there within the *Hamilton's* hull – seen, but unseen. Soon Kyber would relay the order via the warrior pilot, Haite-Caheil: *Kill them all . . . starting with the entire bridge crew.*

Kyber slowed to a halt, reaching the Conductors Officer's wing of the ship. Should he dare to reflect on what his future would hold? Perhaps a seat within the Counsel of Nine itself? It was no secret that several old counsel relics were well past their prime – practically knocking at death's door. He entered the darkened space of his personal quarters, which was kept at a perfect minus 80 degrees Fahrenheit. A blue mist gathered several feet off the deck, scattering as his dark form glided up to his personal crypt, his *Cantonment of Ire*. It was here he found his awaiting, coffin-like, pod. Its top was now silently opening – as if beckoning him in. Hovering there in mid-air, he turned away from the pod, crossed his black skeletal arms over his chest, and elevated himself higher. His legs rose until his body was floating horizontally. His form drifted backward and then downward, light as a breath of air. Soon he was nestling deep within the dark confines of the pod. But his mind had yet to still. *Why?* Hadn't he planned for all possible contingencies?

At last, Kyber felt himself letting go, allowing the dream world to replace reality. He saw ten-thousand of his Varapin warriors in his mind's eye, a moving tide of darkness and doom, streaking across the open cosmos toward a great enemy vessel. Within moments they were upon the enemy's warship, enfolding it within a dark shroud of death.

Chapter 17

Third Drop Location Within the Expanse – Deemed "Open Void of Nothingness"

USS Hamilton, *Bridge*

Captain Galvin Quintos

The 2nd Fleet had gathered into close formation for its third manufactured wormhole jump. Jointly, XO Tannock and I had arranged things, so we were working a staggered duty shift. I felt that keeping an experienced commanding officer on duty would be essential as the fleet faced rising odds of meeting up with unwelcoming alien forces.

The forward Halo-Display came alive with a new feed. Fleet Commander *Elitetan*, Roger Brice, looked upbeat as he prepared to address the fleet. "We will be arriving at an area of space no Earth human has ever ventured into. He almost smiled, "There's a good reason for that . . . there is nothing there. Our scientists tell me we can expect an expanse of warm-hot intergalactic medium, something called a WHIM. The WHIM can be described as a web of hot, diffused plasma gas stretching boundlessly within this region of space."

I looked over to Science Officer Derrota, who had emerged from the CIC to watch Brice's announcement. We looked at each other, and I raised my brows questioningly – *Was what the Fleet Commander saying, true?* Derrota shrugged and shook his head simultaneously.

Brice continued. "While we will be dropping into this *nothingness* void, best we go to battle stations. Spacecraft Carriers, *Enterprise* and *Louisiana,* will be topping off our fuel tanks upon completing the jump. And we will take this time to ensure our respective vessels are in tip-top shape. Ship-wide Maintenance crews have been cleared for double-shifts. Remember, idle hands are the devil's playthings . . . so we will all take this time to bring this fleet up to the highest battle readiness levels."

I suspected he was attempting a smile, but it looked more like he was taking a satisfying crap. Someone subdued a chuckle, making several others amongst the bridge crew chuckle in turn; soon, everyone on the Bridge was laughing. I wondered if something similar was happening upon the ten other fleet warship bridges. At a minimum, Fleet Commander Brice would have thumbnail visual feeds into each bridge. Most likely, he wouldn't hear the laughing, but he'd most certainly see it. I almost felt bad for the man. The Halo-Display returned to the view of open space and the fleet.

Within minutes, our helmsman had the final coordinates

locked in for the manufactured wormhole jump. Lieutenant Pristy looked back at me, "Going to battle stations, sir."

I didn't like the idea of jumping into an area of space where there was, potentially, a dangerous spacial aberration taking place. Overhead, the battle stations klaxon alarm came alive. What was this WHIM thing he was talking about? This web of hot, diffused plasma gas . . . one the stretched boundlessly within that region of space. *Why even go anywhere near there?*

Our manufactured wormhole loomed massive before us.

Chen said, "Orders, sir?"

I really didn't like this and had to fight to keep my heart rate in check. I felt familiar mental paralysis begin creeping into my decision-making processes. *Not now!* "Go ahead, lead the fleet into the wormhole, Helm."

Someone on the bridge screamed – and it wasn't a woman. The *Hamilton* shook violently, as if being struck by multiple missiles at once. The 2nd Fleet had emerged into total chaos. It was a sort of weird, hellish hailstorm. All around the *Hamilton* were twirling mini-sun-like fireballs traveling at thousands of miles per hour. On the display, I watched as both the *Billings* and the *Gallaher* took direct hits in their aft sections.

Lieutenant Pristy yelled over the klaxon's blare, "Redistributing power to aft shields, sir!"

Hardy was at my side, "We're caught in the middle of a Miasma Burn . . . a kind of river of obliteration, Cap!"

"A what?"

"Miasma Burn! Some believe these spinning house-sized

balls of torrid plasma eventually combine to form new baby stars."

"Well, right now, we're taking them right up the tailpipe!" I yelled. "How wide is this river thing?"

Derrota, out of breath, joined us. "They can be substantial, Captain, up to a light-minute's distance in width."

Lieutenant Pristy announced, "All ships reporting inability to break free . . . to navigate out of this . . . whatever the hell it is."

I could see a nearby vessel was being pummeled by the fiery balls of plasma. I gestured to it, "The *Gallaher's* in trouble."

"Yeah, and her shields are dropping," Pristy said. Then she said, "*Hamilton's* shields are holding at seventy percent," anticipating my next question.

I looked to the Halo-Display – hoping to see Brice's face appear and provide some form of desperately needed direction.

"Hardy, what does your inner LuMan say about these things?"

"LuMan describes a Miasma Burn as having no positive mass, it being mostly plasma, but it does have substantial negative mass . . . a type of gravity which is far more than what any of our ships will be able to break free from!"

"So, you're saying we're totally fucked," Derrota added.

Hardy's face display was expressionless. "Basically, yes,"

I yelled, "MATHR Hail Chief Porter!"

Craig Porter sounded stressed. "A little busy here, Captain!"

"Our HyperDrives . . . can they pull us out of this mess?" I asked.

"No way, Cap. We're already pushing them to full throttle . . . and as you can see, we're not moving."

"Captain, another ship going critical," Pristy said.

Contact the *Capitol* . . . see what Elitetan Brice is directing the fleet to do – "

"Captain, it *is* the *Capitol* . . . Elitetan Brice's ship . . . Oh God, her shields just went down!"

Shit! Someone else needed to be making fleet-command decisions. I knew that wasn't supposed to be me. Well, until that was ironed out, I said, "You still there, Craig?"

"Still here, Cap."

"Rush-jump us. Rush-jump the whole damn fleet!"

Okay, at this point I should explain things . . . there are two distinct manufactured wormhole jumping methodologies for US Space-Navy starships. The preferred – and recommended – means is to manufacture a wormhole with its pre-prescribed jump in and out coordinates, then carefully maneuver the vessel, or a fleet of vessels, into that spacial anomaly's yawning mouth at slow, sub-light, velocity. The second means, called a rush-jump, is far more dangerous, and currently forbidden for US Space-Navy vessels to even attempt – due to prior losses of ship assets and crew personnel. On the positive side, there is no lag time with a rush-jump, no slow-and-precise entry to a wormhole with relative safety. No, rush-jumps take place at FTL velocity; synchronized, ships are jumped in an instant. It's a Hail Mary move for one ship to attempt, and an insane proposition when jumping an entire fleet. Because of the danger level, the option can only be initiated from Engineering and Propulsion, not from the Bridge.

Porter continued, "Galvin there's another issue . . . *Hamilton's* jump springs have only partially recharged, so they'll blow, I guarantee it. They'll blow, and maybe take the aft half of *Hamilton* with them!"

"Just do it, Craig! Rush-jump the damn fleet!"

"Are you sure —"

We all yelled simultaneously - Hardy, Derrota, Lieutenant Pristy, and me, "Just jump us!"

We jumped.

At first, I thought the Halo-Display was malfunctioning. All I saw was a distant, amber-colored swath of light dissecting the contrasting blackness of space. Then I realized what it was. "That's the river . . . that's the Miasma Burn?" I asked.

"Correctamundo," Hardy confirmed.

"Damage report, Lieutenant."

Pristy tapped at her console for a few more moments. "As far as *Hamilton* is concerned, almost all her damage is within Engineering and Propulsion. Jump springs are toast; there was a confined explosion. Three crewmen dead." She looked back at me, "Craig's fine, but he's really, really pissed off."

"Lieutenant let's deploy a few sensor-drones so we can get a better visual of the fleet. Crewmember Grimes, hail the *Capitol.*"

"Yes, sir." Shaking his head, "She's not responding, sir. But distress calls are now coming in from several other vessels."

The Halo-Display finally came alive with a visual perspective of the entire fleet. Several ships had taken direct hits and had breached hulls, evident by vaporous debris spewing into space.

Our Fleet command ship, the *USS Capitol*, a Heavy Battleship and the second-most powerful vessel within the fleet, now looked adrift and completely dark. As the opposite side of the slow spinning vessel came into view, I could see much of the hull had been blown away, exposing the vessel's internal skeletal framework and multiple open decks. Hundreds of electrical sparks flashed brightly where power conduits had been torn apart. A bluish-grey vaporous cloud of debris seemed to cling to that area of the ship. I leaned forward and squinted my eyes – yeah, there were bodies, many bodies, floating lifeless within that cloud.

I knew I could ask MATHR for her sensor assessment but preferred to keep the information a tad more private. Keeping my voice down, I said, "Hardy . . . life signs on board the *Capitol?*"

"Sir, once the *Capitol's* aft shields had given out, three consecutive plasma balls tore through the ship's stern and progressed forward through the entire ship, incinerating everything in their path along the way. Everyone on board died in that instant. A crew of twelve-hundred-fifty, including our Fleet Commander, Elitetan Roger Brice, is gone."

The entire bridge crew was listening to Hardy's report. Now, heads lowered – several wept openly. I was sure friends, and perhaps family members, had been on board the destroyed Heavy Battleship.

"Crewman Grimes, establish a micro-wormhole laser

transmission back to Earth – Fleet Command will need to be appraised of this . . . setback."

"Aye-aye, sir."

FTL comms were commonplace within the realm of 22nd Century starships – having the ability to leap-frog back and forth via micro-wormhole laser transmissions. With that said, intergalactic text/voice/video-feed messaging was by no means instantaneous. Conversations were typically an exercise in patience – one fraught with prolonged delays.

My armrest Halo-Display suddenly came alive. With a glance over her shoulder, I knew Lieutenant Pristy had initiated it. It was a readout of the Mission Directives, ones I had already looked at in their entirety – well, at least the main bullet points. But what Gail had highlighted for me was the *fine print* – this was the overall command hierarchy structure of fleet Captains, useful for instances such as now, when the 2nd Fleet had just lost its commanding officer. I reviewed the list. After Fleet Commander *Elitetan* Roger Brice, came Captain J. Johns (better known as Captain JJ) of the *USS Louisiana*, a female officer I knew to be tough and competent. Next, Captain Taiger of the *USS Starlight*, more commonly known as Captain Tiger. I was fourth in line, as Captain of the *USS Hamilton*. I was relieved, realizing I did not want the responsibility of saving humankind riding on my shoulders.

"Sir, Captain JJ is requesting a closed-door meeting between all ship Captains and their top officers to convene . . . like, right now."

We assembled in *Hamilton's* Captain's Conference Room. XO Tannock looked bleary-eyed, apparently having been awakened by this most recent ordeal. Also in attendance were Science Officer Derrota, Lieutenant Pristy, and Security Chief Mattis. Chief Porter had too many issues to deal with in Engineering and Propulsion to be here. Hardy was present, but not seated at the table. It had been over twenty minutes since Captain JJ had requested the meeting.

Suddenly, Captain JJ appeared up on the display, looking frazzled. She had a crop of short bright red hair and the bluest eyes I'd ever seen, eyes that portrayed both intelligence and nervous tension. "Sorry for the delay." She seemed to choose her next words carefully. "Captain Quintos . . . this is a closed feed. I have already spoken to the other Captains and their teams prior to this call."

"I don't understand. What's this all about?" I shot a quick glance around the table and saw that my team was just as confused as I was.

"I'm going to be frank with you, Captain. This mission has been a clusterfuck since day one. It was ill-conceived, and subsequently, has been poorly-implemented. Hell, it's a miracle we've sustained as few asset and personnel losses as we have. But it's not my job to assess the prior competency of Elitetan Roger Brice. Undoubtedly, there will be a set of review boards within Earth's Fleet Command to do just that."

I said, "Granted, things have not gone well early on –"

She cut me off, "We've already lost several key warships and thousands of essential crew. I've lost dear friends. If it were at all possible, I'd give the order to turn this fleet around to regroup back near Earth. But that's not an option. The Thine, Pleidian, Human alliance is spread too thin. Recently, the Grish have been making further inroads into allied space. And now, with the Grish and the Varapin potentially joining forces, well . . . we're in trouble. We're in big trouble."

Chapter 18

None of this was new to me, and I really didn't know why Captain JJ was wasting my time with it all.

She took a sip from an oversized coffee mug. "Just prior to this most recent jump, Elitetan Brice shared with me a high-priority transmission he'd received from Fleet Command. Yet to be substantiated, the approaching Varapin fleet may have been joined by one or more additional fleets."

"How would Fleet Command even know such a thing?" I asked.

"It's above our paygrade, Captain. But there's been speculation that we've jump-deployed a number of cloaked recognizance stations into the Andromeda Galaxy over the past year. Perhaps we've intercepted Varapin ship-to-ship transmissions. That's just my guess – and might be total bullshit. In any event, our already-impossible mission may have just gotten far more difficult. Difficult, and perhaps, unwinnable."

"If there's intelligence we're unaware of . . . intelligence that

affects our mission parameters, we need to have it. And not sec-
ondhand. If there are cloaked recognizance stations, we need to
have direct interface with them."

"I've made that same point. It's being looked into."

My TAC-Band was practically vibrating itself off my wrist.
Chief Porter had been giving me text updates about a radiation
leak with one of his reactors. I inwardly prayed it had nothing
to do with the Zathium in the ship's ADAP fuel mixture. I
glanced over to Hardy, knowing full well he would be eavesdropping on my TAC-Band messages. I gestured with my chin
toward the door – *Get over to Engineering and Propulsion to see
what you can do to help.* Hardy hurried off.

"Captain . . . are you listening to me?" Captain JJ said.

"Yes, apologies, just putting out fires . . . trying to keep that
figuratively." I looked at her, not even attempting to hide my
annoyance. "Captain, every second we're sitting here talking
to you, my officers and I are not doing our jobs. Unlike the
Louisiana, *Hamilton* has been damaged. And let's not forget,
with her jump spring technology, she is our ticket forward."

She smiled, "Direct, decisive, and action-driven."

"I beg your pardon?"

"Captain Quintos. I'm thirty-two years old, and I am the
youngest Captain within the 2nd fleet, other than you. All the
other captains are in their forties and fifties. Yet, not one of
them has ever had direct fleet command. Most have never had
the kind of battle experience you have had. You are a decorated
officer with a sorted, less-than-stellar record."

"Thank you, I think . . ."

"Simply put, I can't do this. And after a lengthy discussion with the other captains, neither can they. This mission is far too important."

A knot in my stomach was forming.

She continued, "Look, I don't lead by consensus. But I do listen to my peers. You, Captain Quintos, need to be leading this mission . . . this fight . . . this fleet."

Fuck.

"I can't order you to accept this duty."

Good! I don't want it.

"But an Admiral certainly can." Captain JJ half smiled as the video display split from one into two feeds. And there it was, the craggy old face of my friend and mentor, Admiral Cyprian Block. He looked as though he'd aged five years since I'd last seen him.

He did not look particularly happy to see me. "Don't fight this, Galvin," he said. I knew the audio and video were slightly out of sync due to micro-wormhole laser link transmissions over immense spacial distances, "I have no time for any of your nonsense. You have been elevated to Fleet Commander for the duration of this mission. Just do what you do best. But know this, screw this up, and I'll knock your rank down to petty officer." There was humor in his eyes, and the corners of his lips twitched up. His expression turned serious again, "I will not blow smoke up your asses, Captain. With the latest intel coming in, it is doubtful the 2nd Fleet will weather the enemy's far greater numbers and technological superiority. I'm sorry to lay this out to you in such matter-of-fact terms. I am confident you will all deal with this reality with honor and profession-alism . . . the US Space-Navy, hell, *Earth*, owes each of you a debt that can never be repaid. Know that your sacrifice will give us much needed time, time to mount an appropriate offen-sive here, back home." Clearly holding back his emotions, the admiral cleared his throat. "On a more positive note, Captain JJ's request for direct interface to our recent classified cloaked assets within Andromeda has been approved. Your MATHR AI should already be decoding the data transfer as we speak. Good luck, Galvin. Good luck to all of you."

The Admiral's feed went black. Nobody spoke for almost a minute.

"Orders, Captain Quintos?" Captain JJ said as her feed now filled the entire display.

"Well . . . in light of this new information, I think we need to rethink our strategy. I estimate we'll be here in this no-man's-land for at least a few more days. You, me, and the other captains need to meet . . . in person."

"I'll set it up, sir. JJ out."

One by one, I looked to each of my fellow officers. "I'm going to be leaning on each of you more than ever. Our first priority will be getting *Hamilton* operational and battle-ready. I'm heading back to Engineering and Propulsion now, XO, you mind cutting your off-duty shift a little short?"

"No problem. You'll find me on the Bridge."

I said, "Derrota . . . I want you back in the CIC, poring over that decrypted Andromeda data from a scientific perspec-tive. XO and Lieutenant Pristy, why don't you come at the data from a more strategic military vantage point. I'll make Hardy available to you as well. One more thing: I've been counted out before. *Hamilton's* been counted out before. Don't believe the Admiral's conjecture concerning our imminent demise.

I arrived within Engineering and Propulsion, finding the air heavily-laden with soot particles. There was a rancid chemical smell, and I appreciated it when a crewman offered me a filter-breather, which I placed over my nose and mouth. "Where's the Chief?" I asked.

"With Doc Viv . . . keep heading aft. Off to the left, near the reactors."

"Radiation levels?"

"Nominal . . . it's safe if you don't hang around in there too long, sir."

I was surprised to hear that Doc Viv was here. I'd heard we'd lost three crewmembers due to an explosion, but nothing about there being other injured personnel.

I found the doctor and the Chief in the control room, adjacent to the main reactor area. Four others were in there as well – each, huddled together, no more than four feet tall and wearing heavy brown environment suits – the Thine scientists.

Entering the control room, my eyes were drawn to the window facing the reactor area. Inside, a seven-foot-tall ChronoBot was doing *something* with a metal wrench, half the size of a man. I noticed one of the reactors was damaged, an area charred with a black crust. Hardy was busy bolting down a curved patch panel over what looked to have been a significant breach. The radiation in there would be lethal to any biological being.

Doc Viv, leaning over the fifth scientist, sprawled out on the deck, was talking to the Thine alien in a calm, soothing voice. "Just relax . . . we're going to take good care of you, Molngong. We'll get you over to HealthBay, get you all fixed up . . . okay?"

I noticed she was holding one of his gloved hands, while Craig was holding his other.

"Captain Quintos," one of the Thine, off to the side, said. I now saw it was Coogong Sohp and was relieved that it wasn't him, lying there on the deck.

"Coogong, what's happening here?"

"Molngong Leth was working within the reactor area when the explosion took place. He is dying, and the wonderful doctor and your Chief of Engineering are spending time with him as he passes."

Coogong didn't look particularly phased by the situation – maintaining his typical, pleasant expression behind his helmet's faceplate.

"You don't seem to be all that upset, if you don't mind me saying so, Coogong."

The worm-like being put his hands together in a steepled prayer-like gesture, hands that I knew were totally robotic within that bulky suit of his. "Captain, Molngong's spirit-force has already joined with that of my own. Rest assured, he is fine, and here with me now. The doctor and your friend, Craig, are speaking with what is little more than a mindless, empty carcass. One that will cease breathing at any moment now."

"So, you're saying they're wasting their time?"

"Well, it seems to be making them feel better."

Both Doc Viv and Craig were now looking up at us. She said, "You know we can hear you, right?"

I shrugged.

She let go of Molngong Leth's hand and let it fall to the deck. Craig did the same. Looking annoyed, Craig said, "I have a shitload of real work to do around here."

I said, "That reactor in there . . ."

"Damage from one of those white-hot plasma spheres . . . it was able to penetrate our shields. Things could have been a hell of a lot worse," Craig said.

"So, nothing to do with –"

"Zathium? No. Well, at least, not directly."

"Is that patch going to do the job?"

"Should be fine. And I don't see there being any long-term damage. The new jump springs will be installed over the next day or so. Just so you know, we don't have an inexhaustible supply of those things." He stood, glanced down at the body, and shook his head. He gave me a crooked smile before hurrying out of the control room.

Doc Viv gave the now-dead Thine alien a couple of pats on his chest. "I'll have a tech come for the remains." She stood and peeled off the light blue gloves she'd been wearing. "My totally unnecessary work here is done," she said, looking past me to Coogong.

My TAC-Band vibrated. "Strange, never had a text message from a Symbio-Poth before. Seems there's a big commotion within the town of Clairmont. Want to check it out with me, Doc?"

She looked at me for an extended second or two. "Sure, why not?"

Chapter 19

Standing together within the GravLift, swaying ever so gently back and forth, my eyes lingered on the diamond ring on her left hand. I thought of asking her about it and who she'd gotten engaged to. Maybe it was someone I knew. The truth was, I really didn't want to know. The adage, *ignorance is bliss*, came to mind.

"What's this about?"

Her question had caught me off guard, and she saw my confusion, "Clairmont. What's happening in Clairmont?"

"Oh. Um, not really sure. Something about an intruder."

She nodded. "Guess we'll find out in a minute, we're almost there."

Thirty seconds later, the lift doors opened, and together we stepped into the little hallway that led to the garage. Walking with her, she paused and looked up to me, concern furrowing her brow. About to say something, suddenly, a frantic-looking

Shawlee Tee Symbio-Poth rushed toward us down the passageway.

"Oh, thank goodness! Please come . . . we must hurry."

We followed the Symbio-Poth Empress into the garage where other Symbio-Poths were busy, once again, changing a tire and looking beneath the undercarriage of a 1950s-era car.

"This way," she said, pausing momentarily as an old Buick rumbled past us, then hurrying across the street.

I heard her murmuring to herself, which seemed strange since thinking wasn't something a glorified robot would typically do – but there again – I knew next-to-nothing about Symbio-Poths.

Reaching the opposite sidewalk, she took off running. We ran after her, leaving the 'Jerry's Pawn' and 'Meats' storefronts behind us. She yelled back, "Hurry! Please hurry!"

My eyes strayed over to an 18-wheeler parked along street, the same one I'd seen the night before. Workmen, *Symbio-Poths*, were unloading pieces of various ride components for the fair. Looking back down the sidewalk, I noticed Shawlee Tee was gone. *Shit!*

Fortunately, Doc Viv had been paying better attention than me. Beneath a hanging hand-painted sign in the shape of a cupcake was the establishment's cursive name, *Baby Cakes*. Doc Viv swung the door open, and we both went inside, the delicious-smelling aromatics accosting my olfactory senses. There were fragrant yeast and vanilla smells, as well as strong cinnamon and chocolate wafting through the air. Enclosed glass shelving displayed decadent sweets: decorated cookies and cakes, fresh-baked pastries, and colorful candies. A pretty young hostess wearing a black and white striped dress with matching bonnet stood at an opening between the display cases; wide-eyed, she pointed to saloon-style doors, still swinging back and forth on their hinges behind her.

We rushed past her, pushing through the doors entering the kitchen. Everything one would expect to find in a baker's galley was here – stainless steel sinks and worktops, large mixing appliances, stovetops, and ovens. But no Symbio-Poths.

"This way," Viv said, heading for another exit. Pushing through the door and leaving the kitchen behind us, we entered a wide, dimly-lit hallway – one that looked to be a kind of backstage access to all the shops situated along the street. We stopped and listened, both hearing it at the same time. Somewhere close, there was a commotion – voice, a man's and, perhaps, a woman's. We headed down the hall to the right and soon reached our destination.

Shawlee Tee was pacing back and forth, quietly murmuring to herself again. As we approached, she looked both relieved and exasperated and pointed to a nearby metal stairway leading up to a second-story catwalk. "He's up there. I tried to stop him. Asked him to stop . . . he's not supposed to do that sort of thing. It's not permitted. Not permitted, here." Her eyes were pleading with me – an outstretched finger pointing upward.

"Stay with her," I said to Viv, already heading for the stairs. I took the risers two at a time, the soles of my boots clang-ing loud like an angry church bell. By the time I'd reached the catwalk some thirty-feet up, my mind had conjured up all kinds of scenarios, like a Symbio-Poth having gone haywire and banging its head against a wall. But it wasn't that. In the darkness, I could see the room was staged as a small-town law office, or an accountant's office. There were three individuals here – one of which was lying still on the floor, a young man wearing a business suit. Standing before me, I saw a bare-assed man with his pants gathered down around his ankles. Lying prone before him, I saw a patch of fabric – the familiar black and white striped pattern worn by the Baby Cakes hostesses. Pinned down atop the office desk, the hostess was struggling to free herself. She was saying, "Stop . . . please stop. Go away. Go away. Please stop . . ."

I fully-comprehended the scene before me: an older man with longish gray hair was obviously raping the hostess Symbio-Poth. Only when the man looked back at me did I recognize who he was. It was that stowaway investor – it was Talco *fucking* Wentworth.

He smiled ruefully back at me, "Want some of this?" He laughed with soul-less malice that sickened me. "These dumb Poths come with all the bells and whistles, Cap . . . if you know what I mean."

I could now see his captive's face – the pretty hostess was staring back at me, her eyes filled with anguish and despair.

There have been few times in my life when rage completely took over my mind and body, to the point I no longer had any control as to what happened next. This was one of those times. In three strides, I was upon him – one hand taking a fistful of his long hair, the other tightly wrapped around his neck. I yanked him up and then backward, pulling him off balance. He flailed and having his pants all gathered around his feet the way they were, he was incapable of putting up much of a fight. I wanted to humiliate him. That, and kill him.

In choking gasps, he croaked out the words, "Let me go! I didn't know . . . it was a mistake . . . bad judgment . . . don't you know who I am? You need me . . . Earth needs me!"

I continued to drag the thrashing piece of shit out of the office and away from his victims. Then, I bent him even further backward, practically inverting him to the point his neck rested on the catwalk's metal railing. I could feel his disgusting Adam's apple gyrating beneath my palm, like a small animal struggling to free itself. Tightening my grip, I watched as his tongue waggled out through gaping lips. His eyes were bulging – *good*. I leaned down and spoke softly into his ear, "You like raping defenseless women, more like girls, dirtbag? Is that what gets you off, shithole? Well, now you're going to know what if feels like to really get fucked, yourself."

Keeping a fistful of hair in my left hand, I let go of his neck. He gasped and struggled to fill his depleted lung with air. I saw the short-lived relief in his eyes.

Behind me, I heard Doc Viv's calm voice say, "Galvin . . . don't do – "

I reached down with my free right hand and took hold of Talco Wentworth's bunched up trousers, and said, "Heave ho, motherfucker!" With all my strength, and in one fluid motion, I yanked his bound legs upward higher and higher until his shoes were up above my own head. Gravity and momentum took over as the rapist did a backflip over the banister. I watched as he dropped ass-over-teakettle in the air until he was out of my sight. There was a resounding *crack!*

I turned, letting out a constricted breath. Doc Viv was now attending to the Hostess Symbio-Poth, helping her off the office desk.

I saw Shawlee Tee taking tentative steps up the stairs. She took in the scene.

"I'm sorry. I'm so, so, sorry, Shawlee," I said. "There's no excuse for what's happened here."

She pulled her eyes away from Doc Viv and the Hostess, looking back at me. "You threw that man over the railing."

I shrugged. "I only wish I could do it again . . . maybe a few more times."

"You know, we're going to have to explain this, right?" Doc Viv said over her shoulder. She was kneeling down next to the motionless businessman on the floor. She'd placed a finger on his neck as if checking for a pulse. Catching herself, the doctor looked to Shawlee. "Can he be . . . saved? Is that the right word for it?"

Shawlee nodded. "Doug Lewis, Clairmont Attorney at Law, but he was never alive, not really. Symbio-Poth's have a kind of internal cut-off switch for when things get . . . well, you know, too overwhelming. We'll get him – and her – back to our area behind the bowling alley. Wipe their memories . . . get them cleaned up."

I noticed that the Shawlee Symbio-Poth used the vernacular,

him and *her*, when referring to the robots. I wondered if she thought of them as more than just automated beings.

Doc Viv stood and said, "Without Wentworth, our deal with Juno 5 will be as good as dead. Don't forget, Zathium was going to be the game-changer that would give the Alliance a fighting chance against our enemies."

"He deserved it, and worse."

"Of course, he did! But breaking his neck for self-gratification may have just cost us the war, Galvin."

Shawlee Tee was shaking her head. "I saw him fall. He didn't break his neck, only his arm. He's alive." She touched her ear. "I can hear him whimpering."

"Maybe I should drag his ass back up here and try again. Double or nothing, I'm sure I can kill him next time," I said.

Viv rolled her eyes. "Best I check on him."

I said aloud, "MATHR, contact Chief of Security Mattis. Tell him we need a team here at my current location."

Standing outside on the sidewalk, I watched as a three-man security detail escorted Talco Wentworth down the street. He was holding a limp right arm with his opposite hand. He yelled over his shoulder, "This isn't over, Quintos! You made a big mistake here today. One I won't soon forget!"

Doc Viv said, "It looks to be a compound fracture of the humerus. He'll need to stay in HealthBay for a few hours."

"Fine, but I want him back in the brig tomorrow, pending official charges."

"And what charge will that be? Malicious intent against

a machine? With his money and influence, he won't get convicted."

"Hey, whose side are you on, here?" I said.

"Look, I know he's a piece of shit. So was his brother, apparently. But right now, he's the US Space-Navy's golden child. With those he knows, his influence, he could make things uncomfortable for you. Maybe get you demoted, or even kicked out of the service."

"I can't worry about that. He's scum."

"You could apologize to him. Let bygones be bygones, that type of thing."

"Not likely. At least, not in this lifetime. What the hell is that all about?" I said, gesturing toward the now far-more-crowded sidewalk. The townsfolk were exiting their small businesses and shops, heading away from us.

Doc Viv said, "They look to be going into the little church, there, at the far edge of town."

I squinted my eyes, which activated my ocular implants, implants I hardly ever found a use for.

"Weird . . . it's not Sunday. Wonder what's going on," she said, now heading down the sidewalk with the myriad of like-minded Symbio-Poths. "Come on, let's check it out."

By the time we'd reached the small, white-steepled church – in dire need of a coat of paint – the adjoining parking lot was almost full. I counted ten cars, one of which I recognized as the same T-bird from the garage. For the umpteenth time, I marveled at the level of detail having been afforded this mock township. By the time we'd reached the steps leading to the scuffed and marred double-oak doors, I was about to tell Doc Viv that I needed to get back to the bridge. I'd already spent far too long here, as it was. That's when I saw them. Seemingly the last few, other than Viv and me, to head into the church.

"What is it?" Viv asked, seeing my expression. "You look as though you've seen a ghost."

Suddenly feeling lightheaded, I didn't answer her. But her comment wasn't all that far from the truth.

Chapter 20

The church was packed to the rafters, and I knew a good many people here. It was unsettling to have my past so abruptly thrust into my present.

Doc Viv was scanning the pews for any available seats while I was scanning the pews for something else – my family. I'd seem them climbing the stairs outside just moments before – my mother, father, and my older brother, Eric.

Viv knelt down and retrieved a sheet of paper off the floor, a flyer of some sort. Others in the congregation were holding the same sheet of paper. Viv held it up so we could both read it. At the top was a grainy photo-image of a serious-looking man who, presumably, was the chaplain.

Emergency Town Meeting

All to Attend, Thursday, July 2nd, 2:00 pm

In a few words, the flyer explained the importance of all

townsfolk attending the gathering and that certain *beneficial* changes were coming to the town of Clairmont.

Doc Viv said, "You didn't notice?"

I was still scanning the full pews, "Notice what?"

She tapped at the grainy picture of the chaplain with her forefinger.

I took another look, leaned in closer, and said, "Shit!" a bit too loud.

Several standing nearby made an indignant face. "Is that Thomas Trent?"

To my left, a familiar voice said, "Galvin! Stop goofing around. We saved seats for you. You can bring your little friend with you. Hurry up!"

My jaw dropped as I looked into my mother's young, pretty face, now standing at my side. Slender, she was wearing an emerald-green dress that reached just above her knees. Gold-hooped earrings swiveled and reflected rays of sunlight coming from a side window. She had her hand on my arm and tugging me away. "Come on!" she said, in a hushed, annoyed voice.

After making eye-contact with Viv, the two of us followed her to a back row of pews off to our left. We side-stepped, doing our best not to step on anyone else's shoes. There was an open space, wide enough for three people, being reserved by Eric. Next to my brother sat my father, who was wearing an old tan-colored corduroy sportscoat. I remembered him wearing that same threadbare coat – one which I'm reasonably sure was the *only one* he owned. At the moment, he was not looking all-too-pleased with the commotion we were making.

Once seated, I realized the rest of the congregation had settled down. There was a lull as everyone stared intently toward the still empty podium. I looked to my left, taking in the faces of my family. They were not merely good approximations or close resemblances; these Symbio-Poths were perfect. Perfect to the point that there was now a growing ache within my chest – *God, how I've missed each one of you.*

Eric glanced my way. If I was ten or eleven here, he would be twelve or thirteen. He made a face at me, then pretended to pick his nose and eat the booger. My mother glowered at him, "Do you want to sit in the car? That can be arranged, young man."

A flash of color caught my eye several pews up and over to our right: a young boy wearing a crimson-red baseball cap with a black howling-coyote logo above the bill. My heart skipped a beat. It was Scotty Miller. Scotty's mother leaned in closer to her son and whispered something in his ear. Immediately, Scotty removed the hat and placed it in his lap. Both the boy and his mother looked to their right, to the stubbled, unkempt, looking man sitting there. A thatch of bedhead hair stuck up straight like a peacock's plume atop Mr. Miller's head. He looked to be three sheets to the wind, and as he swayed a little, his wife placed an arm around him – a solid anchor for turbulent seas. I swallowed hard and tried to look away from the young family, the same family I'd seen incinerated as their Volvo HoverCar erupted into a ball of fire off a small country road. Hard to believe that had been close to twenty years ago.

I forced myself to look away. I took in the faces closer to

me. As the moments passed, more of them went from unfamiliar to *somewhat* familiar. So, this is what it was like here – before the world came tumbling down around the four of us on that fateful night, *an anniversary just two days from now.*

A deep, familiar voice seemed to fill the confines of the little church. "It is written in the book of Genesis: 'In the day that God created man, in the likeness of God made He him. Male and female created He them, and blessed them, and called their name Adam, in the day when they were created. And according to the second chapter of Genesis, Eve was created by God, by Yahwe, by taking her from the rib of Adam, to be Adam's companion.'"

A low rumble of voices steadily rose from the pews.

Standing there at the podium, Chaplain Thomas Trent looked out upon the town of Clairmont. One side of his upper lip had pulled upward into a sneer – the man was making no attempt to hide his condemnation for this gathering.

He continued, "Unlike Adam . . . and unlike Eve, you, here, are not made by God. You are an abomination. I cannot pray for your souls . . . that of which you do not possess."

I wasn't aware my hands had balled into white-knuckled fists. "To hell with this," I said, ready to stand and put an end to this bullshit.

Doc Viv placed her hand over mine, "Wait . . . let's see how this plays out."

Interesting . . . while she was watching this more like a spectator at a performance, like a play, I'd lost all perspective and was ready to throw Trent out on his ear.

The doors of the church suddenly swung open, clattering loud enough to make everyone jump in their seats. A lone figure, seemingly bigger than life, stood within the door's threshold. Silhouetted with the bright mid-day sun behind him, the man's head swiveled left and then right. He stepped forward, allowing everyone to see who had barged in with such irreverent gusto. A smile crept onto my lips; I recognized him at once. As a child, I both respected and feared this mountain of a man. I liked Reverend Goudy Forest. He was everything Chaplain Thomas Trent was *not*: principled, equitable, and honorable came to mind.

He stepped forward into the church, and only then did I realize he wasn't alone. As robust a man as Reverend Goudy Forest was, Sheriff Conway Tiff was not –Tiff was slight and unimposing, as well as gawky and apprehensive. Even as a kid, I knew, *hell, everyone knew,* that Tiff had an innate capacity for avoiding confrontation. It wasn't so much he was cowardly as it was that he prized self-preservation above all else. Skeletally thin, he wore a combover hairstyle to hide his balding pate.

"You will purge yourself from my pulpit, Chaplain . . . and do so at once," Reverend Goudy Forest said, so loudly that I suspected his voice carried outside and halfway into town.

Looking indignant, Trent squared his shoulders, "I am the ship's Chaplain by contract. This, here, is a mockery. One I intend to –"

Reverend Forest stepped aside to reveal the far smaller individual dressed in his ill-fitting dark green uniform. "Sheriff, please remove this . . . this *intruder* from our house of God."

I had fallen into a similar state of mind as Doc Viv's, observing the situation much like a spectator. So, when Chaplain Thomas Trent's eyes found and locked onto mine, I almost turned to look behind me, thinking he was staring at someone else.

"Captain Quintos . . . how can you condone this degradation of *human* spiritual law?

All heads turned toward me. Without glancing to my left, I felt the eyes of my family boring into me. I stole a glance to my right, seeing Doc Viv's bemused expression. She was enjoying this. In that moment of indecision, what came to me was just how important my next few words would be. How willing was I to embrace this make-believe town with its parody of real townsfolk over the alternate reality that I was, in fact, *Hamilton's* commanding officer, and not an eleven-year-old boy with zero authority here? My eyes met those of Reverend Goudy Forest, still towering over the rest of us, standing halfway up the center aisle.

"Do not tempt fate, Captain," Trent said with guile. "This is one moment that can come back to haunt you for many years to come."

It was almost imperceptible. One of Reverend Forest's eyebrows arched up ever so slightly. A subtle taunt: *How far are you willing to let this play out, young man?*

So, I did what I would have done as a ten or eleven-year-old boy; I made an exasperated face and shrugged. Viv stifled a chuckle.

Reverend Forest raised a palm toward the front of the

church, "Sheriff . . . do your duty and remove this individual from my pulpit!"

To his credit, Sheriff Tiff rousted enough courage to stride past the reverend, a hand on the butt of his Colt revolver, and headed toward the front of the church. With his other hand, he gestured for Chaplain Trent to come down off the raised dais.

"This should be good," Viv said, sitting up higher, straining to see better.

His eyes narrowed to near slits; it was as if Trent was attempting to fire laser beams into my very soul. Clearly, the man was far more consumed with his hatred for me than any reverence toward God or spirituality.

As the chaplain stepped down, Sheriff Tiff attempted to take hold of his arm. In an exaggerated overreaction, Chaplain Trent jerked his arm away, "Don't you dare touch me, you ridiculous fool."

While Reverend Forest strode forward toward the pulpit, Chaplain Trent and Sheriff Tiff exited the church's front. I heard them descending the cement steps outside.

"Where will the sheriff take him?" Viv asked.

"There's a small police station not far from the garage in town. I think there's a jail cell or two in there."

"Oh, come on, you don't really think the chaplain will be tossed in jail, do you?" She said, her eyes alive with something, perhaps mischief, stoked by the continuing drama.

Before I could answer, my TAC-Band began to vibrate. "I'm needed on the Bridge. You staying?"

She nodded, "For a little while. No surgeries today . . . and this is fascinating."

Chapter 21

Both Derrota and Lieutenant Pristy were waiting for me within the CIC, hunched over a data display.

"What do you have for me?" I asked, approaching them.

Derrota said, "Good to his word, Admiral Block has provided direct links to those three separate, cloaked recognizance stations previously deployed into Andromeda."

"And?" I said.

Lieutenant Pristy said, "And two of them have no relevant data . . . non-eventful, like watching grass grow."

"And the third?"

"Pay dirt. MATHR had to do some pretty amazing feed enhancements . . . that Varapin fleet was close to a half light-year away from our droid," Pristy said. "Go on, play it for him, Stephan," she said.

The projected 3D display revealed an area of open space with an abundance of twinkling stars, sitting immobile above the console for a full minute. Pristy must have sensed my growing impatience and said, "Just another few seconds, Captain."

The first of the Varapin vessels to come into view, nothing like anything I'd seen before. Certainly, nothing like any US Space-Navy warship. These looked almost organic, animalistic, in form. I couldn't ignore a feeling of doom creeping into my psyche, as more and more alien warships came into view.

"It's hard to judge the size of those ships . . . at least without a reference point – " I stopped talking as one particular warship came into view. It was much, much, larger than the others. I'd seen a feed of this ship before: *The Sintchu.*

I remembered Admiral Block's description; *This impressive-looking vessel is the Varapin Empire's* Sintchu. *Four miles long and a half of that wide. And like the revamped USS Hamilton, she is a dreadnought of unfathomable technology and power. Make no mistake about it; the* Sintchu *is the Hamilton's direct counterpart.*

"The *Sintchu,*" I said.

"Undoubtedly," Derrota said.

The vessel was not only enormous but inexorably formidable – threatening – like a great bird of prey readying to strike. Without thinking, I said, "I honestly don't see how we can go up against such an enemy . . ."

Derrota said, "Then, you're really not going to like this next part."

I continued to watch as the entire fleet, maybe a dozen warships, were unceremoniously met by two additional Varapin fleets – both larger and with more warship assets. "Holy Christ," I said.

Lieutenant Pristy said, "Intercepted data tells us additional fleets are *Wrath of Power*, along with *Revenge of the Heart*. They have joined the *Rage of the Gonjun Ract* fleet and, together, are headed our way."

"So, we can confirm Admiral Block's assessment. Our impossibly dismal odds have just – "

"Taken a turn for the worse," Pristy said, finishing my sentence.

I continued to stare at the projected display. Using two fingers, I expanded the view, zooming in on several smaller, bulbous-looking crafts. "What are those?"

"They refer to them as Ravage-Class landers," Derrota said. "They're both a ship-to-ship assault-style craft, as well as a ship-to-ground assault-style craft. The Varapin also have advanced fighter crafts – Cyclone Death Fighters – that I'm afraid our Arrows would be no match for. Anyway, these Ravage-Class landers are their attack vessels of choice when invasions are imminent. We're still going over the data, but I assure you, they are beyond lethal."

"Of course, they are." Then, I remembered and said the late Zan "Gunny" Mattis's profound words, "We're so fucktipated."

Derrota and Pristy looked at me blank-faced. *Shit.* It was my job to encourage my crew. To motivate them and give them hope – even when there wasn't any. I said, "We just need to figure things out. We're certainly not going to beat the Varapin by conventional means . . . going up against them head to head. That just means we're going to have to outsmart them."

The two officers nodded but said nothing. They knew my

words were hollow. They knew we were *fucktipated*. Then, something occurred to me. I turned around and scanned the CIC. I took a couple of steps and peered into the Bridge. "Anyone seen Hardy, lately?"

By the time Derrota and I entered Engineering and Propulsion, I'd received four separate High Priority messages – three from Chief Porter, and one from Doc Viv, who was currently on her way to meet us here.

We were directed to the reactor area. There, we found Chief Craig Porter pacing back and forth within a passageway, like a first-time expectant father in a hospital corridor. Except that this wasn't a happy occurrence of birth; just the opposite, he was considering the possibility of death.

Seeing me, the Chief looked relieved, but also at the end of his emotional resolve. "Galvin, you have to believe me, I had no idea there was a problem. The damn ChronoBot is . . . well, it's fucking indestructible, right? We all know that."

"Just slow down, Craig. Tell us what's happened with Hardy. I'm sure he's okay." I looked down the passageway to where I had last seen the irreverent robot, there, within that damaged reactor chamber wielding that gargantuan wrench. "What happened when he finished in there? Where did he go? Where is he now?"

The Chief looked at me as if I had three heads. "He didn't go anywhere!" He tried to calm himself. "The son of a bitch never left the chamber. A tech, wearing an environment suit, only found him by accident . . . Hardy had apparently keeled over sideways and was pinned behind that patched reactor."

The impact of the Chief's words sunk in. "Wait, are you telling me Hardy's dead . . . or near dead?"

"Yes, Galvin, that's exactly what I'm saying. There's a small crack or something at the back of his head. He was unaware of it. I'm sorry, Galvin. It was too many hours subjected to extreme amounts of radiation, finding its way into his biological AI."

I noticed Doc Viv was standing at my side – I hadn't seen or heard her arrive.

Derrota said, "You're no expert in complex machine robotics or Artificial Intelligence, Craig."

"Or the physiology of organic brain matter," Doc Viv added. "Take us to him. Hurry, every second counts. He's more than a fucking machine."

"Screw you, I already know that, Vivian," Craig said.

I placed a hand on the Chief's arm, "Just take us to him. We're all just running a little hot here."

Hardy had been moved into the same compartment where the now-dead Thine scientist had been taken. The ChronoBot was seated on the deck with his back up against the far bulkhead. His teardrop-shaped head was lulling to one side, and his usually-animated digitized face was black and lifeless. I knelt down next to him and took the closest of his heavy mechanical hands in mine. About to speak, I waited for my emotions to settle – the lump in my throat to dissipate. The number of close friends I had was few; I couldn't afford to lose another. Truth was, I had no better friend than Hardy. What made this moment all that much worse was the fact that I often - almost always - took him for granted. As often as this strange ChronoBot irritated the hell out of me, I wondered how I would continue without him. There would never be another individual in my life who would have my back the way Hardy had.

"He's dead," I said.

The ship's propulsion system's sound – a low, consistent hum – seemed to grow louder within the claustrophobic compartment.

Doc Viv, taking a knee on Hardy's other side, looked saddened and defeated. She looked up to Derrota. "I'd have to look at his biomass AI subsystem. But he doesn't seem to be," she looked over to me, "responsive. To be alive."

Derrota said, "How about we get him delivered over to HealthBay? We can both take a look."

"I'm sorry, Galvin . . . I know you two were close," the doctor said, getting to her feet. "Best you keep your expectations low, though. Are you coming?"

I shook my head. "I'll stay with him a little longer."

As Derrota and Doc Viv turned to leave, I saw it. A flicker. At first, I thought it might be my eyes playing tricks on me; a small cluster of micro-sensor lights on Hardy's digitized face momentarily went active. Perhaps, a sort of death-twitch human bodies can exhibit, even hours after a person took their last breath. I stared at the flat, black face display, mentally willing it to happen again. "Come on, you big idiot . . . come on."

"He's gone, Galvin. I'm sorry," Doc Viv said from the passageway.

I'd thought she'd already left. "Yeah, I guess you're right. Let's get him moved to HealthBay."

I emerged from HealthBay feeling even less confident about Hardy's prognosis than when I'd left him in Engineering and Propulsion, three hours earlier. There'd been no further indication he was mentally cognizant of what was going on around him. Sure, Derrota had promised to get more accurate diagnostics readings later today, but it was obvious: Derrota and Doc Viv were not encouraged.

In general, there were just so many unknown aspects regarding ChronoBots. Most people didn't realize ChronoBots were old – like *three-hundred years* old – and had been originally manufactured as quasi-indestructible war machines by the *Sheentah*. Most of the ChronoBots were gone now – maybe a hundred remained within the galaxy – and none of those had an interfused human persona residing within their wet biomatter AI component, such as a long-gone 48-year-old Bostonian SWM Crewmember named John Hardy.

Stepping out into Deck 10's main passageway, I saw a small crowd had converged nearby HealthBay's entrance. I recognized most of them, but I first saw Lasalle, an SWM crewmember sitting on the deck reading an old-fashioned printed book. LaSalle tilted the book up so I could read the title: *The Essential Wisdom of the Founding Fathers*. I knew LaSalle was a true scholar in his own right when it came to early American history.

LaSalle said, "I wasn't aware just how much George Washington detested war." He held up a finger and flipped back several pages in the book. "'My first wish is to see this plague to mankind banished from off the Earth, and the sons and daughters of this world employed in more pleasing and innocent amusements than in preparing implements and exercising them for the destruction of mankind.'"

The irony of our Founding Father's words was not lost on me.

"How is my friend . . . I'd like to see him, even if he's asleep. Maybe I could read to him," Lasalle said.

I shook my head, "Doc's not letting anyone else in there right now. Space is limited."

"Then, is it all right if I sit out here . . . while I'm off shift?"

"Sure . . . and I promise you'll be the first to see him if anything changes."

"Uh . . . Cap? How's Hardy doing?" another crewman asked.

I turned to see five concerned faces staring back at me. Only now did I realize I'd missed this odd bunch of misfits. The leader of the small band of marines was Sergeant Max Dryer. His copper-colored hair and abundance of freckles gave him a boyish look, although I knew from past experience, he was one tough Marine. To his right was Grip. Big, Black, and all muscle – even unarmed, he looked lethal – a tightly-coiled snake, capable of striking at a moment's notice. Then, there was

Wanda, with her strands of aqua-purple streaked hair; she, too, was tall and muscular – a badass chick who had no problem telling it like it was. Finally, there were the huge twins, Ham and Hock. There weren't two wits between them, but they had heart and were loyal through and through.

I'd been told that most of my previous crew had opted to serve with me again here on *Hamilton,* but these weren't US Space-Navy service members; they were Marines. There again, Major Doc Viv wasn't Space-Navy, either. At that moment, I felt both honored and humbled by those willing to continue serving with me. "Hardy is . . . well, not doing so well. We're thinking radiation poisoning affecting his organic AI. Somewhere along the line, he'd cracked his head. Could have even been back at Ironhold Station."

Wanda said, "You look all defeated, like you've given up. What's the matter with you? He's one of us. We don't give up on each other."

I looked back at the scrappy young Marine, tempted to tell her how impossible the odds would be for Hardy to recover. But she was right. "Thank you, Wanda. Hardy deserves better from me. I'm not giving up. I just miss the annoying clod."

"Yeah, he really is annoying," Grip said. "Recently, I found my bunk had been moved. It was bolted upside down to the ceiling. Not sure how he did that . . ."

Everyone laughed. Grip said, "Hardy somehow changed the duty roster, so I was cleaning toilets in the head, double-shifts mind you, for a week straight."

More laughter.

I said, "I know you all want to see him, let him know you all have scores to settle with him. Let's just see how it goes."

Max asked, "We going into battle soon, Cap? You know we're here, we're ready for whatever you throw us into."

I didn't answer right away. I made serious eye contact with each of them. "I'm going to be honest with you. Yeah, soon, we'll be going into battle against the fucking devil himself." I stepped closer to Wanda, knowing she was this crew's very heart and soul. "You'll need to dig deep and bring everything, I mean *everything* you have, to this fight."

Without missing a beat, she said, "Cap . . . don't you worry. We heard about them . . . those Varapin. We'll be sending those motherfuckers straight back to hell. You just tell us when you need us. We'll be ready."

Chapter 22

Sprinting down Whale's Alley, checking my TAC-Band, I saw Lieutenant Pristy's latest message – informing me I was late for my own meeting.

I entered the Captain's Conference Room to find most seats filled. There sat the remaining Sr. Officers of the 2nd Fleet. The Captains were in full dress greys, which was not only unnecessary but weird. Shipboard jumpsuits were the standard dress for all crew, as we were well into the operation. My second, XO Eli Tannock, was amongst them and seated to the right of the open seat at the table's head. Everyone stood as I headed for my chair.

"Apologies, everyone. Please sit, we have a lot to discuss."

A Captain with wavy salt-and-pepper hair remained standing at the opposite end of the table. He cleared his throat, "Captain Longbottom of the Billings, sir. In your absence, your XO, Tannock, has been filling us in on some of your thoughts . . . your ideas for dealing with the Varapin."

I nodded, forcing myself not to look at Tannock. I had discussed none of my ideas with him – so the ideas had been his own. Ideas that he'd passed off as mine.

"The idea to set a trap . . . of course, cloak all our assets and go sensor-passive is fine, right in line with fleet protocol. But where to position our warships, anticipating where and when the enemy fleet will arrive . . . that's a potential problem."

Of course, that's a problem! That's why I would never have come up with such a hair-brained scheme. "Captain Longbottom, thank you for your input, and I agree. I apologize, I have not had the opportunity to update XO Tannock with more current strategies." Only now did I glance toward my XO.

Longbottom took his seat, and another Captain stood. *Why do they keep standing up to talk like that?* "Captain Witherspoon, of the *Gallaher,* sir. If I may, we, several of the other officers and I, have some, um . . . perhaps more creative approaches –"

I held up a hand, "Captain Witherspoon, please take a seat. And let's all just stay seated here forth. Not sure where the need for that standing rigmarole got started."

All eyes went to XO Tannock.

I continued. "And the whole cloaked ambush idea was a stupid idea on my part. No need to pussyfoot around things . . . we're here to have a frank discussion. Screw unnecessary formalities, this is far too important."

"We were thinking of using the Heisman / Lock strategy . . . first used back in 2166, where the 9th Fleet had encountered two Grish patrols. A highly effective flanking maneuver –"

I interjected, "Unfortunately, we nearly lost that battle,

even with a two-to-one superiority in asset numbers, Captain
. . ."

"Sorry . . . I'm Captain McAvoy, of the *Mighty,* sir."

"Thank you, Captain McAvoy." I let out a breath as I
looked about the table; many of the men and women here had
ten to fifteen years on me; one or two may have had twenty
years, but they had little – if any – real battle experience. It
wasn't an accident I'd been saddled with this 2ⁿᵈ fleet and these
well-intentioned – but mostly situationally inexperienced –
officers. They, no, *we were all* expendable in the eyes of Fleet
Command. That was a tough pill to swallow, considering my
past relationship with Admiral Block. In some ways, he'd been
more of a father to me than my own.

"Let me be blunt. We, the US Space-Navy's 2ⁿᵈ, Fleet were
not sent out here to prevail. We were sent out here to diminish
the enemy's assets and to slow them down."

"Why do you say that Captain?" said Captain "Tiger"
Taiger, who I recognized from the *Starlight.*

"He's right, Tiger," Captain JJ of the *Louisiana,* said.
"Admiral Block pretty much admitted to that fact."

The older Captain pursed his lips, "Okay, Captain JJ, I'll
buy that. Maybe some of our older ships may be considered
expendable for the greater good, sent out here to buy time to
defend against the Varapin fleet. But to sacrifice the *Hamilton?*
She's the damn jewel of the US Space-Navy, for God's sake!"

Captain Taiger scratched his chin. "I can't explain that.
That makes little sense to me."

But it made perfect sense to me. The *USS Hamilton* was

not a US Space-Navy asset. It was a Captain Galvin Quintos'
personal asset, which was unacceptable to many within Fleet
Command. But talk about shooting oneself in the proverbial
foot! The room had erupted into multiple side conversations.
Voices were getting heated. Things were quickly getting out of
hand.

I checked the time on my TAC-Band – *they should be here
soon.* On cue, Captain Wallace Ryder entered the conference
room. I stood and motioned for him to take my seat. Then
three others entered the conference room, which brought
all the cross-talking to an immediate stop. Chief of Security
Alistair Mattis walked in, along with one of his security people
and their shackled prisoner, Talco Wentworth.

"What's going on here, Captain?" JJ said, eyeing the new
arrivals.

"First of all, let me start by saying . . . there is no way we
can defeat that approaching Varapin fleet. No way in hell. Sixty
superior technology warships with, undoubtedly, more experienced officers, including myself, at their helms."

"I think we've already established that," JJ said.

"Well . . . I, for one, don't like playing the patsy. I don't
like being served up as the sacrificial lamb and done so under
misrepresented mission parameters."

For the first time, Tannock stood and spoke, "Captain
Quintos . . . I must interject. It is clear where the direction of
this conversation is going. So, let me say this: we are officers
within the US Space-Navy. We don't get to pick and choose
which orders we follow. We certainly don't have to like our

orders – but follow prescribed orders we must. Stay true to protocol. If not, there would be anarchy. A total breakdown of authority. As you, undoubtedly, have surmised . . . I am here to ensure that you are reminded of these simple facts. Your less-than-stellar service record proceeds you. Do you think the others in this room are unaware of your multiple, often fla-grant, violations? Your disregard for authority?"

The notion that Tannock was a *plant* here on board the *Hamilton*, was not news to me; and, probably not news to anyone here. But for him to stand and make such an announce-ment in front of my peers hadn't been expected. It would alter the direction of our relationship from this point forward. *So be it.*

"Thank you for your input, XO Tannock."

I looked about the room. "Anyone uncomfortable with the direction I'm taking things henceforth – which I assure you will be, um, unconventional – is free to leave now. There will be no repercussions on my part. But rest assured, my purpose here is not to lead this fleet into what would have been a certain demise. Again, any battle with the Varapin will not be won by fighting by conventional means or following protocol."

I scanned the faces around me. Several of the Captains looked to be undecided.

I said, "For those who share XO Tannock's view on the matter, all I ask is you do nothing to impede the strategies we will be implementing. That, and you follow my orders."

I waited a full minute, and no one rose to leave. "XO

Tannock, I believe your services are required back on the bridge. If you would be so kind . . ." I gestured toward the exit.

Inwardly fuming, Tannock's pallor darkened into scarlet. He looked about the conference room, his gaze a condemnation of all those who had not sided with him. He left without saying another word.

Captain Taiger said, "You better know what you're doing, son . . . I have a feeling all of our asses will be hanging out to dry after this."

I turned my attention to Captain Wallace Ryder. "Captain Ryder, how do you feel about taking a little road trip?"

"Um, sure, what did you have in mind, Captain?"

Two jumps back, we had a little run=in with both the Ramdei and Clouse Veng."

"Yeah, as I remember, they weren't thrilled with our presence within their respective territories."

"True. Although, Centurion Goben of the Clouse Veng Empire was more than a little interested in our jump technology."

Stern glares came at me from all the officers in the room. "Now hold on, before you jump to any conclusions. We need help, and we need it fast. I'm proposing that we offer our Clouse Veng friends an opportunity to technologically leapfrog over their enemy, the Ramdei . . . but do so at a heavy price."

Captain Taiger said, "We don't have clearance to offer advanced tech, such as jump technology, to unvetted alien civilizations. This is common knowledge, Captain Quintos."

"You are one-hundred percent correct, Captain. And that

is why I've instructed Lieutenant Pristy to reach out to Admiral Block. We'll need his sign off on what is officially referred to as a Form CLV-1109937. For those of you not familiar with that form, this will provide for two things. One, the Clouse Veng will be entered into an official evaluation process with Space Command, initiating a mutual trial alliance between Earth and them."

"And the second part?" Captain JJ asked.

"Second, the Clouse Veng will be provided a working sample of our jump technology – jump drives that can be implemented within an entire fleet of ships."

The conference room erupted into mayhem.

"The same aliens that nearly destroyed the *USS Brave!*" One Captain said.

"No way can we trust them with such advanced tech!" Another Captain exclaimed.

"Are you out of your mind?" Captain JJ asked.

"This is crazy . . . no way!" Captain Taiger bellowed.

I let them squawk for a while longer before slamming my hand down on the table. "Okay, okay, settle down!"

They did so, but no one looked pleased.

"As I was saying, the Clouse Veng will be provided with samples, but not fully-operational samples. The US Space-Navy is not new to this process. The sample technology will stay operational within a limited timeframe; I'm thinking a month or two. And we maintain a remote kill-switch, one that can be activated from anywhere and at any time of our choosing. It's understood; having our own jump technology used against us would not be prudent."

"And what do we get in return?" Captain Styles from the *Brave*, asked.

"I thought that was obvious," I said. "Their help going up against the Varapin. If there's going to be a cavalry riding in to save the day, I assure you, it won't be from the US Space-Navy . . . it'll be from the Clouse Veng. Any other objections?"

Captain JJ said, "Go on, Captain Quintos. Lay out the rest of it."

"Captain Ryder will be commanding a small squadron of Arrow Fighters along with our Hub Gunther Craft . . . which is large enough to hold any loaner equipment, while still not depleting our necessary war assets here."

I placed a hand on Ryder's shoulder. "You'll be leaving within the hour, Ryder. Pull your team of pilots together. Oh, and take Sergeant Max and his squad of Marines along with you on the Gunther. Lieutenant Pristy will be contacting each of her logistical counterparts within the fleet as to what spare spring drives will be required of them."

"So, you're taking our spare spring drives?" an unfamiliar captain asked, looking none too happy about it.

"Yes, not all, but most. It's the only way this plan can work. And don't forget, *Hamilton* will continue to jump the fleet herself, so chances are, you won't even need your onboard spring drives. Remember, if we don't make the deal sweet enough, the Clouse Veng will tell us to go piss up a rope. You may need to get creative."

Ryder said, "And why am I taking a squad of Marines with me?"

I didn't answer the question.

"Fine. Looks like I have a lot to do in a very short window of time. I'm heading out of here," Ryder said.

"Good luck, Captain Ryder. Needless to say, a whole lot is riding on you and your team," I said.

He nodded and left the conference room.

I next turned my attention to Talco Wentworth, who had been quietly standing off to one side, along with his security guard and Mattis. If there was any possible way around this, I would have been happy to put this arrogant bastard behind bars for several years. Instead, I needed his help.

Wentworth held out his still shackled hands. "If you would be so kind, Captain. They are most uncomfortable."

His obnoxious, superior, highbrow voice made me want to deck him. Instead, I nodded to Mattis to do what the rapist techno-wizard was asking.

"Do you know why you are here, Mr. Wentworth?"

He combed his fingers through his long hair and smiled. "Of course, I do. Zathium. Everything revolves around the miracles Zathium can offer the US Space-Navy."

Chapter 23

I addressed the room, "I'm assuming we all know about Mr. Wentworth's involvement with acquiring Earth mining rights for Zathium on Juno 5?"

"Some kind of miracle mineral. Heard it can enhance Hyper-Drive performance . . . something like that," Captain Longbottom said. "It's being tested here on *Hamilton*."

"Please explain the details, Wentworth," I said.

Wentworth looked put out at having to go through this again. "Goriom, Zathium, and Pilorium are actually far more than simple minerals . . . they are exotic quantum particle elements. Currently, Zathium is being tested on several of the *Hamilton's* primary systems."

I didn't want to get into the myriad of problems Zathium had already caused for *Hamilton's* Pleidian Weonan modified propulsion system, so I moved the discussion along. "Tell them how Zathium can affect the fleet's overall battle capabilities," I said.

Wentworth smiled, "What if I told you there was a means to enhance the fleet's shields . . ." *the arrogant shit was using his same spiel as before,* "to provide ten times the protection against any of our enemy's energy weapons, rail munitions, or even smart missiles? And that the output of your FTL HyperDrives could be tripled, if not quadrupled. And those newly installed spring jump drive components could potentially double your manufactured wormhole distances?"

Captain McAvoy said, "I'd say those are some pretty boastful claims. But even if they are true by one-half, a US Space-Navy warship would be in a position to dominate virtually any enemy encounter."

I wanted to warn my fellow officers that Wentworth was a scoundrel and an opportunist, *that,* and taking him at his word would be risky, but I needed these officers on my side. Soon, they'd be taking some significant risks, something I was sure they were unaccustomed to doing.

"You have enough for the entire fleet, Mr. Wentworth?" Captain JJ asked.

"Unfortunately, no. A discussion never came up where such a large quantity would be required."

"Then why are we even talking about this?" Captain Taiger asked, looking annoyed.

I rolled my eyes. *Bullshit! Of course, Wentworth would have taken this possibility into account. He hadn't become one of the wealthiest people on Earth by not thinking ahead. Unless I was wrong . . .*

Wentworth scratched his chin, acting as if an errant thought had just crossed his mind. "Hmm . . ."

Here it comes . . .

"Nah . . . best not to even go there," he said dramatically with a dismissive hand.

"Go on . . . what are you thinking?" JJ coaxed.

"Well, there is a slim possibility that a synthesized version of Zathium will be ready for testing soon." Wentworth turned his gaze toward me. "That is if you would allow the good Major Leigh to complete her work on the project?"

"Doc Viv isn't −" I cut myself off. I remembered she had mentioned she and Wentworth had started some kind of an LLC venture together. Perhaps that had something to do with synthesizing Zathium. "Last I checked, Doc Viv's experiments weren't quite ready for prime time yet," I said, ignoring the conspiratorial look Wentworth was giving me.

"Why don't we have the good doctor join us . . . she can share her latest developments," Wentworth said.

I really didn't want to get this far into the weeds with all this, but seeing the other officer's now-interested faces, I'd boxed myself into a corner. I messaged Doc Viv on my TAC-Band and asked her to join us.

Ten minutes later, she was striding into the Captain's Conference Room looking, of course, beautiful, but also unsure as to why she'd been summoned here.

"Ah, Doctor Leigh, thank you for rushing right over. I know you're busy," I said. *Like hanging around a mock church service in our little town of Clairmont.*

"No problem," she said, glancing about the room. "How can I be of service?"

Captain Longbottom spoke up first, "Mr. Wentworth was telling us about your experiments with synthesizing Zathium."

If sideways glances could kill, Wentworth would already be laid out on the deck. Recomposing herself within a millisecond, she said, "I wasn't aware my experiments on Deck 47 had been cleared for open discussion."

Wentworth offered up a half-smile and said, "Major, you can blame me for divulging that secret information. Take it from me, it won't be the last time we cross the line of improprieties going forward."

She gave the older man a disapproving glance, but went on, anyway. "Understand, desperate times call for . . ."

"Desperate measures," I interjected, wanting to move things forward.

She now looked like a child stealing morsels from the cookie jar. "Okay, fine. Yes. The experimentation had started in my lab back on Earth, and I've had my team continuing the work here onboard *Hamilton*."

Sure, why not? Go ahead and conduct secret experiments without my knowledge. I'm only the fucking Captain of this ship. "And why don't you share with the group your progress to this point, Doc?"

"Slow, but steady. We believe we have successfully synthesized the element. But we're at a point where several years of testing will confirm the synthesized product, which we now call *ZathSyn*, is stable and safe. The Thine scientists, in addition to following the tests of the original Zathium onboard *Hamilton*, are helping me with that, as well."

"A couple of years?" JJ said, looking from the doctor back over to me.

"Yes. We don't want another fiasco like what happened here —"

I cut her off before she spilled too many of those beans. "Back to your tests. I'm going to be frank with you, just as I have with everyone here. We've been sent on what amounts to little more than a suicide mission. I'm sorry if that makes you uncomfortable."

"I'm a big girl, Captain. No need to patronize me."

"Good. So, let me lay this out for you in blunt strokes. I want every ship within the 2nd fleet to have an advantage, even if it's marginal, prior to going into battle with the Varapin. If you're concerned with causing damage to ship hardware . . . well, we weren't expected to return home anyway."

She looked up, as if she could see all the way up into the 47th Deck. "I have no problem giving it a try. Manufacturing ZathSyn to that scale will take some reconfiguring of the lab . . . but that's doable." She looked over to Wentworth. "But I'm a minor shareholder. Ultimately, decisions about the product and its manufacturing reside with its primary owner, Mr. Wentworth."

He was already nodding his head. "Yes, I have been working with the US Space-Navy as part of a long-term contract. But still, this is a proprietary, privately owned, synthetic. I cannot in good conscience —"

"Drop the aggrieved act. What's it going to take, Wentworth?"

Looking as if he was pondering the question, I pictured my hands wrapped around his throat again.

"For one, all charges dropped . . . for my previous acts of, um, poor judgment."

"Fine."

"And if we do survive this battle with the Varapin, you provide me with a percentage of ownership in this ship . . . in *Hamilton*."

"No." I looked over to Doc Viv. "Do you have everything you need to proceed without Wentworth's future involvement?"

"Sure. He's not a part of the day-to-day science. But it is his product."

"That's fine. I'm going to borrow it in the name of the US Space-Navy as a necessity of war. If we live through this, Mr. Wentworth can take me, *hell*, the US Space-Navy, to court. That is, once he's finished with his other legal issues . . . like the rape of –"

"Fine!" Wentworth said, clearly not wanting me to expound further on his misdeeds within the town of Clairmont. "You may borrow the ZathSyn product for the duration of this mission. But all charges need to be dropped. And any record of the . . . situation wiped from the ship's records."

I turned my back on Wentworth to address the Captains. "We'll need to move fast. Please have your ship's engineering teams brought up to speed on our plans. Note that the use of this ZathSyn is more of an additive to our ADAP fuel supplies.

Hardware modifications should be minimal," I said, glancing over to Viv and Wentworth for confirmation. They both nodded.

Quiet and introspective-looking, the captains were now getting to their feet. Not one of them looked comfortable with the direction things were taking, with the 2nd fleet about to go completely off-book in terms of approaching the Varapin fleet. These men and women were contemplating their careers' future fate, weighing that aspect against potentially increasing the odds of survival for their crews and themselves.

As the other officers filed out, I asked Doc Viv to stay behind for a minute.

She said, "You want to know what happened after you left, don't you?" There was an air of vivacity, of enjoying life, about her. It took me a second to catch up; she was talking about Clairmont and what had transpired in the church after I left.

"I was going to ask you about Hardy, actually. If I can come by and see him?"

"Oh, okay . . . hold on." She tapped at her TAC-Band for several seconds, going back and forth with what I assumed was one of her nurses or med-techs. "Sure . . . come on, walk with me. But I warn you, he's not showing much sign of improvement."

As we hurried along toward the bank of GravLifts, I had to ask. "Okay, spill it. What happened after I left?"

She laughed, "I knew you wouldn't be able to hold off asking for long."

"Yeah, yeah, get on with it."

"Let's see, when did you leave?"

"Um, Reverend Forest had shown up with Sheriff Tiff. They got Chaplain Trent off the pulpit and were taking him to jail, I guess."

We both laughed at that.

Viv, becoming more serious now, said, "It was strange. I was going to follow the contingent taking Trent off to the pokey, and your mother stopped me."

"My mother?"

"Um, your Symbio-Poth mother."

"Huh, what did she say?"

"She said that dinner is at six –"

"You mean 1800?" Galvin quipped.

Doc Viv rolled her eyes. "At six, and not to be late. She's making chicken and dumplings. And your favorite, pineapple upside-down cake."

I was already shaking my head. "No. I can't be running off to –"

Viv said, "I'm to come, too. I told her we'll be there. She calls me your 'little friend,' like we're both still ten."

"Eleven, actually . . . that's how old we are to her . . . to them. All right. I guess I'll meet you at the garage at quarter to six."

"What should I wear?" She asked, looking as if she was enjoying this far too much.

I shrugged, "I guess what any eleven-year-old girl wears on a farm."

When we arrived at HealthBay, Doc Viv pointed me toward

Hardy's room as she headed farther back into the department's surgery section.

I found Hardy sitting in a chair that looked far too small for his oversized frame. There were no less than twenty-five small devices distributed onto mechanical body's arms, legs, and torso, including several on his head. Derrota was there. He looked up from a tablet he was studying with a furrowed brow.

"Galvin, I wasn't expecting you . . ."

I nodded, but my eyes were on Hardy. I saw that his typically animated face display was pitch black – *lifeless.*

"Look, I'm trying everything I can think of to bring him back," Derrota said defensively.

"I know you are, Stephan. You still think it's that hairline crack in his noggin that allowed radiation to –"

"Seep into his AI bio-matter?" Derrota said, finishing my sentence. "Truth is, I'm not sure about that, or anything. That crack looks to be pretty old. It could have occurred decades, or longer, ago. Why only now is the ChronoBot more subject to radiation than in the past?"

I shrugged. "Older? Nothing lasts forever. Even ChronoBots, I suppose. Stephan . . . level with me. Is he dead?"

"No. Not dead. In fact, my sensors are detecting flurries of discrete transmissions. Perhaps he's trying to communicate, I don't know. But it's a jumble of mismatched frequencies that seem to be meaningless. Not even MATHR can make heads or tails out of them."

"Have you tried talking to him?"

"To Hardy? Of course, I have."

"Yeah . . . how about LuMan?"

"No. I just figured Hardy would do the communicating, as he has in the past. As you well know, we usually can't shut him up."

I stared at the motionless robot. That was true, but LuMan was the robot's original, core identity. I knelt down and said, "LuMan, this is Captain Quintos. Status report!"

There was no change – *or was there?* I leaned forward, coming within a foot of the ChronoBot's face display. "I think I see something in there."

Derrota leaned in too. "I don't see anything . . . wait, oh yes, there it is . . . it's very faint. Random sensor lights going on and off."

I could smell Derrota's Indian cuisine lunch on his breath, probably something like murg makhani.

I said, "This is what LuMan typically displayed prior to Hardy inhabiting his psyche. But never this faint."

Suddenly, we both jumped back at the sound of LuMan's synthesized voice. "Status report . . . status report . . ."

Derrota and I looked at each other. I said, "That's at least something, right?"

"Indeed." Derrota placed a hand on the robot's shoulder. "LuMan . . . can you provide us with a diagnostics overview of your internal systems?"

"Primary hardware systems operating nominally. Error . . . Error . . . incompatible base command . . ."

Derrota and I exchanged a baffled look.

"I wish I could examine his internal software processes," Derrota said.

"You can't do that?"

"Uh-uh, remember, these ChronoBots were designed for battle conditions. Their AI routines are protected, shielded from outside tinkering like nobody's business," he said.

I said, "LuMan . . . what is the condition of Hardy? Can I speak to Hardy?"

It was several moments before the robot answered. "Hardy has been expunged."

My heart dropped. A part of me may have guessed that to be true, already. "Listen to me carefully, LuMan. You need to do anything . . . everything you can to get Hardy back again. That is an order!"

LuMan's face display momentarily came back to life with a myriad of blinking on-and-off sensor lights. A moment later, the ChronoBot looked lifeless again.

Derrota said, "I can run more tests. Maybe give it another hour. I'm sorry, Galvin, but I'll have to release him into long-term storage after that."

Under my breath, I said, "Damn it, Hardy . . . do something in there."

I left the two of them and headed out of HealthBay. Halfway to the GravLifts, MATHR was hailing me.

"Captain Quintos, you are needed on the bridge. Captain Quintos, you are needed on the bridge."

Chapter 24

LuMan's head suddenly rose, and his face display came alive with the activity of bright, blinking sensor lights. He transmitted a reciprocal acknowledgment burst back to his Varapin contact:

> *Orders acknowledged . . .*

Just as LuMan's sensors and visual perspectives were being accessed, the encrypted bidirectional connection, in turn, provided LuMan with a view into the cockpit of the cloaked Cyclone Death Fighter sitting just off *Hamilton's* portside.

LuMan watched as Haite-Caheil activated a virtual joystick. It was now poised, hovering, above the fighter's flight console.

The ChronoBot stood and began removing the numerous medi-sensors the science officer had adhered to his head, torso, and mechanical appendages. As directed, LuMan established a new passive connection with MATHR, something he had been doing routinely in recent hours. This allowed him to transmit relevant information, such as Fleet status and individual ship logistics, overall mission directives, personnel files on all officers and junior officers, and a myriad of other pertinent information that the approaching Varapin armada would use before encountering this abominable excuse for a battlegroup.

Making his way out of HealthBay, he noticed several humans seated there – congregating oddly outside of the medical facility.

LuMan strode with purpose toward Deck 10's bank of GravLifts. The ChronoBot's AI interface node had been elegantly hacked and bypassed, allowing full access to deep-kernel processing functionality. LuMan, one of the most advanced robots in the galaxy, had been reduced to little more than a remote-controlled, walking-talking, toy - something that was not lost on the bemused Varapin pilot now wielding the joystick.

The ChronoBot extended both chrome-plated arms, whereby mini plasma canons snapped into place, one on each of his mechanical forearms. Next came the sound of swivel-mounted shoulder cannons and similar thigh-mounted energy cannons, now also snapping into place.

LuMan had little choice but to follow the simple orders provided to him: destroy all lifeforms encountered. Destroy the *Hamilton*. Approaching the GravLifts, LuMan's target tracking processes locked onto the five-crewman waiting for the lift doors to open.

"Hardy! Hey . . . Hardy . . . hold up, man! It's me, LaSalle."

Ignoring the voice behind him, bright blue bursts of energy pulsed from LuMan's dual forearm weapons. In the blink of an eye – a combination of head shots and upper torso shots and all five humans had been killed where they stood.

"Holy shit! Oh my God . . . Hardy . . . no!"

At the GravLift doors opened, LuMan strode inside. He turned to see the astonished, stunned, face of SWM Crewman LaSalle. *Interesting* . . . this human had not been among those personal dossiers uploaded to Haite-Caheil – although he felt he somehow knew this person. LuMan raised his forearms, target tracking already locking on. The crewman dove out of sight just as the lift doors closed before him. LuMan tapped in the Deck 12 destination. Within moments, the lift doors were expanding open again, and LuMan was striding out into the *Hamilton's* crowded Whale's Ally. Alarm klaxons suddenly came alive, and MATHR was providing emergency information.

"Deck 12, active shooter! Deck 12, active shooter! Security personnel to Deck 12."

The ChronoBot's destination was the ship's bridge, where he'd been instructed to obliterate the *Hamilton's* control functionality and the vessels Sr. Officers. Each of LuMan's weapons came alive – separately locking onto all surrounding targets within the passageway. Energy bolts were literally firing out in every direction. Crewmembers, stunned and paralyzed by what was happening, were mowed down in abrupt and emotionless efficiency.

LuMan was aware that Haite-Caheil, onboard the Cyclone Death Fighter, was right there with him – at least, virtually. One of LuMan's internal display readings provided a numerical counter, which was now advancing well into double digits. It was the status count of crewmembers having been neutralized thus far.

LuMan's guns went suddenly quiet – heat rising from searing hot muzzles. All indications were, there was no one left alive within the ship's main passageway. The seven-foot-tall chrome robot hesitated, experiencing momentary confusion . . . *strange*. He surveyed the corridor one more time before moving toward the bridge entrance.

Chapter 25

Captain Galvin Quintos

I arrived on the bridge to find XO Tannock perched upon the Captain's Mount, literally sitting on the edge of his seat. "Hold your fire!" Tannock barked. "I want that craft captured and undamaged!"

I couldn't really tell what was happening up on the Halo-Display. "Sit-Report, XO," I said, now seeing that *Hamilton*, clustered within the rest of the 2nd Fleet, had deployed several Arrow Fighters – their ghostly outlines indicating they were cloaked.

Gesturing toward the display. Tannock said, "Captain, we may have gotten a small break here. It's cloaked, but we know there's a Cyclone Death Fighter out there. Must have jumped in here undetected. The odds of us even detecting the Varapin fighter would have been astronomically small. But thanks to the latest Pleidian sensor upgrades . . . we've got a passive sensor lock on it. Pilot has no idea we know he's there."

I thought about the repercussions of what my XO was telling me. Potentially, the Varapin now know a hell of a lot more about the 2nd Fleets whereabouts and capabilities than we do them. *Shit!*

The XO extracted himself from the Captain's Mount, and I took his seat.

"Seems as though that Cyclone Death Fighter is just sitting there shadowing *Hamilton*. I've deployed three Arrow Fighters, cloaked, of course, and they're moving in. I would have contacted you, Captain, but the situation was unfolding fast . . . I had to make decisions –"

"That's fine. But this isn't going to work," I said.

"Captain?" Tannock said.

"Even if we manage to creep up on this Varapin fighter undetected, which is doubtful, the last thing we want is for that pilot to panic . . . maybe self-destruct." I looked over to the CIC and saw Chief of Security Mattis speaking to another crewmember. I yelled and waved at him, "Alistair!"

He hurried over to me, "You bellowed, Captain?"

With all MATHR's new upgrades, any possibility she can hack into the nav controls of that Varapin fighter?

"Doubtful –"

I said, "Hold on a sec." I checked my TAC-Band, which was not only vibrating but audibly chiming to the point of distraction. I'd been ignoring it up to this point, but that was no longer an option. I saw it was a message from SWM Crewmember, LaSalle.

LaSalle: WATCH OUT – HARDY'S GONE MAD! FIRING HIS WEAPONS!!

Then I heard it. Weapon fire emanating from out in the passageway. I stood and scanned the fully-manned bridge and CIC areas. The over-abundance of crew here was primarily due to a series of recent anomalies. First, the high probability of that Varapin Cyclone Death Fighter was within spitting distance of *Hamilton* – which was being investigated by Chief of Security Mattis's group over within the CIC. Next, I'd learned from previous TAC-Band updates that Derrota and his team were embroiled in issues about MATHR; apparently, her security protocols had been breached, perhaps even days earlier. And last, as the 2nd Fleet was converging for its next jump forward, Lieutenant Pristy was at Tactical, Chen at Helm, and Grimes was at the Weapons station – even young Ensign Lorric Plorinne was involved, although I had no idea what he was doing. There wasn't an open seat to be found on the bridge. We had a full house, and there was an out-of-control killer robot on the loose – one that was undoubtedly headed this way. From above, MATHR blared warnings of an active shooter.

Everyone stopped what they were doing, now looking to me for directions. As their Captain, as their leader, I was responsible for keeping human losses to a minimum. *But how does one stop an out-of-control ChronoBot?* A wave of anxiety followed by the now-familiar feelings of paralysis crept into my consciousness. My breath caught in my chest. I managed to yell out just one word, "Hide!" Yeah, it was a lame thing to say – but, hey, it was all I could come up with at the moment.

The ChronoBot entered the back of the Bridge with his forearms extended, shooting bright bursts of plasma fire. While everyone around me was diving for cover, I still hadn't taken my own advice to hide or do anything other than stand there, mesmerized by this great chrome war machine in action. Hundreds – no, thousands – of individual energy bolts now encompassed the room. The bulkheads were alive with sparks, glittering showers of light. Systematically, station consoles were being targeted; more sparks, more mayhem, and disaster. Yet, I stood there and watched in fascination. It took a near strike to my head, an errant plasma bolt coming within an inch of my nose, for me to move. But I didn't dive for cover behind the Captain's Mount or cower next to Lieutenant Pristy at Tactical. Coming out of my momentary DOPTSD paralysis, I straightened my shoulders, raised my chin, and walked deliberately toward the ChronoBot. A ChronoBot that had been programmed to be my protector. We were all dead, or soon would be, anyway – there was no stopping this mechanical killer - no one here was even armed. Sure, undoubtedly, a security detail was already en route, but they would arrive here long after we were all little more than charcoal blocks. So, I kept walking, maintaining an expression of disinterest on my face. And then, I was there, standing right in front of the looming robot. The ChronoBot stopped firing – heat emanating from the muzzles of his six energy canons – energy cannons which were now all pointed at my head.

The roar of absolute silence enveloped the Bridge. I said, "Are you done?"

The ChronoBot stared back at me, its face display a wild flurry of blinking sensor lights. I stole a glance to my left and then to my right. There wasn't so much as a tiny scorch mark on the surrounding bulkheads – the wonders of SmartCoat. Keeping my voice as calm as I could manage under the circumstances, I said, "Lieutenant Pristy, Gail, . . . tell me you're still alive."

"I'm still alive," came her soft words from somewhere behind me.

"Mattis, Derrota . . . Chen?"

Three more shaky voices affirmed they were still alive.

"Look around, people . . . Is anybody injured?"

Lieutenant Pristy affirmed what I already knew to be true. "I think we're all okay . . . somehow."

I took another step closer to the ChronoBot. I could reach out and touch it; I was that close. "Hardy . . . you in there?"

The wild flurry of blinking on and off sensor lights had rearranged; soon, a close approximation of a face began to appear.

I made a twirling motion with one finger. "Um . . . it's upside-down. Your face. You need to flip it around."

The familiar hand-drawn-looking *Hardy* face flipped around to normal. I said, "Can you put away your weapons, please?"

All at once, the ChronoBot's weaponry withdrew into their individual compartments as chrome-plated panels slid back into place.

"Thank you," I said. I waited. Rushing things would not be a wise move.

Hardy raised one mechanical finger in the air, a *just one moment* gesture. I nodded.

And then, he was back. I knew it from the ridiculous expression on his digitized face and the different, more human-like way he was now standing.

With his typical Beantown accent, he said, "What a clusterfuck!"

"Really? That's all you have to say after the total shitstorm you just unleashed on this ship and crew?"

Hardy raised his hands in mock surrender, "Hey . . . don't look at me. This was all LuMan and that Varapin pilot's doing. And you might want to show a little gratitude."

"How so?" I asked. The feeling of relief was making my knees wobble – but I stayed upright.

"As you've now discovered, the Varapin are highly advanced. They have a wicked level of technology. LuMan tells me for close to three hundred years, his consciousness has never been so completely absconded with . . . well, other than by me, but that was his conscious choice. What Haite-Caheil was capable of doing –"

"Haite-Caheil?" I repeated.

"The Varapin pilot. Who, by the way, is unconscious. I

recently altered the atmosphere mixture within the cockpit of his Cyclone Death Fighter."

Only now was I aware that a small crowd of bridge crew had assembled around us. I caught Lieutenant Pristy's eye. She nodded ever so subtly; she was okay.

Derrota said, almost sounding angry, "How would you do that? Screw with that fighter's air mixture like that? You have a lot of explaining to do! The death toll out in the passageway alone must be –"

"Hey, hey . . . take a breath, all of you, there's no death toll. Yeah, it took a while for me to take back control of LuMan's shanghaied AI processes . . . I'd been more or less hiding until I could figure out what to do, how to extricate ourselves from the alien's advanced coding. But nobody's been killed. Yes, the Varapin pilot was certain he was killing crewmembers, scores of crewmembers, it was all a deception, but I made sure every shot, every plasma bolt, went askew."

"*You* did that?" I said, making no attempt to hide my disbelief.

Hardy's ridiculous face was suddenly replaced by the big 'S" of the Superman logo. "Oh, you of so little faith . . . hey, it may have taken me a little while to, well, get control of things, but didn't I come through in the end? Huh? Didn't I?"

I looked about the bridge. "Someone give me a status report . . . what's still working in here. And what's happening with that Varapin fighter. And everyone, get back to your damn stations!"

"Uh . . . Captain?"

I turned to see Don Chen kneeling over the motionless body of one of the bridge crew.

He looked up, "I think he's dead."

"That's not my fault!" Hardy said.

I recognized the top of Captain, *XO*, Tannock's head. *Crap.*

Derrota was the first to join Chen at the side of the body. Together they turned the man over onto his back. Tannock's eyes were open and fixed in the kind of death stare I'd seen too many times before for there to be any doubt. My XO was obviously dead.

"There don't seem to be any visible wounds or scorch marks," Derrota said, continuing to inspect the body.

About to message the doctor, I saw that I was too late. She was already running into the Bridge, a small medical device strapped over one shoulder. Reaching the body, she unshouldered her medical equipment and quickly got to work, attaching what I recognized as a ventricular defibrillator on Tannock's now-exposed chest. She yelled, "Clear! Everyone stand back!" She engaged the device, and immediately Tannock's chest expanded and rose, as several hundred volts of electricity pulsed into the dead man's body.

Tannock drew in a desperate breath and coughed. Blinking, he looked around the room.

Under his breath, Hardy said, "Christ, like a cat . . . the man's got nine lives."

Doc Viv continued checking the XO's readings. Without looking up, she said. "Looks like he had a heart attack. I was aware he had the beginnings of coronary heart disease. We were treating it with medication . . ."

I glanced toward Hardy, who was making a face. This was no time for him to be childish. I said, "Hey, act your age, ChronoBot."

Back at her station, Lieutenant Pristy said, "Captain, Bay Chief Mintz says we've got that Varapin fighter secured within the bay and under guard."

I scanned the bridge. Security Chief Mattis was gone, undoubtedly, already heading for the flight bay.

Chapter 26

I'd left Ensign Plorinne in charge of coordinating any necessary Bridge repairs – of which there seemed to be far fewer than expected. Hardy, good to his word, had done an amazing job diverting the blasting of critical ship technologies. Prior to my leaving the Bridge, maintenance techs were already milling about, fixing or replacing any damaged components.

My first stop (or should I say *our* first stop, since my protector in chief, Hardy, was now back at my side), was HealthBay. Stepping out of the GravLift on Deck 10, I said, "And the whole crack thing at the back of your head. The radiation?"

"LuMan prefers to call it a fissure. Not so much a crack as a manufacturing defect. No radiation had ever penetrated this big beautiful head of ours. What I, *we*, had encountered within that reactor chamber was a near-total AI processes shutdown. Perhaps the alien's biggest mistake was not considering me. Sure, the LuMan core was down for the count, but I was still there, watching. The other mistake he made was allowing for a multiplexed bidirectional communications link. Yeah, he was controlling LuMan, but in time, I was, in turn, dinking around with all the controls inside his fighter. I didn't know what controlled what, but eventually, I figured things out. Once I'd gotten his cabin air mixture unbalanced, and he was unconscious . . . I brought LuMan back to life – enough to eradicate the Varapin coding changes."

"And you're sure you got it all? That it can't happen again?"

"Positive. I apologize for letting it happen in the first place. Sorry I became such a liability."

For once, Hardy wasn't putting on a wisecrack face – he meant what he was saying.

"All's well that ends well," I said, as we entered HealthBay.

I was surprised to see that several beds were occupied. These patients looked to have non-life-threatening injuries – bandaged heads, arms in slings, a nose splint. Several doctors, and twice as many nurses, were busy attending to other patients with injuries not severe enough to be issued a bed.

"By this evening, we'll kick all of them out of here," came the familiar voice to my left. "All the injuries were incurred by trying to escape him. Falls mostly." Doc Viv tore off her bloody scrubs followed by her just-as-bloody gloves. She looked about her department with a measured glare. "This could have been a whole lot worse." She put her attention onto Hardy. "Captain, I'll have to ask you to send your ChronoBot out into the passageway. These patients . . . just the sight of him – "

"Sorry, Doc, but no. Hardy's not going anywhere and what damage was done was not his fault. In fact, if it hadn't been for

Hardy's intervention, these people . . . hell, *all of us* would be dead." Raising my chin, I gestured to Hardy to get started.

"What's he doing?" She asked.

I didn't answer her, deciding that actions spoke louder than words. Hardy moved over to the closest bed, where the woman crewmember looked up at the robot, practically cowering. Hardy lowered himself down to one knee, at eye-level with her.

"I am so sorry, Petty Officer Rice. I tried to keep everyone safe."

"What are you talking about? You're the cause of my injuries . . . all of our injuries," she said, accusingly.

"Kind of . . . um, you ever see the old movie invasion of the Body Snatchers? The first one was best, from back in 1956. Sort of campy, but . . ."

Doc Viv said, "You know he's a nitwit . . . only making things worse, don't you?"

"Maybe so. But his lame attempt to make amends will, I hope, mean something to her."

"And he's going to do this with all of them?"

"Absolutely."

"Ugh," she let out a breath, shaking her head. She saw me turn to leave and said, "Where you off to?"

"Flight Bay. We have a new guest. If you will, please send Hardy after me when he's finished here."

"All right. Hey, Quintos . . . don't forget about later."

"Later?"

"Dinner on the farm."

It took me a minute to make sense of that. "There's no way

I'm going to make that date. I have a ship to run. A fleet to command . . . I can't be running off to the land of make-believe. I have responsibilities, Viv."

"First of all, it's not a date."

My eyes shot down to where the diamond had been on her left hand. Of course, the ring would be gone while attending patients.

"And second, I think you may want to reconsider that position."

"Why? I'm sure my Symbio-Poth mother will understand."

"Quintos, I wasn't going to tell you this, but I feel it's important. The Symbio-Poth you believe to be Shawlee Tee . . . well, she's not a Symbio-Poth. No way."

"Say what?"

"You're not a doctor. I am. I'm trained to know the difference between a biological being and a close-looking – amazing, really –construct."

"Wait . . . what are you saying? The *real* Shawlee Tee, Empress Shawlee Tee, is here, aboard my ship?"

The doctor didn't reply.

"Shit. I thought this was, I don't know, frivolous. An eccentric extravagance by a   young woman –"

"She's not a woman, Quintos. She's Pleidian Weonan through and through. They play by a whole different set of rules. I suggest you don't fuck with her designs."

"Look, Viv . . . I'm not stupid. I can see where she's going with this re-creation of my past. Going down memory lane. Maybe she feels that by me reliving my past, somehow, I can exorcise my demons. But it won't work. I am who I am, and I've accepted things the way they are . . . I did that a long time ago."

"Fine. But do you really want to do anything to mess with Earth's most valued alliance? Empress Shawlee Tee may not be overseeing the Pleidian's day-to-day war efforts. She has generals and admirals, not to mention her political appointees. . . ambassadors, and such for that. Instead, she chose to be here. On this ship. You need to see this through."

Fuck.

She said, "Don't be late." I watched her disappear down the passage toward Surgery.

I arrived in the Flight Bay to find a cluster of at least one hundred gathered around what I assumed was the Varapin craft. Nearby were two old Plopper crafts, which I assumed had been used to latch onto the fighter and transport it here.

I wove my way through the congestion of Arrow Fighter pilots, mechanics, flight crew personnel, and others to the front of the crowd. And there it was – an actual Cyclone Death Fighter. To say the fighter was ominous and threatening would be an understatement. Larger than an Arrow by half, the matte-black alien craft was more predatory and bird-like than the Arrow's sleek lines.

Derrota and Mattis were here, talking to Bay Chief Frank Mintz. Derrota was clearly unhappy with the assemblage around the alien ship. "We need to move everyone back . . . no one fully understands Varapin technology."

Security Chief Mattis chimed in, "Stephan's right, who knows what hidden dangers lurk within this vessel. From a security standpoint, this area needs to be cordoned off."

Chief Mintz held his ground, "Well, that's all well and good, but I need this craft moved first. Look around, my friends . . . nothing's moving in or out of my bay as long as this alien monstrosity is blocking the bay entrance."

I joined the arguing threesome. I knew from past dealings with Bay Chief Mintz, he was a cantankerous, unbending old coot. Here in his realm, even I - captain of the ship - would be arguing until my face was blue. "Chief, you have another area . . . someplace out of your way, we can move this craft?"

The Chief gnawed on what was left of a soggy cigar while peering deeper into the flight bay. "I guess we can hover-cart it to the Hub Gunther's berth . . . as long as she's not here . . . that should suffice."

The Chief's words reminded me of the mission I'd sent Captain Ryder on recently, along with several Arrow pilots and a certain band of misfit Marines. I needed to touch base with Wallace soon and get a status report.

"Good," I said. "Let's do it, get it moved." I turned to face the onlookers. "Anyone still standing here gawking in another twenty seconds will be cleaning toilets over in the Marine bar-rack's head. Let me remind you, these are the same toilets that twins Ham and Hock use when taking their morning craps."

Everyone laughed, including the grumpy Chief of the Flight Bay. As the crowd dissipated, I saw Hardy headed our way. *Good, just in time.*

As a flatbed hover-cart was being positioned beneath the Varapin Cyclone Death Fighter, my eyes leveled on the craft's cockpit section. "Hardy, I need you to be at the top of your game here. Tell me that alien is asleep and incapable of ruining my day any further."

"Hard to tell. The Varapin are like no other species. Stories about them abound . . . all are more than a little creepy. They're like the living dead . . . creatures that prefer things to be cold . . . like, *real* cold. Supposedly, their Warrior Pilots are without equal in the galaxy."

I said, "Maybe their own galaxy; hopefully, not ours. But I guess we'll just have to see about that."

Chapter 27

Vicinity of Nebula Sh 2-289, USS Hub Gunther

Captain Wallace Ryder

They had arrived close to the mission's first jump coordinates two hours earlier. Off in the distance, the ultra-bright blue star, LSS 86, was a constant reminder of what recently was lost here, within this turbulent quadrant of space.

Ryder's head throbbed, listening to the constant back and forth smack talk between the six jarheads. When Quintos had suggested he take along the irreverent band of Marines, he was fine with the added security they'd provide the mission. But now he was having second thoughts at bringing them along.

Grip said, "So, Ham . . . you grew up in Oklahoma, right?"

"Uh-uh, Arkansas," Ham said.

"That's right, Arkansas. I hear you can marry your own

sister, or cousin, there in Arkansas . . . your parents are cousins, right? That would explain some things."

Both Wendy and Max chuckled.

Ham said, "I don't think that's any of your business."

Hock, his twin brother, said, "Ham, Mom and Dad . . . they ain't cousins. Grip's fucking with you."

"I already know that. But I think they *were,* like, second cousins . . . maybe. Heard that from Aunt Tobi."

More laughter.

Tuning out the band of idiots, Ryder tried to adjust his weight within the pilot's squeaky bucket seat – there was an untamed spring loose in there that had been relentlessly jabbing him in the left ass cheek for close to six hours now. The old Hub Gunther, a powerful workhorse of a ship, was actually the corporation's name that made this particular spacefaring vessel – one that was not originally military grade. The unattractive, beat-to-shit, but surprisingly-roomy vessel, would comfortably hold a crew of fifteen to twenty. There was a large aft hold designed for hauling raw material such as mineral deposits, in the back, beneath big metal overhead doors. Basically, the ship was like a deep space dump truck. Having been modified before leaving *Hamilton,* the Hub Gunther had been outfitted with a comprehensive weapons package, cloaking capabilities, and the latest wormhole manufacturing jump spring technology.

Ryder had jumped the four crafts – the Hub Gunther and three Arrow Fighters – into what he'd recently learned was Vroghn-Maign Territory.

Max plopped down next to him in the co-pilot's seat. "Want to go over this one more time, Captain?" Max asked.

"What's there to go over . . . it's not like we have much of a plan, Sergeant."

Max stared out the forward window.

Ryder said, "Fine . . . we uncloak the Gunther, but not the Arrows. I toggle on an emergency distress beacon, and we wait for the Clouse Veng to arrive."

"And hope it's not the Ramdei that comes snooping, instead," Max added.

"We make it clear we are no threat . . . just an Earth vessel, simply scouting mining locations in the area. That we were led to believe this was open, frontier, space. Then undoubtedly, they'll want to board us."

Max nodded. "And that's when we'll cloak ourselves, and with the help of those Arrows out there, start creating a little havoc amongst their fleet."

Ryder said, "And once we've proven we're a legitimate threat, we'll request a face-to-face pow-wow with that big tumbleweed alien himself, Prime Centurion Goben."

"Seems simple enough," Max said. "But a lot can go wrong. We're making a shitload of assumptions. Mainly that their technology won't be able to track our cloaked ships."

"That, and this Goben character will even be interested in making a deal."

"He'll be interested . . . he made that clear when we were here previously," Ryder said.

They sat in silence for a few minutes before Ryder checked

in with the three Arrow pilots and let them know things were about to get crazy.

Max turned in his seat, "It's showtime, people."

Ryder was impressed to see how quickly the Marines transitioned from being six stooges to six badass combatants. He heard them reviewing their gear, Tagger sidearms being checked, and the low hum of Shredder plasma rifles cycling up to full power.

Ryder toggled the Emergency Beacon switch to ON and watched as several new warning indicator lamps came alive on his control board. To prepare for this very moment, a tank of black smoke had been rigged near the aft propulsion exhaust cone. Ryder flipped another switch to start venting that shit into space.

"Now, we wait," Ryder said.

They didn't have to wait long. And, immediately, Max's prophetic words had come back to haunt them: *But, a lot can go wrong. We're making a shitload of assumptions.*

The fleet moved in on them like a tidal wave. No less than twenty large warships, and, according to his board (which was lit up like a Christmas tree), each had weapon locks on the Gunther. This fleet was definitely Clouse Veng.

"Incoming!" Max yelled. "Looks like two, no, three missiles!"

Ryder was well aware of the three inbound smart missiles. The ship's AI, not coincidentally named *Gunther*, in a calm male's voice, announced:

"Take evasive action. Take evasive action. Impact in twenty-six seconds."

Ryder said, "Huh, fusion tipped . . . looks to be set for proximity-triggering. Old tech, but effective."

"Damn it, Ryder!" Max yelled.

"Impact in twelve seconds."

Max looked over at Ryder. "Hello . . . do something!"

Ryder casually tapped at his console and then took up the nav controls. Going into cloaked mode was not supposed to have an effect that could be physically detected, but he could swear he felt *something* – a kind of tingle. On the low-tech flat display before him, he watched the three still-cloaked Arrow Fighters taking evasive action. With four seconds to spare, Ryder banked the Gunther hard to starboard while gunning the propulsion system to its maximum thrust. Although the g-force compensators were doing their best to keep up, he was pinned to his seat. The thumping sounds of tumbling, unsecured Marines behind him, along with their grunts and groans, put a lop-sided grin onto Ryder's lips. "Hold on, everyone!" he said, far too late to be useful.

The Hub Gunther was invisible and imperceptible to the Clouse Veng warship's sensor arrays. The three smart missiles were now drifting off course, searching aimlessly to regain their respective target locks.

Although only one of his three Arrow pilots was female, Ryder said into the open channel, "Okay, boys and girls, who's ready to cause a little trouble? Over."

Lieutenant Akari James – her call sign appropriately designated as *Ballbuster* – was the first to respond, "Copy that. Oh, and I'm more than ready. Let's rock and roll. Over."

Ryder, a well-known lady's man within Earth's Space-Navy, had, in fact, been *rocked* by the petite and feisty Akari James on multiple occasions. But now that he'd been promoted to Captain, he'd be making more of a conscious effort to quell his, *say*, primal impulses. That, and his heart – much to his chagrin and frustration – still belonged to another, although she'd made it clear she wasn't interested. But he would not give up on Doctor Vivian Leigh, at least not yet.

Like Ballbuster, his other two Arrow pilots, Lieutenants Rick Plumb (aka *Rags)* and Stan Kent (aka *One Shot),* were among the very best of the 2nd fleet's - or any other of the US Space-Navy's fleet. Ryder watched as the three Arrows separated from their tight formation, each heading off toward a warship of their own to pester. Ballbuster was closing in on what looked to be a light battleship.

"Weapons going active. Over," she said, as bright red Phazon Pulsar bolts peppered the battleship's underbelly.

The Hub Gunther was headed for the largest of the warships, a heavy battleship, the same one the fleet's Prime Centurion had been commanding. Listening to the open channel chatter, he was hearing reports from his Arrow pilots that all the ships were already showing varying degrees of damage to their aft sections.

Ryder said, "Do me a favor, Max . . . press that button over there on the board. No, not that one, the one next to it."

"What is that?" Max asked, pressing the button.

"You just initialized our new forward rail canon."

Approaching the heavy battleship's bow, getting larger by the second, Ryder thumbed down the firing controls.

Chung, Chung, Chung, Chung . . .

Vibrations coming from the big rail cannon were shaking the deck beneath their feet. The Clouse Veng warship's shields were insulating them from the barrage of incoming rail spikes.

"Hmm, okay, let's try Phazon Pulsars." Ryder tapped the appropriate button, and bright red energy bolts were now streaming toward the target. It was evident the Pulsars were indeed penetrating and causing damage to the heavy's outer hull.

"Captain?" Came Akari's voice, an octave higher than normal.

Ryder said, "Go ahead, Ballbuster . . . I can see you on visuals. I think we can wrap this up. We've clearly gotten their attention. Over."

"Cap! I have a fucking problem. I've completely lost cockpit control . . . and I'm being sucked into this, whatever the hell it is . . . maybe a Destroyer."

Ryder felt a knot forming in his stomach. He said, "Rags? . . . One Shot? Give me your dispositions. Over." Ryder waited but heard only static. "Ballbuster . . . let me hear your voice again. Over."

Only static.

Max said, "I don't see them. No weapons fire."

Ryder said, "Gunther . . . I need an update on my three Arrows."

"All three Arrow Fighters have been contained within an arresting field and are currently being drawn into the Frigate, Toth Ho Malto, which translates to –"

"Quiet, Gunther!" Ryder tried to think. He knew the band of Marines was right behind him, taking in the implications, just as he was. "Shit! Shit! Shit!"

"Talk to me," Max said.

"It's simple. We assumed that just because the Clouse Veng didn't have wormhole manufacturing capabilities or cloaking, they didn't have any other advanced tech, either. *Fuck!* The Alliance doesn't even have that kind of arresting field . . . tractor beam tech."

"So . . . we're screwed?" Wanda said.

He maneuvered the Hub Gunther farther away from the fleet. Ryder huffed out a breath, motorboating his lips. He said, "Gunther, how were the Arrows captured?"

"Several of the Clouse Veng warships are equipped with what is akin to ship-to-ship virtual netting devices. Although the Arrows could not be seen or tracked via

sensors, they were detected once they had breached these invisible nets. At that point, the arresting fields were engaged."

"And you're only telling me about this now?" Ryder said, already knowing the minimally-intelligent AI would not answer such a rhetorical question.

Max said, "So . . . okay, they know about the three Arrow Fighters. But not us, right? Not the Gunther?"

Ryder stared out the forward window. "I assume that's true. But come on, the pilots will be tortured . . . God, what a mess."

"I guess it's a good thing you have a band of top-notch Marines trained for just this sort of situation."

He chewed on that for a moment. "Maybe it's time I contact Prime Centurion Goben, see if we can work out some kind of trade here."

Max said, "Yeah, that could have worked well before . . . when we were holding all the cards. But our bargaining power went to hell when our three pilots were taken."

Wanda said, "Why didn't we just hail this Prime Centurion Goben right from the get-go? Why fire on their fleet at all?"

"I talked about this with Captain Quintos . . . without the 2nd Fleet here, the sheer dominating prowess of those warships, he felt the Clouse Veng wouldn't take us seriously. We had to show them that even our little contingent could wreak havoc. Then when we hailed the good Prime Centurion Goben, we'd be communicating from a position of power."

"So, how'd that work out for you, huh?" Wanda said. "This was never a well-thought-out plan."

Ryder let her jab go. *She was right.* "The original plan will still work. We have the technology, the Spring Drives, that they want."

No one said anything for a full minute.

Grip, with his deep baritone voice, broke the silence, "You still cannot negotiate from weakness. I get it, it's why we came here with guns blazing . . . but now we've lost the upper hand. We make our presence known, those tumbleweeds will just take those Spring Drives sitting in our hold and kill all of us."

"So, we not only need to rescue our pilots, we need to increase our bargaining power. Take something essential . . . something dear to them," Wanda said.

Ryder thought about MATHR and how she'd been able to hack each of this fleet's AIs and ship-wide networks. Gunther was certainly no MATHR. Ryder said, "Gunther, how deep into that Clouse Veng Destroyer, where our pilots are being held, can your sensors penetrate?"

"That will not be necessary, Captain Ryder. Previously, MATHR had logged all the internal specifications of each ship within this fleet."

"Wait . . . you're saying we have detailed intel to work from?" Max said. "Deck layouts . . . passageways, compartments?"

"Yes, along with potential targeting locations, such as main power grid junctions, command centers, their respective armories . . ."

"Okay, okay, I get it," Ryder said. He turned around in his seat and scanned the equipment the Marines had brought along with them. "Those battle suits there . . . tell me about them."

Max said, "The latest and greatest . . . made of hardened alloy kamacite, with helmet faceplates configured with nearly-impregnable diamond glass. Of course, we have shoulder-mounted auto-tracking Phazon Pulsar weaponry." Max turned to look at the impressive-looking suits hanging shoulder-to-shoulder on the bulkhead. "Oh, and these suits have the latest enhanced Thine technology stealth capabilities, as well. No one will see us coming until it's too late."

"I see there are seven suits . . ."

"Yeah, we brought an extra one along with us . . . that one there might even fit you," Wanda said with a smile.

Ryder was aware Wanda was flirting with him. Keeping his mind on business, he said, "Okay . . . maybe things aren't quite as dire as I thought."

Chapter 28

Captain Galvin Quintos

I stepped out of the lift onto Deck 72/73, still feeling irritated. I'd given up on finding a way out of coming here this evening. Sure, Empress Shawlee had coerced my actions, not by brute force but through kindness and gentleness.

So, I'd been busy. For the last three hours, I'd been talking to the other Captains, planning, strategizing our next moves. The consensus was to move up the timeframe for confronting the Varapin fleet. With luck, we'd cut the spigot of leaked information that had been going from LuMan out to the Cyclone Death Fighter, and back to the alien fleet. Undoubtedly, they knew all our jump schedules, our initial battleplans, such as they were. No, we weren't going to dramatically alter our odds of beating the Varapin, but we could switch things up a little, beginning with a surprise attack. I'd also reviewed Ryder's encrypted micro-wormhole laser-link message. *What a clusterfuck that was.* That mission had always been a Hail Mary move but losing three pilots right from the start was disheartening. Well, it would be up to Ryder to get the trolley back on its tracks and earn that new promotion.

I knew Hardy was lurking somewhere behind me. I told him I didn't want to see him tonight. If he was going to play protector, it would have to be from afar. And if I spied even glint of his chrome form, I'd have him dismantled – not that I could really do such a thing.

Entering the Clairmont Auto Repair through the back door, I found Doc Viv sitting on a stack of tires and tapping on her TAC-Band. She'd obviously been busy with a clothes replication – wearing faded jeans, cowboy boots, a simple yellow blouse, with a matching ribbon in her blonde locks. She was stunning.

She looked up as I approached. "You're late." She stood and dusted off her backside with several provocative spanking motions.

I said, "Yeah, well, the chicken and dumplings will just have to wait a bit. Shall we go . . . get this over with?"

"Come on, let's try to make the best of this, Quintos. You look like you could use a little stress-relieving diversion right now."

Since the large roll up doors were all closed for the day, we exited the garage via the entrance door, which had conveniently been left unlocked. Outside, the sun was setting, and this mock world had taken on a rich, golden tone that made me miss home – miss Earth.

"Now, will you look at that," she said, looking back over her shoulder at me with a smile so bright and enthusiastic I thought my heart just might stop beating right then and there. She said, "Who would have thunk . . . that a vintage pickup truck would be sitting here like this . . . and with the engine idling, to boot?" She moved around the front of the old two-tone Ford F150, opened the door on the passenger side, and climbed in.

The truck seemed oddly familiar to me. I realized this was the combustion engine precursor to the hover-truck my family owned as a child. By the time I was situated in the driver's seat, Viv was fiddling with the radio on the dash. As she spun the dial, music from the 1950s blared through a tinny-sounding speaker. She shook her head. *Spin, spin, spin.* Even though the snippets of songs were some two-hundred years old, I still recognized Elvis, Nat King Cole, and Tony Bennett. She settled for *That's Amore,* by Dean Martin, and sat back.

I examined the archaic controls and must have looked confused because Viv said, "It's a three-on-the-tree configuration. Put your foot on the brake, that big peddle down there." She leaned over and pulled the lever, ". . . you put this on D, for Drive. The big round thing in front of you is the steering wheel."

"I know what a steering wheel is; I'm not a total idiot."

"Good. Then get your foot off the break and step on the gas."

It took me a few minutes to get the feel of things, but soon I was king of the road, window rolled down with my left elbow propped there. We cruised through the town heading west. Shop owners were closing up for the night – we exchanged several waves. Mr. Peterson, from the Vinyl Visions record store, yelled a friendly, "Howdy folks!" Doc Viv had the soles of her boots up on the dash, and she was now singing along with Sinatra, *Young at Heart*. How she knew the words was a mystery to me.

As Clairmont was soon relegated to my rear-view mirror, Viv must have noticed my dour expression. Coming up on the left was where it had happened. The Volvo HoverCar in front of us had been going slow. It had been weaving back and forth over the yellow lines.

"Hey, . . . cowboy," Doc Viv said, bringing me back to the here-and-now. She was making a demure, coy expression. "You know, I've never been out of the big city before, cowboy. I'm sure glad you know your way around these parts . . ."

I laughed. "Yeah, Clairmont is one big city. Well, stick with me, kiddo, I'll keep you safe out here in the boonies . . ."

The rural mock Indiana countryside slid by us like fleeting memories. Up ahead, I could see the dirt drive turnoff. It wasn't the first, or second, or the third time I'd marveled at the level of detail, the intricacies, the care taken to make all this so authentic.

"You okay?" Viv asked, now facing me, with her back up against the passenger door. I smiled, getting a momentary glimpse of what it must have been like dating her as a teenager. She hadn't lost those qualities – a measure of innocence, along with a good measure of flirty tease.

I said, "See that old oak over there?"

She nodded.

"Eric, my older brother, and I used to climb that to the very top. You can see the outskirts of town from up there. Few days before leaving here, Eric lost his grip on that bottom branch and dropped to the ground . . . sprained his wrist."

The driveway, little more than a dusty two-track, was leading us to a small farmhouse up ahead. My memories of the place had my childhood home looking far larger – less ram shackled, less-dilapidated, looking. Was this the same as I remembered? Yes, and no. I grew up in the 2150s, not the 1950s.

"Not all that impressive, huh?" I said, my tone apologetic.

"Oh, I don't know . . . I think some would call this the American dream."

I slowed the old Ford as we approached a sagging front porch that hadn't seen a paintbrush in decades. Stopping, I put the truck in park and turned off the key. We let the billow of road dust settle a bit before opening our doors. We got out of the truck – a breeze stirred the stifling hot air. Somewhere out of sight, I heard shirts snapping on a windy clothesline.

Coming around the truck's front bumper, there was the scream of unoiled hinges and the *Slap* of the screen door slamming shut. My mother had come out to greet us. She stood there, waving a dishtowel at the lingering dust. "Oh, for goodness sakes, Galvin . . . you should have parked over by the shed."

She was wearing a robin egg blue-checked dress with a

white apron tied around her waist. Strange, she probably wasn't much older than I was now. She was pretty – and all business. She took her job as a housewife and mother of two monsters seriously. "Good to see you, Vivian . . . hope you like chicken and dumplings . . . it'll be nothing fancy here."

"I'm sure it'll be wonderful, Mrs. Quintos."

Looking somewhat flustered, my mother said, "Eric's getting cleaned up for dinner, and Dad's around here some-where. Why don't you two track him down and drag him back to the house? Supper's in ten minutes." With that, the hinges screamed again, and the screen door clattered shut.

"Come on, I'll give you the grand tour. Oh, and watch your step. Like walking through land mines . . . between all the chicken, cow, and goat shit, you'll need to keep one eye on the ground at all times."

"You have chickens? Goats? Cows?"

"A few of each . . . at least we did in my world –" Just then, we were interrupted by the sound of five or six clucking chick-ens coming around the side of the house. *Symbio-Poth chickens?*

Viv laughed and knelt down as the angry-sounding birds swarmed around her looking for food. "I'm sorry . . . I don't have any seeds for you today."

"Come on, let's go find my dad," I said as we passed the corner of the house. The sound of a whining starter motor was unsuccessfully coaxing an engine to start.

"God Dammit! You worthless piece of –"

"Carl!" my mother's voice shot out from the open kitchen window. "Watch your language! Kids are about!"

Chapter 29

We saw him over by the barn. The hood was up, and it was as if he was being eaten by a metal monster – my dad's legs could be seen protruding out from the engine compartment. He was wearing striped, grease-stained overalls. An oily red rag hung down from his back pocket.

I moved to the front fender and looked into the shadows. "Hey, Dad." It was strange how easy it was to become eleven again.

"You know what a 5/16th socket is, boy?" he asked.

No clue. Finger-searching through the metal box of sockets, I found the 5/16th whatever-the-hell-it-was and handed it down to him. I saw Doc Viv wander in through the open barn doors. I said, "Um, Mom says it's suppertime."

"Well, this bucket of bolts won't fix itself, will it?"

"Guess not."

"Tell Mom, I need five . . . five minutes."

"Okay."

A scream emanated from the barn. *Shit!*

Dad cursed, banging his head somewhere beneath the hood.

I hurried into the barn and squinted into the dim shadows. "Viv . . . where are you? You okay?"

"No, I'm not fucking okay."

I tracked her voice to the left of the stalls. I saw Betsey, the old sway-backed nag peering over her gate. On the ground was Doc Viv, sitting up with her two hands raised, as if waiting for a nurse to come slip gloves over her fingers; I could tell she was covered with something dark.

"Shit! . . . I'm covered in shit!"

It took all my willpower not to laugh. I'd warned her about land mines, and the one she'd found was huge. And wet. Probably from one, or maybe both, the dairy cows.

Eric ran into the barn, followed by my father. While Eric pointed and laughed, my father scowled. "Well, don't just stand there gawking, boy, help her up."

I did as told, not wanting to touch her outstretched hand. She looked disgusted as I pulled her to her feet.

"She's covered in shit . . . like, from head to toe," Eric said, pinching his nose between two fingers.

"Go get your mother, Eric," my father barked. "Tell her what happened."

I said, "Welcome to life on the farm. Aren't you glad you came along?"

"Do you really want me to answer that?" she said, craning her head around to see her backside and legs.

Two minutes later, my mom was bustling into the barn

holding a stack of clothes. "Now I can't guarantee anything will fit you, young lady. But we can't have you coming into the house with that muck plastered all over your derrière. There's an outside shower spigot along the other side of the barn. You'll need to rinse off."

My mother held out the stack of clothes to her. Seeing the wet dung on Viv's hands, and thinking better of it, she handed them to me. "Carl, Eric . . . in the house. Give the girl some privacy."

"God, I stink. I think I might throw up," Viv said, making a gagging sound.

"You're a doctor . . . I'm sure you're used –"

"Put a sock in it, Quintos. Take me to the stupid spigot thingy."

We found it outside on the other side of the barn. Basically, a garden hose clamped to a showerhead, mounted high. A bar of soap was wedged behind the spigot nob. Viv got undressed, and I nervously looked for a place to put the clothes.

"Just hold on to them. And turn around, for goodness sakes."

I did as told while listening to the sound of rustling clothes and her continued verbal grumblings. My eyes leveled on the old Buick in front of me, its hood still open; that, and the passenger-side mirror. I'd like to say I averted my eyes, doing the gentlemanly thing by not watching her strip down to her natural bare-ass splendor. But I couldn't have, even if I'd wanted too. Her slim, well-toned body now glistened beneath the cascading flow of water. She lathered herself using the bar of soap

— her backside, her legs, her flat belly, and finally, her breasts. Her nipples had gone hard from the frigid water. She looked up and let the water splash onto her face. There was something oddly familiar about her form, her body — although I'd never seen it before. *God, she's beautiful.*

"If you're done acting like a perv, maybe you can hand me that towel on top of the clothes?"

Our eyes met within the chrome frame of the Buick's passenger-side mirror. The smirk on her lips made it clear that she'd known all along I'd been watching her. She'd turned sideways and had one arm draped across her breasts. "Sometime today would be nice . . ."

I handed her the towel, "Sorry."

"No big deal, it's not like I have anything you haven't seen before."

Turning away, I thought about that. *Had I? Seen her . . . more accurately, felt her? Was that her, those months earlier, in that hot springs pond within Hamilton's Japanese garden? That night all I could see in the darkness was the sporadic glint of light upon the placid water. And then, the woman had come to me, a lithe naked form. She'd place a finger upon my lips — we were not to speak. She'd pushed my hands away; I was not to touch. She'd made love to me and then was gone without a trace.* Nah . . . it couldn't have been her. *Or could it?*

Ten minutes later, the five of us were squeezed in around the kitchen table. Eric, twelve, was making popping sounds with his mouth and playing with his fork. *Had I been that annoying?* Probably worse.

I looked at Viv. She was wearing a yellow dress with a white collar and big white buttons; one of my mother's, no doubt. Viv's still-damp hair was tied back with a ribbon. It was uncanny how well she melded into this 1950s time period.

My mother said, "Best if everyone just hands me their plate so I can do the serving," She grabbed my dad's, pilling a heaping scoopful of Chicken and Dumplings onto his plate and repeating the process for each of us. I waited for my father to take the first bite, somehow remembering that we did all those years earlier. Taking a mouthful of the chicken and dumplings, I was almost overwhelmed with nostalgia – an abrupt craving for this simple past life. A simple family with uncomplicated day-to-day concerns. Love from two parents and the close bond of a brother, one I'd yet to realize the importance of.

"Now, tomorrow, we'll need to get an early start."

"Tomorrow?" Viv said.

"Yes, the fireworks won't go off 'til dark, but the parking will be impossible."

I was already shaking my head. "I can't . . . I have – "

I felt Viv's perfectly-placed kick nail my left shinbone beneath the table. Her knitted brows were telling me to shut up. I took another bite and tried to think of anything other than Scotty Miller and the Indianapolis Coyotes baseball cap perched on his head. Then, the fireball resulting from my father's reckless, murderous actions. I looked at the man now. This was the time I still loved him. He was bigger than life – I'd wanted to be just like him. And within twenty-four hours, I would learn to disrespect him, hate him, like none other. I put down my fork; I'd lost my appetite.

"You not feeling well, sweetie?" my mother said, looking concerned. She reached over and placed the back of her palm on my forehead. "Uh-huh, I think you're a tad warm. Maybe you should lay down."

"I'm fine, Mom." I picked up my fork and ate. *Why, Shawlee Tee? Why did you create this town for this period of time – one of the worst times of my life? Why are you tormenting me like this?*

Feeling myself falling into a funk, I noticed Viv's left hand. She wasn't wearing her diamond ring. Thinking back, she hadn't been wearing it since we'd met up in the garage. Mood elevated, I said, "Dad, think you'll get the Buick running by tomorrow?"

"I don't know, maybe if you help me after supper, we can get her to turn over."

"What about me?" Eric said, looking wounded.

"Oh, I have another job for you, Mr. snicker-at-someone-when-they-fall-in-cow-dung . . . you'll be shoveling out the barn tonight."

"Ah, Dad! Come on . . . it was funny. You thought it was funny too, didn't you, Vivian?"

Doc Viv looked at the twelve-year-old boy for a long moment and then smiled. "Yeah, it was funny." She laughed, and the rest of us laughed, too.

My dad coughed and reached for his glass of water. I noticed there was a slight tremor to his left hand – that, and he looked to be having a tough time breathing. *A defective Symbio-Poth. A malfunction of some sort?* Doc Viv was watching him closely, as well.

My TAC-Band started to vibrate; then, Viv's did the same. Even before I could lift my wrist to check things, a large shape appeared at the kitchen window.

Eric screamed.

My mother screamed.

My father abruptly stood, his chair falling backward, clattering onto the linoleum floor behind.

"Easy, everyone . . . it's only Hardy, a friend." I noticed that my Symbio-bot family had gone into a sort of robot-trance, and I assumed they had been progammed for "on hold" when my actual life's activities came into play. "He's here for me, and he's harmless." *Kind of.*

The ChronoBot's upper torso and head filled the kitchen window, and he was making an ominous face – he'd chosen that of a creepy jack o' lantern with a toothy, Cheshire Cat grin.

"Enough with the face, Hardy. What is it?"

"We need to go, Cap . . . the Varapin alien has awakened."

"Okay, I'll be down to Flight Bay in a few minutes."

"Awakened and escaped. The alien is in hiding. Oh, and there's been a death."

I said, "You could have led with that." I briefly wondered why the hell the robot was here instead of searching, tracking down the alien pilot. Then I remembered, Hardy's primary concern would always be protecting me, first.

Hardy and I, along with Doc Viv – still wearing what I'd learned earlier was called a *circle dress* – arrived at Flight Bay. There were more than a few gawking glances in her direction; she looked like she was dressed for a garden party.

Chief of Security Mattis was there, barking off orders to several armed teams readying to move out. Sprawled out close to the Varapin fighter was one of Mattis's security forces – he was obviously dead. Doc Viv knelt next to the body while I remained standing at her side.

"Good God . . . look at him," she said.

I was doing just that – and what I saw chilled me to the bone.

Hardy said, "Yeah, that's what they do . . . the Varapin. They suck the life force right out of you. And that's what's left behind . . . a husk of a corpse."

She read his embroidered name and rank on his suit: "Seaman Larry Baxter, Security Forces."

The man's face had been reduced to a kind of purple, shriveled-up prune. "Tell me we are tracking the whereabouts of the pilot. Between yours and MATHR's advanced sensors, not to mention security cameras –"

Chief Mattis stepped into the conversation, "What we have is . . . total crappola. Apparently, these Varapin ghouls aren't exactly alive in the same sense other organic life is alive. And, apparently," Mattis said, looking to Hardy for verification, "This Varapin pilot has tech that distorts our onboard cameras and sensors."

Doc Viv stood up, "I'd like to do a complete autopsy on Baxter here. I've called for a med-bot to retrieve the body and deliver it to HealthBay."

"Is he safe . . . you know, to be around? Who knows if he's been contaminated," Mattis said, glancing down to the shriveled corpse.

All eyes went to Hardy.

"I'm not picking up any errant alien viruses or parasites. And no macro-sized robotics, no nanobots, crawling around on him. . . so no, nothing that can harm anyone that I can tell."

"But we still have a killer alien loose on this ship," I said.

"More like a vampire," Doc Viv said with a shrug.

"At least it doesn't fly like a bat," Mattis said.

Hardy made a new, wide-eyed face.

"What? Spit it out," I said.

"I believe the Varapin can . . . hover about."

"What does that mean, *hover about?*" I asked, quickly losing my patience.

Hardy said, "I'm drawing upon LuMan's databanks. Don't forget, he's been around for centuries. There are, um . . . encounters reported within Andromeda, of beings that match the description of the Varapin. And those reports speak of beings that most definitely hover about. And a couple of more things; they are strong . . . very strong. That, and they are capable of brief amounts of time in open space."

"You mean, without an environ suit . . . without a space-suit?" I asked.

"These are unsubstantiated reports."

I looked at Mattis. "I want this ship locked down. I want every one of your security forces searching. And we still have Marines on board, a full company. . . 243 jarheads. Get them rousted and coordinated with your teams. Find this pilot and find him fast!"

"I'd suggest one more thing," Mattis said. "Sidearms, any Space-Navy personnel trained for combat, should be armed with a tagger until further notice."

Exhausted, I caught myself yawning. I checked the time on my TAC-Band. I'd been going pretty much non-stop for close to thirty-six hours, and I needed to get a few hours' sleep. I hailed Lieutenant Pristy, "When was the last time you had some rack time?"

"I just came off six hours, so I'm well-rested. Is it true there's a killer alien hiding somewhere on board?"

"Yes, look, you'll be doing double-duty until further notice."

"I figured; you need an XO."

"Bingo. I'm heading for my quarters . . . just need a few hours before I drop. Anything comes up, wake me."

"Copy that. Sweet dreams, Captain."

"Sweet dreams?" Doc Viv repeated.

"Never mind that. Please let me know what you find out about Baxter."

"Will do." She did a little half-spin that made the hem of her circle dress flare outward, exposing more of her long, perfect. legs. "You know where to find me."

By the time I made it to my quarters, I fell into my bed,

fully dressed – too tired to remove my boots and too tired to turn down the covers. Momentarily, I thought about the killer alien onboard and almost roused myself, out of guilty feelings. Instead, I closed my eyes and fell fast asleep.

I awoke feeling like a human trampoline with someone jumping up and down on my back. As my cognitive senses cleared, and I saw who was standing next to the bed, I realized it was Hardy. "Stop! I'm awake already."

"There's a problem . . . several problems, actually. You weren't answering your TAC-Band."

I looked at my wrist. My TAC-Band wasn't there. I remembered, then checked under my pillow. Retrieving it, I saw there were several unread, urgent messages. Yawning, I said, "How long have I been out?"

"Tracking your bio-readings, I'd guess five hours, ten minutes and thirty-six seconds. More importantly, our killer Alien has been busy."

I sat up and swung my legs over the side of the bed. Putting on my TAC-Band, I glanced at the most recent message.

URGENT! Captain Quintos, you're needed on the Bridge.

I hurried over to the head, left the door open, and said, "Sit Report, Hardy. Tell me everything."

While Hardy spoke, I changed into a fresh officer's jumper; there was no time for a shower.

"It looks as though the pilot was moving towards Engineering and Propulsion, three different crewmembers spotted *something dark and fast- moving.* One of those was Chief Porter."

"Craig saw the alien?" I said, strapping on my tagger holster rig.

"He's in HealthBay with gouges, claw marks to the chest. Lucky to be alive is my guess."

"He's okay?"

Hardy hesitated a moment, "According to his chart, he's fine. He'll be released within the hour."

"You shouldn't be reading patient charts, Hardy. They're supposed to be private, confidential information."

"Absolutely . . . couldn't agree more."

Why do I even bother? I strode toward the exit of my quarters. "So, tell me about the Alien. Where is he, *it*, now?"

"Still aft in the ship."

We were within Whale's Alley and headed for the Bridge when Hardy abruptly stopped. A light bulb symbol suddenly appeared on the ChronoBot's face display.

"What?"

"I know exactly where the Varapin Pilot is hiding."

"How? Where?"

"Craig's DNA."

"On its claws," I said.

"Yup. It's on its claws. And he's hiding . . . currently, Engineering and Propulsion area.

"Go. Head aft, find him!"

Hardy was already protesting.

"I just need to check in on the Bridge," I pointed, "which is right over there. I'm right behind you. Go!"

Reluctantly, the ChronoBot did as ordered. I hurried off toward the Bridge. According to multiple TAC-Band messages, they had their own emergencies for me to deal with.

Chapter 30

Lieutenant Pristy was seated on the Captain's Mount, and like everyone else on the bridge, she was staring, transfixed on the Halo-Display.

"Lieutenant . . ." I said, stepping to her side.

"Oh, Captain . . . I think we have a problem," she stood and was about to step down from the raised mount.

"Stay, I'm headed right back out again. Tell me what's happening here."

"Fleet's converging, and it was moving into formation for our next jump."

I'd already gathered as much, seeing the tight arrangement of the 2nd Fleet on the display, but I let her continue.

She pointed, "We came across that." She tapped at the controls on the armrest, and the display zoomed in.

"Some kind of drone?" I asked.

She nodded, "It's operational. Transmitting. Stephan is

analyzing the signals now. He thinks it's Varapin; what we would call a Prospector Drone."

I said, "Uh-huh, sent out ahead of a fleet to do spacial reconnaissance . . ."

"Here he comes now," she said, gesturing toward the CIC.

As a brow-furrowed Derrota approached, he said, "This isn't good, Galvin."

"It's just a drone, Stephan."

Derrota said, "The Varapin utilize similar micro wormhole laser link comms as we do. What's caught my attention - and now MATHR's attention – is, for no better term, signal propagation, although that's not really accurate either –"

"Stephan!"

"Sorry. I'm talking about the time it takes for the laser link signals, coming and going from this drone, back and forth. It's way too fast. If the Varapin Fleet were, let's say, thirty light-years distance, the delay would be several hundred nanoseconds."

"How long is the delay?"

"Almost none . . . maybe twenty nanoseconds."

"So, you're saying the Varapin Fleet is what? Within days of us?"

"You're not understanding what I'm saying, Galvin. They are here . . . no more than one manufactured wormhole jump away. So, unless you're fully prepared to go to battle, like, *right now*, you cannot make this next jump."

I looked back to the display and at the small Prospector Drone. "And they know we're here. They can jump in at any time and catch us off guard."

The three of us looked at each other. I said, "Lieutenant, go to battle stations. I looked over to the Comms Station, which Crewman Don Chen was currently manning. "Inform the other Captains . . . bring them up to speed on the situation."

"Aye, sir."

I said, "Lieutenant, we're sitting ducks, here in this tight formation. Where are we? What's around us?"

Nothing, really. A dwarf Spheroidal Galaxy, NGC 185 . . . also known as Caldwell 18, which is a type 2 Seyfert Galaxy - a small satellite galaxy of Andromeda. But it's not any closer than our previous jump stop-off. And it's not in the direction we were heading."

"So, nothing."

She tapped at her tablet, "Wait a minute, MATHR's just updated, resolving local celestial objects. There is a remote star system that sits out here in the expanse - in the middle of nowhere. Blue dwarf star, thirty-six exoplanets." She looked up and made a face. "That's a lot of exoplanets. Hey, three are goldilocks worlds . . . interesting. This system isn't charted. Not sure anyone knows about it. Unnamed, as far as I can tell."

I smiled. "Gail . . . new orders. Get us there. The whole damn fleet. And we're not jumping."

Slowly, she nodded her head.

She knew why. Two tracking indicators: One, even relatively small manufactured wormholes causes warping of space-time, produced by the influx of very powerful gravitational forces. The Varapin would know we'd jumped in, and then back out again. Two days - or even weeks – after a ship or a fleet, in our case, has made a jump, highly advanced sensors, such as those utilized by the Varapin, can track what's called a *radiation pull*. Basically, that's a swath of resonating ship-propulsion exhausts, mostly radiation, pulled into the mouth (and on into the throat) of a wormhole, providing a virtual, directional arrow-pointing in the direction the jump was made.

"You'll set a fleet course for our new, unnamed, star system . . . but take an alternate round-about course getting there. Let's not leave any easy radiation breadcrumbs for them to follow."

"And you want me to do all this myself, Captain?"

"I don't know . . . you ever want to sit in that chair full-time?"

"I do."

"Then you'll need experience giving orders. That, and taking risks along the way."

"Aye, Captain."

"All warships stay on battle stations," I said.

"Oh, and Captain?"

I turned back to her.

"What about that?" She said, pointing to the Varapin drone.

"Right before you move the fleet out of here, . . . blow it up."

Her face lit up as she smiled. "Copy that. I love blowing shit up."

Leaving the bridge, I hailed Hardy.

"Go for Hardy."

"Talk to me . . . tell me you know where the pilot is."

"Captain Quintos!"

I looked up to see the very last person I wanted to see right now. "Ah, Chaplain Trent."

"I'll have you know, I sat inside that . . . that ridiculous jail cell for hours!"

"You'll have to walk with me, Chaplain . . . I've got an emergency situation aft."

"Whatever." He hurried to keep up.

"The good news, you're out, a free man. I hope you're planning to stay on the right side of the law going forward." I said. I could tell by his expression that he didn't appreciate my humor. "How did you get out, anyway?"

"I broke out." He said, unable to conceal his grin. "It was like one of those old-time movies. I used the blanket from my cot to pull the keys off a nearby desk. Ingenious, if you ask me."

I nodded appreciatively. Obviously, it had been a setup, an easy means for the Chaplain to escape and flee the town.

"Clever, Chaplain. But I'm not so sure I'm okay with *Hamilton's* Chaplain being a jailbird."

He chuckled at that. "I have to admit. It was exhilarating. You don't think I'll be drawn to a life a crime now, do you?"

We'd reached the bank of GravLifts. "We can only hope, Chaplain." The lift doors opened, "I have to leave you here . . ."

His face was serious again. "I'm not done discussing the town Chapel, Captain. You can't keep me from my flock."

The lift doors closed. *What flock? They're not even real people!*

Remembering my TAC-Band, I said, "Hardy! So, where's the alien pilot?"

"Oh, are you talking to me now? I didn't want to interrupt such an important conversation when a killer Varapin is on the loose."

"Don't be a smartass. The pilot?"

"He's been on the move. I have a good idea where he is, though . . . hold on. Yes, I've found him."

"Where, exactly, are you, Hardy? Best you wait for backup . . . Mattis' teams, the Marines."

"Unfortunately, there won't be time for that, Cap . . ." Hardy disconnected.

I said, "MATHR, direct this GravLift to as close to Hardy's current location as possible!"

Her voice filled the lift,

"Redirecting to Deck 18, Zone G. Hardy is located outside of Environmental Conditioning, Level 3."

I mentally pictured that part of the ship. The massive air filters were in there, and much of the ship's atmospheric gasses were combined there to the correct percentages, the proper mix amounts of nitrogen, oxygen, carbon dioxide, and so forth. Was the Varapin there to screw with the ship's breathable air? *Maybe.* But wasn't there something else about that area of the ship? Yes, it was cold in there, *very* cold. There was something Mattis had said about the Varapin fighter – how, when Hardy first remotely opened the cockpit, a frigid mist had spewed out. Yeah, the Varapin liked it cold.

By the time I'd arrived at Deck 18, Zone G, I'd already

been communicating with Chief Mattis, ensuring Hardy had spoken to him and that his security forces had been deployed. They had, and Mattis was in the process of getting Marines strategically positioned within Zone G to ensure our alien friend would have zero possibility of escape.

By the time I'd reached Environmental Conditioning, Level 3, as indicated by the large orange block lettering high on the bulkhead, I had to weave my way through a dozen or so battle-suited combatants, each armed with a Shredder rifle. Chief Mattis and Marine Colonel Drake Bonell were standing at the entrance, and both were barking off orders. Bonell was the commanding officer of all *Hamilton's* Marines, and also those onboard all other 2nd Fleet forces, as well. I may have been the commanding officer here in space, but once his forces' boots landed on another planet – or even another ship –Bonell outranked me. I'd recently had words with the Colonel over my mission deployment of Sergeant Max Dryer and his crew. He didn't like that I'd cherry-picked a team from his company; that was *his* job. Hey, the two of us just didn't like each other, plain and simple.

The Chief and the Colonel saw me approaching. I said, "Hardy?"

Mattis jacked a thumb over his shoulder. "Went on in there several minutes ago. I told him to stop and wait for instructions, but –"

Colonel Bonell interjected, "But the damn robot has no discipline. Not surprising, that seems to be a theme on this ship."

I let that go. I knew Bonell and XO Tannock were friends. I hailed Hardy, "What's your status, big guy?" I'd gone a bit overboard to sound casual, knowing it would irritate the Colonel.

"Well . . . Captain, I've found our alien pilot."

"Good. We need him alive."

"Yeah . . . are you absolutely sure about that?"

"Of course, I'm sure. What's going on?"

"I really, really want to kill this motherfu –"

"Hardy! Just tell me your situation."

"The Varapin has, well . . . wrapped itself, its cloak thing, around my head and shoulders. He's strong, and is attempting to force my head up, to have me look into his ugly face."

I heard several grunts coming from Hardy.

"He's not strong enough to succeed . . . the little weasel. Anyway, we're communicating. LuMan has the Varapin fighter pilot's dialect stored within his memory banks. Haite realizes there is a biological component to my AI infrastructure . . . and wants to suck the life out of it."

"Can he do that?"

"Nah . . . no way."

"Okay . . . what else? What else does he want?"

"Other than to kill everyone on board? He wants to escape, for starters."

"No surprise there," I said.

"Look Cap, there was an SWM team working in here . . . I guess doing filter maintenance. All were wearing environ suits. Cap, seven of them . . . they're all dead; they look like dried prunes behind their torn, open faceplates, like the guy in Flight Bay. Their environ suits are shredded . . . bloodied messes. Interestingly, it was done postmortem - some real anger issues with this alien. So, I'd really like to kill him now. Start by pulling his scrawny arms out of his sockets."

"Hold on to that." I turned to look at Mattis and Bonell, who'd been listening to our conversation.

"I say, let your robot tear the fucker apart," the colonel said.

Mattis shook his head, "Negative on that. We need whatever intel he can provide us."

"Agreed," I said. That Varapin Fleet is almost upon us. Haite, there, may give us something useful that can help, even if unintentionally."

Chapter 31

Hardy was losing patience with the alien. In truth, it would be a simple task to kill him, to snap those bony arms wrapped around his head, or those legs wrapped around his upper torso.

Hardy said aloud, "There are laws, restrictions, placed on Space-Navy personnel. Outright torture has been outlawed for centuries."

The alien had yet to stop trying to force Hardy's head back. "That is good to know, half-breed machine. The Varapin do not have such ludicrous, counterproductive limitations placed upon them. Torture . . . I wonder, do you, mechanical man, have pain receptors . . . do you writhe and cry out when intolerable agony invades your psyche?"

"Not so much."

"Where are you taking me, obtuse machine?"

"To an adjacent area of the Environmental Conditioning department. Where this area is cold with a constant sub-zero temperature, there's another section." With his head still covered by Haite's body and cloak, Hardy was now walking with his arms out, Frankenstein-style. Hardy's proximity sensors were more than sufficient for him to amble about without what was equivalent to his eyes, but he wasn't used to doing so. Hardy was conscious of the Captain's further attempts to hail him, but he ignored them.

Hardy stepped down onto a metal platform leading to a narrow catwalk – which swayed back and forth under Hardy's thousand-pound girth.

"Where are you taking me, annoying, obtuse machine?"

"We're almost there . . . just a few more steps and we'll be entering what's called Hygienics, another temperature-controlled area, used to nullify organic properties in the atmosphere. So, there's both radiation and, well, I'm sorry to say, heat. *Lots* of heat." Hardy stopped at the airlock hatch to manually input the proper code for access. *Click! Click! Clack!*

"You will stop. I order you to stop, immediately!" the alien demanded.

The airlock hatch slid open, and Hardy stepped inside the small intermediary chamber. It felt significantly warmer.

"You will stop. Stop now. Return us to the cold. You must return us . . ."

"Oh, come on, Haite. We haven't even reached our final destination. The Hygienics area is impressive." He tapped in the code at the other airlock hatch. *Click! Click! Clack!* The hatch opened, and hot searing air filled the space around them.

"You know, most *organics* would be wearing a heavy environ suit before even thinking about coming in here."

Hardy felt the tension around his head start to ease; the Varapin's arms were already losing strength, its breathing becoming labored. "I know, you're thinking it's visually such a striking sight . . . all those big amber furnace burners towering overhead. Some say it reminds them of the deepest regions of Hell in here. But come on, how would anyone know what Hell really looks like?"

Panting and gasping for air, the alien said, "You said Space-Navy . . . does not permit . . . torture."

"Yeah, that's sort of a grey area with me. Am I part of the crew? Ahh . . . yes, and no. But this isn't torture. It's simply a friendly tour of one of the more interesting areas of the ship. Does the heat bother you?"

"What . . . do . . . you . . . want?"

Hardy pulled the Varapin from atop his head and held him there out in front of himself for several long moments using one mechanical hand. "You are one ugly son of a bitch, Haite." He let go of the Varapin and watched as the alien dropped to the searing-hot deck plates.

Screams of agony erupted from the dark form's gaping jaws. With effort, Haite rose, but hovering seemed to take all his strength – like an exhausted hummingbird losing its battle with relentless, overpowering gravity.

Hardy noticed movement within the airlock chamber. The Marines were coming. Their battle suits would not compensate for heat for long.

"You asked what I wanted," Hardy said.

"Yes . . . anything."

"Lie to me, and I'll leave you in here. You'll slowly cook to death. Maintenance crews will have to scrape your crispy dried remains off the deck with a shovel."

Hardy briefly wondered if a Varapin would know what a shovel even was.

Six Marines poured out from the airlock, Shredder rifles raised and pointed toward the Varapin. Hardy opened the comms channel with the Captain.

"Dammit, Hardy! What the hell are you doing in there? Is the alien still alive?"

"Oh, sure. We're just having a little quality mano-y-mano time. Getting to know each other. He's excited to tell you about himself . . . tell you anything you want to know, in fact."

"Well, drag his ass back out here. I'll talk to him."

"Best if he stays right here, where he has more impetus to be forthright."

"Fine. Can he hear me?"

"Yup. I'll translate your every word."

"Ask him about the Varapin fleet . . . how many warships are coming?"

The alien didn't wait for Hardy's translation, surprising him by speaking English. "*Rage of the Gonjun Ract, sixty-two warships of unparalleled technology and prowess. A fleet that will destroy your archaic 2nd Fleet, will destroy humanity, destroy Earth . . .*"

Hardy saw that the hovering form had descended and was

just a foot above the deck. A deck so hot, it had the nearby Marines shuffling from one foot to another. Hardy grabbed the alien pilot by the back of its cloak, which seemed to be made of an organic substance – like a natural growth from its skeletal shoulders, maybe similar to a human's hair or toenails.

"Weaknesses . . . I need to know any weaknesses. Vulnerabilities we can exploit," Quintos said.

Hardy could tell the Varapin was fading fast. Still clutching the alien, he moved away from the closest burners – back toward the airlock where the air was easily two hundred degrees cooler. Almost immediately, Haite perked up. Hardy repeated the Captain's question, "Fleet weaknesses and vulnerabilities we can exploit. Tell me now, or I'll take you back over to the burners."

Overwhelmed by the heat, the Marines were now back-stepping out of the Hygienics area – back into the airlock.

Hardy observed as Haite-Caheil, the elite Varapin Empire Cyclone Death Fighter pilot, answered Captain Quintos' questions. But Hardy knew when the alien was lying – the Varapin had a kind of "tell" when being dishonest. Haite raised his head and arched his back ever so slightly. So, Hardy took it upon himself to motivate a more honest response. *Snap!* One arm and then, *Snap!* the other arm was broken within Hardy's mechanical grasps. After shrill cries and a good amount of flailing about, the Varapin pilot continued with only the truth.

Where Hardy's inner LuMan would have felt no remorse torturing the pilot, Hardy actually did. He did not enjoy inflicting pain. But Hardy's more human psyche had been mentally replaying the bodies of the seven innocent SWM crewmembers lying there within the adjacent compartment. Anger and the need for reciprocal justice had fueled his actions. He so wanted to end the life of this despicable excuse for a life but knew that would be taking things too far. It would affect his relationship with the Captain. So, now that all the questions, at least for the moment, had been answered. Hardy carried the limp, semi-conscious being out of the hellish Hygienics area and into the far-cooler airlock. By the time Hardy had made his way back through the ice-cold Environmental Conditioning section, then out through the second airlock, the alien pilot was coming around. This was an amazing, robust, creature, he thought, like Earth's cockroaches – enduring within the most extreme conditions. It was clear why the Varapin had risen to the pinnacle of the Andromeda Galaxy's proverbial food chain. Undoubtedly, that could be true for the Milky Way Galaxy, as well.

Hardy dropped the alien at the feet of Captain Quintos and Colonel Bonell.

"Is he alive?" the Colonel asked.

The Varapin pilot's dark form began to rise on his own volition. Hardy placed his heavy foot upon his sagging cloak, driving Haite back down onto the deck. "I suggest he be confined," Hardy said. "This is a most resourceful and dangerous species."

The alien twisted its head around to peer up at the captain. A sort of growl emanated from his hideous jaws. Hardy took in the captain's expression - unease, and something else.

Chapter 32

Ryder and Max had gone back and forth debating which of the Clouse Veng warships to infiltrate: the Destroyer where the three Arrow pilots were being held or the Heavy Battleship, commanded by Prime Centurion Goben. Ultimately, Max had made the strongest case for hitting the Heavy Battleship, its name translating to *The Mighty Tree,* or *The Mighty Oak,* something akin to that.

As it turned out, thanks to MATHR's previous Clouse Veng fleetwide network hacking, there was something, indeed, precious and irreplaceable on board the fleet's command ship. But it wasn't as much a *what* as a *who.*

There had been too much information to weed through, so besides Ryder and Max combing through the files, two other

Marines, Wanda, and Grip, joined in. Both Ham and Hock, not having the necessary attention spans for such work, spent the time checking and rechecking their assault gear.

Everyone was suited up into their respective battle gear. Their helmet HUD,s were well-suited for displaying the myriad of diagrams and textual information.

"I've got something big," Grip said sounding excited.

"That's not what I hear," Wanda said.

Grip continued, "As I'm sure you've all read, the Clouse Veng are bio-plant-based beings, right?"

"Go on," Ryder said, continuing to read from his own HUD.

"It seems *The Mighty Oak* has a highly-secret and extremely well-guarded life-repository."

Wanda feigned a yawn, "Fascinating."

"What I think I understand is, they, the Clouse Veng, are worried about their future prospects . . . as a species. And not just from fighting with the Ramdei, who are more similar to bipedal humans. The Clouse Veng aren't born, they're spread, say like a dandelion on Earth; they grow from seeds. They reproduce asexually by seed, and they are capable of producing other viable seeds without the need for any kind of cross-fertilization, a process known as apomixis."

"How would you even know such a thing?" Wanda said, a little more respect in her tone.

"My mother's a botanist," Grip said. "Anyway, over the past millennia, the Clouse Veng's population has been taking a hit. Basically tanking. Their seeds aren't reproducing like they should."

"For shit's sake, Grip, get to the point," Wanda said. "We get it, these house plant aliens have a real problem."

Grip went on, "Okay, so that gets me back to the secret onboard repository. It's a repository of seeds."

No one spoke.

Looking frustrated behind his faceplate, Grip said, "This is big. Look, on Earth, we have the Svalbard Global Seed Vault. It's an actual temperature-controlled building located on some little Norwegian island called Spitsbergen. In theory, if there was some kind of worldwide blight – or even nuclear annihilation - this would be Earth's backup plan for survival. This is like that but much, much more important to the Clouse Veng. We infiltrate that life-repository, and we hold the keys to the Clouse Veng realm."

It took another two hours to produce an operational mission plan. What was coming next, an actual boots-on-the-deck kind of combat, was not within Ryder's skillset. He'd let Max take the reins for this next part of the mission.

Ryder watched Max as he worked with his team. He admired - even envied - the close-knit camaraderie they shared as Max took time to go over things again, mostly for Ham's and Hock's sake. "We'll be splitting up into two squads." Max looked over his team. "Wanda, your team has Hock and Captain Ryder. I'll take Grip and Ham."

Ham and Hock looked at each other.

"Get over it, you're twins, not conjoined twins," Wanda said to the now-confused looking duo.

Max continued, "We're not breaching the Heavy's hull . . . they'd detect it, and there's a whole lot easier way in. We fly in. We've already established their sensor tech cannot detect the cloaked Hub Gunther. We just have to avoid crossing through any of their virtual nets. I believe Gunther has made adjustments and can steer us away from any of those."

"So, I'm stealth-flying us into their flight bay? Right under their noses?" Ryder asked.

"That's the plan." Max looked at Wanda. "I'm counting on you to breach this life-repository and grab up as many seeds as you can carry. You'll head back to the Hub Gunther, hopefully undetected."

Ryder said, "And your squad will be making a commotion at another part of the ship?"

"That's right. We'll head for the armory and set off some fireworks. As things are now, the life-repository is far too well-guarded for Wanda's squad to penetrate."

"Actually, I don't usually do the penetrating, dear," she said, dead-panning.

"We need to pull a good portion of the guards away from the repository."

Ryder nodded. "We all meet back up in the Hub Gunther, leave the way we came, and contact Prime Centurion Goben with an ultimatum."

Ryder looked at the others. "You know, a hell of a lot can go wrong with this plan."

Wanda snickered, "Welcome to the Marines, flyboy . . . yeah, we can shit the bed in any number of ways, but that's pretty typical. We adjust. We adapt. And then we bring home the win."

They'd plotted a roundabout course through the Clouse Veng fleet with the AI's assistance – a course that obverted several virtual nets strung between pairs of warships. Back at the Hub Gunther's controls, Ryder piloted the old mining vessel - with its noisy propulsion system of constant creaks and clanks, wondering how the fleet's sensors could *not hear* them. But there again, sound waves didn't migrate through the void of open space. Still, Ryder held his breath as the cloaked Hub Gunter came within several hundred feet of the closest warship.

Wanda was in the copilot's seat next to him. Like the rest of them, she was battle-suit ready for the mission, but her faceplate was open; he could see her face as she spoke to him and those behind. He stole a quick glimpse at her full glossy lips, finding them sexy. *Huh – She's wearing makeup now. Which wasn't there earlier.*

"Did you hear me?" she asked, now looking at him straight-on.

"No . . . I was thinking."

"I said you need to stay close to me when we reach our LZ. Do what I tell you to do without hesitation."

Ryder gave her mock salute, "Copy that . . . I'll be a good Marine soldier, I promise."

"Marines aren't soldiers," she said, not appreciating his backtalk. "You do know, this mission, some of us probably won't make it back. Maybe none of us will make it back."

Now it was his turn to get annoyed. "And you know, every time I fly an Arrow into battle, there are high odds I won't be returning to the flight bay. Or worse, one of my people won't be coming back. So, I don't need reminding of the risks of combat, lady."

Momentarily wounded, it was as if he'd slapped her face, and Ryder immediately regretted his stupid knee-jerk response. She sat back in her seat, then closed and darkened her faceplate. She was one of the toughest people he'd ever met, but that didn't mean she wasn't also a woman with feelings.

Ryder chided himself once more, before saying," Coming up on the Heavy's flight bay entrance." The glowing energy field reminded Ryder of an aqua-blue swimming pool, all lit up at night.

Wanda said, "Watch out for that shuttle heading in there before us."

"I see it," Ryder said, relieved she was still talking to him.

The Hub Gunther passed through the energy barrier, slowing to a near-crawl. There were several smaller, and a few larger, vessels down below – their loud drive engines idling. *Good*, because otherwise, the Hub Gunther would most definitely be heard in here. Ryder leaned forward in his seat and looked for a spot to set down.

"How about over there," Wanda said, pointing to what looked like a metal mezzanine deck, far back within the bay."

"I like it. It would be well out of the way. But the Gunther's a heavy MF-er . . . we'd be taking a chance that those metal supports will give out." He gave her his best one-sided smile, "But hey, let's give it a shot." He goosed the ship forward and then swung the Hub Gunther one hundred and eighty degrees on its center axis. "We should be right over the mezzanine," he said.

Max leaned between them. "Shit. I think we've been made."

Ryder followed Max's gaze out the forward window to a group of four of the tumbleweed looking aliens. It looked as if they'd turned to face in their direction. Ryder held the Gunther in place, and once again, held his breath. Over the years, he'd seen countless alien species, but these had to be the weirdest.

He wanted to land –and fast. But initializing the landing thrusters, even while cloaked, might yield noticeable visual anomalies. No one spoke, no one moved. Ryder had already begun assessing his best firing solution while making an escape.

"No, they're not even facing us," Wanda said. "You can make out their faces if you really look for them . . . and those faces are looking toward that shuttle that landed a bit ago."

"Speaking of that shuttle . . . look who's being led out of it," Max said.

Following single file, three human pilots were being led at gunpoint down a gangway. First was *Rags*, then *One Shot*, and bringing up the rear, *Ballbuster*. Their helmets had been removed, and he could see their dour expressions. Ryder made a few taps on his TAC-Band and said, "Hey Ballbuster, don't look so grim, things aren't as bad as they seem."

Raising her head, she casually glanced around the flight bay. Ryder knew Lieutenant Akari James had heard his voice via her auditory implants. A bemused smile crossed her lips and then was gone.

"We're cloaked . . . situated on the mezzanine off to your right. I just wanted to let you know we'll be coming for you. We have some other business to take care of first, so be ready."

She nodded, just before being prodded in the back by one of her Clouse Veng guards with an energy weapon. She yelped and dropped down to one knee.

"Looks like that hurt like a bitch," Wanda said.

"I'm taking us down," Ryder said. "Cross your fingers this thing holds us."

As the Hub Gunther's landing struts made contact, the mezzanine shuddered and shook beneath its weight. Ryder, Wanda, and Max scanned the flight bay for any indication their presence had been detected. It hadn't. Realizing he may not be back here, depending on how things transpired, he recorded a short micro wormhole laser-link transmission message for Quintos. He updated him on the three pilots' abduction, how he and the Marines had landed the Hub Gunther within the Clouse Veng's warship, and gave a brief description of what they were planning on doing going forward.

Ryder shut down the Gunther's drive and stood. Within sixty seconds, the six of them, still cloaked within the Gunther's stealth system, were descending the aft under-belly ramp. Once on the mezzanine, Ryder contacted the ship's AI, instructing it to raise the ramp and seal up the ship —and let him know if anyone approached the ship.

Together they descended a long, winding ramp; apparently, these tumbleweeds didn't do well with steps. Once on the flight deck, and according to plan, the two squads split up. Max, Grip, and Ham headed for one passageway, while Wanda, Hock, and Ryder, headed for another – their prearranged routes showing on their helmet HUDs. An immediate and obvious thing: passage headroom was limited since the Clouse Veng were more wide than tall. The teams were forced to hunch down as they ran.

Ryder, following behind Wanda in the lead, held up a fist, signaling to hold up. They followed her example, as she put her back up against the right-side bulkhead. A couple of unarmed alien crewmembers were heading toward them, both chattering away, excited about something. Being this close to them, Ryder was struck by how little density there was to the tumbleweed's biostructures. Thousands of little twig-like branches stemmed from a central green Jell-O-like glob. Their faces, if you could call them that, had eyes and a mouth, of sorts – all suspended by slightly larger branches. Limbs, such as legs, arms, hands, were formed as needed on the fly, multiple twig branches combining to enable an odd sort of walking. Ryder assumed the same type thing would happen when branches needed to fuse for activities like pickling something up or pushing open a door.

It took them another ten minutes to locate the life-repository, deep within the heavy battleship's bowels. Here, the bulkheads were reinforced with added structural girders all over the place. During their research back on the Hub Gunther, they had discovered that this area of the ship was totally self-contained. It could even be jettisoned in an emergency, and it provided for basic self-propulsion and navigation capabilities, like a ship within a ship.

Wanda spoke quietly over their comms, "That's the vault hatchway right up ahead. So, we're going to hold up here."

Grip said, "I count twenty-two hostiles . . . eight milling around down here, nine on patrol along that catwalk above us, and I see three, so far, through that little window."

Ryder had counted the same number of aliens. The window Grip had referred to was midway up the hatch leading into the vault.

He watched as the security teams moved about. The alien's weapons were shaped nothing like their own Shredder's, although they did have a protruding muzzle. Strange, it looked as if their weapons were mysteriously floating out in front of them. Only upon closer inspection could he see smaller twig-like branches wrapped around what would be the gun's stock.

Ryder listened to the open channel; Max and his boys had located the ship's armory and were attempting to breach its hatchway now.

The Gunther AI had provided them with all the necessary passcodes, so Ryder was wondering what was taking so damn long. Having seen his three pilots on board, he wanted to expedite things, moving on to the rescue phase.

"Damn it!" Max spat. "God forbid they have anything

resembling a regular fucking doorknob here. They must use multiple twig fingers to open this thing. Ryder paired his HUD to Max's to see a small feed of what the Sergeant was looking at. Sure enough, it was a weird and intricate mechanical latch-type device. *Why don't they just blow the damn door?* There again, blowing the door to an armory could take out the entire ship.

Max said, "Grip, get over here . . . we'll have to use twenty of our human digits."

Twenty fingers and thumbs worked on the device, while Gunther AI was providing detailed instructions via comms. The problem was, Ryder supposed, was that as long as Max and Grip were there screwing with the hatch, anyone could attempt to enter or leave the armory.

"Got it!" Max said.

Ryder watched as the hatch door swung open and Grip and Max hurried inside. Ryder unpaired his HUD; he'd need all his attention on what was about to happen here.

Max and Grip were hefting backpacks filled with explosive charges, and Wanda shouldered a similar pack. There was no guarantee that entering passcodes into whatever kind of weird key interface would work. If necessary, they could resort to blowing away the hatchways of this particular vault. But now, looking at this vault door, as big and formidable as any bank vault back on Earth, Ryder doubted that any amount of explosive charges could make a dent on the thing.

He felt it, first coming up through the deck, followed by the distant sound of an explosion. Wanda said, "There goes the armory. Look alive people . . . we're up to bat!"

A klaxon came alive nearby, a sound so loud it hurt Ryder's ears - even through his helmet. The security teams around them went still, looking momentarily perplexed. Suddenly, commands were being barked – orders issued. Half of the tumbleweeds up on the catwalk were now coming down a nearby spiral ramp – one alien had mis-stepped and was literally rolling down the rest of the way.

It was only by chance that Ryder looked to his left in time, jumping aside as two Clouse Veng charged past. He felt one of them brush against his battle suit. A twiggy face looked back in his cloaked direction, but the alien soldier kept moving. It was then that the life-repository hatch swung partially open – a tumbleweed was sneaking a peek to what was going on outside. With so much commotion going on, Ryder's crew must have been impossible to ignore.

Wanda didn't hesitate – neither did Grip. Ryder felt a shove from behind to get moving. "Go, Ryder . . . move it," Hock said.

The squad pushed into the half-opened hatch and into the life-repository, causing the curious Clouse Veng to roll backward like an out-of-control whiffle ball. Wanda was the first to fire her Shredder, followed by Grip and Hock.

Ryder saw that there were more than three Clouse Veng crewmembers in this exceptionally large compartment – there were at least ten. He also noticed their Shredder's Phazon Pulsar bolts were doing absolutely nothing to these excited, angry aliens.

Only three aliens were armed, and they were blindly firing

back at them. The loud overhead klaxon was making it hard to think, let alone do anything else. It was then that Ryder took a direct strike to the middle of his chest. Flung hard into Hock, he gasped for air. Hock shoved him away while Ryder staggered, trying to stay on his feet. He wondered if he'd cracked a rib or two, imagining that this is what it would feel like getting punched by a ChronoBot. A series of energy bolts crackled as they flew past his head, missing him by inches.

Wanda yelled, "Ouch! You little fuckers!"

Grip fell back, holding the side of his head.

Hock, a blackened scorch mark evident on his battle suit between his legs, grabbed his privates and groaned.

Like most of this operation from the get-go, this mission continued to unravel into a never-ending shitstorm; three technically-advanced Arrow fighters had been seized with three of the fleet's best pilots on board. And now this squad was being handed their asses in a basket by three ugly shrubs. It was at this moment, with energy bolts crisscrossing all around him, he thought of Quintos and the trust his best friend –and his commanding officer – had placed in him. Quintos had given him just enough rope to hang himself. He knew he wasn't Quintos; sure, Ryder was good, maybe even a great pilot, as was Quintos. But Ryder, as an officer, as a Captain, now? He brought a good amount of baggage to the party; he drank too much, and he was characterized as a relentless womanizer. He knew that's how Vivian saw him and why she'd never let him back into her bed again after their one tryst. And based on today's clusterfuck of events, this Captain of *Hamilton's* Arrow pilots would be finished; that was if he even survived the next few seconds. *Enough with the pity party.* Ryder lowered himself down to one knee, raised his own Shredder, and took careful aim. He positioned his virtual crosshairs on one of their green, central, Jell-O globs and squeezed the trigger. *Thwack!* A splatter erupted onto the back bulkhead. A thousand twigs blew apart and outward – a dandelion blown into the wind.

"What did you do?" Wanda yelled over their comms.

"Aim for their green blob," he yelled back.

Thwack! Thwack! Thwack! Thwack! Within ten seconds, the bulkheads were dripping with green goo, and twig shit was swirling in the air all around them.

Chapter 33

Ryder hadn't known what to expect with this life-repository place, but it wasn't this. As he stood there, taking in the abundance of life around him, he simply stared, dumbfounded. The expectation had been something akin to what was on Earth in that seed vault that Grip had talked about on the ship. Perhaps there'd be row after row of shelving units, and innumerable shelves with containers filled with one type of humdrum seed after another. *This was not that.* This was amazing, and the implications of what they were doing here now weighed heavy upon his shoulders. Dread gripped at his heart – at his very soul.

"They're like plant puppies," Grip said, as several small green organisms scampered about on the deck in front of them. Obviously intelligent, they were playing – jumping, rolling, wrestling with one another.

Ryder drifted farther back into the compartment. Yes, sure, there were rows and rows of shelving units here, but they weren't filled with sedentary seeds. No, here there were thousands, hell, *tens* of thousands, of botanical baby organisms which were alive and interacting with each other – they were communicating!

Wanda joined him at his side, "There are so many species . . . such a diversity of life here."

Ryder looked at her. Her suit had taken several hits – scorch marks cratered her helmet, torso, and legs. With her faceplate open, he could see moisture brimming in her eyes. "We're, what . . . supposed to take these life forms? This wouldn't be war-time robbery, it would be blatant kidnapping." She looked at Ryder and went from near-tears to laughing out loud. A happy sprout of some kind had scampered up Ryder's battle suit and was now sitting on his shoulder, its little face far more defined than those on the tumbleweed aliens.

Grip and Hock, both entwined with playful, passenger-greenery – looked as crestfallen as Ryder felt.

Hock said, "I don't want to hurt no baby plant thing. Just wouldn't be right. Didn't sign up for that."

Grip said, "I know Earth's survival is in the lurch and all. We need bargaining power . . . but I'm with Hock. I can't do it. Can't be taking any of these plants away from their home."

Ryder's comms crackled, and he heard Max's voice. "We're back, safe and sound onboard the Hub Gunther. And Captain, you'll be happy to hear that we have three relieved pilots sitting here with us. A successful mission from our end. Wanda . . . Ryder . . . what's your situation with the vault? Over."

Ryder and the other three of the squad had heard Max. No one knew what to say.

Eventually, Wanda said, "Um, we ran into some complications . . . hold for the time being."

Ryder said, "You hear that?'

"What," Wanda said.

He said, "The klaxon . . . it stopped." But the others weren't looking at him; they were looking past him. Slowly, Ryder turned around. There were no less than twenty armed tumbleweeds, all pointing their weapons at them. One of the Clouse Veng

stepped forward. As he spoke, Ryder's auditory implant translated his soft-spoken but all-too-serious sounding words, "I am Prime Centurion Goben. So much as twitch, and you will be killed where you stand."

Ryder heard Max's voice over their comms, "Holy shit . . ."

Prime Centurion Goben said, "Humans, again, you invade our home-space. Why? To annihilate our young . . . our future?"

Wanda looked as if she was about to answer him, but Ryder spoke up first, "No. We wouldn't . . . couldn't do that. Um, we're actually here to ask your help."

The Clouse Veng fleet commander looked to be stymied by this response. So much so, he turned to look at the Clouse Veng next to him. Strange, the more Ryder observed this weird, plant-alien – the more he was able to discern slight changes in expression. A tightening twig movement here, a slackening there.

"Dare I say you have a most perplexing method for gaining our support. You have brought death and destruction to our people . . . I cannot imagine any reason why your lives shouldn't be terminated immediately."

Ryder raised his palms in a *hold on a moment* gesture. "Have you ever heard of the Varapin? Come from the Andromeda galaxy . . . dark hooded beings, hover around, and suck the lifeforce from their enemies?"

Once again, the Clouse Veng were talking amongst themselves. The increased tension in the compartment was palpable; even the baby plants had become still.

"Not by that name . . . but yes, the beings you call "Varapin" have ventured out to nearby territories. Word has spread to other regions, and to these regions of space."

"They're coming, Prime Centurion. A Varapin fleet . . . some sixty great and powerful warships. Their ultimate destination is my home world, Earth."

"You are at war with these vile beings?"

"Well, we weren't . . . but it's complicated."

"Then simplify it. I'm sure I'll understand the gist of what you have to say."

"Earth . . . humanity has been at war with the Grish – who are also vile beings. We humans have alliances with two other civilizations, the Thine and the Pleidian Weonan. The Grish, who are losing territories they'd previously gained, have reached out to the most ruthless and powerful adversary they could find . . . the Varapin."

"Fine . . . I see your plight and understand your unfortunate circumstances. Perhaps I can even see why you have gone to such ridiculous methods to gain my people's attention. But this is not our fight. As you well know, we have our own enemies . . . our own turmoil to deal with." Prime Centurion Goben was already turning away." No. It is not in our best interest –"

"Did I mention we come bearing gifts?" Ryder said.

Goben slowed. "We already have your Arrow fighters. Our scientists will dismantle them and reverse engineer the technology –"

Ryder held up his TAC-Band. "I will destroy them remotely. Do it right now. We're probably soon dead anyway."

Prime Centurion Goben turned back to face him. "You must do what you must do."

"The gifts I was speaking of are far more advanced technology and will provide you with a victory over your enemy, the Ramdei. That, and Humanity would like to create a war pact between our two civilizations. Something you had asked for only recently, no?"

"Only then, I was not so certain of your kind's true nature." He used an assemblage of twigs to gesture toward the green-slimed bulkheads.

Ryder was trying to think of something else to say when the fleet commander said, "What gifts? Although I can't imagine it will make any difference."

"How about the ability to manufacture jump wormholes."

Now, this had Prime Centurion Goben's attention.

"And I'm not talking about simply handing over the technology . . . I'm talking about providing you with operational jump spring systems . . . enough of the actual hardware to outfit your entire fleet. And I have it here, close by."

"Why didn't you just come to me first? Before all this?" Again, he gestured toward the bulkheads.

"I don't know – a dumb decision. We honestly didn't think you would take the offer seriously. That or you'd be more inclined to steal the technology . . . seeing that our bargaining power was non-existent. We'd be forced to destroy our own vessels, a no-win situation. But I must tell you, coming here . . . seeing this place, the abundant young life . . . we wouldn't have harmed any of them."

"I know this . . . I was listening to your translated communications. We know your cloaked ship is there within our flight bay. I personally watched as your three pilots disappeared into it. But I do believe you will destroy that vessel and yourselves, if necessary. You are warriors, and that comes with the job, no?"

Ryder didn't need to answer him. He continued to hold his TAC-Band up with a finger poised to destroy the Hub Gunther and all those within it. He thought of the feisty, Akari James, and how the Universe could ill afford to lose such an amazing woman.

"I am a mere commander; such important decisions are above my station. You will stay here, amongst our offspring . . . our future. Although I trust no harm will come to any of our Clouse Veng progeny, these energy rifles will stay trained on your heads. When I return, I will have my orders. Stay, play . . . get to know us."

With that, Prime Centurion Goben hurried from the compartment.

Chapter 34

Unnamed Star System – Expanse beyond the Milky Way

Captain Galvin Quintos

The 2nd Fleet was hopelessly outmatched. Yet. I'd come up with a glimmer of an idea on how to deal with the Varapin, thanks to a conversation I'd had with LaSalle just days earlier. He was on the bridge making repairs – we were still having technical issues with one of the consoles – a result of LuMan's earlier shooting spree. It was then that LaSalle and I got to talking.

"Still reading that book about, what was it . . . something like the Framers of the Constitution?"

"The book is called *The Essential Wisdom of the Founding Fathers*. And no, I finished that one. I'm on to a book about the inventive methods used by the early American rebels, and how they'd found ways to even the odds with far better armed and far more organized British troops."

"It's amazing that the colonists were to able mount such a defense," I said.

"Not just a defense, Captain . . . an offense."

LaSalle was on his hands and knees, now peering up at the underside XO Pristy's Tactical station. "This thing is shot to hell, excuse my French, sir. I can get things patched up temporarily, but ultimately, this station should be replaced."

"What do you mean, offense?"

LaSalle took a seat on the deck while thinking about my question. "Keep in mind, the American revolutionaries did, eventually, put together a regular army. But in the beginning, it was all about unorthodox tactics – tactics that played a huge role in the colonies securing their independence. Up until that point in time, wars, battles were fought out in the open. Soldiers were presented in tight formations. Today, we know that's crazy, but it was simply the way things were done back then. But the revolutionaries weren't about to come out into the open where they could be annihilated by such superior firepower."

None of this was new to me; every kid in grade school learned about this.

LaSalle continued, "No, The British got a taste of how the Americans would fight on the very first day of the Revolution; I'm sure you already know that, sir."

I nodded.

"It was the infamous "shot heard around the world" . . . the

Battle of Lexington and Concord, where the British regulars marched through the Massachusetts countryside."

I could almost picture it as LaSalle recounted the battle.

"The ragtag Americans were an . . . aberration. They didn't mass in front of the British as they'd expected. Instead, these Yankee scoundrels slithered on their bellies and fired from behind trees and stone walls. Captain, I can't tell you how much this infuriated the British field commanders. How dare these insolent American peasants *not play* by the proper rules of war! It was a matter of honor for the British. This was not the kind of open gentleman's fight that the British had expected; instead, these tactics took a devastating toll on the British regiments. Long after the Battle of Lexington and Concord, the Americans would hone their guerrilla warfare skills . . . use military tactics like conducting ambushes, instigating sabotage raids – all kinds of hit-and-run tactics. They concentrated on being highly mobile and flexible, which enabled them to fight such a larger, less-mobile, more traditional military."

By the time LaSalle had finished his lecture from beneath the acting XO's console, I had the kernel of an idea. We'd be taking up strategic positions within this planetary system. No, it wasn't a long-term strategy, but as every warship Captain knows, the first few minutes of interstellar warfare often dictates the decisive end result. If I could position our assets well out of the direct line of fire, primarily energy-weapon fire, we might just tip the odds.

Chen, on Comms, interrupted my ruminations. "Captain,

we have an incoming laser link transmission . . . looks to be from Captain Ryder."

Finally. "Play it."

I listened to the recording and then had Chen play it again. The good news, if there was any, was there weren't any KIAs as of yet. But Ryder had sounded dispirited, perhaps even remorseful that things hadn't gone as planned. But what plan? There never really was a viable ops plan; I'd sent that crew out there as a Hail Mary and, for the most part, told Ryder to improvise, to find a way to get us, the 2nd Fleet, Earth, Humanity, some help. It was a suicide mission, except that I'd refused to acknowledge it at the time.

"Captain, 2nd fleet's approaching the Galvin-Gail star system . . . ETA, ten minutes."

"Hold on there, Lieutenant . . . Galvin-Gail?"

"Uh-huh, I named it."

"You did, did you?"

"It's allowed. It's in the SPC-NAV-OPS manual. Want me to show you the specific reference? Any uncharted interstellar celestial object, or objects, can be provided appropriate nomenclature, subject to the review and approval of US Space-Navy Command . . ."

"You could have just called it the Gail star system."

"No, I like that our names are there together . . . seemed more appropriate."

"Fine. Instruct the fleet to hold up here, Lieutenant."

"Don't you mean, XO?" she said, sending a furrowed glance back at me.

"Sorry . . . of course, Acting XO."

Up on the Halo-Display, the distant star system with its blue dwarf star and thirty-six exoplanets came into view. The sight was breathtaking.

Standing at the side of the Captain's Mount, Derrota said, "Like our Solar System, the exoplanets are situated within the same basic elliptical plane. The three goldilocks region worlds are much like Earth, with oceans, land masses, and one particular world which looks to have a compatible atmosphere. Oxygen levels are a little rich for humans, but it would be breathable, just the same."

I nodded, taking in the system's sheer size, easily five times that of our Solar System. "Intelligent life?" I asked.

Derrota glanced down at his tablet. "Life? Yes. Intelligent? MATHR's on the fence about that."

Without turning around, I gestured with a raised hand for Hardy to join us. I knew he preferred to stay at the back of the Bridge, occupying the same spot with his back up against the bulkhead. Not that he didn't sometimes wander around, but he'd most definitely fallen into a routine of making that spot his home base.

Both hearing and feeling his stomping approach, I said, "You heard my question, I surmise."

"I have ears like a Labrador. My long-distance sensors have not detected any technology . . . no spacefaring vessels, no terrestrial machinery, and atmospheres are pure, void of emission pollutants."

"So, no aliens, no people –"

"I didn't say that, Captain. There are, indeed, aliens . . . people. I can't tell you what they look like. Just that there are primitives on that world. Approximately three million, on a world twice the size of Earth."

Derrota was nodding his head, "A little late, but MATHR concurs. I'd like to send a recognizance droid there to –"

"Chenland," John Chen blurted from Comms.

"Oh, come on." I shot an angry look toward XO Pristy. "See what you started?"

For some reason, the rest of the Bridge thought that was funny. "Fine, submit your nomenclature request along with the XO's."

Derrota continued, "As I was saying, I'd like to send a recognizance droid down to Chenland to acquire more data."

"Go ahead. Let me know what you find there."

Derrota ambled away, his attention back on his tablet.

"Lieuten– Um, XO, let's have the fleet take up their pre-determined positions within the system. Everyone stays out of direct line of fire." That was true for energy weapons; certainly not smart missiles. But I was going to grab every small advantage I could find at this stage.

"And you still think the Varapin will arrive along the same vector we just arrived from?" She asked.

"I do. They already have a good idea where we are . . . and that we have their fighter craft and pilot. Maybe we'll activate the fighter's homing beacon, something like that."

She shook her head. "That'll be suspicious. It's going to, what? Miraculously just turn back on?"

"You're right, there'd be nothing subtle about that. This species hasn't become the preeminent force within Andromeda by allowing even the smallest slight from an enemy to go unchallenged. I know it's lame, but maybe have it flicker to life . . . go on and off a few times, like it's faulty."

From her expression, she thought the idea was less than stellar. I said, "The point is, they'll come. Now, the real question is: what else can we do to even the odds before they get here?"

XO Pristy said, "Captain . . . getting fleet requests to start their deployments of RPPTs."

She was referring to self-contained Remote Phazon Pulsar Turrets. Relatively new within the Space-Navy's weaponry arsenal, these cloakable, tank-like vehicles were designed primarily as land-to-space weapons. Their Phazon beams were capable of penetrating even the most resilient ship's hull. That is, once that warship's shields had been breached. So, from orbit, these drop-deployed weapons were not the end-all solution, but merely one more trick up our sleeve. Each of our 2nd Fleet warships had six RPPT's within their respective holds – except for *Hamilton*, which had nine.

As *Hamilton* held back, I watched as the rest of the 2nd fleet, a Battle Group of ten Earth warships, invaded this once tranquil-looking, star system. We were interlopers, marauders here. Soon, death and destruction would follow.

XO Pristy said, "I've requested we trade places with the *USS Starlight*. That way, we'll be taking up position behind Chenland . . . they'll be behind exo-25."

"Best you don't get overly attached to that world, there. Something to think about when naming things." That reminded me of the Clairmont farm and a cow I'd named as a kid: Lacy. A calf that eventually grew into a fine cow. A cow that, ultimately, ended up at Mr. Springer's 'Meats.' I'd cried for days. My thoughts turned to the mock town taking up Decks 72 and 73. I wouldn't be going back there any time soon – Empress Shawlee Tee would just have to get over it. Right now, I had far more critical things on my plate, like the survival of the human race. We'd been sent here to gain the alliance some well-needed time to prepare. I wanted more than that.

"XO . . . you have the Captain's Mount," I said, getting to my feet.

"Where you off to, Captain?" she asked, getting up from her Tactical Station.

"First, to see how your predecessor is doing in HealthBay. Then, to see our prisoner."

With Hardy close on my heels, I entered a quiet and deserted HealthBay. The lull before the storm. A passing nurse directed me to Recovery, back within the Surgery Center off to our left. "Hang here, Hardy. I won't be long."

I found Captain Eli Tannock sitting up in bed, sucking something green through a clear straw. Upon entering, I saw the holographic avatar, projected above Tannock.

"That thing's going to drive me to drink. Pops on and off every time there's any kind of movement in here."

I watched the revolving, amorphous human shape with its

multi-colored organs exposed, constantly updating metatag descriptions; I could see how the thing could be annoying. "I guess it gives the doctors an up-to-the-minute visual of your . . . condition," I said.

"I know that. But it's a reminder my body parts are no longer my own."

My eyes went to the strip of white bandage along his sternum. Tannock pulled down on his hospital gown, "Doc says there won't be much of a scar once they do some flesh-scaping."

"Does it feel any different?"

"Not really. It was a genetic fast-grow. No issues, no anomalies, supposedly a perfect replacement heart. I'm as good as new and ready to go back to work, Captain."

I offered an encouraging smile but thought of Lieutenant Pristy and how much she loved being the ship's XO. "You just take it easy for now. Follow the Doc's instructions, and we'll see about things."

"I'm coming back to the Bridge, Captain. I'd appreciate your support in the matter."

"Of course. But like I said, it's your doctor who makes that determination." I offered up a smile and a little go-get-em' punch to the air before leaving.

In the passageway outside, I found Doc Viv leaning against a bulkhead with a bemused smile.

"You know, he's ready to be released. Healthy as an ox, in fact."

"Look, we're about to go into battle . . . stress on that new heart you gave him will be, well, stressful."

"Got it, the stress will be stressful. Any other words of wisdom for me?"

I felt my shoulders slump. "Come on . . . Can't you keep him here . . . for just a while longer? Maybe . . . please?"

"Fine. But you'll owe me."

"You got it. Anything." I left the Surgery Center, collecting Hardy along the way, and together, we headed aft. I needed more information from our reluctant prisoner.

We found Haite-Caheil, Cyclone Death Pilot, levitating horizontally within his confinement cell. Impregnable diamond glass separated us from the dangerous alien, and I was thankful for that.

I looked over to an armed nearby Security Forces guard, "How long has he been like that?"

"As long as I've been on shift . . . four hours and counting. Creepy if you ask me."

"He's in pain," Hardy said. "Think this is how he's dealing with it."

"Pain?"

"From when I broke his arms. Imagine it's uncomfortable."

"Ask him if he wants us to treat his injuries," I said.

"Fuck him. You saw what he did to those SWM guys . . . Nah, let him suffer."

"I'm not asking for your permission. See if he wants medical attention, Hardy."

The ChronoBot had come up with a new way to exhibit

his irritation. His face display showed a zoomed-in view of two beady eyes and two scowling eyebrows.

"Don't be so dramatic."

Hardy moved closer to the glass partition and spoke into an intercom speaker. "Hey, you, sleeping beauty . . . need help with those arms?"

The Varapin pilot didn't stir, didn't answer.

I said, "Maybe you should speak to him in his own language."

"He understands what I'm saying."

"Well, then, step aside, I'll speak to him myself."

Hardy did as he was told, and I stepped up to the speaker. "Haite-Caheil . . . why not let me fix your arms? In ten minutes, a medical bot can be here, setting the bones for you."

I waited for a reaction, but none came.

"Feels a little chilly here. Downright arctic . . . I think I'll have the heat turned up. Maybe a few hundred degrees." I had no idea if that was even possible, but I thought it was worth a try.

The alien, still levitating, turned his head our way. "Leave me in peace . . . I have provided you all the information you are going to get."

And Haite-Caheil had, indeed, provided much information, details of the combined fleets, *Wrath of Power* along with *Revenge of the Heart* – which had joined with the *Rage of the Gonjun Ract*. According to him, the *Rage of the Gonjun Ract* and sixty-two Varapin warships, now just hours away from our current location, were far superior, technologically, and in

numbers, to our feeble US Space-Navy 2nd Fleet. With prod-
ding, Haite had provided the more specific capabilities of the
Varapin warships – their energy weapons and railgun-type
cannons, their shields and cloaking technologies, their wormhole jump capabilities. He knew the technical details, the actual
hard-core specifications, far beyond anything I'd have been
able to relate about our own warship assets. Chief Mattis had
overseen the interrogation, and he'd asked the right questions.
He'd even asked what the pilot knew about our own fleet, the
specifications, and capabilities he believed we possessed. He
knew everything, an incredible amount of detail concerning
Hamilton's firepower compared to the Varapin's counterpart,
the *Sintchu* – which was much larger and more formidable
than *Hamilton*. Yes, LuMan, while under the influence of
Haite-Caheil, had provided far too much information. But
what the alien pilot had *not* transmitted back to his superiors
was anything concerning our Zathium enhancements. Either
LuMan had been able to hold back those details, or he hadn't
known about them. Hardy didn't know, and his inner LuMan
was coming up blank. Needless to say, this was, potentially, a
big break. As things stood, the approaching Varapin fleet would
be undervaluing the *Hamilton's*, in fact, the entire 2nd fleet's
prowess and capabilities.

"Leave me be . . . I have nothing more to tell you," said the
Varapin pilot, looking away. "To heal, all I require is quiet . . .
solitude."

"There's one area you did not assist us with: the *Rage of the*

Gonjun Ract, tell me specific missile targeting weaknesses . . . vulnerabilities."

"You waste your time," Haite said in a soft and fading voice.

I noticed a speaker mounted above the top diamond glass ceiling. "Guard, that speaker. Can you selectively direct sound to that?"

The guard, Crewman Silverman, looked puzzled by the question.

Hardy said, "According to the ship schematics, the answer is yes."

I tapped at my TAC-Band, doing a database search. "Huh . . . that's interesting," I said.

"What's that?" Hardy said.

"I just did a search of the most annoying, irritating, song of all time."

"What did you come up with?"

"A little tune from way back in the late 1990's. It's called *Vengaboys, We Like to Party.*"

"Never heard of it."

"You wouldn't have . . . it's from two-hundred years ago." I looked to the guard, who seemed interested in our conversation. "I want, *Vengaboys, We Like to Party*, piped into this cell at full volume. It's not to be turned off, no matter how much our prisoner complains."

The guard looked up to the ceiling and scratched his chin.

"Cap, we don't want Crewman Silverman to overexert himself. I've already taken care of it . . . the miracles of wireless technology. Your musical choice has been queued up and is ready to go. Full volume . . . one-hundred-and-twenty-five decibels." Hardy said.

"Play it."

The sound of an old-fashioned automobile horn blared from the speaker. Then the music blared so loudly I had to cover my ears. Granted, it was a catchy little tune with a good, solid beat. *Da daaaa da, Da daaaa da, Da daaaa da,* then the vocals came in, *We like to party, we, we like to party . . . We like to party, we, we like to party . . . We like to party, we, we like to party . . .* Okay, a little repetitive, but I could see how it could make one feel like moving their feet. At twenty-seconds into it, I was already getting annoyed. At a full minute, I wanted to kill somebody. Only then did I glance toward our captive alien. He was on his feet, his hands were covering what I assumed were his ears. He was saying something, but the music was way too loud to make it out.

I pointed to one of my own ears, "I CAN'T HEAR YOU! I'M GOING TO LEAVE NOW . . . BE BACK LATER TO CHECK ON YOU . . . ENJOY THE MUSIC . . . IT'S ON AN ENDLESS LOOP! I smiled and offered up a friendly wave.

Chapter 35

About an hour had elapsed since I'd last dropped in on our Varapin prisoner. He was now crouched and huddled into a corner within his cell. *Vengaboys – We Like to Party* was still blaring from the overhead speaker. I gestured to Hardy with a slicing motion across my throat for him to cut the music. I let the welcome silence linger a few moments before speaking.

Looking at my TAC Band, I said, "Huh . . . go figure . . . the Vengaboys have another tune, kinda similar to *We Like to Party*, that I think you'll like."

Haite rose and turned to face me. "What is it you want to know?"

"I told you, targeting vulnerabilities. I'm looking for ways to even the odds, or at least, improve our odds."

"When you are the preeminent power within your realm, there are no vulnerabilities." He hesitated, ". . . and there is your answer, Captain Quintos."

"That's it? Your only insight?"

"Tell me, what do I get in return for any further assistance?"

"Other than you being allowed to live? What do you want?"

"I will not be allowed to return to my people. Being abducted is considered a disgrace, an embarrassment to the realm. The simple fact that I have not committed *Shiktong* . . . suicide, only furthers my dishonor."

"Why haven't you? With your strength, surely you could have sufficiently banged your head against a bulkhead . . . something like that."

"True enough. But I do not wish to die. What I request is something my military does not practice . . . but yours does."

"Go on."

"*Safe haven*, I believe, is the term?"

"And why would we trust you not to screw the US Space-Navy at your first opportunity . . . are you not offering to do the same to your own people, now? Add that to the fact, you've ruthlessly killed crewmembers on board this ship. Eight to be exact. That cannot go unpunished."

"I have had much time to think within the walls of this small security hold. Captain Quintos, one who has already been stripped of any honor cannot regain honor where it was lost. Not really. But honor, personal honor, can be born anew somewhere else."

"I don't know about that. Maybe a traitor's honor."

"Honor, just the same. For me, it is preferable to death. I wish to pursue safe haven. And I will, willingly, take up arms against the Varapin to prove myself to you."

"I don't believe you. No one would."

"Again, allow me to prove myself to you."

"Yeah, well, I don't know how I'd be able to do that, without further endangering my crew or ship."

"But I do . . . I have a plan."

A part of me wanted to leave this area of the ship right now, before I was pulled into the manipulations of an enemy, an enemy probably was more intelligent than me. But I could not ignore the fact that I was more than a little intrigued. I said, "Fine . . . but here's the first price you will pay if you are playing me."

"Playing you? What is this 'playing you' phrase?"

"Duping me, conning me, tricking me . . ."

"Ah . . . yes, I understand."

"I'll shoot you in the head where you stand and not give it a second thought. So, before you begin, best you take that seriously into account."

"May I proceed?"

I glanced over to Hardy. His face display was an uncommitted swirling of white pixels.

I said, "Go on."

Hovering a foot or so off the deck now, the Varapin floated closer to Hardy. "There is a commonality to all Varapin space battles. At this point, our approach to conquering the inferior is the same; by now, it is rote, a series of pre-planned militaristic actions that, inevitably, never fails."

"And by knowing these actions in advance . . . we can, what? Throw a monkey wrench into the works?" I caught myself using a phrase he couldn't possibly know. "We can disrupt their rhythm . . . make them second guess themselves? Something like that?"

"After a millennium, the Varapin have experienced the full spectrum of potential defensive measures. What they do not anticipate intellectually, their advanced technology will do anticipate for them."

"So, we need to trick them. Let them think they have already won when they haven't? Give me an example of how we can do that."

The Varapin pilot, recovered even more now, steadied his deathly gaze upon Hardy. "Your ChronoBot, here, may be the key . . . I do not believe my superiors are aware he is no longer under my – Varapin – control. We could use that to our advantage."

"Careful saying *we* and *our*. That's still to be determined. Go on."

"My Cyclone . . . it is still in one piece? Still operational?"

I looked at Hardy. His face display showed a big thumbs up icon.

Again, I said, "Looks that way. Go on."

"My suggestion is to have this clever robot pilot my Cyclone Death Fighter back to the Varapin fleet, specifically, back to the *Sintchu.* From there, you will have a most powerful ChronoBot onboard the most powerful dreadnought of the Galaxy . . . of *any* Galaxy."

I stared at the hideous pilot for a long few moments, unable to speak. It was fucking genius, and I had to restrain myself from high-fiving Hardy. *Hell*, high-fiving the alien.

"It's . . . something to consider. Maybe." I said.

Chapter 36

I couldn't sleep that night. After tossing and turning for an hour, I got dressed in shorts and a tank top, and within ten minutes, was entering *Hamilton's* Gym, alone. I'd ordered Hardy to spend every minute he could within the Flight Bay and the Cyclone Death Fighter, verifying from the craft's stored comms messages that Haite was telling the truth. We needed to confirm that, as far as the Varapin were concerned, Hardy – more accurately, LuMan, would be expected to still be under Varapin influence. The ChronoBot also needed to familiarize himself with the fighter's – and subsequently, Varapin – technology.

The Gym, like the rest of the ship, had undergone a beautifying and technological transformation. Pristine white SmartCoat covered the bulkheads, and the exercise machines were new. It would take me far too long to figure out how to use any of them, so I decided to head up to the running track, instead. At least that hadn't changed much, but it was prettier and smelled better than before.

It was nice having the place to myself as I ran, thinking, and putting my recent decisions through a myriad of mental stress tests. Two hours later, physically exhausted, and my shirt drench with sweat, I realized I hadn't been able to nail down anything conclusively. Every part of my decision-making was based on a roll of the dice . . . nothing was definitive. My main worry was if this would be an epic shitshow, and were the Varapin going to steamroll right over the 2nd Fleet? Even my most basic orders, to slow the Varapin down long enough for the alliance to be better prepared, could very well be a joke. Admiral Cyprian Block, the EUNF U.S. Space-Navy's Executive Five Star Fleet Admiral, was counting on me to *at least* do that. Getting more depressed by the moment, I changed gears. I spent the next half-hour trying to poke holes in Haite's idea of sending Hardy into that Varapin dreadnought. What could go wrong? For one, I could lose one of the most advanced and effective fighting machines ever known to mankind. Second, there was no guarantee that LuMan couldn't be turned again, only adding to the forces coming up against the 2nd fleet – and ultimately, Earth. And finally, I might be losing a good friend, one who had risked his life, several times, to save mine."

Making it back to my quarters, I showered and caught a few hours of sleep. I awoke when my TAC-Band began to vibrate. Without opening my eyes, I said, "MATHR, who is that?"

"It is the reminder you set for your 0700 meeting with Chief Craig Porter in Engineering and Propulsion."

"What time is it now?

"0645."

I opened one eye, half-expecting to see Hardy standing there. Then I remembered, I'd ordered him to spend all his time with the Varapin fighter.

I was ten minutes late for the meeting. I arrived at Chief Porter's office and found it crowded – standing room only.

"Oh, how nice of you to join us," the Chief said.

"Yeah, yeah . . . what did I miss, Craig?" I asked, surprised to see Wentworth was here along with three of the Thine scientists. The always-friendly Coogong Sohp, cleared the faceplate of his environ suit, offering me a welcoming smile. I saw Doc Viv, half- sitting/half-leaning on the edge of the Chief's desk, stifling a yawn. The one I hadn't expected to see here was Captain JJ, with her bright red hair.

I was just about to ask to be brought up to speed when two more people entered the already-packed office: XO Tannock and Chaplain Trent. *Terrific*. Neither had been invited – but I was too tired and honestly didn't care enough to send them away.

Wentworth clapped his hands together three times, where once would have been more than sufficient. "We have much to go over, so best we get started."

I caught Craig's eye – he shrugged and rolled his eyes.

"Amazing progress on all fronts. Much better than expected, wouldn't you agree, Doc?"

Doc Viv said, "Mm, oh yes," although the sarcasm was lost on Wentworth.

"As you directed, Captain, our Zathium syntheses endeavor proceeded and . . . you'll be happy to learn, was a success. We then tested ZathSyn with an ADAP fuel sample. No problems there, none whatsoever. What's more, ZathSyn had been determined to be a better match for *Hamilton's* unique Pleidian propulsion system – better than our original Zathium additive."

I kept waiting to hear the "but" in his self-congratulating speech, but none came. With so much good news, I didn't know what to say.

"Now, the attractive Captain JJ has something she'd like to add," Wentworth said.

Her cheeks flushed at the inappropriate compliment. *Wentworth really is a tool.*

She said, "We tried the stuff. I was a little nervous . . . wouldn't want the *Louisiana*, having a good portion of the fleet's fuel reserves onboard, stuck out here in the middle of nowhere. Coogong Sohp and his colleagues were there to ensure that no mistakes were made. A Space Carrier's propulsion maintains three separate systems, three big drives, three fuel reservoirs. We made the modifications to just one of them. The one drive alone outperformed the other two combined, and by a wide margin. Power outputs are through the roof . . . which will impact FTL progression, shield performance, and a host of other ship systems. So, I'm sold. I've given the order to have the other propulsion systems upgraded." She looked over to me, almost daring me to object. I didn't. The 2nd Fleet wasn't expected to return home to Earth. Another roll of the dice, at this point, was just fine with me.

Wentworth was beaming.

The Chief leaned in close to me, "How do you think he maintains that tan out here?"

"I have no idea."

"I hear he's much older than he says he is . . . like eighty or ninety. Maybe drinks that stuff . . . or gives himself a Zathium enema each morning."

That made me chuckle.

"As time permits, we'll have the rest of the fleet powered with the ZathSyn additive by this time tomorrow," Wentworth announced.

"Hold on there," I said. "We could be attacked literally at any moment now. The Varapin, like the 2nd Fleet, will be cloaked . . . we won't have much of a warning. I can't have any of our assets out of commission, even for a minute. So, you'll have to work within those constraints."

I moved over closer to Doc Viv, who was looking bored.

"No problem, Captain," Wentworth said. "No vessel needs to go off-line, not even for a minute, as you put it."

"Just the same, I'm leaving it up to the individual ship Captains to determine if they want any upgrades made to their warships. That means no heavy-handed sales pitches, understood?"

"Of course! Hey, I'm all about free will, Captain."

Under her breath, Viv said, "Oh brother, you mean just like you were all about free will when you raped that poor Symbio-Poth?"

A sparkle of light caught my eye. The engagement ring was back on her finger, and this time, she caught me looking at it.

I sat down on the desk next to her. "So, no problems earlier . . . with the synthesizing process. Seems things progressed awfully fast."

She shook her head, disgusted. "No surprise. It was all an act for you. He had had no doubts about being able to synthesize Zathium because he'd done it all before. It was almost like he'd choreographed the situation. I guess this is how the rich keep getting richer."

"You too, since you're a part of the LLC, he set up."

"Maybe," she said unconvinced. She looked at me, "I forgot to tell you, the empress, Shawlee Tee, she's gone."

"Gone? Gone where?"

"Home, I guess. Said she had her Schooner here. Things apparently are not going well back home; she needs to be with her people. She wished us well with the Varapin and has faith that we will survive the ordeal."

"Survive is not the same as prevail," I said.

"She also said that I was to get you back up to Clairmont afterward . . . she made me promise."

"We'll see . . . who knows what will be left of the old girl."

She looked at me, questioningly.

"*Hamilton* . . . her days are probably numbered. The Varapin will be targeting her first."

"Is it too late to put in for a transfer? Maybe I should ask Cap JJ over there if the *Louisiana* needs another surgeon," Viv said with a lopsided grin.

My next stop was Flight Bay. As expected, Hardy was there familiarizing himself with the Cyclone Death Fighter. The one I hadn't expected to find there was the murderous Varapin pilot, Haite-Caheil. Granted, t six of Security Chief Matti's armed guards encircled the fighter, all with their weapons trained on the ghoulish-looking alien. *Just the same, I should have been consulted beforehand on this.*

Haite was hovering in the air, while Hardy was standing on a wing, leaning into the cockpit.

"I wouldn't have agreed to this, Hardy!"

He straightened and looked down at me. "Sorry, Cap. But if we're to get going within the hour, I needed to –"

"Hold up. You said, *we're*. Who are you going with?"

"The creepy alien. He's coming with me."

"No. No way."

"Yes, way."

"He's our enemy. He'll get you, and the rest of us destroyed. Why would I even consider such a stupid thing?"

"Because he promises to be good."

"Ha-ha, that's funny. I want him back in his cell."

"Cap, I've given things a lot of thought. The Varapin wouldn't allow this fighter to approach, let alone reenter their flight bay, with just me at the controls. No, this grim reaper-looking dude has to be in the cockpit with me."

I looked at the Cyclone. "Looks pretty cramped in there."

Hardy glanced inside the cockpit. "We talked about that too. He'll have to sit on my lap."

I almost laughed out loud but maintained a stern expression. "And once you're inside the alien ship, the *Sintchu* . . . what then?"

I pretend to be LuMan and under their control. I'm a good actor . . . in the third grade I played Peter Pan for our class talent show."

"Be serious, a lot depends on you wreaking a whole lot of havoc on that dreadnought. And I'd like to get you back here in one piece, too."

"Probably not much hope of that, Cap . . . sorry to say." For once, he actually knew the seriousness of the situation, and he wasn't making one of his ridiculous faces.

"And if the pilot turns on you, before or after you get onto that ship?"

"I've taken precautions, but, yeah, there's a good amount of risk here that I'll just have to live with. Look, Cap, I'll snap his neck at the first indication he's turning on me, and he knows it."

"I don't know. He'd be arriving back to his own kind . . . probably be the hero. Certainly not the disgraced prisoner he is now. All that gibberish that he should have committed suicide . . . I didn't buy it."

The Varapin pilot spoke for the first time. "Captain, as I

have told you, my career with the Varapin is over. Your robot has ensured that. The memory banks of my fighter provide a detailed accounting of my deceit. That will become more than evident to them soon after we land. As we discussed, my intentions are to align myself with US Space-Navy; nothing has changed. That is, if I survive."

Hardy said, "Yeah, I wouldn't count on that too heavily, demon-breath . . . I suspect this story ends with you and me –"

"Hey! Knock it off with the gloom and doom crap, Hardy. I don't want to hear it."

Five minutes later, I watched as Hardy, the Varapin pilot, and the Cyclone Death Fighter accelerated out from *Hamilton's* flight bay. Just like me sending Ryker away with the band of Marines, this was another ill-formed, half-cocked plan, one set in motion and having little to no chance of success. Sadness pulled at my heart as I watched the distant blue tongue of afterburner flames – now disappearing into the blackness of deep space. I had too few friends to be losing any more like this.

Chapter 37

ChronoBot Hardy

Considering the circumstances, piloting the Cyclone Death Fighter was enjoyable, even exhilarating, for Hardy. But having the Varapin perched there upon his lap --not so much. As a ChronoBot, his olfactory senses were keen – more acute than that of a German Shepherd – and this alien had an unpleasant smell about him. Hardy had been trying to equate this particular smell with something from his childhood growing up in rural Boston, Massachusetts.

"I got it . . . my old, sweaty, high-tops. Yeah, my gym shoes . . . that's what you smell like, Haite. Not a fond memory."

Not as tall as Hardy, he was able to see over the Varapin's head. They had left the system, the Galvin-Gail planetary system, five hours and seven minutes earlier. He glanced down, observing the back of Haite's hooded head. Hardy had little doubt the alien was a duplicitous killer, but there again, some of what he'd said may have been true.

"There . . . Rage of the Gonjun Ract . . ." came the alien's voice, breaking the silence.

Hardy had already noticed the magnificent alien fleet, off in the distance, a minute earlier. Strange, how his long-range sensors hadn't detected a thing until they were almost right upon the Varapin. The 2nd Fleet would have been equally surprised. Hardy recorded a message and sent it off to *Hamilton*. It wouldn't be long before Crewmember Chen, who would be on Comms right now, would receive it and inform the Captain. If for no other reason than that, this mission could already be considered a success.

Hardy said, "By now, your Cyclone Fighter has been detected. Any moment, you will be hailed."

"And you wonder if I will warn my people."

"The thought had crossed my mind."

A series of blinking lights came alive on the dashboard. A voice, almost as grating and annoying as that of Haite's, filled the cockpit.

"Answer . . . request clearance to land within the *Sintchu's* flight bay," Hardy ordered.

The Varapin pilot did as told, and as far as Hardy could determine, had provided no kind of clandestine warning. Waiting, with clearance yet to be given, Hardy said, "Best you let them know I'm here. Probably detected my presence, anyway."

Hardy didn't like how the Varapin language sounded, but

it fit with how the aliens looked. Haite relayed, as if it was an afterthought, that he had the ChronoBot onboard. "A gift for Conductor Sprin-Rop Kyber, if he so wishes."

Another full minute passed without a response from the *Sintchu.*

"The Varapin are a suspicious people . . . they will suspect treachery."

"I already know this may not work," Hardy conceded. "But, remember, you will be the first to die, if it doesn't."

"I have a thought," Haite said, ignoring the threat, and then continued speaking to the *Sintchu.*

Hardy listened as the pilot casually offered to jettison the oversized robot prior to landing, as if he cared little if the robot would be joining him. He went on to say the mechanical oddity was no longer of any importance and had fulfilled its function.

Clever touch, Hardy thought.

Eventually, permission to land was granted, but Haite was told, sternly, that any deviation from landing protocol would be met with dire consequences.

Hardy knew Haite was in trouble. He'd disobeyed direct orders by not staying with the human's 2nd fleet.

Haite said, "I will take us in from here, robot. They will notice if you do not navigate this Cyclone precisely as a Varapin pilot would do. Once we land, you speak only when spoken to. And use LuMan's voice."

Hardy did not appreciate the Varapin's bossy tone, but let it go.

As the Varapin fleet grew in magnitude before them,

Hardy's already-heightened sense of dread doubled, then tripled. Even with LuMan's knowledge base of other great alien fleets, this was incomparable. Although cloaked, his advanced sensors were able to make out the vessel's outlines, as if looking at illusory forms beneath an ocean. These were huge, ominous-looking warships – winged birds of prey on the hunt. And the largest of them all, the *Sintchu,* could not have looked any more threatening.

"We're in way, way, way over our heads . . ." he said aloud.

Haite slapped Hardy's two large mechanical hands away. The *Sintchu's* gaping flight bay loomed before them. As immense as *Hamilton's* was, it would be dwarfed in comparison. They passed through the energy atmosphere barrier, one which separated the cold vacuous void of space from the dreadnought's inner atmosphere.

"You guys keep things pretty dark in here, I see," Hardy said. "All that mist swirling around on the deck . . . and I didn't think you Varapin could get any creepier."

"You should cease talking, robot." Haite piloted the fighter high over a myriad of parked spacecraft; small gunships, Ravage-Class Landers, shuttlecrafts, and row after row – thousands upon thousands – of Cyclone Death Fighters. The craft spun on its axis and lowered down to the deck, positioned perfectly between a Cyclone on the left and a Cyclone on the right. Haite cut the engine and triggered the release of the canopy. Haite wasted no time, extricating himself from Hardy's lap – rising and floating several feet away.

"Was it something I said?" Hardy uttered.

Standing up to his full height, Hardy watched as the Varapin pilot turned to face him. Haite's ugly exposed jaws widened into what Hardy assumed was a malicious, taunting grin. About to make an unflattering comment, Hardy realized he couldn't. In fact, he wasn't feeling quite himself at the moment. And like two fast opposite-moving trains on parallel tracks, he watched – more like sensed – LuMan moving into predominance, as Hardy, once more, moved, powerless, into the deep recesses of ChronoBot consciousness. He wouldn't be faking anything. LuMan *was* taking control. Like a threatening, ominous storm – hooded black figures, dozens of them, advanced from every direction.

Chapter 38

Captain Galvin Quintos

"Go ahead and play it, Chen." I said, hearing that Hardy had made contact. The message was short and sweet.

Have reached the Varapin Fleet. Contact imminent. Enemy is inbound to 2nd Fleet's position . . . these badass warships are cloaked and will be almost impossible to detect. Suggest you have MATHR start scanning high MV-band spectral frequencies. Based on current velocity projections, expect fleet's arrival there at 1326 hours. Good luck.

My heart was already racing as I checked my TAC-Band. It was 1322 hours. *We had only four minutes – if that.* "Battle stations!" I yelled. "XO notify the rest of the fleet. All ship's . . . silent-running from this point forward." Silent-running, an old Earth naval submarine term, now referred to – in modern space lingo – dampening detectable propulsion radiation signatures and stifling unnecessary comms activity.

"Aye, aye, sir," she said.

I yelled over to the CIC, "Tell me you heard that, Stephan . . . MATHR's to scan –"

"Already on it," Derrota said from somewhere within the CIC.

My mind raced as the moments passed. *What have I forgotten? We're all cloaked, check. Stealth recognizance drones deployed throughout the system, check. Propulsion systems around the fleet would be operating within the confines of quiet-running mode, check. RPPT's have been deployed to nearby exoplanets fleet-wide, check. Communications between ships had been halted, check. No direct line-of-sight positioning, check. All fleet warship assets were readying their Arrow Fighter squadrons for fast deployment, check. Crews were manning the magazine compartments and readying munitions, check. And close to one hundred Phazon Pulsar cannon platforms would be activated, testing – pivoting back and forth, left and right, check.*

I said, "Look alive, could be any second now, people . . ."

I sensed more than saw someone arrive at my side.

"Captain Quintos, request my return to active duty."

I didn't have to look at him to know that voice. "Not a good time right now, XO Tannock."

"On the contrary, sir, I would say this is the perfect time."

XO Pristy glanced back over her shoulder. "It's okay, Captain, I can –"

I cut her off, "Tannock, think you can still work a Tactical board?"

"Of course. I may be an old fart, but I've still got my wits."

"Good, because we're going to get really busy here . . . so get up there with Gail . . . you two can split your XO duties . . . someone on *Hamilton*, someone on the fleet. Work together, Gail. You'll be XO1, Tannock, you're XO2 . . . any problems with that?"

Pristy shook her head. Tannock smiled, "It's just good to be working again." He ambled over to the Tactical console, where Gail was already scooting over to make room for him.

I caught sight of Derrota now running toward the Captain's Mount. He was making exaggerated arm gestures toward the forward Halo-Display.

"We see it, Stephan. Good job!" I said. It was the Varapin fleet, and thanks to Hardy, we were seeing *something*, what was typically called an *intorsion-displacement* of space, detectable because MATHR was now scanning the high MV-band spectral frequencies.

"Six-hundred-thousand miles and closing, sir," XO Pristy said. Not hearing a response, she stole a glance backward.

It wasn't so much that I couldn't speak, as I couldn't do *anything*. The sudden paralysis was absolute. Even blinking was out of the question. But what *was* moving incredibly fast was my heart rate. *Oh God . . . not now . . . please . . . not now.*

I saw XO Tannock getting to his feet. He was more-than-ready to take command.

"Sit down, Tannock! He's fine! Sit the fuck down!"

If I hadn't heard her voice and actually saw the words coming from her lips, I wouldn't have believed XO Pristy could muster such an admonishing tone. Gail had come along way – I was proud of her

"I'm fine," I said, coming out of it – my voice having far less strength than I'd hoped for. I sat up straighter in my seat. I wondered how many people on this Bridge knew my recent LOPTSD diagnosis. *Who was I kidding?* Nothing, I mean, *nothing*, stays secret on a US Space-Navy warship.

"Looks like the Varapin are changing course, sir," XO Pristy said.

"Damn it . . . we need them to come to us here in this system."

"Looks like they're going to circle around . . . come in from behind us," XO Tannock said.

I didn't answer for several moments, prompting more eyes to turn toward me again.

"I'm fine, mind your stations, people. *Tannock was right, though.* "XO2 Tannock," I said. "Instruct the fleet to stay in position . . . stick to the plan. Keep comms to a minimum."

"Aye, Captain."

"Crewman Grimes, you ever play chicken back home where you come from . . . Nevada, right?"

"That's right, Captain and yes . . . not much else to do on a Friday night in Winnemucca."

"Well, this time, you won't be behind the wheel of a tricked-out hover-car for this ride. So, Helm, get us around this planet,"

Crewman Chen added, "You mean, around Chenland."

Grimes said, "Um . . . I don't think playing chicken is even an option for MATHR, sir."

"She won't like giving up full nav control, especially within a battle situation," Chen added.

"Then you'll just have to fly by the seat of your pants, Helm . . . go to manual piloting."

"Sir?" Grimes said.

"You heard me."

"Aye, sir, manual piloting engaged," Grimes said, as he took up the rarely-used hand controls now rising up from the Helm station control board.

"Engaging maneuvering propulsion, sir," Grimes said. A moment later, he said, "We're clear . . . orders, sir?"

"I guess it's time we see if this ZathSyn shit is all it's cracked up to be. Easy does it now . . . okay, come about thirteen degrees . . . Good. Now put the *Hamilton* on a direct course for that fleet . . . for the *Sintchu*. Punch it, and don't let up," I said.

Grimes said, "Here we go . . . putting the pedal to the metal, sir."

Hamilton's forward acceleration was nothing less than explosive. Except for myself, thrown back hard into my chair cushions, everyone else on the Bridge was flung from their respective seats. I heard Derrota cursing from the CIC. A moment later, the G-force compensators kicked in, and the crew crawled backed to their stations.

"Estimated collision time, thirty seconds, Captain," Grimes said.

I notice one crewman hadn't gotten up from the deck.

"XO Tannock! You're now also manning the Weapons Station . . ."

"Aye, aye, cloning the weapon's station here to Tactical," Tannock said.

"All forward guns active, Rail Cannons, Phazon Pulsars!" I ordered.

"Twenty seconds," Grimes said.

"Someone tell me we'll be able to get a lock using some of our Smart Missiles!" I queried Tactical.

"Not yet," XO Pristy said, studying her board. "Wait . . . almost . . . almost . . . Yes! We've got a lock . . . I've got thirty, now forty fusion-tipped missiles tracking and ready."

"Fire! . . . Fire all of them!"

Grimes said, "Head-on collision within eleven, ten, nine –"

"Missiles away, sir," came Pristy's excited voice.

And there she was, up on the Halo-Display – right in front of us – the *Sintchu,* and she was no longer cloaked. A collective gasp filled the Bridge. The word *immense* came to mind. With her arched and spread wide wings, her down-sloped nose, she looked as if she was riding some kind of invisible air current, coming in for a kill, like something dark and evil – a living nightmare.

"Down! Skim beneath her belly, Helm," I yelled. Inwardly praying my counterpart onboard, the *Sintchu* hadn't just given the same exact order. I instinctively looked up, half expecting the top few decks of *Hamilton* to be cleaved off from the rest of the ship. Fortunately, there was no impact.

"We're clear of her!" Grimes said. "Oh, crap!" he added,

as he maneuvered *Hamilton* up, down, and around, a blur of Varapin warships following in close to the *Sintchu*, far too many to visually keep track of. Then, all of a sudden, the *Hamilton* was clear of the alien armada.

I said, "Somebody, tell me we caused some damage to that oversized pigeon."

"Not much, sir." XO Tannock said. "The *Sintchu's* shields held strong . . . but maybe . . . looks like some faltering with her shields along her port side, around midship."

"So, no damage? No damage at all?"

"No, sir," XO Tannock said. "But our Smart Missiles have yet to strike."

"We definitely caught their attention, sir. Fleets no longer circling around to the far side of the system," XO Pristy added. "And the Varapin fleet is coming to a stop, they've gone to battle stations, Captain."

"Good, well, maybe that's good," I said.

"Missiles making contact in three, two, one . . ."

The Halo-Display momentarily went solid white – unable to compensate for so many fusion tipped Smart Missiles all going critical within microseconds of one another. I knew that each missile payload had the equivalent of a thirty-megaton nuclear blast.

As the display came back alive, I saw that the *Sintchu* was still there.

"Thirty-eight missile strikes, Captain. Two misfires," XO Tannock said.

"I want an estimated damage report." I glanced toward the

CIC. I knew the men and women in there would be evaluating and making sense of MATHR's latest sensor data.

XO Pristy, concentrating on her board, said, "According to the CIC, the Varapin still don't clearly see our fleet assets . . . but are looking real hard in our general direction. Know we're here . . . trying to get a weapon's lock as I speak. Our cloaking tech must be better than I thought," she added. "Okay . . . damage to the *Sintchu*. Nominal. That port side area where her shields had weakened . . . five separate deck breaches there, and atmosphere is venting. No critical systems are down. Estimated loss of life, seven hundred."

I was still in a bit of shock that *Hamilton*, the pride of the US Space-Navy, had done little to impact this enemy. We'd thrown pretty much everything we had at her, and there was little to show for it. Even more concerning, there was an entire armada still there – all, most assuredly, equally resilient. We had no choice but to continue as planned. "Helm . . . come about slowly. We'll be entering the system with the blue dwarf star to our port side; just the way we want our alien friends to enter the system."

"Copy that, sir," Grimes said.

"Wait, hold on, I'm not done. We need to leave a few breadcrumbs. Not so many that our exact position can be determined, but just enough that they think our cloaking tech isn't as good as we think."

The comms speaker on the Captain's Mount squawked with Derrota's voice, "Best if I do that, Captain. With the Pleidian upgrade, MATHR now has the capability to produce phantom signatures. We'll want them to appear far enough behind us that we can stay clear of any directed missile explosions."

"Good. Get ready, Stephan . . . Helm take us into the system. Take us back to our hiding place behind Chenland . . ."

Chapter 39

"No enemy missiles fired as of yet, sir," Pristy said. "The Varapin . . . maybe half the fleet, are following along behind us. Or what they think is us . . ."

Derrota had not only delivered as promised, leaving the phantom breadcrumbs, but he'd also managed to illusory ship outlines on the Halo-Display, moving methodically and slowly slow the Galvin-Gail star system.

The *Hamilton* came to a full stop behind the blue-green world, *Chenland*. I got to my feet. "XO Pristy," I said. She looked back at me, and I gestured with a slight jerk of my head, *we need to talk.*

We met at the back of the bridge and in a hushed voice, I said, "Look, I don't expect anything to go wrong . . . with me. But I need to know you'll step in if necessary."

"I don't understand," she said, concern in her eyes.

"I'm not sure what I'm going through –"

"You mean the late-onset PTSD . . . I'm sure it's temporary."

"It's good to know what's supposed to be my private medical information has not become so universally known."

"I can't control what I hear, sir. But we think it's temporary . . . it'll pass."

"Be that as it may, you'll need to take the Captain's Mount if the situation arises. You understand what I'm saying?"

"Um, I think so. But XO Tannock, he's like, twice my age, far more experienced –"

"No. I want you."

She looked at me with wide eyes, and there was something else in her hopeful gaze, too. *Shit!* I needed to rephrase that. "I want you because you think more like me. Abstract. Unconventional. We cannot win here, playing by the rules."

She was nodding her head, the weight of what *might* happen already pulling on her slight shoulders.

"Look, I'm fine, Gail . . . I promise. This is a, um, just an in-case scenario. I've already made the command log entry. MATHR will back you up if it comes to that. But again, nothing's going to happen. I'm fine."

"Captain!" Tannock shouted from the Tactical station. "Enemy is closing in."

I gave Pristy an encouraging nod, and we both headed back to our respective stations. Tannock shot Pristy a speculative glance as she sat down next to him.

I studied the Halo-Display as the Varapin warships crept along, their sensors undoubtedly passively scanning for signs of the 2nd Fleet. Within a minute, I would be giving the order to open fire on the enemy. From that second on, our positions would become evident. We might be able to cloak our warships but cloaking the emergence of millions of rounds of rail spikes and Phazon Pulsar beams, would not be possible. And that's why the RPPT's, also cloaked, were such an essential aspect of this plan. If for nothing else, they would become a distraction – something unexpected.

"Captain, the Varapin . . . thirty-two warships are now fully immersed within the system," Pristy said.

"XO Tannock, inform the fleet . . . initialize RPPT's on my order." I thought about that . . . *the next words coming from my lips will be the start of a war. A war with an enemy unparalleled with any enemy humanity has faced – or may ever face. I will be kicking the proverbial hornet's nest, and there will be no means to put those angry hornets back into their nest.* "Fire! Fire Remote Phazon Pulsar Turrets, now!"

Earlier, each 2nd Fleet warship had deployed hundreds of their own stealth recognizance drones – totaling thousands – and were now strategically positioned throughout the Galvin-Gail system. It was now MATHR's job, a simple task for her, to assemble the collective raw video data and provide, amongst other things, a full 3D, omnidirectional, bird's-eye view of the planetary system. I watched as bright blue energy beams came alive, creating a magnificent light show. Yes, the Varapin cloaking tech was good, but not good enough, thanks to Hardy's last message and MATHR's enhanced capability to see those MV-band spectral frequencies. All thirty-two Varapin warships returned fire almost immediately – bright red energy pulses were now crisscrossing open space.

I said, "XO Tannock, instruct the fleet . . . fire at will, fire at will. XO Pristy . . . engage the enemy."

Both Science Officer Derrota and Chief of Security Mattis were at my side. The only one missing was Hardy. It was only then that I realized how close the ChronoBot probably was, because there, up on the Halo-Display, I saw the uncloaked *Sintchu* making its way directly toward *Hamilton*.

An explosion caught my attention.

"That's the *USS Gun,* Captain. Destroyed, all lives lost," Tannock said.

The Gun was one of three corvettes in the fleet. It wasn't a surprise that the smaller vessel would be the first to go down against a more powerful opponent.

"We're taking fire, Captain. The *Sintchu's* unloading on us," Pristy said. "I'm returning fire."

I saw and felt it, as *Hamilton* came under attack. The enemy dreadnought was, indeed, unleashing a hellfire of weaponry. "Shields?" I asked.

Pristy became still. Then, suddenly, she turned around in her seat to face me.

"What is it, XO?"

"They're holding. Our shields . . . their holding at" she glanced back over to her board, "eighty-seven percent. All our asset's shields seem to be holding." She looked over to Tannock. His mystified expression confirmed what she'd said. He nodded, "She's right, Captain."

"I don't understand," I said aloud – confounded. "We're

outnumbered, we're clearly outgunned . . ." Another explosion caught my attention up on the Halo-Display. "Who'd we lose?"

"That's not ours, Galvin," Derrota said, scanning his tablet.

Tannock said, "That was a small Varapin destroyer . . . The *Louisiana* took it out.

"Huh, go figure . . . well, good job, Captain JJ," I said under my breath.

Derrota leaned in closer to me, "Seems we owe Wentworth a good bit of gratitude. You know it's the ZathSyn, right?"

"Yeah . . . clearly a gamechanger." I still hated the guy, but he, along with the Thine scientists, deserved all our gratitude.

"We just lost the *USS Mighty*, Captain," Tannock said.

Another Corvette. Seems there was only so much ZathSyn could do for those smaller crafts.

I saw them up on the display even before Pristy made the announcement, "Incoming . . . eighty-six Smart Missiles . . . all look to be nuclear-tipped . . . deploying countermeasures now."

I stood up, "Let's get those RPPT's on the planet targeting those missiles!"

"On it, sir." Pristy said.

"Too late, I'm already on it," Tannock said with a wry grin.

"Helm keep us moving . . . let's use some of that quick acceleration we've acquired. No sense in giving the enemy a stationary target," I said.

Grimes, at the Helm, said, "Um . . . I suggest you, sir, and everyone, sit down and strap in."

"Good point. Like he says, everyone, strap in!"

The Halo-Display went white with three consecutive flashes.

"Those were all Varapin ship explosions," Tannock said.

Cheers roared up from the Bridge crew.

Irritated, I yelled back, "Knock it off, people . . . that's a total of four out of sixty-two enemy vessels . . . it's not nearly time to celebrate."

I heard Pristy say, "*Shit!*" under her breath.

"Keep it together, XO . . . What's happening?"

"Two updates . . . the rest of the Varapin fleet had now entered the system . . . they're joining the fight."

"What else, XO?" I said.

"Thirteen still remaining nukes are inbound. Contact in three, two, one . . ."

Hamilton shook, and I could hear a clattering of loud noises coming in from Whales Alley. That meant only one thing, our shields had been breached.

"Damage report!"

"Coming in now from MATHR, Captain," Mattis said, scanning his tablet. "Breaches on Decks 5, 6, and 7. Structural damage, including two Phazon Pulsar Turrets taken out of commission. Atmosphere venting . . . still waiting on missing crew or confirmed lives lost."

"Shields at sixty-six percent, and falling," Pristy said.

I unconsciously gritted my teeth. *And so, the tide turns. Think! How do we switch things up again?*

"Captain?" Pristy said, pointing to the Halo-Display. "There . . ."

"I see them. What the hell am I looking at?"

The bridge went quiet as everyone stared.

"Oh no . . . no," someone said behind me.

"There must be dozens of them," Chen said from the Comms station.

Derrota said, "Confirmed . . . those are indeed Varapin Warriors."

"But they're not wearing spacesuits or battle suits . . ." Grimes said.

"I don't think they need them," I said.

"True," Derrota said. "They like the cold, and they can hold their breath for extended periods of time."

I turned to Mattis, "They're heading for our breached decks. Inform Colonel Bonell, tell him to get his Marines prepped and deployed to Decks 5, 6, and 7. We want to take out those invaders before they storm the entire ship."

I remembered what just one of those Varapin killers could do, and that seven crewmen had been slaughtered within Environmental Conditioning by the Cyclone Death Fighter's pilot, and another one on the flight deck. If it hadn't been for Hardy, the body count could have been much higher.

I called after Mattis, "And once the Marines are in place, I want those decks isolated, have all Vac-Gates in the area closed off."

I hoped that would be sufficient – the Vac-Gates were thick and highly-reinforced emergency-deployed bulkheads. Each Deck had multiple gates, and they were virtually impossible to breach without serious explosives.

One of our many dispersed recognizance drones had picked up on the approaching Varapin Warriors – who were now visible up on the Halo-Display. With their hooded cloaks, they were almost as dark as space itself. And they moved fast – certainly not Arrow Fighter fast, but fast.

"How is that even possible, Stephan? The lack of breathable air . . . the frigid temperature . . ."

Derrota said, "2.7 Kelvin. That's about minus 455 degrees Fahrenheit. No. Nothing, no living organism could survive in such conditions. Irreversible protein denaturation resulting in cellular death happens instantaneously at that temperature."

"So . . . are they even alive?"

He pursed his lips, "That's the question I've been pondering. Most definitely not alive in the same sense as that of life on Earth . . . but as we've learned, the Universe has many surprises, many unexplained phenomena."

"Captain!" Crewman Chen said. "Incoming hail from Earth. Encrypted micro-wormhole laser-link. Highest priority . . . it's Admiral Block."

"Open the channel," I said.

The Admiral's face appeared in a separate feed next to that of the approaching Varapin Warriors. His hair was disheveled, and the bags under his eyes were pronounced and dark. His mouth moved, but the sound and video were out of sync. "Captain Quintos . . . I don't have much time. Things have escalated. Earth . . . we're being attacked as I'm speaking to you. Fucking Grish!" The admiral's eyes darted left and right. The man looked beyond frightened – he looked terrified. "Australia

. . . gone. Southern Africa . . . gone . . . Italy . . ." Tearing up, he couldn't complete his sentence. "We need you back here, Galvin, we need the 2nd Fleet, back here, now! Hell, it may already be too late."

XO Tannock interrupted the Admiral, "We just lost the *Gallaher,* one of our Jericho-Class Destroyers."

The Admiral, hearing Tannock's voice, said, "Wait . . . you're under attack? The Varapin?"

"Yes, sir, as we speak."

His eyes closed in resolute defeat. His thoughts were plainly expressed in that one moment of time – that all was lost, that the 2nd Fleet was never expected to survive the Varapin assault. That we would not survive, just as Earth would not survive – all hope was lost.

Why that irritated me as much as it did, I can't explain. But irritate me, it did. "Admiral. Admiral! Look at me, damn it!"

Admiral Block, shocked by my abrupt tone, straightened. His eyes focused.

"You may have given up on the 2nd Fleet, but I certainly haven't. You need us there? We'll be there. And for your information . . . we're kicking ass out here. The Varapin, *pfft,* they're a bunch of pussies. I suggest you take the same advice you've given me over the years . . . never, ever, give up, not until you're dead and six feet under!"

One corner of the Admiral's lips curled up. "A bunch of pussies, huh?" he said.

I nodded, "Uh-huh."

Of course, he knew I was lying through my teeth. "Well

then, go get em', Galvin . . . Just get here as soon as you can. Block out."

The feed went dark. All eyes were on me. "Hey . . . I said what he needed to hear. Now let's get back to it."

"The good news, Captain . . . *Sintchu* has eased up with their onslaught."

Derrota said, "Don't want to incinerate their warriors."

"ETA on their arrival here?"

Pristy said, "It's only a guess, but I'd say five minutes . . . based on their progress so far."

That was my guess too. I hailed Bay Chief Frank Mintz via my TAC-Band. It was still early in the battle for Arrow Fighters to be deployed, but these were abnormal circumstances.

"Go for Mintz!" he said, his voice loud against a backdrop of noisy fighter engines within the flight bay.

"You're aware of the incoming –"

His gruff voice cut me off. "Like a flock of fucking bats . . . yeah, were monitoring them."

"Get a squadron out there . . . I don't want those bats on my ship."

"On it, Mintz out."

"Bad news, Captain . . . The entire Varapin fleet has joined the battle. We have four more enemy warships headed our way," Tannock said.

Chapter 40

Galvin-Gail Star System – *Rage of the Gonjun Ract Fleet, Sintchu*

The ChronoBot

The phrase, *once bitten twice shy,* came to mind as Hardy's consciousness finally emerged from the depth of a deep and debilitating fog. "Hello, LuMan . . . how's it hanging?"

LuMan, devoid of even the slightest smidgen of humor, would not and did not answer the rhetorical question.

Yes, Hardy had been surprised, caught off guard once again, at his and LuMan's inability to ward off the Varapin's technological capabilities to subjugate and dominate their collective AI consciousnesses. But the *once bitten twice shy* idiom had prompted him to be far better prepared this time around - to be ready for anything and everything. So, before landing that Cyclone Death Fighter within the Varapin's flight Bay, he and

LuMan had been inwardly talking, planning, scheming. Most of the crew on board *Hamilton* didn't really understand that Hardy and LuMan weren't two minds fighting for inner domination. LuMan disliked interfacing with humans, or any other organic being, for that matter; but, Hardy thrived on those very same interactions. In fact, he lived for them. No, LuMan and Hardy were as close to being *family* as the technological realm of artificial intelligence would allow; they both had their separate place, which was good, but they were also united in ways. So, they had devised several self-running background programs. Upon entering the Varapin Flight Bay, LuMan probed, found, and then hacked one of the *Sintchu's* more vulnerable networks. Within micro-seconds, tiny self-running *zombie* programs were infiltrating various onboard AI sub-systems. Then, the complete Hardy consciousness began systematically streaming into some of the more obscure memory-bank storage systems within the alien dreadnought. Three systems were tapped: he refuge, *garbage*, collection system on Deck 18, the temperature control system on Deck 9, and the data storage for the life-energy containment cisterns up on Deck 33. When the ChronoBot's AI mind had been totally scrubbed and the mindless robot's thousand-pound hulk thrown into the raw materials reclamation chamber, the Varapin were confident this robot would never – *could* never – be a problem again. What the Varapin had not considered would cost them: tiny wrappings of stacked synthetic mem-strand *tags*, each mere atoms thick, which provided for individualized robot component memory. Not all information was stored within the ChronoBot's typically-busy, central AI. For instance, not the tension regularity for an ankle joint, the return orientation position for a wrist joint, or the open/close status of any one of the ChronoBot's energy canon panels. Like a human's muscle memory, ChronoBots had these innumerable, localized, memory tags that the robot's AI brain could access, as needed. So, when a little self-running timer (one that was *not* a part of the ChronoBot's central AI, but actually nestled within one of these small memory tags within the ChronoBot's left knee joint integration) came active – all sort of small-but-important things took place. In this case, communications protocols were established with another self-running program, one currently inhabiting that cluster of data stored within the *Sintchu's* refuge collection system. Almost immediately, zettabytes of information funneled back into LuMan's AI, both into his hard – and organic – brain matter. Soon, LuMan was sitting up. Then, Hardy's consciousness was reestablished – was *actualized*. Only then did Hardy ruminate on . . . *once bitten twice shy*. Hardy looked around, taking in the heaps of scrap metal and other unidentifiable, discarded materials. Across from him was another robot, obviously of inferior technology, lying sprawled across the heap, a lifeless, abused-looking tangle of metal limbs. Two dull eye sensors within a dented head stared blankly at the nearest bulkhead.

"Where the hell am I?" Hardy asked to no one in particular.

Instead of answering outright, LuMan provided Hardy with the detailed blueprint layout of the *Sintchu*. A big red X marked their current position within what was being referred to as Refuge Depot 200.

Hardy, with LuMan's help, found a *Sintchu* communications channel to piggyback onto and hailed the *Hamilton*. Hardy hoped the ship was close enough for the transmission to reach. For that matter, he hoped the *Hamilton* was still in existence.

Hearing Crewmember Chen's, "Who is this . . . identify yourself at once!" command, brought Hardy a good measure of relief.

"Hey Chen, you know, you've really nailed that authoritative voice thing. It's working for you, big time."

"Hardy?"

Chapter 41

The only positive news was how little damage was being reported as of late. What had become evident during this battle -, not just for the *Hamilton*, but for the rest of the 2nd Fleet – was how the ZathSyn additive had improved our defensive shields' performance to unheard-of levels. The enemy's energy weapons were having little impact. Smart-Missiles were another story, but we were having some success tracking, targeting, and destroying those in flight. None of that meant we were winning the battle. By sheer numbers alone, the enemy would eventually overcome our defenses and prevail through attrition. Seems all we had done, thus far, was forestall the inevitable.

Chen put Hardy's incoming communique through. "Can you believe they just tossed me into a Refuge Depot, Cap? One would think they would, at the very least, find a way to repurpose a perfectly good ChronoBot."

It was a relief hearing Hardy's voice, but there was little time for chit-chat. "Need a Sit Report, Hardy" I said.

Hardy continued, "I've breached the *Sintchu's* network, so getting out of this compartment shouldn't be a problem. Then, I can make my way to the bridge, or propulsion system, and start doing some serious damage there. That is still the plan, right, Cap?"

"Varapin Warriors have reached *Hamilton,* Captain," Tannock said.

He needn't have mentioned that, for we had all watched as the tidal wave of those deathly beings reached *Hamilton's* outer hull. Less than a quarter of their numbers had been taken out en route by our Phazon Pulsar strikes – but it had been almost impossible to get an accurate weapons-lock onto the individual aliens.

"Cap? Hardy said.

"Negative, Hardy. Hold on . . . things are changing as we speak."

Having just returned, and standing next to Derrota, Chief Mattis said, "Hardy, did you mention you'd breached the *Sintchu's* network?"

"That, I have. Well, partially. Doing my best not to be

noticed. Have a small presence within some of the ship subsystem interfaces, rudimentary programs –"

Mattis cut him off, "Hardy, can you implant a worm into the ship's primary network?"

"Already three steps ahead of you there, Chief. That was always the plan. Got one called *Anal Surprise*. If not detected too early, it'll wind its way to the aft part of the ship and burrow into the propulsion system's operating system. From there, the worm will propagate, get into other key systems: environmental, navigation, internal power distribution center, weapon systems . . . you name it. But that'll take some time. And there's a good chance the worm could be discovered before it can do any real damage. These ghouls are as technically-advanced as the Pleidians - or even the Thine. Have redundant firewalls –"

I said, "Just get your worm deployed right away . . . like, right now, Hardy."

"Copy that, Captain. One Anal Surprise, coming up."

"Now, listen to me carefully, Hardy," I said. "I need you back here on the *Hamilton*, immediately. We're being boarded by the Varapin as we speak."

"Escaping this ship might not be so easy, Captain."

"I'm counting on you to figure it out. Good luck, Captain out."

Chen said, "Captain! Just received a desperate mayday from the *Enterprise*. She's lost all nav control. Twelve decks are currently venting to space, and her shields are failing. Their Captain's been killed, and XO Griffin has taken command."

Shit! Leaving the *Sintchu* behind, and no longer keeping

that powerful dreadnought's full attention, brought her power-ful guns onto other, far more vulnerable, 2nd Fleet assets.

"Helm! Get us over there!" I said.

I checked my TAC-Band, which had been vibrating non-stop for a minute or so. "Go ahead, Colonel Bonell."

"We're hunkered down here within Decks 5, 6, and 7, behind closed Vac Gates. All my Marines are taking losses."

I could hear the growing desperation in his voice.

"These hovering fuckers sure can take a hit . . . I mean, how is it Shredder fire can go right through them like that?"

I stared at my TAC-Band, then looked up to the Halo-Display and saw we were approaching the *Enterprise*. Numerous fireball eruptions peppered her hull, while the big Space Carrier had multiple vents spewing atmosphere and debris.

Pristy said, "The *Sintchu* stayed with us. Captain! Oh God, she's now firing on the *Enterprise.*"

I looked to Pristy, to Tannock, then to Derrota. Colonel Bonell's face stared up at me from my TAC Band.

Boom! Boom! Boom! Boom!

The kettledrum in my chest was unrelenting, and I felt my mind reaching a kind of critical mass endpoint. My vision was closing down – a tunnel effect taking place, one that directly corresponded to something similar happening with my hearing. *Huh – is there such a thing, a hearing tunnel effect?* Strange, that at this moment, I would think of Doc Viv – her shimmering, wet naked form standing there beneath that stream of water, there at the side of the old barn. *Who the hell was she engaged to?*

The slap was hard enough to whip my head to the side.

There, standing at the Captain's Mount, right in front of me, was none other than Lieutenant Pristy. My XO was looking both angry and scared. "Snap out of it, Galvin!"

It was strange hearing her call me by my first name. Yes, I'd done it again, lapsed into another DOPTSD stupor. My mind was avoiding having to deal with just one more high-stress calamity. Coincidentally, I'd also just thought of something – something important. "They're energy beings."

"What?" She said, her eyes burning holes through my forehead.

"The Varapin! Of course, energy weapons won't have any effect on them. Hell, Shredder energy fire may be like catnip to them!" I looked back down to my TAC-Band, where a concerned Colonel Bonell looked back at me. "What you need are projectile weapons, Colonel . . . you need good old-fashioned bullets and gun powder. Real firepower!" I stood up and spun around, searching. There, sitting at his station, was the lone Pleidian on the bridge. Having my full attention boring down into him, the scrawny Ensign Plorinne looked as if he might just lose his bowels. "Ensign! I've got a job for you. Tap into MATHR and find out if we've got any close-range projectile-type weapons on board the *Hamilton*."

The Ensign tapped at his pad for several seconds before looking back up. "Armory #4, it's on Deck 13, Zone C. There's a cache of three-hundred AZZ Atchissons there."

"What the hell is that?"

"Shotguns, sir." He looked down and read from his board,

"Says they're fully automatic . . . have an expanded drum capacity of seventy-five twelve-gauge shells."

"Perfect! Now tell that Armory #4 on Deck 13 that you're coming and requisitioning all the Atchissons they have. You got that? Have them ready for you when you get there. You'll want them loaded up onto a hover-cart. You're to deliver them to Colonel Bonell. You can get a maintenance bot to help you."

Ensign Plorinne stared back at me, a deer caught in the headlights.

"Well, move it, Ensign!"

I turned back to face the Halo Display, "Sit Report on the *Enterprise*?"

Pristy was still standing two feet in front of me with a furrowed brow. I turned my attention to Tannock.

"She's on her last legs, Captain," he said.

"Tell . . ." I had to remember her name, "Tell XO Griffin to initiate Abandon Ship protocols . . . have shuttles start bringing her crew over to the *Hamilton* immediately."

Pristy gave me a wary, *you better not pull this shit again,* look before returning to her station. I let out a long breath. The Colonel had dropped off from my TAC Band. I inwardly prayed that his soon-to-be-delivered Atchisson shotguns would be of help to his Marines. The mere thought of those Varapin Warriors getting past them, past our Vac Gates, and moving into *Hamilton's* passageways, scared the living bejesus out of me.

Chapter 42

Galvin-Gail Star System

Sintchu – Refuge Depot

Hardy

Having spent a good ten minutes deploying Anal Surprise into the *Sintchu's* network, Hardy began searching for a viable escape route. It was then that he realized he'd been more than a little too optimistic with the Captain. His ability to escape the confines of this Refuge Depot may have been more wishful thinking than actual fact. He wondered if the blank-staring robot (who he had named "Gus), had once stood where he was standing now, also wondering if there was any plausible way out of this place.

The gentle hum of an electric motor pulled Hardy's attention into the darkness far up, overhead. Hardy's acute motion sensors picked up on the movement before his visual scans had made sense of the dark form descending.

Hardy said, "Have you come to gloat, or have you too, been relegated to this garbage heap?"

"We have little time, Hardy. Soon, my empty Ebom-Pod will prompt a security shutdown. A ship-wide search will come next. As expected, I, having been so easily abducted, have been deemed a disgrace . . . an embarrassment to the realm. My superiors are surprised, perplexed even, that I have not already committed Shiktong. Soon, I will be stripped of my previous honors and commendations. Everything I have become is now lost. I have already discussed the possibility that this could happen with your Captain. Hardy, my personal honor can be born anew . . . somewhere else."

"You mean like on the *Hamilton*?"

"Yes."

"And the Captain agreed to this?"

"He didn't disagree." "I wish to pursue what you call *safe haven*. Hardy, I have decided to take up arms against the Varapin and align my loyalty to Humanity."

"Look Haite, loyalty is more than a word to be thrown about; it's proven by one's actions. Your actions tell a different story, wouldn't you say?"

"I am here, now, ready to assist you. You will allow me to prove myself. That, or we will both be destroyed."

Hardy took another glance around the confined space, the broken robot on the deck. "Fine, but I don't see how you can —"

Before Hardy could finish his sentence, Haite had grasped Hardy's left mechanical arm, and together, they began to rise into the air.

"Escape to the Flight Bay will be difficult. You must do exactly what I say, move when I say move, stop when I say stop."

"Move and stop. . . got it."

"We are not far from my Cyclone. But the Flight Bay is heavily guarded. Do you have weaponry other than plasma cannons integrated into your construct?"

"Nope . . . what's wrong with plasma cannons?"

"Energy weapons are ineffective against my kind."

"How about we deal with that if the need arises?" Hardy said, looking down from where they were, now fifty feet in the air. He wondered if a ChronoBot could survive such a fall. He didn't want to find out. Up above, a shaft of light was piercing the darkness. "That a hatch or an open doorway?"

"Be silent, robot . . . someone approaches."

Hardy had picked up on the movement, as well. Two Varapin's carrying something within a passageway. Then, suddenly, there was a large metal object falling, heading directly for them. Instinctively, Hardy began to flail about, as if that could magically propel him out of the way.

Haite moved them both with the ease of a feather being blown by the wind. Two seconds later, the metal object crashed onto the deck below. *Clang!* Hardy made a cartoonish grimacing face, "Sorry, Gus . . ."

Haite elevated the two of them, bringing them even with

the Refuge Depot's open-shoot access port. It was a little tricky for Haite, as he pushed and shoved Hardy's large and unwieldy form out through the opening – but in time, he managed it.

Once on solid footing, Hardy noticed Haite was moving slower with less agility. *It's good to know these Varapin do get tired and have limits to their strength.*

"This way, robot. Do your best not to clomp so loudly."

"Yeah, walking on tip-toe isn't really a thing with Chrono-Bots, but I'll do my best."

As the two hurried down the passageway, Hardy felt the familiar pull coming from LuMan. His counterpart's primary life directive was to protect Galvin Quintos, at all costs. That was something LuMan's previous master, Coogong Lohp, had programmed into him, at just before being chopped up into little bits. But Hardy shared LuMan's directive, and he didn't like being this far away from the Captain, either.

They moved past several open hatchways where Hardy saw countless oblong enclosures, something Haite had called Ebom pods. He wondered how long Varapin spent lying around in those things. He tapped into the *Sintchu's* network and determined that the ghouls spend virtually all their free time in the pods. No hanging out in the break room, no playing cards with their mates, no dropping a duce reading a magazine – no, if they weren't on duty, they were crashing in an Ebom pod. While he was tapped into the network, he checked on his Anal Assault program. It was still *worming* its way around the aft part of the ship. Having almost been detected several times, the intelligent worm was moving more slowly, more carefully, now.

"This way!" Haite said, hanging back just inside of an open hatch to what was, obviously, the noisy Flight Bay.

Haite hovered there, peering out and looking indecisive. Hardy moved to the hatchway and, like Haite, saw there were too many busy Varapin crewmembers for them to go unnoticed.

"My Cyclone is over there," Haite said.

Hardy counted seven Cyclone Death fighters between them and Haite's craft. But the closest vessel was much larger and, frankly, beautiful. With its sleek aerodynamic lines, reflective obsidian skin, arched bird-like wings, and Varapin-characteristic downturned nose, he realized this ship was something special.

Haite said, "No . . . this is the personal craft of Conductor Sprin-Rop Kyber . . . no one would have the audacity to abscond with the fleet commander's –"

Having heard enough, Hardy was already out through the hatchway and making his way beneath Conductor Sprin-Rop Kyber's lux ride. He looked for an underbelly egress into the ship. Soon, Haite was at his side and pointing a bony black finger, "Pull that latch, there."

One minute later, they were situated within the forward nose of what Hardy learned was called the *Chintagh*. The large cockpit could almost be called a bridge, but not quite. Hardy plopped his large frame down into the pilot's seat and assessed the multitude of controls and readouts.

"I have not flown this craft before . . . I am unfamiliar with the controls," Haite said.

"It's like riding a bicycle . . ." but Hardy let his words trail off. He was reasonably sure that Varapin didn't ride bicycles. "I think I got this. Routing around within the *Sintchu's* network has provided me with a wealth of information. Like the Varapin equivalent of a User's Manual for this fine craft. Ready?"

"You are going to what . . . just lift off and fly this ship out of here?"

"Sure. Do you think anyone will fire on us? Not knowing, for certain if the fleet commander is actually on board or not?"

Once more, Haite raised a twiggy finger . . . "We have been discovered. Look."

Like a swarm of tightly clustered bats, they were approaching from farther back within the bay. Each of these warriors was armed. Hardy's mechanical hands didn't hesitate – he flipped several tiny switches and low-profile levers, and the *Chintagh's* aft drive came alive. Using the hand controls, Hardy brought the craft up off the flight deck. Unlike an Arrow, this craft didn't require noisy, intrusive lift thrusters. He spun the craft around on its axis and shoved the controls forward. Only now, as they were making a fast dash toward the bay opening, did red energy bolts streak by the glass canopy.

Haite glared at Hardy, "Seems they know that Conductor Sprin-Rop Kyber is not aboard this craft!"

With less than two hundred yards to the bay opening, Hardy was feeling somewhat more optimistic. That was until another larger vessel rose off the flight deck in front of them. "What the hell is that thing?"

"Guardian Defender, the equivalent to one of your smaller Gun Ships, although far more capable . . . more lethal."

Little lights on the *Chintagh's* dash flashed, an alarm blared. Haite said, "They have a weapon's lock on us. Best you halt and set her down."

But while Haite was crapping his proverbial pants, Hardy was back, searching the network. After several nanoseconds, rummaging through some three trillion files (most being the equivalent of audio files), Hardy opened a communications channel to the ever-approaching Guardian Defender.

"This is Conductor Sprin-Rop Kyber . . . you will move aside at once!"

Haite said, "That did sound like him . . ."

Now, having to bring the *Chintagh* down to a slow crawl, Hardy spent another moment familiarizing himself with the vessel's onboard weaponry. It was impressive, yet inadequate compared to the brute force of that Guardian Defender. Hardy stole a glance at the small warship – her big guns leveled at them.

Hardy used Kyber's voice once again. "You will move aside at once, Warrior Mongung . . . Warrior Halngto . . . move aside or face the sharp edge of a Crescent Blade!"

Hardy was just as concerned by the scores of hovering Varapin Warriors behind them as the Guardian Defender vessel in front.

"Interesting . . . it seems by using the pilot's respective names, there may be some confusion," Haite said.

But the enemy ship remained steadfast before them. Hardy concentrated on the open space just to the right of the vessel. There would be little wing clearance, maybe three inches on either side of the *Chintagh*. No. Hardy did not feel confident enough in his piloting abilities to chance it. So, he brought LuMan to the forefront, and he took the proverbial co-pilot's seat within. It was then that the real Conductor Sprin-Rop Kyber's voice was broadcast over the open Varapin comms channel.

"Destroy them! Attack! Fire your weapons now!"

But LuMan had already shoved the controls fully forward, all the while incrementally adjusting their rocketing, high-speed trajectory to the right of that Guardian Defender. A metallic sound rang out like the *clanging* of a bell as the starboard-side wing clipped the Guardian Defender's wingtip. Less than a second later, the *Chintagh* had pierced through the energy boundary and was hightailing it out into open space.

Chapter 43

Galvin-Gail Star System

USS Hamilton - Bridge

Captain Galvin Quintos

I watched the Halo-Display as our 2nd Fleet warships traded blows with the Varapin Fleet. We were down to seven from our original eleven warships having left Halibart Shipyards, having lost the *USS Capitol, USS Enterprise, USS Gun,* and the *USS Mighty.* The *Rage of the Gonjun Ract Fleet* had lost twelve, bringing their numbers down from sixty-two to fifty.

Once more, *Hamilton* shook and rumbled.

Pristy glanced back, "Looks like the enemy found a weak spot in our shields, Captain. Two Smart Missiles penetrated Decks 32 and 33 . . . damage report pending."

I hailed Colonel Bonell, "Talk to me, Colonel."

"Well, once we get one of those flying fuckers within our sites, those Atchisson shotguns turn them into dust clouds. It's a beautiful sight. But they move really fast, most of our bullets go astray. Oh, and Captain, we're running low on shells."

"Tell Ensign Plorinne, he'll get you more from the armory."

"Sorry, Captain, but it was the Ensign that told me that, so, once we're out, we're out. More and more of the hooded bastards are coming in. We'll hold them back for as long as we can. Can't we deploy our Arrows, Captain? Get them before they reach *Hamilton*?"

"*Sintchu's* hammering our flight bay, just as we're hammering theirs, neither side can take advantage of their fighters. But I'll come up with a solution, Colonel. Just don't allow for any Vac Gates to be breached. That has to be your priority."

"Doing our best, hope that will be good enough. Bonell out."

"Incoming vessel!" Pristy yelled. "It just emerged, more like *snuck out*, from the *Sintchu's* flight bay, sir. A miracle it wasn't taken out by our Phazon Pulsar fire. Huh . . . that's odd . . . looks like *Sintchu's* firing on her own vessel."

"A Cyclone Death fighter?" I asked.

"No . . . something larger than that. Formidable shielding on that vessel," Tannock said.

Chen said, "It's Hardy, Captain!"

Pristy reached across her console to the board in front of Tannock, "We need to stop firing into that area of space!"

Tannock said, "Hey, I'm on Weapons, little missy!"

"That's Hardy?" I asked, ignoring their immature turf war.

Chen said, "They're requesting clearance to enter the bay . . . but the bay's still being clobbered by enemy fire."

Apparently, I didn't answer soon enough – both Pristy and Tannock turned back to me with trepidation.

"I'm fine, I'm fine," I said. "Just thinking . . ."

I noticed Derrota and Mattis were both looking at me with similar, concerned expressions. I said, "Alistair, how large are those breaches, where the Varapin Warriors are coming in?"

The Chief of Security clearly thought the question was ridiculous. "My guess . . . twenty to thirty feet in diameter on Decks 5 and 6 . . . the breach on Deck 7, bigger, maybe twice that size. It opened up one of our larger cargo holds."

I said, "Chen . . . tell Hardy to pilot that, whatever-it-is he's flying, into that Deck 7 breach . . . land inside that hold."

"But it's wide open to space, sir," Pristy said.

"Yeah, and Hardy's a robot, he'll be fine."

"It's also crawling with Varapin Warriors."

"Again, Hardy's a weaponized top-of-the-line ChronoBot . . . remember, he's built for battle. I know you care about him, but right now, I'm the one sitting at Captain's Mount, XO."

"Aye, sir. Sorry, sir," she added.

Derrota looked to Chen for confirmation, before saying, "Did you notice that Hardy said, *we,* not *I.* As in the plural *we.*"

I thought about that. "Maybe he meant he and LuMan. I don't know."

Derrota tapped at his tablet. "No. MATHR confirms that

it's most definitely two distinct pilots on board that vessel." He looked up, "It's Hardy and one Varapin life form."

"Has to be Haite-Caheil," I said. "He spoke to me while in custody . . . the pilot requested asylum. I didn't believe him, at least, not at the time. Now, not so sure."

"A Varapin wants to join our side?" Derrota said with disbelief. "No way can we allow that alien killer back onto this ship."

"We have bigger fish to fry right now, Stephan," I said, checking my vibrating TAC-Band and seeing Doc Viv's face. "What's up, Doc?"

She sounded stressed, "HealthBay beds are filling up fast, Quintos. Same goes for the Morgue, unfortunately. So, I'm asking you for help."

"Okay, what can I do to assist?"

"I need personnel. My staff is getting overwhelmed. Anyone that has even a smidgen of medical training would help."

"I'll put out the call, but I gotta go." I cut the connection and pointed to Derrota. "Find anyone and everyone who has medical experience and send them to HealthBay."

Tannock said, "We should have a live video feed from that hold on Deck 7, in a second."

"Multiple reports coming in from the fleet . . . Varapin ships are maneuvering in close to our warships, we're talking kissing-distance close," Pristy said. "Oh, boy . . . they're deploying more of their Warriors. And Captain JJ says a breach to the *Louisiana's* outer hull is eminent. Warriors are using some kind of particle-beam torch."

A new feed came alive just in time to see a sleek-looking Varapin spacecraft careening into that *Hamilton's* breached Deck 7 hold. It slammed down hard onto the deck and began sliding sideways as bright yellow sparks sprayed outward and showered down within the compartment. That few moments of illumination depicted a horrific scene – hundreds of Varapin Warriors clustered together, all just waiting to infiltrate the rest of the ship. I knew that, soon, this same scenario would be duplicated throughout the 2nd Fleet. I said, "Just because their weapons haven't been able to penetrate our shields . . . it won't stop them from attacking us from within. Damn it! We need to do something fast."

Movement. I watched as Hardy immerged from the Varapin ship and immediately was engulfed in a sea of black-cloaked beings. But I couldn't worry about Hardy right now. *Think!* Then it came to me. "We need to change the dynamics of this space battle. We need our Arrow Fighters out there taking out those Varapin Warriors."

His voice dripping with condescension, Tannock said, "Well it's just not possible. Not with the *Sintchu* targeting our flight bay – "

I ignored him, "XO Pristy, please tell me our Broadsides didn't get trashed during *Hamilton's* most recent renovations."

"Well, I know they're still physically present, but . . ." She had to reach across in front of Tannock, who was manning weapons at the moment. He made an exasperated expression as she tapped away for several more moments. She looked back at me with a sly grin. "All are operational, sir. Associated magazines are fully stocked with fresh bowlers."

That's all I needed to hear. "Come about, Helm! Bring us abreast of the *Sintchu*. Tannock, since you have the weapons board, I want those portside Broadsides ready for business within thirty seconds."

"Sir . . . this does not seem to be an appropriate time to be taking these kinds of risks –"

"XO Tannock, did you think I was asking permission?"

"No, sir. Bowlers are being loaded via their ramp-injectors now."

I called down to Flight Bay.

"Go for Chief Mintz!" Came the Chief's gruff voice.

"Arrows ready?"

"They've been ready!"

"Good, on my command. Just hang tight."

Tannock said, "Portside Broadsides . . . we're locked and loaded, sir."

Pristy said, "Uh-oh . . . *Sintchu's* propulsion system is coming alive; she knows something's up with us."

"We go where she goes, stay with her, XO!" I said. "XO Tannock, fire all portside Broadsides! Fire now!"

While some of us knew what to expect, not everyone else on the bridge could have possibly anticipated what was to come. It was as if *Hamilton* was in a child's hands – a small toy being viciously shaken about. The dreadnought's big cannons roared to life: *Boom! Boom! Boom! Boom! Boom! Boom!* Everyone was grabbing for something to hold on to.

"XO Tannock, target the *Sintchu's* weapon turrets . . . and target her Flight Bay!" I ordered.

"Trying. With those big guns . . . it's more like point-and-shoot and hope you hit something."

"Sintchu's attempting to flee . . ." Pristy said, her voice raising an octave or two.

"Helm, stay with her." I yelled into my TAC-Band, "Okay, Frank . . . Deploy the Arrows . . . deploy the Arrows!"

I watched as various locations along the *Sintchu's* hull were now erupting into fantastic fireballs."

"Looks like the enemy shields can't stand up to our bowlers," Pristy said.

Understandable. These Bowlers were massive. And like immense bowling balls, each had strategically placed circular finger-like holes all around their circumference. These holes were the dispersal channels for white-hot magnesium scatter frags – which effectively weakened enemy hull-armor plating a nanosecond just prior to impact. Who says just because something's old that it's not still remarkably effective? Sure, I knew this battle tactic would not be the end of the alien dread-nought, not by any means. But we'd counterpunched; the crew and commander of that vessel would know the *USS Hamilton* was not an adversary to be taken lightly.

While the *Sintchu* was being peppered with cannon fire, I stole a glance at the feed showing Deck 7's hold. I had to fight to keep feelings of dread from my mind. Then, I saw movement at the belly of the alien craft. Hardy had re-emerged from a hatchway, and he was holding something big on one of his mechanical arms. And there was a Varapin Warrior at his side.

"That's Haite-Caheil," Derrota said.

"How can you tell?

"He's the only one wearing a band, like a bandanna, wrapped around the top of his head. Maybe Hardy told him to put it on . . . maybe to differentiate himself from the others."

Pristy said, "Look! That's a rail cannon Hardy's lugging around. It has to be one torn out of the alien ship. I can't believe he did that!"

I stared in awe of the ChronoBot. "So, what . . . Haite's holding the munitions canister for him?" I asked – not expecting an answer.

The railgun burst to life, flames spewing from the weapon's muzzle. A blur of projectile rounds shot forth as Hardy swept the cruel weapon from side to side. Haite, standing next to him, fed out a continuous belt of rail ammunitions. The two made for a strange, but effective, duo. All around them, Varapin Warriors were bursting into black clouds of dust. I only hoped Colonel Bonell and his Marines had found adequate cover in time.

"Captain!" Chen was looking at me – his face frozen in terror.

"What is it? Speak, man!"

"It's the *Brave,* sir. Those Varapin Warriors . . . they've breached her outer hull. They're now streaming into the ship from multiple locations. Captain Styles says he's sealed off the bridge but feels it's only a matter of time before they'll be taken, too. He says, one after another, those flying – hovering – aliens are sucking the life force out of each of his crew. Bodies are filling the passageways. He has no doubt he and the rest of his bridge crew will be subjected to the same fate. And soon. He's requesting our immediate action. He's asking that we destroy the *Brave*. To do it now."

"Tell him we'll try to get over there as soon as possible. Tell him to hold on just a little – "

Chen was already shaking his head, "They're just seconds away from breaching the bridge. Captain Styles says he can see sparks coming in from their torches."

Pristy put up a feed that showed the *USS Brave* – her hull a blackened mass of moving cloaked Varapin, like countless ants skittering around a piece of discarded candy. I felt for the Brave's crew – having earlier survived one brutal space attack, now having to endure this. The little corvette was lost, I knew that. Glancing at the faces around me, my Bridge crew knew it, too.

I said, "Chen, open the channel from Captain Styles."

Immediately, chaotic, desperate sounds were being broadcast into the *Hamilton's* Bridge. "Captain Styles . . . this is Captain Quintos . . . are you absolutely sure about this?"

"Yes, Captain . . . hurry. We do not want the life sucked out of us like . . . the others on board. For the love of God, do it now!"

I caught Pristy's eye. I nodded at her.

"Absolutely not," Tannock said, reading our not-so-subtle

signals. "We cannot, we will not fire upon our own vessel. Especially one with living crewmembers!"

"XO Tannock, you have the weapons board. I'm ordering you to destroy the *USS Brave*. I won't allow any further dishonor to come to that ship and her crew. Do it . . . take her out, or I'll command XO Pristy to do it for you."

Red-faced, daggers shooting from his eyes, Tannock said, "No. We don't kill our own people. There's still a chance. No, Captain. Regulations emphatically say –"

"Yeah, well . . . screw regulations. XO Pristy, take out the Brave. Smart Missiles . . . full barrage. Five nukes should do it. Do it now."

"Aye, sir. She reached across in front of Tannock once more. "Missiles away, Captain."

Abruptly, Tannock pushed away from his station and stood. He glowered down at me. "Fleet Command will hear about this atrocity in my report."

Here we go again. I should never have allowed Tannock back on my bridge. "That's fine. You're relieved of duty, XO Tannock. You're to remain in your quarters for the duration of this mission."

He left the bridge without another word. I watched as five Smart Missiles rocketed forth toward the honorable warship, *USS Brave*. I motioned for Chen to cut the audio coming from the doomed vessel's bridge. We watched in collective sadness as the little Corvette was eviscerated in a series of blindingly-bright nuclear blasts.

I said, "Please . . . everyone stand."

In unison, the Bridge crew stood.

Saluting, I said, "Crew of the *Brave*, you honor the US Space-Navy and all humanity with your sacrifice. Heroes, all . . . well done and thank you. Rest now, you've done your part . . . we'll take it from here."

Chapter 44

Crewman Grimes, seated at the Helm, was doing a good job keeping in relatively close to the *Sintchu*, and Pristy was doing equally well, pounding the alien dreadnought with *Hamilton's* Broadsides. But what held my attention at the moment were the multiple squadrons of bright red Arrow Fighters firing their rail spike munitions, not toward the enemy, but toward our own 2nd Fleet assets during synchronized fly-bys as shields were temporarily lowered. It took me a second to understand. Sure, our ships were sustaining minor hull damage, but that was a price every ship captain was willing to pay. *How else were they to kill the invading Varapin Warriors?*

Derrota said, "According to MATHR, tens of thousands of Varapin Warriors have already been killed. And they are no longer being dispatched from enemy fleet vessels."

It had been nine hours since the destruction of the *USS Brave*. I did not regret my actions to have her destroyed, not for a second. But I knew, later, if we survived that long, there'd be repercussions. I'd be held accountable. *So be it.*

Pristy, her voice sounding tired, said, "Captain, enemies now concentrating their fire on our Arrows . . . we've lost fourteen in the last few minutes. Varapin are picking our fighters off. Arrows are making little-to-no impact since they've turned their attention to the enemy warships."

"Call down to Chief Mintz. Have them recalled; they've done their part."

Even with the constant shaking and rumbling from the still-firing Broadsides, I couldn't help noticing Hardy's distinct heavy footfalls entering the Bridge. Sure, I knew he'd survived the ordeal within the hold on Deck 7; he had pretty much single-handedly cleared that compartment and the other breached decks of Varapin assault teams. But still, it did my heart good having the big idiot back here on the Bridge with me. I shouldn't have been surprised, seeing his latest face display. He'd chosen to look like the ghoulish Varapin, complete with extended, bone-white jaws.

"That's disgusting, not to mention in bad taste, Hardy," Pristy scolded.

"Where's Haite?" I asked.

"Turned him over to Chief of Security Mattis. So, to answer your question . . . I imagine he's back in his cell. I promised Haite I'd put in a good word to you. He'd like to become part of the crew, you know."

"That's never going to happen. Let's not forget he's killed eight crewmembers . . ."

Hardy now displayed a digitized, photo-quality face I'd never seen before. Somewhat chubby, certainly not handsome, but friendly-looking. I instinctively knew I was looking at the real John Hardy, perhaps as he would have looked when he was alive some five decades earlier. I felt that saying something, anything, would be a mistake – so I said nothing.

"How long since any of you slept?" Hardy asked, looking at each of us individually.

"I'm at twenty-seven hours," Grimes said.

"Twenty-eight for me," Pristy said.

Chen said, "About that for me, too."

I said, "No one expected this space battle to go on for this long. At this point, we're just trading blows, but even with the damage we're inflicting on the *Sintchu* and a few others . . . the 2nd Fleet cannot withstand seven-to-one odds much longer. Collectively, our shields are being hammered . . . drained. Our mission was to delay the Varapin Fleet. I'd hoped to do more than just that."

Glancing up to the ChronoBot, I saw his face display was showing a little kitten. No, not a kitten. "You're saying I'm a pussy?"

"Who . . . Me? I didn't say anything. But I didn't think you were one to be giving up. Maybe you need a little nappy-nap . . . or some warm milk and a cuddle."

"Screw you," I said under my breath, wondering if he was right. Had I given up?

"Captain! *USS Gallaher's* shields just went down," Pristy exclaimed.

"Where is she?" I said. Remembering the Jericho-Class Destroyer – Captain Witherspoon's command.

"Behind the ninth exoplanet in this system . . . has been fending off seven warships. Oh God, she just blew apart."

The Halo-Display now showed the *Gallaher*. The destroyer had broken apart into three sections. Nearby, seven Varapin warships continued to fire their powerful energy weapons. One after another, all three *Gallaher* segments exploded; clearly, there would be no survivors.

Derrota said, "The Hamilton's shields are holding at thirty-two percent . . . but based on the depletion ratios of our other US Space-Navy vessels, the 2nd Fleet will be completely destroyed within the hour."

"Do we have enough power reserves to jump away?"

Derrota tapped at his template, looking grim. Yes, for *Hamilton*, but not for bringing along the *Billing, Kennedy, Starlight*, and *Louisiana*. The Broadsides are eating up a lot of power reserves."

"So, we could save ourselves, but at the cost of losing the remainder of the fleet."

"*Hamilton* has a crew of many thousands . . . that's a lot of lives that *can* be saved."

"What's the damage to the *Sintchu?* Surely she has to be feeling the pain of those bowler strikes."

"Indeed," Derrota said, with gratification. "MATHR estimated her crew of thirteen thousand has been reduced to eight thousand. One-third of her big energy weapons have been taken out, and her flight bay is in shambles. But her shields are holding at fifty-eight percent." Derrota looked at me with resignation, "She'll outlast us, Galvin. I'm sorry."

I knew we were losing this battle, and if we didn't come up with something fast, we would all die out here while fucking nowhere.

"Um, Captain?"

I felt only dread, hearing Crewman Chen's voice once more. *Was it another plea for help we couldn't possibly give? Was it the last words of another desperate captain?*

"What is it, Crewman?"

Eyes wide, and with his hand hard-pressed into one ear, he said "Sir! It's . . . it's. . . Captain Ryder!"

"Look. On the display, Captain!" Pristy said.

I wasn't sure what I was looking at. It didn't make sense. What I could determine was that it was a whole lot of warships. "What fleet is that?" I said.

"That's not a fleet, sir . . . that's two fleets. On rapid approach, we have both a Clouse Veng Fleet and the Ramdei Fleet."

I now recognized the two distinct warship designs. "There must be hundreds of warships –"

"Two hundred-and-twenty-seven, to be exact," Derrota said.

The first person I noticed on the Halo-Display was none other than Captain Wallace Ryder. He was standing amongst a disheveled band of cocky-looking Marines of which I was thrilled to see. What I was having a hard time figuring out was the strange-looking plants that were, *seemingly*, jumping –dare

I say, playing – all around them. Another familiar being came into view, none other than the big tumbleweed alien himself, Prime Centurion Goben.

Ryder said, "Captain, I've had to make some pretty hefty promises here that Fleet Command may not be too thrilled with . . . things like advanced technology swaps and war-pact alliances, just to name a few. But they're here, Captain. And it looks like just in the nick of time. Would have been here earlier . . . but installing those spare Spring Drives . . . configuring wormhole manufacturing jump tech into alien drive configurations, well, let's just say it was no walk in the park."

Prime Centurion Goben said, "When it came down to it, Captain Quintos, the ones you call *Varapin*, they are not new to our species. But their imminent advancement toward our local space, that cannot be tolerated. We, the Clouse Veng along with the Ramdei, aligned with the Humans . . . together, we will crush this vile petulance here and now."

Chapter 45

Being the commander of what few ships remained of the US Space-Navy's 2nd Fleet, and the commanding officer most familiar with the battle situation, both the Clouse Veng and Ramdei assets were now taking direction from me. By sheer numbers alone, one would have thought the Varapin Fleet would be in trouble – would be losing. But that was not the case. Sure, we'd given our new partners the capability to jump vast distances in the blink of an eye. Still, their inferior weaponry, and more importantly, their lack of cloaking capability and less-effective shielding, were making their warships easy targets for the far-more advanced Varapin.

When it came down to it, this was a simple mathematical equation. Plusses and minuses. Thus far, the only good news was that our 2nd Fleet vessels were no longer taking the brunt of the attack.

Pristy slammed a fist down onto her board. "This is so frustrating! Captain, it's the frickin' *Sintchu*. She's making the big difference here . . . she keeps coming to the aid of her fleet's warships, and here we are following along like a puppy behind her, trying to get her attention with our Broadsides. But again, and again, the *Sintchu's* big guns are taking out any Clouse Veng and Ramdei warships she comes close to."

I'd been more than aware of the same thing, and it was, indeed, frustrating. Getting to my feet, I said, "Keep at it, XO . . . I may have an idea brewing." Heading to the CIC, Pristy yelled after me, "We're down to our last Bowlers, sir . . . ten minutes, maybe fifteen, and that's it."

I already knew that, as well.

I found Derrota seated at his station. *Hamilton's* Combat Information Center was the ship's technological hub, where MATHR was situated, where battle simulations were calculated, smart missiles were programmed, and where tactical best practices were derived. Derrota and four of his direct reports were huddled around a display. I found a seat and joined the group. "Talk to me."

One of the younger CIC guys, Mallory, with a bad case of acne, spoke up first., "The Varapin are just biding their time. Time is on their side and they know it. It's that fucking big bitch of a ship!"

Derrota shot his subordinate a cold glance for swearing in front of the captain, while I tried not to smile.

"We've played out thirty-seven different battle scenarios," Derrota said. "As long as the *Sintchu* remains here in this planetary system, we cannot defeat this enemy. I'm sorry, it is as simple as that."

"So, we get that bitch of a ship out of here," I said.

Mallory, who was unconsciously attacking a whitehead on his chin, said, "There is no way her Captain would leave this system. Why would he, or she, do that?"

I leaned back in my chair and chewed on that. Then I smiled.

"What is it, Galvin?" Derrota said. "It's not like we have any time to spare. If you have an idea, spit it out."

I looked out through the opening into the Bridge. I saw Hardy had taken up his usual on-stand-by location at the back of the Bridge. The ChronoBot's hearing was beyond amazing, and consequently, I knew he had been listening in on our conversation. I said, "Hardy . . . do me a favor, go get the Varapin pilot, Haite-Caheil, and bring him to the CIC. Tell Chief Mattis I'll take full responsibility for him being out of his cell."

"One Varapin traitor coming up, Cap."

Minutes later, Hardy, with a shackled Haite-Caheil in tow, arrived within the CIC. Derrota and his four underlings looked up, startled at the sight of the hideous Varapin. Mallory, a bloody spot on his chin where he'd won the battle with the whitehead, looked as if he might pee his pants.

Haite said, "I was wondering when you would be calling for my assistance."

"Really?" I asked.

Hardy jerked the alien's shackles, "Try not to be annoying."

"On the contrary," I said. "I want you to be as annoying as you possibly can be."

A question mark appeared on Hardy's face display.

I said, "Haite, you made it clear you want to stay here on *Hamilton*. Perhaps find a position amongst the crew. I can tell you right now, officially, that can never happen."

The alien picked up on the operative word, *officially*. "And unofficially?"

"That depends on what happens next. What you're capable of doing."

"Go on, Captain."

"First, tell me you can get me a direct communique into the Sintchu's commander."

"That would be Conductor Sprin-Rop Kyber."

"And?"

"And yes. I can provide you a direct interface with the fleet commander."

"It's not me who will be speaking to this Kyber fellow, it's you, Haite."

His blank stare prompted me to go on. "Tell me. Do you know what it means to taunt someone?"

"Of course."

"Good. You will be contacting this Conductor . . ."

"Conductor Sprin-Rop Kyber," Haite repeated.

"And you will taunt him. You will drive him into enough of a frenzy that he will go to virtually any lengths to destroy you. To destroy the *Hamilton*."

"And the purpose of all this senselessness?"

"Simple. Soon, *Hamilton* will be jumping away. We'll be making it easy enough for the *Sintchu* to follow. We'll do this by leaving just enough breadcrumbs for your brethren to pick up on."

"Breadcrumbs? . . . Ah, I understand the reference. Still, one-on-one, no matter where you end up, the two vessels are not evenly matched. You will be destroyed. No disrespect intended, Captain."

"None taken. Now, these breadcrumbs will provide our exact jump coordinates – where *Hamilton* will be jumping away to. We'll have to make it seem like we've made a terrible, cataclysmic mistake by leaving these coordinates exposed."

"The Conductor is highly-intelligent and will not be easily fooled."

I noticed Pristy standing within the opening between the CIC and the Bridge. "Captain, Bowlers have all been depleted. I'm switching over to Rail Cannons, but – "

"I know, we'll no longer have the upper hand. Instruct the Helm to take us away from the *Sintchu*. Get her following us for a change. In any event, we won't be here long."

She turned away, looking perplexed.

I looked about the CIC for just the right setting. On one bulkhead was a Halo-Display, a smaller version of the one at the front of the Bridge. "There. Stephan, can you display a running countdown timer? It'll have to correspond to the actual manufacturing of a jump wormhole . . . a wormhole we're going to be jumping through in a few minutes."

"Of course. But Galvin, you want to give the enemy our jump coordinates? Why?"

"The coordinates you're going to provide on that display

will not be the exact same coordinates as our *actual* jump coordinates. Close, but different." I looked at the group around me and saw total bewilderment. *Good!*

I explained to Derrota and his team exactly what I had in mind. Could it be done? We'd be jumping far farther than any US-Space Navy vessel had ever jumped before. Only time would tell. Meanwhile, I had Haite-Caheil positioned in just the right location within the CIC; far enough in the background was the countdown timer, clicking off the seconds, with jump coordinates there, as well. But it was nearly impossible to read, out of focus and at an extreme angle. Unless the Varapin used some of their advanced technology, it would be impossible to decipher. Breadcrumbs, nearly impossible to find.

I positioned the ChronoBot in front of Haite, Hardy would be the visual and audio communications relay back to the *Sintchu*. The stage was set. *Hamilton's* actual jump coordinates were loaded into the Spring Drives. I'd brought the Ramdei and Clouse Veng fleet commanders up to speed on my scheme, which had been deemed reckless and hair-brained, with little to no chance of success. But as their warships were being annihilated at an alarming rate, the plan was soon embraced.

I stood before Haite, close enough to pick up on his dank, musky smell. I'd not gotten used to his ugliness. "You want to become a part of this crew. Start a new life? This is your one opportunity to increase the odds of that happening."

"I understand, Captain."

Hamilton abruptly shook, causing me and everyone else around me to stagger about.

Derrota said, "*Sintchu's* now coming at us with all she has. Looking to finish us off and get this battle done with. Shields are down to fifteen percent. Galvin . . . We have only minutes, if that."

I said, Hardy, "Go ahead, open the channel to Conductor Sprin-Rop Kyber."

The voice that answered was raspy and menacing – like something heavy scraping across a metal surface. Hardy's face display showed a cartoonish image of an old-fashioned movie camera. He said, "And, Action!"

Chapter 46

Galvin-Gail Star System

Varapin Empire Warship, **Sintchu – *Bridge***

Conductor Sprin-Rop Kyber

H is beautiful, impregnable *Sintchu* warship. *How had this happened?* Taking out this insignificant fleet was supposed to be effortless - an inconsequential diversion before moving on to Earth. And now, he could hardly look at the view hologram where the Sintchu in her entirety was being displayed. The wreckage caused by the *Hamilton's* big projectile-spewing cannons had been devastating.

Seething anger filled Conductor Sprin-Rop Kyber as he hover-paced back and forth within the expansive bridge. His inner rage continued to build, escalating by the minute. And like the infamous Mount Quantra-Thall, the monumental volcano back on Devastin, an eruption of rage – one of epic proportions – was imminent. So, when the off-ship hail interrupted Kyber's already-tumultuous musings, seeing Haite-Caheil's traitorous face almost put the Conductor over the edge.

Haite made the equivalent of a taunting laugh. "How pathetic you are. You do know you have already lost, yes? Or has your self-importance precluded your ego from facing the grim reality of the situation?"

"How dare you speak to me in such a way. I will have you –"

"Shut up. Shut up, and listen to me, Kyber. I no longer take orders from you. I will do as I choose. And I choose to no longer serve such an incompetent Conductor as yourself. Are you so obtuse that you have not noticed your own officers laughing at you behind your back? That the entire *Sintchu's* crew is equally disgusted by your ineptitude? Did you know they have planned for a mutiny?"

Conductor Sprin-Rop Kyber roared, no longer able to restrain his anger. "How you will suffer . . . you will feel unimaginable pain as I personally wield the Shriek Belt . . . ten thousand thorns ripping and tearing at your anatomy!" But seeing Haite's apparent calm demeanor only infuriated the Conductor that much more. "Where are you . . . you traitorous coward!"

"I am close. I am right here . . . home now, amongst my new friends. I am on the *USS Hamilton*. The same vessel that has turned the *Sintchu* into a heap of bent and mangled metal. This must be such an embarrassment for you. But I must leave you now. I am scheduled to relay all our Varapin technological secrets over to these amiable Humans."

Kyber had to fight to keep his voice steady, "You have disgraced yourself and disgraced the Varapin Realm. Soon, the Rage of the Gonjun Ract Fleet will have destroyed every ship within this star system. Soon, the *USS Hamilton* will also be destroyed. Her shields are failing. Her munitions are depleted." Kyber was reasonably sure that it was all true, and now he produced a mocking smile of his own.

"Oh, how adorable . . . you think you've won." Haite let out a patronizing chuckle. "We care not about any of the vessels remaining behind. Collateral damage. No. When the *Hamilton* leaves this system, it leaves as the victor of this battle. So, take my advice, Kyber, turn back and head home for Devastin. The Rage of the Gonjun Ract has been battered and ruined, a crippled shadow of what that fleet once was. Certainly, not in any condition to continue . . . and certainly, no match for the far superior Human race."

Conductor Sprin-Rop Kyber and the decorated pilot, Haite-Caheil, glared at one another for several long moments. "Farewell, Kyber . . . I'm being told our manufactured jump wormhole awaits us."

Kyber, beyond angry and close to erupting, was at that place where all reason and all good judgment no longer exist. His grotesque jaws opened, about to issue the order to bring the full might of his still fully-operational dreadnought to bear upon the *Hamilton*, when he saw the formation of brightly-colored prismatic spacial distortions. Next appeared the formation of a yawning wormhole mouth.

"Do something!" Kyber yelled. "Stop the progression of that jump wormhole . . . Disrupt that wormhole!"

No less than two hundred of the *Sintchu's* most powerful Dual Vortex Laser Beam weapons came alive – bright red criss-crossing beams of energy culminating into one small area of space. But the command had come too late. Both the jump wormhole and the *USS Hamilton* were now gone.

"Tell me our sensors have tracked that wormhole's end-point!" Kyber said, glaring down at the tactical station's nervous attendant.

"My apologies, Conductor. But the Humans implemented anamorphic distortion waves . . . their end-point coordinates are impossible to track."

"You imbeciles! There must be a means to locate that ship . . . there must be!" Kyber looked to his Communications Attendant. "Play back the communique! From the beginning!"

The holographic display replayed the communique, and soon Kyber was being drawn in, feeling the fury building within.

"There, Conductor Kyber," his second-in-command, Regent Malimand, said pointing. "There is something just out of view there on their display."

Kyber waved away the suggestion, "I see nothing there . . . you waste my time —" But he stopped short and was now reex-amining what his second was still pointing to. Kyber moved closer to the display. "Is that some kind of timer . . . perhaps a countdown timer?"

"I believe so," Malimand said. "And there are numbers there below it . . . perhaps spacial coordinates . . . too difficult to determine for sure."

"I want that image deciphered! I want those coordinates, and I want them now!"

Chapter 47

USS Hamilton, *Bridge*

Captain Galvin Quintos

I was already regretting my decision. *What the hell was I thinking?* Now, within the next instant, we could be jumping into our collective demise.

The prospect of jumping to anywhere near the same vicinity of our earlier 3rd drop location was crazy – was beyond ludicrous. This was the same drop location where we had lost the *USS Capitol* – multi-thousands of crew – and easily could have lost the entire 2nd Fleet. Except for perhaps jumping directly into a star, or maybe a black hole, I knew this was right up there as one of the most suicidal stunts I would ever attempt.

The plan was simple, bait the thus far impossible-to-defeat *Sintchu's* commander into chasing us here. Although I'd queried MATHR, queried Hardy, and queried my Science Officer, Derrota, I found there was no definitive way to knowing if that Miasma Burn river of obliteration – with its spinning house-sized balls of torrid plasma – would still be exactly where we had left it. Hey, conditions change. We had zero previous examples of Miasma Burn Rivers to make any comparison to.

The breadcrumb coordinates we'd discreetly provided for the *Sintchu's* Conductor to follow were the precise coordinates we had used the first time we arrived into this *Void of Nothingness* area of space – and smack dap into the Miasma Burn river. That is, if it hadn't moved. On the other hand, *Hamilton* was now jumping, hopefully, to coordinates nearby, and within a distance to visually witness the *Sintchu's* demise. But we could just as easily be cooked ourselves; in which case, Conductor Sprin-Rop Kyber would have the unique pleasure of watching the *Hamilton* being obliterated. These were the thoughts racing through my mind just before we arrived at our drop location.

"Jump successful, Captain," Helmsman Grimes said with relief in his voice.

Up on the Halo-Display, off in a not-too-distant section of space, was a most beautiful and welcome sight. There, brilliant and sparkling, was that same flowing river of blazing-hot plasma. It almost looked serene – like a golden roadway meandering back and forth upon the contrasting blackness of deep space.

Derrota, Mattis, and Hardy were at my side. And there was one more; I'd permitted Haite-Caheil to remain on the Bridge. One way or another, he would have been partially responsible for what happened next.

Derrota queried his tablet. "The spacial anomaly . . . has not moved. We're approximately three-hundred-and-twenty light-minutes from the Miasma Burn. So, if all goes as planned, the Coordinates we provided should put the *Sintchu* right into the middle of it."

I wanted to say that things rarely, if ever, go as planned, but held my tongue. So, we waited in silence. Five minutes. Ten minutes. Fifteen minutes.

Word had spread of my ridiculous plan, and soon the Bridge was getting crowded by an assortment of Lookie Lou's: Talco Wentworth and the four Thine Scientists, each wearing their oversized environ suits. Chief of Propulsion and Engineering Craig Porter, XO Tannock, who was supposed to be confined to quarters, along with Chaplain Trent, and finally, Doc Viv, who was wearing her baggy scrubs and still managed to, somehow, look sexy in them. *Fine. The more the merrier*, this being such a pivotal moment for all of us. And the truth was, I didn't mind the company. Win or lose, we'd be sharing this outcome.

At thirty minutes into our wait, XO Pristy broke the silence. Turning in her seat, she looked up at the menacing-looking alien, "Maybe you've overestimated the capabilities of your commander –"

It was at that precise moment that the Varapin *Sintchu*, jumped into view.

I stood – the rest of my Bridge crew stood. Still, no one spoke. There she was, the great and powerful dreadnought, *Sintchu*, and she had arrived using the exact coordinates we'd provided. Now, just as the *USS Capitol* had been days earlier, the alien warship was caught within that flaring cacophony of erupting plasma. Cheers erupted from the onlookers. Wentworth awkwardly attempted a high-five with Coogong Sohp. Now seemingly angered by this latest abrupt disruption, the golden river looked to be attacking the warship – devouring the colossal vessel. Within seconds, she was broken in half – and those sections broke again into even smaller sections. Soon there was nothing left of the alien vessel. The cheers and laughter continued around me. Somehow, we had done it. My eyes found Haite-Caheil; he had silently drifted toward the back of the Bridge. He had helped make this happen but had been a traitor to his own kind in doing so. I wondered what emotions he was feeling – did the Varapin even possess emotions as humans do? If his taunting of Kyber and the Conductors rising fury was any indication, they certainly do. At the moment, I wasn't sure what to do with our alien prisoner. One thing was for certain, I would never, ever, trust him.

"Hey, not bad Quintos . . ." Doc Viv said, pulling a rubber band from her ponytail and letting her hair fall free. "So, we've won? It's over?"

"Depends. Let's find out how the rest of the 2nd fleet is faring."

Hand to one ear and intently listening, Chen glanced up as we approached. He said, Captain, established a micro-wormhole laser transmission . . . I've just made the connection . . . Captain JJ wishes to speak with you."

"Go ahead and put her up on the Halo-Display."

Captain J. Johns suddenly appeared on the display – her shock of red hair seemed even brighter than usual. There was a black smudge of grime on her left cheek.

"Talk to me, Captain JJ . . . how goes your battle?"

"No, you first," she said, eyes pleading.

"The *Sintchu's* been destroyed. There's nothing left of her."

I hadn't realized that she, too, had been speaking to me in front of a full bridge. Cheers erupted behind her at the news of the *Sintchu's* demise. Tears welled up in her eyes, and she needed a moment to let the lump in her throat pass. "That is indeed good news, Captain. Well done, sir . . . well done. And I too have good news for you . . . the US Space-Navy 2nd Fleet, along with our Ramdei and Clouse Veng allies, have defeated what remained of the Varapin fleet. Without the assistance of the *Sintchu*, our sheer numbers of warships – not to mention your Arrow Fighters –, gave this battle over to the good guys."

"Excellent, Captain," I said. I'd almost forgotten about *Hamilton's* Arrow Fighter squadrons – all left behind when we'd jumped from the system. "Can you tell me if Captain Ryder –"

"Ryder's fine, Captain. In fact, he and a band of Marines are here on the *Louisiana*."

"Good to know. You might want to hide your stash of liquor from that bunch," I suggested.

"What's the plan, Captain Quintos . . . you're not heading back to this system, are you?"

"No. We won't be going anywhere for several days. That

last jump we made. . . it far exceeded normal jump distance parameters. I suspect we'll be here, making Spring Drive repairs for several days. Best you head toward Earth, we'll coordinate a location where we can meet up."

"Any word from the Admiral? How Earth is faring the attack from the Grish?" She asked.

"That's my next call. I'll keep you informed," I said.

Chen was already making contact with Earth as we ended our transmission. It took a minute before Chen said, "I have the Admiral, Captain. Strange . . . at first, he didn't believe it was me, us, from *Hamilton*!"

That was strangely gratifying, "Put him on the Halo-Display."

I wasn't sure what I'd expected, but seeing Admiral Block, hair all askew, wearing a worn undershirt, was not it. I feared the worst – had the Grish attacks decimated our home planet? Was there anything left of the United States as we knew it? The crowd behind me had grown, but had gone quiet, waiting for the Admiral's update.

I said, "Admiral . . . sorry, it's taken me so long to get in touch. I need to ask you, sir, how are things on Earth?"

The older man cleared his throat and blinked his eyes several times before answering. "I suspect you don't know what time it is here."

"Um, no sir . . . I have no idea."

"Well, it's 0300!" He now realized there was an audience standing behind me and that all eyes were locked onto him.

He nervously looked away, "Tammy . . . get me my damn robe, will you?"

It dawned on me he'd been fast asleep – the reason for the mussed hair and old T-shirt. Chen said, looking contrite, "Um, Fleet Command . . . they put me through to his home in Maryland. Sorry sir, guess I should have mentioned that."

There were more chuckles behind me as the EUNF U.S. Space-Navy's Executive Five Star Fleet Admiral stood and put on his bathrobe. He, too, was now chuckling, "You just wait, Quintos . . . I'll get you back for this." Sitting, his smile faded, "Yeah, well, we're holding our own here with the Grish, Captain. Not to say things aren't bad, but the Pleidian Weonan have come to our rescue. Again. In fact, it's an old acquittance of yours, Fleet Commander Twinwon. His fleet arrived just in time. The Grish ran off with their tails between their legs." Block now looked at me with deep concern. "The real question, Captain, is how is the 2nd Fleet fairing against Varapin?"

I let the seconds tick by and tried to look defeated. It didn't work because XO Pristy, sitting closest to the Halo-Display, was giggling.

"Captain?" Block said.

"We did okay for ourselves, sir. At least for the short term . . . the Varapin won't be a problem."

Chapter 48

Three-Hundred-and-Twenty Light-Minutes from Miasma Burn

USS Hamilton, *Captain's Quarters*

Captain Galvin Quintos

Hamilton had incurred heavy damage from the *Sintchu's* constant, devastating weapons fire. It would be several days before the blown Spring Drives could be replaced, aligned, and rigorously tested. There were numerous radiation leaks, and plasma was now venting into space to relieve pressure buildup within two of the ship's reactors. Hull damage was substantial – a total of eight Decks had been breached. Temporary makeshift patch jobs were being performed by SWM teams working around the clock. One-hundred-and-ten good men and women on board the *Hamilton* had given their lives in service to the US Space-Navy, while close to three hundred crewmembers sustained injuries of one kind or another; fortunately, most were minor. Remaining 2nd Fleet warships, along with surviving Ramdei and Clouse Veng vessels, were preparing for their long trek back to our meetup location. At a minimum, it would take them eight days since they would require appropriate *JDTR's* – those Jump Down-Time Requisites in between jumps.

I'd instructed the second shift Bridge crew to their stations and ordered everyone from the first shift to get some desperately-needed sleep. For me, that was easy. Adrenaline, also called epinephrine, released by one's adrenal glands during high stress or life-threatening situations, is an amazing hormone. It had kept me going for a number of hours without sleep. The thing is, once those adrenal glands stop pumping that stuff into one's bloodstream, and one's mind stops the constant replaying cataclysmic events on an endless loop, the inevitable crash is absolute. I slept for eighteen hours straight. I awoke to hear voices. *Who the hell is here in my quarters?* My TAC-Band was vibrating to distraction – *how long has that been going on?* Opening my eyes was a challenge due to the amount of grit and gunk accumulated during my slumber.

"Get up, sleeping beauty. . . you've got work to do."

I tried to swallow and found that difficult. "Hardy . . . what . . . what are you doing in here . . . what time is it?" I croaked.

"Time to get up and take a shower. Smells like the business end of a jockstrap in here."

"Give me another few minutes." I slurred, drifting back into a wonderful deep sleep once more. It was then that I felt the bed covers being pulled down and cold metal hands none-too-gently taking hold of my upper arms and pulling me off the mattress. I had the sensation of movement as I tried, once more, to open my eyes. Then I heard the sound of running water. It was like being awakened by electrocution. The frigid, ice-cold water had me gasping for breath, as one of my flailing fists found the side of Hardy's oversized head. Still, he continued to hold me under the arctic deluge with one of his outstretched arms.

"Okay! Okay! I'm awake . . . turn on the hot water. And get out of here!" I yelled at the seven-foot-tall ChronoBot.

"Make it snappy, you have a meeting you're already late for."

"You know, it's times like this I wish you'd opted to stay onboard the *Sintchu*."

I heard Hardy's heavy footfalls leaving the head, then his parting words, "Major Vivian Leigh is here to escort you . . . best you move things along, Captain sleepyhead."

Doc Viv's here?

Coming out of the head with a towel wrapped around my waist, I found Doc Viv sitting up in my now perfectly-made bed. She looked radiant there, tapping a message into her TAC-Band. She was dressed casually, snug jeans, a pink, plaid snap shirt, and a white cowboy hat. Her long golden locks fell loose down past her shoulders.

I said, emphatically, "No. No way."

"What do you mean, no way? How do you even know what I'm here for?"

"I'm not going back there."

She stood and stepped in close. Looking up at me, serious as a heart attack, her Stetson's brim came within an inch from my chin. "You are going! And as your doctor, I won't approve you for going back on active duty until you do! Too many freeze-ups. Have I made myself clear, Quintos?"

"Crystal. Do I have to wear a silly outfit –"

"Are you insulting the way I look? Is that really how you want to start this day?"

"No. Sorry. You look fine. Better than fine, you look –"

"Oh, just shut up. Get dressed."

Then, I noticed the clothes on my dresser. Two towering cowboy boots stood sentinel above the pile, and atop the stack was a wide belt with a silver and gold buckle the size of Texas. It glimmered beneath the overhead lights. Looking desperate. I looked back to Viv.

She laughed, "I'll wait for you in the passageway."

We rode together in relative silence within the GravLift. She sent several more TAC-Band messages and then began to hum a familiar melody, but I couldn't remember the song's name. She was in a good mood, and I could tell, enjoying how miserable this was making me. And all I could do was stare at the diamond on her left hand's ring finger. Finally, I asked the question I'd wanted to ask since we'd left Halibart Shipyards. "So, you're engaged, Doc. Congratulations. Is it someone I know?"

A confused crease formed between her brows. As a

realization came to her, she extended the fingers of her left hand. "Pretty, don't you think?"

"Lovely. Looks expensive."

Pfft . . . "Don't you think I'm worth it?"

I had no idea how to answer that. Of course, she was worth it. But the lady was engaged now, I wasn't about to start making obtuse compliments to someone else's soon-to-be-bride."

She let me off the hook with a laugh, "You know, Quintos, you're an idiot . . . you do know that, right?"

"Why am I an idiot? Hey, you don't want to tell me, no skin off my nose. Just making idle conversation."

She rolled her eyes and let out a breath. "I'm not engaged to anyone. This is a fake diamond. My made-up story is I got engaged to an old boyfriend back on Earth while *Hamilton* was being refurbished and while you were convalescing in the hospital."

"Why go to all – "

"Let's just say there's someone here onboard the *Hamilton* – and no, I won't say who – that simply won't take no for an answer."

I had to work hard not to show the relief I was feeling inside. Instead, I just shrugged. "Seems like you've gone to a lot of trouble," I said.

"Did I mention you're an idiot?"

"I think so . . . maybe more than once."

We arrived at Decks 72/73, and soon we were emerging out into the back of the garage. The human-looking Symbio-Poths had left, the day's work of changing tires and working beneath the old Thunderbird complete. My eyes were drawn to the row of high windows on the closed rolling doors. It was nighttime, and I could see the distorted reflections of bright-ly-colored flickering lights coming in from the street beyond. Filtering in from the outside, I heard the kind of cheesy music unique to summertime fairgrounds.

"Don't you just love it? Those are the sounds and," she took in a deep breath, "and the smells of Americana . . . hot dogs and popcorn . . . fast rides and desperate grown men and women screaming like little children."

She looked like she was ten years old, and her excitement was momentarily contagious. But I put a hand on her shoulder as she began to step away. "Wait. Hold on a sec . . . It's been days, more than a week since we've been here. The 4th of July is long past – "

"No, Quintos, today is the 4th of July. At least here in Clairmont, it is. Time is not chronological here. Time is, well, mostly determined by you . . . by your visits here. Empress Shawlee Tee set things up that way. So, you're here at the perfect time." Her smile faded as she saw my pained expression. "Come on, it'll be okay. I promise." With the smile back on her lips, she took my hand and pulled me toward the door.

Outside on the street, we were greeted by my young parents and my twelve-year-old brother, Eric.

"I told you not to run off, Galvin . . . Hello, Vivian, nice to see you. Are you sure it's all right with your parents to be out this late?"

"Yes, Mrs. Quintos . . . it's fine."

My dad stood with his hands on his hips and surveyed the

fairgrounds, taking up Clairmont's Prairie Oysters Street. The place was packed. And the fair-goers were not entirely Symbio-Poths, by any means. It seemed as if the entire crew of *Hamilton* was here. A voice yelled down from above us, "Hey, Cap . . . I mean, Galvin!"

I looked up to see it was SWM Crewman LaSalle, seated within the towering Ferris wheel's top gondola. I waved back with a smile.

"I'm going to find my friends," Eric said, running off before my parents could object. Doc Viv said, "We're gonna go play too," and once again, she took my hand and pulled me deeper into the fair. A part of me wanted to hang with my Symbio-Poth parents; sure, I knew they weren't my real parents, but they were as close to my real parents as I'd ever experience again in this life. I wasn't averse to pretending, at least for a little while.

We passed by the arcade booths, where we saw the blue-glowing Ensign Plorinne playing the Balloon Shooter arcade game. He was trying to line up one of his wide-set eyes to BB gun's muzzle sites. XO Pristy, dressed similarly to Doc Viv in jeans, snap shirt, and cowboy boots, was playfully poking pink cotton candy into Helmsman Grime's face. I saw XO Tannock and Chaplain Trent climbing into a car of the Rockin' Roller Coaster. The two men were holding hands and were snuggling up close to each other. They looked both happy and nervous about the ride.

"You didn't know?" Viv said.

"No, but I'm typically the last to know anything. Good for them . . . I guess everyone needs someone special."

We got in line for the Zipper ride; ahead of us, at the front of the line, was Chief Porter. He hadn't gone with the perfunctory *cowboy* dress code but was wearing his typical off-duty Hawaiian shirt and shorts-and-flip-flops apparel. "Hey, Galvin . . . Viv. Want to take cuts? Come on up."

"Nah, we're good, Craig. Have a good time . . . try not to barf all over yourself." I said.

From behind me, a familiar voice said, "You sure you can handle this ride, Brigs?"

That was my call sign from when I was an Arrow pilot. On three occasions, I'd spent time in one ship's or another's brig for not following direct orders to drop pursuit of an enemy craft, and to RTB – *return to base.* The moniker, *Brigs,* had stuck after my last three-day stint behind bars. Only J-Dog still called me that. I turned to see my good friend, Captain Wallace Ryder. Next to him was the younger, and very cute, Lieutenant Akari James, who was appropriately designated with the call sign *Ballbuster.* I hadn't spoken with Ryder since his mission, and I looked forward to catching up soon. I said, "Hey, J-Dog . . . Ballbuster . . . good to see you both."

It was subtle, but I noticed Doc Viv had tensed and had moved closer to me. And she had yet to look at Ryder. As I said, I'm typically the last to know what is going on when it comes to onboard relationships, but there was clearly something going on between Viv and Ryder. Strange, though – I hadn't noticed any tension between them when we'd met at the Rocket Diner. Was he the one she was trying to discourage with her phony diamond ring? Had the infamous playboy, Ryder, been with Doc Viv at some point? That bothered me, and I had to fight not to show it. Viv noticed my forced smile and gripped my hand tighter. I wanted to throw a tantrum, to wrangle my hand free and tell her that if she was willing to be with someone like Ryder, then I wasn't the one she should be holding hands with. But I didn't do that.

It was only when the two of us were alone again, after climbing out of our Zipper car on wobbly legs, that she said, "I guess I should explain . . ."

"You don't owe me any explanation. You're a big girl."

"Oh, stop it with the fake, *I don't really care* performance." She pulled me around to face her. "We're all entitled to make a mistake, aren't we?"

"Of course. Viv, honestly, you don't have to explain yourself to me. I'm your friend, we're just getting to know each other. I'm not perfect, and I'm certainly in no position to judge you."

The corners of her mouth came up. "Well, you certainly know me as well as Ryder does." She looked away, her cheeks turning pink. "The difference is, you're decent. You're respect-ful . . . you're a good guy, Quintos."

But I wasn't listening to her. I was still replaying her words; *you know me as well as Ryder does.* What the hell does that mean? My mind flashed back to that dark Japanese hot springs and unknown, naked woman who'd rocked my world that night in the water – only to leave without ever saying a word. *Was that her? Was that Viv? Nah . . . could it?*

"It's time to go, Galvin. Eric has a tummy ache."

I turned to see my Mother, Father, and Eric, who had a mustard glob on the right side of his mouth.

"Go?"

"Yes, son . . . say goodbye to your little friend. It's late . . . I'm sure Vivian's parents are worried about her."

About to object, Doc Viv said, "Go. You need to go with them, Galvin. It's okay."

I felt my forehead go cold. My chest was already starting to constrict. It was impossible to swallow. My mother's arm came around my shoulder, and she led me away from Viv, the Clairmont Fair, and the watchful eyes of untold *Hamilton* crewmembers.

"Um, where you parked, Dad?" I said, remembering I'd said those same words some twenty years earlier in my life. *God, I don't want to be here. This is stupid; this is wrong.*

"We parked behind 'Meats.' Mr. Springer said we could park behind his store."

We stopped long enough for Eric to throw up into the curb there on Prairie Oysters Street, while my mother gently stroked my brother's back, reminding him why five hot dogs had been a bad idea. This had actually happened. I remembered the sound of Eric retching and the foul smell that almost got me upchucking next to him. But how could the Pleidian Weonan's have known this – and these all too-convincing Symbio-Poths?

Across the street, other families were leaving the fair. It was then that I noticed Scotty Miller wearing his stupid Indianapolis Coyotes baseball cap. The kid was talking loudly and making exaggerated hand gestures, as he described one ride he'd been on. His parents looked down at him adoringly. *Oh no . . . please no . . . don't let them die again.*

By the time Eric and I were climbing into family truck's back seats, I was hyperventilating. A full-grown, fucking man, and I was hyperventilating like a scared little girl –

"For goodness sakes, Galvin, put on your seatbelt. You're almost eleven, not five!"

A minute later, we were leaving Clairmont's lights and traveling on that dark two-lane road out of town. My parents were squabbling about something, and Eric was moaning about his upset stomach. In that moment, I was no longer the Captain of *Hamilton;* I was almost eleven, not thirty. I was a young boy who knew something bad, something awful, was about to happen. I closed my eyes.

"God dammit! What's that fool doing?" My father barked. The argument he'd been having with my mother – his anger – was now transferred to the swerving Volvo in front of us. My father stepped on the gas to pass. We came up to the other car. It was dark out, and this patch of road didn't have streetlights. The Volvo, going slow, was still weaving back and forth over the yellow lines. Dad was forced to slow down, as it was not safe to pass. "Damn Sunday driver . . . someone needs to teach this SOB a lesson."

"Dear, relax . . . we're in no hurry –" My mother started to say.

"I'm going to get us out in front of this lunatic. That's all there is to it!" He stepped on the gas again, and we were soon parallel with the other car. The Volvo swerved and almost clipped the truck. My dad tried to maneuver around the Volvo, this time on the right side, but the Volvo swerved toward us on that side too.

I noticed I was holding a small stuffed animal in one hand and a milkshake in the other. *When . . .* I took a sip, just as I had some twenty years earlier. It was icy cold. Vanilla.

Dad's pickup and the old Volvo were now driving side-by-side on the narrow country road. I could see into the other car's backseat. There was the boy wearing the Indianapolis Coyotes baseball cap. He looked back at me and flipped me the bird. *Oh yeah – now, I remember he did that.*

"That's Scotty Miller," I said to my Mom in the front seat.

The Volvo suddenly jerked to the right and clipped our truck with a loud *Clank!* The truck's driver side mirror went flying off behind us. At that moment, I watched as my dad went from angry to furious. Instead of slowing down, letting the other car have the road, my dad pulled the steering wheel hard to the left, knocking the Volvo off the road. Turning around, I watched as the smaller vehicle practically went airborne. One moment it was there on the road next to us, the next, it was shooting off at an angle out into the open field. I screamed, my mother screamed, and Eric screamed. My dad slowed the truck, and we all watched as the Volvo rocketed nose-down into a ditch or gulch. Seconds later, the car exploded. Yellow light filled the truck's cab. I caught sight of my mother's horrified face – the shock and terror in her eyes. *Oh god . . . I want this to stop now.* She screamed, "Carl! We have to turn around!" Eric began to cry as my mother pounded her fists on my father's arm and shoulder, "Stop the truck! Damn it, Carl, Stop the truck!"

I was both mesmerized and paralyzed with fear. I was ten, going on eleven, and my world was coming unhinged again. As he had done twenty years earlier, I waited for my father to step on the gas and flee the horrible scene. I waited . . .

But my father didn't step on the gas. Instead, he cranked the old Ford's steering wheel around and around, powering the big truck into a U-turn that took us off onto the road's shoulder. Soon, we were bouncing and jostling across the open field headed for the distant flames. *Wait! No, this isn't what happened. This isn't my life.*

My father swerved around the skeletal rusted remains of an old broken-down tractor and came around a big mound of dirt. The truck skidded to a stop; both my father and mother already had their doors open and were running toward the gulch on the other side. Eric was still fumbling with his seat belt, but I was already out my door and chasing after my parents. I didn't want to see the exploded car – that young family being burned alive – but my legs kept running anyway. I couldn't stop. I ran, winded, trying to see, but the fucking mound of dirt was obstructing my view. I slowed, my face already grimacing in preparation for what I was about to see. Would I see the up-ended Volvo – the charred bodies of Mrs. and Mr. Miller and their son, Scotty? Finally making it around the mound, I saw the raging fire's bright flames reaching high into the night's sky – that, and the large, blackened propane tank beneath them. *Propane tank?* The big tank had been pierced by some kind of agricultural tiller rig, like the kind pulled by a tractor when plowing a field.

I looked for the Volvo and found it some thirty feet farther back within the gulch. *I don't understand.* By now, my Mom and Dad had reached the Volvo and were helping the Millers out of the wrecked car. Mrs. Miller was crying, as was little Scotty. Mr. Miller was limping and holding a palm over his chest. I heard Mrs. Miller say the words *heart attack on the road,* which explained the swerving. But more importantly, the wrecked Volvo hadn't actually exploded. Instead, the Volvo had hit the metal tiller thing, which, in turn, had been propelled into the propane tank, causing it to explode. *But no . . . that wasn't what happened. Or was it?* I tried to blink away the tears now filling my eyes as I watched my mother holding and consoling Mrs. Miller. Everyone was alive. Everyone was just fine. I was on my knees, now feeling the heat from the nearby raging fire. I was a grown man, and here I was on the verge of sobbing. *What is happening to me?*

Arms came around me, pulled me in close. It was none other than Empress Shawlee Tee, and she was on her knees, right there next to me. "You came back . . ."

She held my face in her hands. So strange and so alien-looking, but also so beautiful. Her eyes were kind and loving – looking at me now, it was as if she could see into my very being – my very soul. "Breathe, Galvin. This is the reality you never knew. This is the truth. The Millers did not die here that dark summer night all those years ago. Yes, your father's actions caused a crash, but no one died."

"Shawlee, twenty years ago, we didn't turn around. We didn't go back to see – "

"No. You rushed home . . . loaded up your vehicle and were gone before the morning light. Your mother and father avoided reading anything about Clairmont . . . not wanting to face a young family's death one night on a dark rural road. But they wouldn't have found such news; it hadn't happened that way. No, your parents didn't turn back and help the Millers from their vehicle; another family did that. But this is what you needed to see, to experience." She kissed my cheek and gently stroked my face. "Oh, Galvin, it is time you forgive your father and mother. And forgive yourself. It will take time, but if you allow that needed inner healing to take place . . . you will be fine. You are my brother, Galvin, and I love you. I will always be here for you. This was necessary, I hope you forgive me." Once more, she kissed my cheek and then was gone, walking off alone into the darkness.

Epilogue

I was cleared by Doc Viv to return to the Captain's Mount for the remainder of the voyage home. She was hesitant to do so, and I couldn't blame her for that. Over the course of the mission, I'd frozen - locked up - on several high-stress occasions. She assured me that I'd get through this period in my life, eventually, but only by doing further work. Something told me that she'd be happy to assist. But reiterating, Delayed Onset PTSD was not something that would magically go away after one, albeit enlightening, Clairmont exposure therapy.

Captain Eli Tannock had not been pleased with me being authorized for duty and had made his views on the subject quite clear to the doctor. Even with the total success of the mission against the Varapin, I suspected he would be making a big stink to Fleet Command. Yes, I'd given the order to fire upon the invaded, perilous, *USS Brave* – perhaps that was a court martial offense. *So be it* – I'd deal with that, if and when, it came.

But for now, the crew of *USS Hamilton,* was in the mood to celebrate. We had persevered through another tumultuous, impossible, mission – a mission we had not been expected to survive. We had proven Fleet Command wrong. This crew, this amazing great warship, had been victorious against an opponent of far greater numbers, and of far more advanced technology.

Sitting here in the Captain's ready room, putting the finishing touches on my mission briefing to Admiral Block, I looked up to see there was someone standing at the open hatchway. Wearing form-fitting attire, I didn't recognize her at first; her headband was fitted with two cat-like ears.

"What are you supposed to be? A Leopard?"

She reached around, found her long tail, and waved it at me, "No, silly, I'm a Jaguar. Spots are completely different."

I nodded while keeping a serious expression – it took all my willpower not to let my eyes wander over her wonderful feline curves.

She said, "You know, the party's already started."

I'd heard MATHR make the announcement an hour earlier. It was an all-hands costume party in the town of Clairmont. Tomorrow, that little town on Decks 72/73 was being dismantled. But tonight, it was being made available for celebrations. The Fourth of July rides and arcade games were still there; the only requirement for admission: you had to come wearing a costume. I hadn't planned on attending. Wanted to give the crew a chance to relax, let their proverbial hair down without the ship's CO putting a damper on things.

Tilting her head, Doc Viv made a *meow* sound. "You're coming."

I shook my head.

"I have a costume for you."

"What kind of costume?"

She turned and gestured behind her. A moment later, a seven-foot-tall ChronoBot entered my ready room. Hardy was wearing a ridiculously large Stetson atop his odd-shaped head, a blue snap button western shirt, oversized blue jeans, gargantuan cowboy boots, and – to finish things off – bright yellow chaps. He looked ridiculous and I couldn't keep from laughing out loud.

He looked at me with a faux hurt-feelings expression that made me laugh even harder. Viv was laughing too, and while I was about to shoo them both away, Hardy brought out what he had been hiding behind his back. There, hanging on a hanger, was another costume. One that was even more ridiculous than his.

"I'm not wearing that!"

Viv said, "Yes, Captain sourpuss, you are."

"Are those . . . um, lederhosen?"

"Uh-huh . . . you're a Bavarian barmaid . . . barman, you'll be serving beer to the crew tonight. No arguments."

Fifteen minutes later, Doc Viv, Hardy, and I, emerged into the throng of costumed crewmembers within Clairmont's congested Main Street. Loud dance music was being piped in from above, all the carnival rides were running, and every arcade stand was packed to the gills.

I felt a pat on my behind, "Nice lederhosen, Skipper . . ."

A sexy-looking Cleopatra strode past me. I said to no one in particular, "Please tell me that that wasn't XO Pristy . . ."

Hardy said, "Hey, I have a surprise for you, Cap!"

I was afraid to ask. Hardy's face display had changed into the symbol of an old-fashioned record on a turntable. The song that was playing suddenly changed. Thundering down from above came the unmistakable sound of a car horn followed by the now all-too-familiar lyrics from *Vengaboys – We Like To Party.*

The End

Thank you for reading **USS Hamilton – Miasma Burn** book two in this series. If you enjoyed this book, PLEASE leave a review on Amazon.com—it really helps!

To be notified the moment the next and all future books are released, please join my mailing list. I hate spam and will never, ever share your information. Jump to this link to sign up:

http://eepurl.com/bs7M9r

ACKNOWLEDGMENTS

First and foremost, I am grateful to the fans of my writing and their ongoing support for all my books. I'd like to thank my wife, Kim—she's my rock and is a crucial, loving component of my publishing business. I'd like to thank my mother, Lura Genz, for her tireless work as my first-phase creative editor and a staunch cheerleader of my writing. I'd also like to thank Sarah Mayor for her fine work editing the manuscript as well. Others who provided fantastic support include Lura and James Fischer and Stuart Church.

Check out my other available titles on the following page.

Made in United States
North Haven, CT
14 December 2021

12809309R00248